THE ORCHID'S CHILDREN

Series

Books 1-3

By Amber Fawn

PLAYLIST

CONSEQUENCES

SAVING SWEET SIENNA

BROTHER'S REVENGE

To those who understand that blood doesn't always mean family.

PART ONE:

CONSEQUENCES

CHAPTER 1:
TROUBLE

Marcus

Under the fading streetlights, my heart races as I join my cohorts, a tight-knit group of misfits with an obsession for trouble. With each stolen engine we rev, we defy the tedious routine-filled lives that attempt to suffocate us. Trouble is easy. Petty crimes have become second nature. Relay theft is as simple as tying a shoelace. Even so, the adrenaline rush is something I'll never get used to. The buzz. It consumes my mind entirely, dismantling any rational thoughts I may have left. That pull of adrenaline has become too strong to resist. It's like primal instinct.

I'm fully aware that at almost twenty years old I should be spending my Tuesday very differently. At 3 a.m. sleeping would be the obvious alternative; playing a game or even going to a club if you're the more '*rebellious*' type. But that's too normal. Too stable. We were never given that opportunity.

Tonight's car is one of the better ones we've 'borrowed'. Starting the engine and hearing the growl of that exhaust is intoxicating; there's no sound quite like it. I press my foot on the clutch and rev the engine loud, just to add a little extra danger. Pulling off unnecessarily fast just so I can feel the car's power rush through my body. Rolling the windows down and blaring the music loud enough to feel the speakers pound is essential. Non Negotiable. I'm in control. That's where I like to be. Sienna touches my arm from behind and leans forward with a concerned look on her beautiful face.

"Is that a new tattoo?" She asks.

"Yeah, my mate did it for me at his house a few nights ago."

"You're gonna run out of space for them soon." I can't help but smirk at the adorable dose of genuine concern in her voice.

"Does that turn you on?" I ask, raising an eyebrow at her, forcing her to behave and sit back in her seat.

Such a pretty little thing.
"Marcus, look!" Skylar shouts.
I turn to my right, knowing exactly what I'm about to see. The others. Specifically Dean.

The pungent scent of marijuana punches its way through our windows and the thumps of their music match up almost perfectly to ours. Gorgeous. I look past Delilah who's sitting leisurely in the passenger seat, of course; their lovey-dovey relationship makes me sick. Dean is grinning assuredly from ear to ear, knowing full well he's about to speed past us. He puffs his joint before shouting over.

"In a bit, mate!" he laughs.
I've been challenged.

I put my foot down to the floor and hear the wheels squeak from under me. The wind whips us through the open windows. I catch glimpses of Dean smirking and Birdie waving smugly out of the back seat window as we alternate between first and second place. The road is ours. Traffic lights are nothing but an obstacle right now. I weave in front at the bend of the road. I know I'm pushing my luck, but the thrill has a hold of me. It has me hostage. Dean takes my risky move as a provocation. *What a surprise.* We reach the motorway, the unofficial-official final stretch. Almost instantly I hear a wheel spin from the side of me and I'm forced to swerve out of the way as Dean cuts me up, beeping the car horn to mock me as he knows his move gives me no choice but to slow down. He brakes slightly to allow me to catch up.

"Better luck next time, ay?" he gloats.

"Don't flatter yourself, you got lucky" I say, jokingly trying to protect my pride. We cruise for a while just taking in the moment. Letting it engulf us. Allowing it to teleport us back to when we were kids, just for a little while. I'm zoned out, in a world of my own. I'm happy. Through my daydream, I vaguely notice Dean dart off abruptly and Sienna leans through from the backseat to switch off the music.

"Uh Marcus, what are you waiting for exactly?" she says in a soft but panicked tone. I catch the flashing lights in the rearview mirror and sirens are suddenly flooding my ears. I'm jolted back into reality.

"Fucking drive!" Skylar yells. My foot hits the floor and we're all pushed back into our seats. The force of the acceleration is unsettling this time. We're in trouble.

"Call Dean, now." I instruct as I swerve bluntly onto the slip road. Residential areas are the best for a chase. They make it easier to veer out of sight. They're tight, cluttered.

"Yo" I hear from Skylar's muffled phone speaker.

"Where should I head?"

"Lose 'em and get to Orchid's, bro. We'll get the gate open."

"Sounds good."

The key to a police chase is to keep your cool. Think logically. Outsmart. With every turn I navigate, I'm planning the next five. My dad taught me how to drive; how to handle high speeds. He tells me I'm a natural-born driver. In fact, that's about the only nice thing he's ever told me. Getting caught isn't an option. Isn't something that even crosses my mind. I don't get caught. I figure everything out. The girls are alternating between gripping the grab handles and the back of the front seats. Albeit this is due to the abrupt turns, not fear. They know they're in safe hands.

I'm gaining ground now, naturally. They're struggling. I'm closer to the meeting point; a mere few minutes away under normal circumstances. Time to end the chase. I accelerate for the last time, pushing the car to its limit. This area is etched in my memory; I know every road, alley, and dead-end like the back of my hand. After a couple of ridiculously fast turns, I become very aware of the lack of flashing lights in my rearview mirror. The sirens are fading. I approach the gate. Open, as we agreed. I swerve into the dirt road and through the open gate; my wheels spinning out as I decrease my speed. Driving in, I pull far enough to vanish from view. Engine off. Silence. We instinctively lower our heads, a reflex more than a necessity, and listen to the coppers race past behind us. They've been outwitted.

Checkmate.

CHAPTER 2:

ORCHID'S

Marcus

Without exception, the realisation of what had just transpired is always comical. I understand it shouldn't be, yet it always manages to elicit a chuckle. The novelty never wears off. Those brief moments of lifting our heads, sharing an exuberant glance, and truly comprehending that we've pulled it off once more. Turning to the front, I rub my hand on my forehead and I can feel my arrogant smirk forming. Skylar leans in from the back, checking my expression, and soon enough, she's giggling along with me. Both of us revelling in a conceited sense of relief.

Meanwhile, Sienna is likely a beautiful bundle of stress in the backseat.

Dean opens my door, laughing hysterically, with his joint still in hand. Admittedly, seeing him without one would be an odd sight. The smell of weed follows him. It lives on him. Sunken into his skin. It's one thing we have in common.

"You alright?" he asks, still lightly chuckling.

"Wonderful." I reply, somewhat sarcastically. Stepping out of the car and onto the pothole-ridden dirt path, Dean boisterously pats my shoulder, as if he were a proud father.

We stand together and look towards the building. It's a moment of perfect stillness, only broken by the sweet melody of birdsong just beginning. The sky is yet to start its transition from darkness to light. The doors stand sealed, the windows barricaded. Debris litters the car park, an unsettling testament to neglect. There's a faint 'Orchid's Children's Home' sign that somehow clings on, a ghostly reminder of the past. My heart faintly aches with memories from the years I spent inside. What was once a place I thought of as my home now stands empty and forgotten, like a lost soul longing to be remembered.

"It's been a while." Delilah says softly.

"Yeah," I mumble, nodding my head, as the echoes of laughter and conversation that once filled the rooms now fill only my head. Though in reality, they had been replaced with eerie silence.

"Let's go in!" Skylar suggests. I immediately look to Sienna, knowing she wouldn't be fond of the idea.

"I'm not sure about that." She responds, fishing for our agreement.

"Why not?" Birdie questions. "Scared there might be ghosts?"

Sienna lets out a nervous giggle.

"Come on, It'll be good." I reassure her.

I wrap my arm around her for comfort as we slowly head up to the entrance, gathering our varied thoughts. More and more memories rush back to me with every step I take and I feel my heart racing in anticipation. The car park where I first learnt to ride a bike. The front steps that I used to draw on with chalk. The now-boarded-up windows we would throw snowballs at in the winter. With one foot pressed firmly to the wall Dean begins to pull on one of the boards.

"Bro, gimme a hand." Together we manage to pry it off and get through to the smeared, dusty window beneath. I take a short peek in whilst disposing of the wooden board but the inside is nothing but darkness. Dean begins scanning the car park as the girls peer through the window with their phone flashlights. He sets his eyes on what he's looking for and walks assuredly towards it. After picking up a large brick, he turns around to face the window and whistles. The girls look over at him as he signals with his hand for them to move out of the way. After taking a second to perfect his aim, he proceeds to launch the brick cleanly through the window. Classic Dean, smooth as smooth could be.

"Easy peasy." Skylar says, practically leaping through the now shattered window. I'm often unsure if she contains even a single drop of fear in her body. Dean follows, climbing effortlessly inside and instinctively turning back around to lift Delilah through. I'm aware that she is petite, but with the way Dean lifts her, I can't help but imagine she is entirely weightless. Following it up with a swift smack to her behind once she had safely reached the floor. A connoisseur of charm. I move toward the jagged, broken window, navigating its edges cautiously as I make my way inside. The glass shatters underfoot, emitting a distinct crunch as I land in the pitch-black space. Without a moment's pause, I extend my hand, reaching out to assist the girls as they navigate their way through the same window.

Once we all are inside, I retrieve my phone and activate the flashlight, casting a beam into the darkness that surrounds us. With a deep breath, I steel myself, gazing ahead, a peculiar sensation settling within me. Standing in the building that had once been so familiar, but now feeling like an unwanted guest in my own home. *Well, I am trespassing after all.*

The living room. Our living room. If I can still call it that. The peeling walls and cracked ceilings remind me that it's no longer the place I knew. Feelings of nostalgia wash over me. Our dead silence is screaming in my ears. Ringing. Most of the furniture has been removed, except from the sofa we would squeeze onto for movie night, now tattered and worn. Dean picks up an old gaming controller from the floor and dusts it off. He vaguely scans his eyes past all of us, who are watching him attentively, and lets out a light smirk.

"Mad." he murmurs as he stares back at the controller, turning it around as if to analyse it. I can practically feel him replaying the memories in his mind. We continue walking through the rooms; our kitchen now entirely empty. Dust and cobwebs consume this place. I step into the bathroom and catch a glimpse of my face in the cracked mirror. I didn't think it would ever see this version of me. I had never imagined that this very mirror would get the opportunity to reflect my now adult self. *Trippy.*

Exiting the bathroom, I instinctively pull the door closed behind me, though the reason remains elusive. Perhaps habit, or maybe a simple gesture of respect. With each step through I'm inspecting every wall, every floorboard, every item that remains. It's as if I'm strolling through a personal museum, surrounded by the exhibits of my own past.

The office. We were never allowed in here. Which ironically made it the most appealing room; despite the fact that, to my knowledge, the only thing living inside was paperwork. Boring adult paperwork and the suffocating aroma of coffee. Stepping inside now I feel like I'm breaking the law. *Yet again, that's probably because I am.* Entering the room I feel somewhat disappointed. As a kid, it appeared vast, holding an air of mystery and grandeur beyond comparison. In reality it's just an office. A dull, little office. I pull out the chair and take a seat, just because I can. Evidently the others feel the same way, as they take their places on the few other chairs, the desk and the floor.

"This office is shit." Birdie states. You can always rely on her for a profound summary.

"That's one way of putting it." I reply with a soft chuckle. Skylar slowly stands up off the desk and approaches a large filing cabinet. She tugs several times on the drawer but it doesn't budge. She sighs, a touch dramatic, then glances over at me, silently beckoning for assistance. I scratch my head and point my flashlight towards the hideous, dark-wood desk in front of me in search of a solution. A couple of pens, a stack of sticky notes, a broken lamp and '*aha!*'. A paperclip.

"Here." I say, throwing her my tiny discovered treasure.

"Perfect, thanks." She gets to work immediately and begins straightening out the paperclip, leaving the ends bent. It's as if the method is deeply ingrained in her mind. It must be. She inserts one curved end into the keyhole and begins to turn. Left. Right. Left. Right. Finding the correct unlock position. Click.

"Voilà!" She exclaims. Her fingers begin flicking through the contents and she tilts her head to briefly read the titles of each document. She lets out a small excited giggle and turns quickly to face us.

"All of our old files are in here!"

"No way." We seem to all respond in unison, our eyes widening. She nods her head happily.

"Who's up first then?" Dean asks, rolling a new joint.

"That would be..." With determination, she resumes sifting through the files, her head slightly tilted in concentration. This time, her search is meticulous, her eyes scanning each page with rigour. She pulls out the first file and walks back over to the table, placing it down firmly. Meeting my gaze, she pivots the paper to face me.

"Marcus Bear."

CHAPTER 3:
MARCUS BEAR

Marcus

Everybody gathers at the speed of light around the desk, leaning in to get a glimpse of my file.

"Aww," The girls screech in time with one another. My baby photo staring up at us. My unkempt hair and red flushed cheeks. Those eyes, full of hope and curiosity. Not knowing what life was, or what it had just thrown at me. It's bittersweet. Reading a summary of my childhood, written by a social worker or volunteer who likely didn't truly know me. Somebody who condensed my early life into a single form before heading home to a family of their own. But the truth is they probably cared for me. Tried for me. Thought they were helping me. Thought they were stopping me from becoming exactly what I am today.

CHILD INFORMATION RECORD
GREAT BRITAIN

NAME: MARCUS BEAR

DATE OF BIRTH: 21/06/2004

DATE OF ARRIVAL: 02/12/2006

REASON FOR ADMITTANCE: UNSAFE HOME ENVIRONMENT

ANY FAMILY STILL IN CONTACT: NO

ELIGIBLE FOR FOSTER/ADOPTION PROGRAMMES: YES

PERSONAL NOTES:

Marcus arrived at orchids at the age of 2, after social workers were called to his home following reports of consistent drug use by his mother. They found his home environment to be unfit and unsafe. His mother did not fight for custody and voluntarily admitted him to Orchids childrens home and cut all contact from that point. His father could not be located at the time.

Marcus' biological father made contact with Orchids and gained full custody on 18/09/2018.

It goes without saying that I have always been aware of the fact I was abandoned by my mother. It was never a secret. Even so, there was just something very different about seeing it written on a piece of paper, in black and white. It's all right here, and it's all so hard to read. Looking back now from my newly-adult perspective, it's hard to not feel a sense of bitterness. The thought of ever walking away from that sweet child is alien to me.

I sit here now as a young man who has just spent his night 'borrowing' cars, evading the police and breaking into a building and I can't help but wonder if things may have turned out differently for me, if my mother would have kept me. Maybe my life could've been better. Maybe I would've been a good person. But then again, maybe not. Maybe I would've ended up just like this anyway.

I love my dad. I know he loves me too. I'm thankful for him giving me a home. An actual home. But I can't forgive him. Never. Looking down at this piece of paper and seeing those dates. 2006. 2018. Where was he for all of those years? I've never gotten an answer. How can you wait that long? I feel like the other people in my life haven't really thought to question it. In fact, not a single person ever has, but me. It makes me feel like I'm crazy sometimes. *'Aren't you just so happy your dad finally found you?'* Over and over. How could it have taken that long to 'find' me? I stayed in a children's home just a few streets away from where he lived. It makes me wonder, how genuine was his search? Did he put in any real effort, or was he even searching at all?

"Wow, you were here for a long time." Delilah says, snapping me out of my resentful daydream. I scrunch my nose and push away the paper; pretending I'm not interested. In reality, I'm just trying to avoid any conversation about it.

It's a strange concept, isn't it? I spent my whole childhood in this place, with my friends. We lived it together. I knew nothing else but this place and them. The fabric of my existence woven alongside theirs. This was my home. My normal. They're my family. Yet, talking to each other about the very reasons we were there in the first place is pretty much considered a no-go.

"You alright?" Dean asks, gripping my shoulder, joint still in hand.

"Yeah, fine mate." I respond with a slight chuckle. Skylar's gaze shifts to me with a gentle, caring expression, holding it for a beat longer than comfortable, almost crossing into an intensity that breaks the moment. Eventually, she turns around and starts walking back towards the filing cabinet.

"Who's up next then?" She says smiling. She starts flicking through files once again but stops quickly. A smirk forming on her face. She prances back to the table and places the file down.

"Only the greatest, most beautiful, most perfect person in all of the world."

CHAPTER 4:
SKYLAR FARMER

Marcus

The atmosphere whilst looking at Skylar's file is completely different. It's funny. The room feels lighter. We all let out a few chuckles whilst reading through, including her. The truth is Skylar never cared about being here. Never cared about hiding away from her life here, or why she came here in the first place. In fact, I'm not sure Skylar truly cares about anything. She's one of life's luckier people; not because she hasn't had any issues. Quite the opposite. She just has an incredible ability to take a problem, no matter how big, and simply flick it away like a bug. She does what she wants and says what she feels. Never seen her cry. Never had her bad actions catch up to her, nor do they seem to affect her. A fearless, guiltless individual.

CHILD INFORMATION RECORD
GREAT BRITAIN

NAME: SKYLAR FARMER

DATE OF BIRTH: 03/03/2005

DATE OF ARRIVAL: 02/11/2017

REASON FOR ADMITTANCE: BAD BEHAVIOUR

ANY FAMILY STILL IN CONTACT: NO

ELIGIBLE FOR FOSTER/ADOPTION PROGRAMMES: YES

PERSONAL NOTES:

Skylar was admitted to Orchid's at the age of 12 due to years of uncontrollable bad behaviour. She was removed from her secondary school after just a few months for truancy and threatening another student. Her parents contacted police and had her removed permanently from her home when she had snuck out in the early hours of the morning to meet with older friends and engage in illegal activity.

Skylar was adopted on 19/01/2019 and is settling very well.

"How the actual fuck did you manage to get adopted so fast with a record like that?" Birdie says laughing and shaking her head.

"Not to mention the face practically screaming *'trouble'*." Sienna adds. Skylar rolls her eyes and laughs along with us. As I listen to the group joke about Skylar's file, I admire her carefree attitude. The world is like her playground, and I envy that.

As I alternate between reading and looking at her I can't help but think of her as somebody who has truly mastered the art of living. Seeing her as a different species to me altogether. It has to be innate. Why can't I embrace life with the same fearlessness and self-assurance that she exudes? What sets her apart from the rest of us? Can I learn something from her '*example*'? Do I want to? Maybe it isn't as easy as it seems, to not care. Maybe not caring is more work. More strain. Though if that's the case she certainly doesn't show it.

"The real question is who let me take any kind of picture with those earrings in and my roots not touched up?" Skylar says with a disgusted look on her face.

"That makeup though." Birdie adds, with an approving look. "You should definitely do a dark lip more often."

"Alright alright. Who's next?" Dean says, rubbing his forehead.

"Aww, are we boring you, Dean?" Skylar says while sarcastically pouting her lips.

"When are you not?"

"Touché." And just like that, Skylar snatches her file, deftly folds it to fit into her back pocket, and saunters back to the filing cabinet. Her smile lingers as she swiftly plucks the next file, stealing a glance for herself before returning to us. She climbs up to take a seat on top of the desk this time and crosses her legs. She winks playfully at Delilah before placing down her record.

CHAPTER 5:
DELILAH FRANKLIN

Marcus

I don't even have to look, I can simply feel everyone smiling. Not that her file is anything to smile at; but because we're proud of her. Happy for her. A kind, loving soul. If any of us deserved a family it was her. If anybody deserved a happy ending after being here, it was her. I can still remember the day she came back to Orchid's, shy and reserved, but always with a gentle smile on her face.

I knew immediately she was special. Always eager to help others, to lend a listening ear. She had become like a little sister to all of us over the years. She's the glue holding us together. I mean, she deserves a medal just for putting up with Dean's bullshit.

CHILD INFORMATION RECORD
GREAT BRITAIN

NAME: DELILAH FRANKLIN

DATE OF BIRTH: 20/03/2005

DATE OF ARRIVAL: 11/05/2006

REASON FOR ADMITTANCE:

VOLUNTARY ADMITTANCE

ANY FAMILY STILL IN CONTACT: NO

ELIGIBLE FOR FOSTER/ADOPTION

PROGRAMMES: YES

PERSONAL NOTES:

Delilah was brought to Orchids by her mother at the age of 1 after she found she wasn't capable of parenting Delilah due to her mental state following the death of Delilah's father. Her mother committed suicide just days after bringing Delilah into our care. She was adopted by her grandmother on 29/08/2006

Delilah was returned to Orchids on 07/03/2012 following the unfortunate death of her grandmother and has been entered into the adoption programme once again

Delilah was adopted on 24/06/2016

After reading, Delilah kisses her fingers and touches them to her anklet. The anklet her grandmother gave her. I don't think she'll ever take that off. I wish I had gotten a chance to meet her. I wish I could've thanked her for giving Delilah the early childhood she deserved. She allowed Delilah to grow into herself. To keep her warmth and her hope despite everything the world threw at her.

Had she arrived at Orchid's earlier, I'm not sure she would be the Delilah we know now. It's as if her grandmother was a guiding light for her, and still is. She used to always talk about how strong she was. I mean, after losing her child and taking Delilah in herself; having to hide her grief for her sake, it's no wonder she passed on that resilience.

I observe Delilah, noticing the subtle rhythm of her deep breaths as emotions bubble beneath the surface. Her eyes glisten with tears as she takes one more deep breath. She looks up and notices me staring.

"I just miss her, you know?" She says quickly wiping her tears with her sleeve. I nod in comfort as Dean wraps his arm around her and kisses her head. I can almost feel the weight of their love for each other. Despite the fact that they couldn't be more opposite, it's hard not to feel a sense of awe at how much they've been through together and how deeply they still care for one another. So opposite that they're almost identical. That's what makes them work. Their differences are irrelevant. The experiences they faced together have bonded them for life. You can't get away from somebody after sharing this home with them. They'll always be in your mind. In your heart. We're a part of each other whether we like it or not. More than a family.

"Should we stop looking through these?" Skylar asks, concerned.

"No." Delilah replies, wiping tears that had fallen down to her chin. "I'm fine. It's actually been pretty nice having some time to reminisce."

"You sure, baby?" Dean asks. Delilah looks up to him and nods. Taking it as a cue, Skylar moves to fetch the next file, easily locating it and chuckling as she carries it to the desk. There's a collective understanding among us as she approaches; the identity of the file's subject is evident to everyone.

CHAPTER 6:
BIRDIE KING

Marcus

There are many ways I can describe 'princess-Birdie'. Problematic, self-obsessed, high maintenance, sneaky, a diva. An instigator. The definition of manipulative. The list goes on. She definitely takes on the 'fiery red-head' stereotype to the highest degree. The last kind of person I would ever choose to be friends with. The odd one out. Flawed. But I love her of course.

As exhausting as she can be, she stuck by us all. She's honest, sometimes way too honest. Reliable. Safe. Strong. That's all that truly matters and I wouldn't have it any other way. She's an important piece in our puzzle and life wouldn't be the same without her. Though I can confidently say I fear for any man who ends up with her. *She'll eat them for breakfast.*

CHILD INFORMATION RECORD
GREAT BRITAIN

NAME: BIRDIE KING

DATE OF BIRTH: 13/12/2004

DATE OF ARRIVAL: 23/05/2008

REASON FOR ADMITTANCE:

NEGLECT

ANY FAMILY STILL IN CONTACT: YES

ELIGIBLE FOR FOSTER/ADOPTION

PROGRAMMES: NO

PERSONAL NOTES:

Birdie arrived here at Orchids at the age of 3 after being removed from her parents custody when she fell from a window in the property and neighbours had made a report of neglect. Social workers removed her from the home and her parents are currently fighting to regain custody of her.

Parents are in regular contact.

Birdie's parents regained full custody on 01/02/2017

Birdie's file is funny to all of us. Birdie is funny to all of us. Because the truth is she never should've been at Orchid's in the first place. She never fit in here. Her story was an unfortunate but fairly simple one. She comes from an amazing family. Well, a snobby family if we're being blunt, but a loving one nonetheless. She was a bratty child and she misbehaved. Her parents never abused her, never neglected her. The fall was nothing but an accident, but Birdie is a drama queen. Always has been. Unfortunately, so was her neighbour.

Her parents remained steadfast by her side, advocating for her relentlessly during her time here. It was evident to all of us that they would eventually gain custody. The odd one out. Her experience was nothing like the rest of us. Orchid's was more like a holiday home for her. Always going out for trips. Always being sent money and gifts. A pampered little princess.

I probably should be envious of her. She had everything I didn't. Money, family, security. But I'm not. Not at all. That life isn't for me. The standards. The pressure to be perfect all the time. The false smiles at all those black-tie-snob-conventions they call 'get-togethers'. Not to mention the uncomfortable clothing. I could never handle it. Maybe that makes her stronger than me. In all honesty, I feel for her. She lives in a whole different world, a comfortable but lonely one. It's like she's living in a cage wrapped in gold. I don't think she'll ever be able to reveal her true genuine self, if there is one. She fears disappointing people. Underachieving. To me that sounds like a nightmare. To constantly be on display as a perfect example of what somebody else thinks is ideal.

Even here at Orchid's where the standards are significantly low, I struggled being myself. But Birdie, well, she's on a whole other level. It can be sad to watch. I mean it when I say she doesn't fit in with us, but I worry sometimes that she doesn't really fit in anywhere. She's just existing. Living a life that was never truly hers to live.

"What's so funny?" Birdie asks, with a playfully offended attitude. Nobody responds, there's no need to. Instead, we all exchange glances, silently acknowledging the irony. Here we are, all struggling to find our place in the world; committing petty crimes for fun, yet we find humour in the one who has her life the most together. I glance over to Birdie. She's still laughing, but something in her eyes tells me she isn't truly happy. I never believe she is. Maybe deep down she feels guilty. Or maybe I'm projecting my insecurities onto her. Who am I to judge? Maybe she's completely content being a pampered princess. All I know is that I wouldn't trade places with her for anything in the world. Sure, my life is filled with a lot of shit, but at least I have the freedom to make my own terrible decisions.

Skylar stands up and makes her way back to the filing cabinet.

"Let's move on, shall we?" She says, still giggling slightly. Her fingers begin rummaging once again and she swiftly grabs the next file to place on the desk. The mood dampens.

CHAPTER 7:
SIENNA SAUNDERS

Marcus

Sienna and Birdie are polar opposites, with one exception. They don't fit in, but in very different ways. Sienna is dorky. Quiet. Anxious. Beautiful. Sweet. She was never made for this life. She sticks with us because we're all she knows, but she's too good for us. She struggles to keep up, knowing deep down this isn't what she wants. She loves us, sure, but we're holding her back.

I know she wants more for herself, but she's never been able to break herself free from the safety net we've created. If she was honest, she'd rather be at home right now, reading a book. She'd wish for a drama-free life. A simple life. A life that isn't filled with people like us. A life with her true family, not crime, drugs and endless therapy sessions. Something quiet. Happy.

CHILD INFORMATION RECORD
GREAT BRITAIN

NAME: SIENNA SAUNDERS

DATE OF BIRTH: 14/03/2005

DATE OF ARRIVAL: 22/09/2010

REASON FOR ADMITTANCE:

EMERGENCY ADMITTANCE

ANY FAMILY STILL IN CONTACT: NO

ELIGIBLE FOR FOSTER/ADOPTION

PROGRAMMES: YES

PERSONAL NOTES:

Sienna was brought to Orchids at the age of 5 by police as an emergency admittance directly from her school after her parents were involved in a fatal car accident. She has found settling here a huge change and has recently been secluding herself more. She will be monitored closely and has been given extra counselling sessions regularly.

Sienna was adopted on 20/12/2015

'*Everything happens for a reason*'. Well, Sienna is the reason I know that's bullshit. What reason could there be for what happened? For what justified purpose does a child go through losing both of her parents at once? I can't even imagine the pain. Dragged away from a life of unconditional love and happiness and ending up with us. She deserved a life of success. She deserves normal teenage troubles. Maybe sneaking out a couple times or arguing with her parents about how messy her room is. Instead she's stuck with a bunch of reckless, selfish write-offs who think we're invincible.

I remember the time the others had pressured her to smoke weed with us. She coughed and gagged like she was about to throw up. I could've killed them that day for fucking with her innocence. *Only I get to do that*. Though I thought in some ways it would help her. In reality it just made her more paranoid and anxious. She hated feeling like she wasn't in control of herself. And yet, she stuck around. I can't help but feel responsible for that. Knowing I played a role in dragging her down this path with us.

Sometimes I wonder what would happen if we just let her go. If we leave her behind. Would she finally get the peace she deserves? Maybe go off to university and find a normal group of friends. Or would she spiral out of control? It's a scary thought, but one I can't help thinking about. I just want to change things for her. I don't want to be the reason she's stuck in this life forever. Plus I'm secretly too selfish to let her leave.

"You've always been so beautiful." Delilah says, admiring Sienna. She scrunches her nose, rejecting the compliment.
"Thank you, but-"
"There's no *'but'*" I interrupt. Sienna looks at me almost as if she's confused. "You're beautiful, sweet." I continue. She briefly smiles at me before looking down and fidgeting nervously with her hands. I wish she were easier to

read. I can't work her out, but I so desperately want to. I watch her gorgeous curls bounce around as she lifts her head back up to smile at me. I can tell that I make her nervous. She makes it obvious for me, maybe on purpose. I suppose that's a good thing, yet I can't seem to get through to her the way I want to. It's like every time I feel something may be developing between us she builds a wall around herself.

There's just something about her that draws me in. I can't help myself when it comes to her. Maybe it's that infectious smile. Or maybe it's the look she gives me when she thinks I'm not paying attention. Whatever it is, I want it. She's my sweet angel. I want to give her the life she deserves. *Of course*, the darker side of me wants to pin her down. Break her. To have my way with her. Wrap my hand around that pretty little neck. But it doesn't matter what I want, because every time I get closer, she pulls away. I can't force her to open up to me, because I know how much she's been through. I'm just waiting for the day that she'll let me in.

I suddenly realise through my daydream that the whole room is silent. I zone back in and see them all smirking at each other. Everybody can tell I'm flirting. I'm sure they always can, yet she's never directly addressed it. Never flirted back. Well, not vocally at least. Just with her body language, and her eyes. *Always her eyes*. Those beautiful golden eyes. Like pools of rich, inviting honey. Sometimes I'm sure they light up with a mysterious glint, as though she has secrets she's not ready to share. I feel like she's playing a very long game with me, and I can't help but play along. I'm like a moth to a flame. Sometimes I worry that it's all just wishful thinking. What *I* want. Maybe she just knows deep down that she's too good to be with somebody like me. If that's the case, then she's right.

"You two done staring at each other yet?" Dean asks, raising an eyebrow. I rub my hand on my head and laugh gently, now praying for the moment to pass by.

"Well then …" Skylar says smugly, "moving on."

"Not much suspense for this one is there?" Dean says, leaning back into his chair. Skylar approaches the filing cabinet to grab the last file, flicking her fingers through once again. Searching, and searching. And searching. We all look at one another in confusion. She turns to us and frowns.

"Hm … Dean's file isn't in here."

"It's probably too long to even fit in there." Delilah jokes. Dean looks angrily at her, in an obviously playful way, before letting out a smirk and gripping her thigh tightly.

Skylar uses the paperclip once again to open up the other drawers. Regardless of how many times I watch her do this, I can't help but be impressed. Where did she even learn it from? Where did she learn half of the things she does?

I vaguely glance back at Sienna to find her staring at me, her doe eyes wide and hazy. I raise an eyebrow and she quickly turns away. *Very cute of her to think I wouldn't notice.* I scooch myself closer to her and whisper a husky warning in her ear.

"Keep looking at me like that and we're gonna have a problem, sweet." She tries her best to hide her tiny smirk before standing up and moving somewhere else.

Skylar suddenly stops searching before pulling out a folder and popping it open. She reads for a few seconds and bursts out laughing. I guess she found it. She walks towards the desk still laughing hysterically, struggling to get any words out.

"Well the good news is, I've found it. But the even better news is that it's in a folder titled '*For the young offenders unit*'" Everybody erupts into laughter, including Dean who is now covering his eyes. Of course Dean would have his own separate folder. Why would he not? It's Dean. He takes one more puff of his joint and leans forward, his hand not leaving Delilah's thigh.

"Here we go."

CHAPTER 8:
DEAN DOUGLAS
Marcus

Dean Douglas. How do I even begin to describe Dean Douglas? I think 'an absolute fucking nightmare' would be a good start. He's a problem. A lost cause. The type of person who enters a room and indirectly demands your attention. Not in a good way, not at all. Rather in a way that would make the majority of people run a mile in the other direction.

He's blunt, disrespectful and has a temper that could rival a volcano on the brink of eruption. I don't think there's a single person who has had the pleasure of being in his presence that he hasn't lashed out at. He's a dangerous person. He's constantly leaving a path of destruction behind him. He's beyond change. Beyond any help. Dean is Dean, and you either deal with it, or you leave.

CHILD INFORMATION RECORD
GREAT BRITAIN

NAME: DEAN DOUGLAS

DATE OF BIRTH: 01/12/2004

DATE OF ARRIVAL: 07/01/2017

REASON FOR ADMITTANCE: ABUSE, DANGEROUS BEHAVIOUR

ANY FAMILY STILL IN CONTACT: NO

ELIGIBLE FOR FOSTER/ADOPTION PROGRAMMES: YES

PERSONAL NOTES:

Dean arrived at Orchids at the age of 12 after his mother filed a police report against him following a physical altercation between him and his father. Dean is showing worrying signs of anger and general bad behaviour including physical altercations with other children, personal drug use (cannabis) and leaving the home without permission. Must be closely monitored by staff.

Dean was found by the police after stealing a member of staff's car for a joy ride whilst in possession of cannabis. Staff did not press charges but Dean was taken to spend a year in a young offenders unit on 08/03/2019

He's a force of nature and his behaviour is alarmingly unpredictable. Even his words carry a sharp edge, capable of cutting through the toughest of skin. I certainly don't like to be on his bad side and as hard as it can be to admit, I'm afraid of him. I suppose it doesn't help that he is definitely physically intimidating. Around 6'1 and broad. And yes, whilst he may be a few inches shorter than me and he's not particularly muscular; he's toned and he's incredibly strong. Far stronger than me and far stronger than most people he comes across. Trust me, I've seen it all with Dean. I've seen him fight, throw objects across the room, break tables, you name it. But that's not what scares me about him. I fear his mind.

I've seen him manipulate people and situations to get what he wants. He's charming when he wants to be, but that charm is always laced with danger. It's like you're walking on eggshells around him, never quite knowing when he's going to snap. One minute he'll be laughing and the next he's storming out of the room, slamming the door so hard the walls shake.

Despite this, he's a brother to me. I admire him, and for some reason, I seem to crave his approval. I've seen glimpses of vulnerability in him, rare moments when he's let his guard down. There's this sadness in his eyes sometimes, like he's carrying the weight of the world on his shoulders. I can tell he's battling a lot in his mind. It's like he's permanently exhausted. Constantly on the verge of explosion, and his unyielding rage is the only thing driving him. There are moments where I see an entirely different side to him. Like when he's with Delilah of course.

He treats her with such a gentleness, as if she's made of glass. He's smooth and charming. Perfect to her, somehow. He's a complex person, with many layers; and he's my best friend. A huge part of who I am. It's a constant struggle. Having to constantly remind myself of the person I know he truly is underneath the mean facade. To care about him so deeply. The part of him that's redeemable. Struggling to find equilibrium between his virtues and flaws.

Seeing the image on his file is disturbing. He looks completely broken, and so extremely young. Thinking that this was the Dean I first met is alien to me. He looks so vulnerable now. So hurt. The giant bruise on his tiny face is harrowing; especially knowing the circumstance. Yet at the time I can remember thinking it made him look strong. Tough. Threatening. I can assure you that those tears welling up in his eyes were gone as fast as they arrived. He wouldn't let anybody see him cry. No way. He was playing the tough guy character right from the start. He had to. It's how he protects himself. The epitome of '*Hurt them before they can hurt me*'.

"Shit, that's a hefty bruise." Skylar states.

"Yeah, he fucked me up that's for sure." Dean begins to laugh, almost nervously. He's hurting, I know he is. I wish he would just say it. The room gets uncomfortably silent. We're all thinking the same thing. We can see he's in pain but saying the wrong thing can make him snap, and trust me, nobody wants that.

"That was fun." Delilah says smiling, likely desperate to break the silence and make sure Dean doesn't have too much time to think. Dean having time to think is a recipe for disaster. It's all for damage control. He presses a tender kiss onto Delilah's forehead, understanding her intentions, before sitting forward, his gaze fixed on the floor. The weighty silence settles in once more, and this time, I sense the responsibility to break it resting upon my shoulders.

"Maybe we should carry on looking around." Dean briskly stands up and nods his head in agreement.

"I don't wanna look at this shit anymore." He snaps, placing his hand on Delilah's back, leading her out of the room. I look at the others; they look back at me and our eyes do the speaking. We're aware of the need to maintain an upbeat atmosphere for the sake of Dean, at least for the remainder of the evening.

I let the girls leave the room first, not because I'm a gentleman, but because I want to soak in the room one last time. *The big, scary office full of mystery and secrets.* Yet as I stand, towering over the furniture that lives here, I let it sink in once more, that it's really nothing but an office. A boring, crappy little office. I'm putting my innocence into perspective. The big dreams I had. All of the insane ideas and plans. None of which came to fruition, clearly. I'm back here, in this now-abandoned children's home after stealing another car. Failing in every aspect of my life. A loser with no purpose. That isn't what my younger self would've wanted. Not for any of us. I take one last moment before ducking through the doorway and closing the door behind me. Glancing to my left, I notice the others making their way upstairs, prompting me to follow suit. Each step I take feels like a moment to absorb everything around me.

The barren walls, the peeling paint. The dust and debris scattered across the wooden floor. I remember the days when all you could hear was the echo of children's laughter through the walls and the pitter-patter of feet. Getting told off for trying to bring our bikes inside. And as we grew, the sounds of thumping music and doors slamming were the usual. But today, I hear nothing but a haunting silence and creaks of doors that I'm sure never creaked before.

CHAPTER 9:
UPSTAIRS

Marcus

As we make our way upstairs I attempt to shake away these melancholy flashbacks and focus on the present. It doesn't work. 1, 2 ,3, 4, 5, 6, 7, 8, 9, 10, 11, 12, 13, 14. 14 steps. As a kid, I had a habit of counting each step as I ascended or descended the stairs. I'm not sure why. It's not as if I was expecting that number to somehow change. The girls are chatting away, in their own little world. It's as if they're oblivious to the fact that the ghosts of our past are lurking in every corner of this place.

My mind is a blur as we move from room to room. The tiny upstairs bathroom with broken tiles and rusty pipes. The room that once belonged to the girl is now completely bare, devoid of any belongings. Nothing but moulded walls and torn-up floorboards. A completely smashed window with cold air pushing its way through. Though, it feels much clearer than I remember. Probably because it isn't covered in clutter. Or that my eyes and throat aren't burning from the fumes of hairspray and perfume, smacking me in the face. I always used to wonder what they'd talk about. In all honesty, I still do. Though it's unlikely I'd ever understand it anyway. Girl talk isn't exactly my specialty. If it was, Sienna would be mine already.

Only one room is left now. The bedroom I shared with Dean. The door, shut. Just how I had left it. Part of me doesn't want to open it. I'm not sure I can handle being hit with the memories. I left everything here. There wasn't a single thing I wanted to keep. When my Dad came to take me with him, that was the start of a new chapter for me. Or so I thought. New chapter, same shit. I turn the stupidly-loose knob and push the door open. Turning back to look at Dean as I make my way in. He shoots me a comforting glance and follows my lead.

Everything floods back and crashes into me like a wave. The room, the smell, the sounds. All of my stuff. My entire childhood exists inside of this room. I make my way over to the single bed that's pushed up against the wall. The chequered grey duvet I left is just lazily placed on top of the bare mattress. The wall, once adorned with my cherished bike posters, now stands bare, the torn remnants lying desolately on the bed. Dean's hand finds its way to my shoulder, offering a reassuring touch amid the melancholy scene.

"You good, bro?" He asks.

"It's a mess." I respond. This seems to be the only thought I can articulate. For some reason, it's making me angry. It feels like our space isn't being respected. Yes, I know it's not our space anymore and maybe I shouldn't care at all. But I do. Why? Nobody else seems to. I'm zoning into every single scuff on the walls. Every single broken piece of furniture. I make my way over to our wardrobe and open it, half-expecting to find my old clothes still hanging there. But it's empty, not a single piece of fabric left behind. I feel my blood boiling up inside and my breathing getting heavy. I turn to face Dean, who is still standing by my bed, a look of understanding in his eyes. He knows exactly what this room meant to me. To the both of us.

I look at the walls again and spot the old writing from when Dean and I had planned to escape. '*Escape*' as if this was some kind of a prison. We wanted to leave this place behind. To go as far away as possible. Somewhere. Now standing in this room, I realise how foolish we were. Just kids. Dreaming of a life we didn't understand and were so painfully far away from ever having. Confronting the reality of my situation and accepting the fact that my life didn't pan out the way I always wanted is a hard pill to swallow. I close my eyes and take a deep breath. It's time to leave.

"Let's go." I say, my voice cracking slightly. As everyone starts to exit, I follow suit, moving with the group. But a sudden pause halts my steps, my gaze drawn to the corner of the room behind the door. The slightly lifted floorboard. That's when I remember the things I had hidden. I immediately crouch to the ground and begin pulling up the floorboard. It's much easier to lift than I remember. I swallow as I feel the memories flooding out of this space on the floor.

As I pull out the cardboard box from beneath my heart is racing and adrenaline is running through my body. It's been years since I've even thought about this box. It's as if my younger self is reaching out to me, trying to remind me of the things I once held dear. Shoving them in my face. With shaky hands, I open the lid to reveal a pile of photographs, some trinkets and a few drawings. The pictures are blurry and worn but the meanings of them are still so fresh. Some of them are pictures I had taken on my old disposable camera, and others are pictures I had been given. I can feel everyone watching me closely as I flip through to the bottom of the pile.

A photo my mother had given the social workers when she passed me over. Of us. I had pretty much forgotten what she looked like by the time I was old enough to understand. This was the only reminder of her I ever had growing up. No matter how much I despise that woman, I didn't have the heart to throw it away. So I kept it, but I kept it at the bottom. Always at the bottom. That fucking photo. I wish she would've just kept that stupid fucking photo. But that would've been too selfless. She had to give me that one extra problem. One extra thing to deal with; to battle in my mind. The woman is cruel by nature.

She wanted me to know what she looks like. To never forget what she looks like. She wanted to leave me with a teaser of a mother I never got. But me? She couldn't care less. Never cared to see what I looked like as I grew. Never called to see if I was okay. Never contacted at all. Nothing.

As I sit on the floor, staring at the photograph of my mother and I, I feel a knot forming in my stomach and a lump in my throat. I begin seeing stars and the room starts spinning. It's as if all of the emotions I ever had towards her are coming back in full force. All at once. Cutting through me like knives. I quickly shove the photo back to the bottom of the pile and slam the lid shut.

My sweet Sienna crouches down next to me with her hand on my back. I look at her in the eyes as her face fills with concern.

"I'm here." She says, "Take a moment, please." She accepts the box from my grasp with a deliberate slowness, her eyes never leaving mine. I reach out, resting my hand on her knee, steadying my breath. With a firm press of my palms against my eyes, I attempt to stave off any impending tears. Seeing my mother's photo again after all of this time had hit me harder than I could've anticipated. It's like opening an old, deep wound that never healed.

She was a stranger to me, yet I longed for her to have been different. Waited up every single night just hoping she would walk through the door. Constantly living in denial. I had tried to rationalise that maybe she just couldn't take care of me. That maybe the story I was told was a lie and, in reality, I was taken away from my loving mother by some *evil* police officers. That she was fighting desperately every day to get me back. But if I was honest with myself, which I am now, deep down I knew she just didn't want me.

Summoning the strength, I rise to my feet, and Sienna stands beside me, her hand a steady presence on my back. Though the others cast their gaze in my direction, no words escape their lips. Dean's firm grip on my shoulder is accompanied by a silent inquiry in his eyes, asking how I'm holding up. I respond with a nod, signifying that I'm alright. He moves past me toward the spot of the missing floorboard, crouching down to retrieve something hidden within. Rising to his feet, he turns around, revealing a book in his hand.

CHAPTER 10:
THE BOOK

Marcus

"What's this then?" He says smiling at me. "'*Defeating the Dragon*' Written and Illustrated by Marcus Bear, 04/02/2016." My cheeks flush with embarrassment as I try to snatch the book back. Dean, of course, doesn't let this happen.

"It's just a stupid storybook I wrote."

"Still writing stories at 12?" He laughs.

"11 actually."

"Oh my bad, that makes all the difference." We all laugh and he begins trying to remove the clasp. His face stiffens as he clearly struggles to do so.

"Struggling there, tough guy?" I say jokingly. He smirks and motions a '*shh*' to me with his finger. Despite his persistent efforts, the clasp refuses to yield, drawing out the amusement among us. Even Dean joins in the laughter, scratching his head in mild bewilderment. Altering his hand position, he makes another attempt, but the outcome remains unchanged; no luck.

"Let me try!" Skylar demands snatching the book. She studies the clasp for a moment, gently brushing her fingers across the carved surface. She starts pulling, her jaw clenched in frustration as she mutters something under her breath. Despite her efforts, it remains steadfast, refusing to budge.

"Come on then, Miss Lockpick." Dean teases.

"Here, I'll do it." Birdie snaps. Everybody takes turns trying to defeat the lock, but to no avail. Surely it can't be that stuck? My turn. I grab the book and turn it to examine the lock. It's a standard book lock, the kind that should open effortlessly. I glance at everyone with a puzzled and judgmental expression before attempting it myself. With one finger I pop open the lock and '*BOOM*'...

A sudden, powerful force escaping from the book, ricochetes off of every wall surrounding us in a frenzied dance. Not a loud noise, but rather a deep and resonant sound that made the entire building vibrate. As if a giant hammer had just struck the ground, sending a ripple through the air and pushing us backwards. It lasts maybe a few seconds yet it feels like an eternity. My ears begin to ring intensely, feeling as though they might burst. My eyes start to water and my heart is beating wildly, pounding through my chest. We frantically look at each other, every face covered in panic. Immediately we're drawn to the abrupt sounds of pouring, heavy rain outside. Nobody speaks. We all stand frozen, unable to comprehend what we've just experienced.

"What the fuck was that?" Birdie says, her voice trembling. We all exchange glances but don't have any words. No answer to her question; because none of us know the answer. Though all of us long for the answer. I glance down at the book in my hands as I'm shaking uncontrollably. A book can't do that, it's just not possible. I look back up at Dean who is staring at me intensely.

"It's just thunder, surely." He says, trying to convince himself.

"Bro, what kind of thunder does that?"

"You got a better explanation?" I look at the book once more and begin flicking the clasp open and closed with my finger before looking back at Dean, saying nothing, but my movements are speaking for me.

"*Ahh* okay, so we've found a magical fucking book? Is this really where we're going right now?" He's right, it's crazy to even think something like that, but what other explanation could there be? I shrug my shoulders and Dean rolls up another joint as his hands are shaking terribly.

"What do we do?" Sienna asks, looking up at me in fear. I look at her and shake my head. I don't know what to tell her. With a heavy heart, she lowers her head, and I instinctively pull her close, wrapping my arm around her, providing a tight embrace for comfort. Dean takes a long puff of his joint.

"Read it." He demands.

"I don't know if that's a good idea, man." He begins slowly walking towards me and laughing vaguely.

"So you're telling me, you think you're some kind of *chosen one* who has not only found a magical book, but written a magical book and you're not even gonna read it?" We stare at each other for a few intense seconds.

"He's right Marcus, we have to read it." Skylar interjects. "What if there's something important in there?"

"There won't be, Sky, it's a shitty little fantasy storybook I wrote as a kid. Dean was right, it had to be thunder." The room fills with an awkward, lingering tension as I wait for somebody else to move on the conversation. I turn my focus to the rain outside; pounding down in a heavy rhythm onto the roof. Creating a background noise that is strangely soothing to me. Like a lullaby, calming my racing heart and anxious thoughts.

"Maybe we should get going." Delilah suggests.

"I agree." Dean responds, taking another drag. He briskly grabs Delilah and leads her out of the room, the rest of us following closely behind. As we make our way back to the broken window we climbed in through, I'm not taking in the building anymore. Not thinking about the memories I made here. I'm thinking about the book in my hand. The bang. The sudden storm. None of it makes sense.

We reach the smashed window and all I can hear is the relentless downpouring of rain. I pull up the hood of my jacket and climb my way out, the shards of glass cracking underneath my feet. We all run back to the cars, more than ready to call it a night. As the car doors shut, the silence is definitely noticeable. We all sit for a moment, exhausted, soaking up our thoughts.

"Marcus, are you okay?" Sienna asks.

"Yeah, sweet." I shoot her a smile through the rearview mirror. "I'm all good." She smiles back briefly and turns to look out the window, mesmerised by the pouring rain. Dean beeps a few times from the other car, before driving off recklessly. I turn on the car, 5:23a.m.

As I drive slowly, my mind is full. So many thoughts are racing through my head that I'm not thinking a single thing. It's all a blur. My head is thumping and my eyes are strained. The rain continues to pour down heavily, creating a white noise that echoes through the empty streets. I pull up to Skylar's house, my eyes barely staying open.

"See ya!" She shouts, smiling, as she gets out of the car, slamming the door behind her. Somehow still full of energy. *That girl can't be human.* I watch and wait for her to get inside safely. Well, *Safely* for Skylar, meaning I watch her climb onto

47

the top of her porch and pull herself up through the top floor window. She waves enthusiastically at me and I nod back before turning to Sienna. Curled up on the back seat, fast asleep, using the seatbelt as a pillow. Suddenly my mind isn't so busy. All I can think about is how beautiful she is. How angelic. My sweet girl.

I start up the car again, whilst smiling ear to ear, and drive it back to where we had taken it from. As I step out, grabbing the book from my lap and tucking it into the top of my joggers, I'm making sure to be as discreet as possible; trying not to make a single sound. I open the door to the back seat and give Sienna a gentle shake to wake her.

"Hey," I whisper. She stirs and rubs her eyes in the most adorable way possible before looking up at me. "You wanna just stay with me tonight?" She nods her head and smiles, shutting her eyes once again. I unbuckle her seatbelt and carefully lift her out of the car, shutting the door slowly with my elbow. As I take the short walk back to my house with Sienna in my arms, I'm at peace for the first time in a while. The only sound that fills the air is the soft chirping of birds. These moments, with just the two of us, hold a special place in my heart, even when not a single word passes between us. I feel grateful for the trust she puts in me; at this moment, holding her in my arms she's the only thing I care about. Protecting her. I'd kill for her safety.

I want to understand her. I want to know what to say to her, what she wants. Whatever it is, I'll do it. I want to be more than a couple of friends who flirt and that's it. I want us to do more than just 'like' each other.

That is, if she even likes me.

As I navigate the dark and quiet streets, all I can detect is her head resting on my chest, rising and falling with my breaths. Feeling her warmth seeping into my skin, I realise just how much I crave her affection. I want so desperately to kiss her, but I don't want to ruin any moment. I don't want to risk our friendship. While a friendship may not be exactly what I want, I'd take that any day over not having her at all. As I reach my front door, With one hand, I clutch my keys tightly, while the other remains a steady support around her. I unlock the door and lead us inside, the comforting warmth of home wrapping around us. Taking deliberate steps, I guide us up the stairs and into my bedroom, ensuring a gentle closure of the door behind us.

I carefully settle her onto my bed, tucking the duvet cover snugly around her for comfort. I take a deep breath before taking a risk and gently pressing my lips against her forehead. She stirs a little before settling back into her slumber, the light from my desk lamp softly glowing on her skin. I begin taking off my shirt when I'm abruptly snapped out of my current paradise. The book.

CHAPTER 11:
'READ IT'

Marcus

I hold the book in my hands and stare at it. Flicking the clasp and tutting nervously. Dean's instruction is repeating and repeating in my mind on an endless loop. 'Read it.'. It's pretty pathetic. Incomprehensible. Am I scared? Scared of a book I wrote myself? But it isn't just a book anymore, is it? It's a book that seems to have caused a fucking explosion and sudden storm. Am I losing my mind? I shake my head, trying to clear it and throw the book onto my desk. I need to sleep. To make the most of this moment with Sienna. But as I slip into the bed beside her and try to settle, my mind can't help but wander back to the book. It's sitting there smugly on my desk, taunting me. Impossibly, I can feel its presence in the room with us. It's like there's a weight in the air.

I try to push the thoughts away, instead focusing on Sienna's peaceful breathing and the warmth of her body next to mine. But it's no use. It's calling me. I can't just ignore it, can I? What if I'm not going crazy? There could be something important inside. What's the worst thing that could happen? I sit up in the bed and crack my neck, my mind made up. I'm procrastinating and I can't ignore it any longer.

I climb back over Sienna and take a seat at my desk, glancing over at her to make sure she's still asleep before I open it. I hold my breath while opening to the first page, in preparation for another 'bang'. It's fine. No noise, no rain. Nothing at all. I take a breath of relief before my attention is brought to my childish drawings and terrible, sloppy handwriting. My skills were definitely not at the right level for my age. But is that surprising?

'The animals were asleep peacefully in the village, when suddenly they were awoken by the sounds of rain and thunder crashing above the houses and a loud ROAR in the distance. They all emerged from their homes, and to their horror, they saw the very scary 'Derpy Dragon' rapidly approaching. Panic set in as they realised that their village was in grave danger.

'Baker kitty' immediately got to work, using her magic to whip up medicine potions and remedies to give the animals strength in battle. 'Sakura fox' scrambled desperately to protect the nearby flowers, while the army worked feverishly to fortify the village defences. But then, disaster struck, 'Shy spider' stumbled and fell, injuring one of her many legs. With one of the animals vulnerable, the animals had to move even faster to prepare. Time was running out.

At last, the Derpy dragon arrived, accompanied by his loyal sidekick who is 'definitely a Froggy'. The chaotic battle began and the village was soon awash with flames as the dragon breathed fire on the homes and shops. Despite their fear, the animals fought back valiantly, determined to defend their

51

beloved home. All of a sudden, the dragon began losing energy, and fell to the ground, dead.

King 'Mint choc chipper' and Queen 'Milk 'n' cookies, deer?', who had been watching from the safety of their castle, waited for the dragon to die before emerging from the castle to inspect the damage brought by the dragon. Together, they closed the gates once again to protect their village.'

After reading I pause, almost expecting something crazy to happen. Maybe an explosion? A bang? Some kind of surreal beam of light like they have in the movies? Nothing. Just my bedroom. It's simply a tale straight out of a storybook—a mere thunderstorm. Why did I even entertain the thought of it being something more? Almost amusingly anticlimactic. With a quiet chuckle, I close the book, letting go of any lingering expectations. I try to seal the clasp which, for some reason, no longer closes fully and turn off the lamp. Once my eyes begin to adjust to the darkness, I make my way back into bed. As I lay down next to Sienna, she stirs again and shifts slightly closer to me. Taking another risk, I wrap my arm around her, pulling her close to my chest; the soft sounds of her breathing mixed with the chirping of birds outside lulling me to sleep.

Waking up a few hours later, Sienna's head still resting on my chest, everything feels right. I feel so weightless. So content. I trace my fingers over her cheek and make my way down to her neck, memorising every curve. I pull away from her gently, trying not to disturb her sleep, and grab my phone to check the time. 10:14. I get out of the bed quietly and decide to make breakfast for us.

As I brush my teeth and make my way to the kitchen the only thing on my mind is Sienna. My sweet. She's all I want. She's the only thing holding me together. The only thing in my life that makes me want to be a somewhat-good person. I stand still and glance around the kitchen, trying to decide what to make. Bacon sandwich? Pancakes? Too simple. I need her to know that I'm a good cook. Not that she would even care. She's too nice. A full English. That's it. I open the fridge and take out some eggs, bacon, sausages, baked beans and mushrooms and start cooking. The smell of sizzling bacon fills the room and I can just feel myself smiling. It's the perfect morning.

Taking a sip of my tea, I hear her faint little footsteps behind me. My heart is pounding with excitement and the butterflies in my stomach begin to race. I fix my hair and turn around to see her standing in the doorway wearing one of my hoodies and rubbing her eyes. It's an adorable sight which forces me to try and conceal my smile. I know I have to play it cool, but fuck, it's pretty much impossible when she looks like that.

"Good morning, sweet."

"Good morning." She replies with a smile, looking around at all the food I'm serving up. I nod subtly, feeling very proud of myself. I know I'm impressing her.

"I hope you're in the mood for a full English breakfast, *Marcus Bear style*." I say with a smirk as I set down her plate. She laughs and takes a seat at the table, pouring herself a glass of orange juice.

"You're good to me." she says taking a bite of bacon.

"And you're mean to me. In fact I'm the only person you're ever mean to," I pause, "and that really turns me on." She rolls her eyes and pouts, trying to conceal her smile. I can hardly focus on eating and can't stop myself from staring at her; the sunlight pouring through the window and bouncing off of her skin.

"You got plans today?" I ask.

"College is supposed to be today's plan." I check the time on my phone and smirk before flipping it to show her. 11:37.

"*Shit.*" I say sarcastically. "Too late for that now I guess."

"What did you have in mind?" I shrug nonchalantly, trying to come up with an idea on the spot.

"Wanna go for a ride?"

"No. Not the bike."

"What's wrong with the bike, sweet?"

"I hate the bike."

"You don't mean that."

"I absolutely mean that." We both laugh and look at each other for a few seconds before I stand up and grab the bike key, tossing it in my hand.

"I'm serious, Marcus."

"So am I, *Sienna,*" I raise my eyebrows and wait for her to change her mind.

"Fine, but no speeding."

"Okay, no speeding." I promise as I reach out my pinky finger. She stands up slowly, rolling her eyes and locks her pinky into mine.

"Maybe a little speeding." I tease as she walks towards the front door.

CHAPTER 12:
LEAVE THE CITY

Marcus

We make our way outside and I can feel the cool breeze on my skin. The sun is shining, but what's funny is that if Sienna wasn't with me I probably wouldn't realise it. I'd be cooped up in my room with the curtains shut, smoking weed and wasting yet another day of my life. I grab my helmet and toss it to Sienna before hopping on the bike. I start the engine and rev it a few times before motioning for her to climb on. She does so reluctantly, wrapping her arms tight around my waist as I slowly begin to push off. The feeling of her heartbeat through my back is indescribable, like she's a part of me. I take things easy at first, not wanting to freak her out too much, but as we hit the open road I can't resist the urge to speed. I glance back at her briefly and she seems nervous. But excited at the same time.

We ride for hours through winding roads; the sun shining down on us. I can feel her grip tightening every time I pick up speed, and it's almost reassuring to feel her trust in me. Eventually, we start to pass by fields and farms and I can see cows and sheep in the near distance. The air begins to smell like freshly cut grass and wildflowers, which makes a refreshing change from the constant scents of petrol and cigarettes back at home.

Places like this make me feel like I'm taking my life for granted. Like I'm missing out. I'd do anything to live in a place like this. I take a deep breath and let out a laugh, glancing back at Sienna. We eventually reach a small clearing near a river and I decide to park the bike, both of us climb off and take a moment to breathe in the clean air. I stroll over and take a seat on the grassy bank, briefly dipping my fingers in the water.

The water feels stimulating and cool against the skin of my fingertips and I watch as it ripples and fades away. Sienna soon joins, sitting down beside me and staring out into the fields. We sit in a comfortable silence for a while. Peace. Quiet. I look around and take in all the vibrant colours and the gentle sway of the tall grass in the breeze. Vibrancy is rare for me. More often than not, everything seems grey. Desaturated. I riskily place my hand on Sienna's leg before removing it quickly and deciding to roll up a joint; lying back to take a drag. Looking up at the sky I feel like the kid I never got to be. Safe and secure.

"Isn't this just the ideal place to be?" I say, closing my eyes. "I hope we can leave that fucking city one day."

"I agree," She replies lying back with me. "But it has some positives."

"Such as?" She pauses in thought for a moment.

"The lights at night time are pretty beautiful."

"*Ah yes,* the lights. They definitely take my mind away from the never-ending traffic, crippling pollution and high crime rates."

"You say that as if you aren't constantly adding to those high crime rates." We both laugh and look into each other's eyes.

"How do you do it?" I ask.

"Do what?"

"Find the good in everything." She shrugs and looks back up to the sky.

"Everything bad has something good. You just have to look for it." I take a moment to think about her answer; the sound of the river flowing in the background.

"A rabbit!" She shouts, practically leaping to her feet. I sit up slowly resting my arms up on my knees and take another puff. Across the river, a small brown rabbit sits, quietly observing from the other side.

"I wanna cuddle it."

"You can't cuddle a wild rabbit, beautiful." Before I can even fully finish my sentence she has taken off her shoes and socks and started rolling up her very baggy jeans.

"What are you doing?" I laugh. She doesn't respond as her mind is entirely fixated on the rabbit. Finding a shallow part of the river broken by rocks, she starts stepping across with her hands flicked upward, like a little princess. With every step, the rabbit is becoming more aware of her presence and beginning to distance itself.

"It's okay, bunny." She says, softly. Her face fills with determination and she begins to rush. As she takes her next step I notice her foot slipping, almost in slow motion, and she falls onto the rocky edge of the river.

"Sienna!" I shout, knowing it's impossible to catch her. I quickly throw my blunt and run into the river; the water almost reaching up to my knees. I quickly lift her up and carry her out of the water and onto the soft, swaying grass.

"Are you okay?" I ask.

"My leg hurts pretty bad." I look down at her leg and see a small amount of blood sitting on top of a significantly large scrape. I swiftly make my way to my bike and start searching through the rear compartment to locate my first aid kit. As I open the kit and take out some antiseptic spray and a bandage, I notice Sienna staring at me. Her eyes filled with amusement, as if she's discovered a whole new part of me. She looks down, but I can see a smile tugging the corners of her mouth. I gently crouch down beside her and spray her wound. She winces briefly, clutching my hand tight.

"Sorry, this might sting a bit."

"It's okay. I'm sorry I ruined the peaceful moment."

"You didn't ruin anything, sweet" I reassure, bandaging up her leg. "Just a little mishap, that's all." She looks up at me and suddenly our eye contact is very intense. I feel my heart pounding and there's a silence between us, as if the world around us has frozen in time. I'm entirely captivated by her. Her eyes, the way she looks at me, her hair, her lips, her skin. That tiny hand gripping mine. My mind is racing with a million thoughts at once, each telling me to stop being a coward; to tell her how I feel.

"I'm in love with you." I confess. She looks shocked as her mouth opens slightly and her eyebrows scrunch, but I can't stop there. "There's nobody like you, Sienna. Nobody. And I'm sorry if this is a lot to take in but I just can't pretend anymore."

"Marcus," she says, shaking her head.

"Look, I know you're above me. *Believe me,* I fucking know that. I'm not the best man there is, far from it, but I also know that nobody else will love you the way I do." She doesn't respond, or move, but her eyes begin to widen. I start leaning in and she does the same. Her beautiful little face, flushed with nerves.

"We should go." She says abruptly. *What?* I look down and try to register what just happened, before pulling away and clenching my jaw in embarrassment. Staring into the abyss, I slowly lift her to her feet, cherishing the touch of her hand, and begin methodically packing away my first aid kit. The action is mechanical, a physical distraction. I can see her from the corner of my eye, standing awkwardly beside the bike as I walk to grab our helmets.

"Marcus I'm sorry, it's not you. I just-"

"It's cool." I say, cutting her off and passing her the helmet, our hands brushing briefly as she takes it. We both slip them on and mount the bike, the engine roaring to life.

"Ready?" I ask, looking back. She nods and wraps her arms around me, squeezing me tight for some reason. Everything she does is confusing. This can't be in my imagination. Is she scared? Playing with me?

As we drive back towards home, I can feel a tension we've never had before. I've ruined everything. My heart begins to sink lower and lower with every passing moment. I should've kept my mouth shut. But I was so close. I notice her grip loosen, both physically and emotionally and I'm kicking myself. All I can hear is the engine. Each time we stop I can feel her eyes on me, but I don't want to look back. I don't want to see her face, flushed with disappointment or confusion. I don't want to explain myself. As we finally pull up to her house, I park the bike and take my helmet off, turning to face her. She's avoiding eye contact but is forced to look at me while returning the helmet. She smiles at me briefly.

"Thanks for today, I had fun." She says softly.

"Of course, sweet."

"I'll uh… text you later?"

"Yeah, cool." We both force a smile but I know I can't let her go like this. She begins walking away but I impulsively grab her hand and pull her to face me. Those perfect eyes staring right into mine.

"I didn't mean to make things awkward."

"It isn't awkward." She lies.

"Oh *really*? Because it feels pretty fucking awkward to me."

"I just need time to think, Marcus." She turns and walks away, not looking back. I wait for her to get inside and I snappily put my helmet back on. As I ride home, way faster than I should, I can't help but feel like everything is falling apart. My heart aches as I go over every word I said to her, over and over. I can't lose her.

Before I walk back into the house I check my phone, hoping she'd messaged me. But there's nothing. No message. Nothing.

"You've fucked it." I murmur to myself. Home shit home.

CHAPTER 13:
FAMILY DYNAMICS

Marcus

Walking back through the door feels so wrong. I feel entirely helpless. I should be doing something to fix this. Tossing my keys onto the side table, I walk through to the kitchen and grab myself a beer from the fridge.

"There 'e is!" My dad shouts, stumbling into the kitchen. His 'demon dog' following closely behind. The last person I want to see right now. "Y'alright mate?"

"Yeah dad, I'm good."

"Where ya been?"

"I just went for a ride."

"On your own?" I take a deep breath as I open my beer and begin drinking, knowing this conversation is about to go south.

"Nah, with Sienna."

"Ahh, Sienna ay?"

"Yup."

61

"She ya girlfriend yet?"

"No, she's not." He begins laughing obnoxiously and raging anger starts to build up inside of me. I take another swig of beer and look him dead in the eye; as usual he doesn't take my hints to shut up.

"*Cor*, you move a bit slow don't ya mate?" He continues to laugh and hits my shoulder. My mind is thrown back to the files we had found.

"That's ironic." I mumble under my breath. His laughs quickly softens.

"What was that?"

"I said, that's ironic." He has the nerve to look at me with confusion.

"What you tryna say?"

"Well, I don't know about you but I'd say that taking over 10 years to *find* me was pretty fucking slow."

"Excuse me?"

"You heard me." I start, "I stayed 15 minutes down the road in a children's shelter and you actually expect me to believe you were making any fucking effort to find me? You weren't doing shit."

"You have no idea what I was doing out there, boy. Watch your fucking mouth."

"Or what?" I walk up to him and lock my eyes to his. I'm seeing red.

"I'm your father."

"So you keep reminding me. If only you'd bothered to show up when I *actually* fucking needed you. I brought myself up. I had to take care of myself while you were off doing your own thing. You're a complete joke." He takes a step closer to me, his breath smelling like whiskey and cigarettes.

"Say one more word boy, I dare ya."

"I'm not a boy. I'm a grown man now. You missed that part, remember?"

Suddenly, he lunges at me with a closed fist and gives me no time to react before I feel the impact of his hand against my jaw. The pain is sharp and intense, causing me to lose balance briefly and stumble backwards. The room falls silent as we both stare each other down. His eyes are filled with a burning rage and I can feel my heart rate increase rapidly. I catch a glimpse of the vein pulsing in his forehead. The anger and resentment between us is palpable, vibrating in the air like an electric current. The room feels so much smaller now and I can taste the copper of blood in my mouth. I want to kill him, but instead I freeze entirely. Without saying a word he turns and begins walking to the front door.

"Scumbag." I say, shaking my head.

"You better be gone by the time I get back." he responds, slamming the door so hard I can feel the house shake.

I stand there, alone in the kitchen, trying to process what just happened. Anger, sorrow, and frustration interlace within the tumult of my thoughts. I hear the sound of my dad's car engine roaring outside as he speeds away, leaving me behind once again. *Deja vu.* Seeking solace, I take another sip of beer, endeavouring to pacify my frayed nerves, and walk over to the sink to splash my face with water. The chill of the cold water is relieving against my burning skin. I grab my phone from my pocket and text Skylar, asking if I can crash at her house. Her family treats me like I'm one of them. Sometimes I wish I was. Her home has become a welcoming escape zone for me, like an oasis in the chaos of my life.

I head upstairs and start packing a bag. It's not the first time I've had to do this, but I have a different feeling now, *and a much bigger bag.* There's no going back this time. As I'm about to leave the room a peculiar sensation creeps in; a nagging feeling of forgetting something vital. Pausing, I pivot to survey the room, and there it is staring me in the face. The book. I couldn't care less about that book. I had forgotten it even existed for years whilst it was left to rot under a floorboard. But I do care, subconsciously. I quickly grab it and stuff it into my bag before heading out.

I hop on my bike and ride towards Skylar's house, my mind still reeling. The wind rushes through my hair, momentarily distracting me from the swirling thoughts. I try so desperately to focus on the road ahead but everything is passing me in a blur. I'm riding recklessly, but this time, it's not deliberate. The blaring of multiple car horns pierces the air, more than usual, directed at me, but I'm at a loss about what I'm doing wrong.

Miraculously, I arrive at Skylar's house, despite navigating the route without a single conscious thought. Disembarking from my bike, a heavy weariness settles in. I can tell I'm both emotionally and physically drained. I crack my neck in an attempt to alleviate some tension before advancing toward the door. The faint, comforting sounds of laughter and chatter emanate from the living room window.

I take a deep breath and knock on the door, setting aside my unease. Skylar opens the door almost instantly, with a concerned look on her face.

"You okay?" She asks.

"Yeah, just another argument."

"Marcus, your face-"

"I know. Don't worry about it."

She moves to the side, staring in shock at my jaw, it must be bad. I step inside, gently slipping off my shoes and leaving my bag on the stairs. Skylar guides me into the living room, where her parents are cosily seated, engrossed in a film.

"Oh my goodness!" Her mum shrieks, jumping off of the sofa. "Darling what happened?" I shrug it off and reach out for a hug instead.

"Was it your old man?" Her dad asks, standing with his arms crossed. I nod to him.

"Yeah, things just got heated. I'm fine though." Her parents exchange a worrying glance before her dad takes a breath and speaks again.

"Well, you stay here as long as you need to, okay? I'll set up the spare room for you in a bit." He says, placing a comforting hand on my shoulder. I feel a lump forming in my throat and I'm forced to swallow my emotions. At this moment I'm wishing for a different life. For a life with parents like hers; ones who actually care about me instead of seeing me as a burden, punching bag or inconvenience. It's all so foreign to me. Did I not deserve it?

My mind wanders to memories I've been suppressing; memories of loneliness and feeling unwanted. I feel an overpowering wash of sadness for my younger self. For that little boy who deserved better. Skylar's mum thankfully saves me from my own thoughts and returns me to reality by gesturing me out of the room.

"Come on Darling, let's get you sorted out."

I follow her into the kitchen, taking a seat at the large dining table while she rummages through the drawers. Skylar walks in shortly after, grabbing herself a small stack of biscuits before taking a seat next to me. I take the moment to collect myself and relax; the warmth of Skylar's home soothing me. Her mum grabs some antiseptic cream from a first aid kit and grabs a seat opposite me. She gingerly begins to apply the cream to my wound, leaving me with a sharp, stinging sensation which quickly cools and spreads outwards across my hot and swollen jaw.

The sensation is almost refreshing as I begin to feel it disinfecting. The scents of the cream and air freshener mixed with the sound of Skylar's brothers laughing upstairs is creating a heartwarming atmosphere that I long for. I close my eyes and take a long breath, a slight smile forming on my face. Feeling a hand rest on top of mine, I open my eyes to see Skylar's mum smiling at me.

"Feeling better?"

"Yes, Thank you."

"No need to thank me, Darling. We just want you to be alright."

"Do you wanna talk about it?" Skylar asks, taking a bite of her final biscuit. I look at her and shake my head briefly.

"It's just the usual shit."

"I know just the thing you need." Her mum says suddenly, standing up and walking to the bottom of the stairs. "Boys! Come down! Game night!"

In no time, Skylar's younger brother bounds down the stairs as her mum quickly scurries off to grab the games.

"Marcus!" He exclaims, running to me for a bear hug. Her older brother following, slightly less enthusiastically, behind and greeting me with a simple nod of the head.

"Y'alright bro?"

"Yeah, all good."

"You been in a fight?" he asks.

"Nah, it's nothing man."

We spend the rest of the night playing through all of the board games they have and eating snacks, the tension from my day dissipating slowly. The sounds of laughter and the joy of both winning and losing fills the room and I feel like a part of the family once again. My mind letting go of the turmoil and becoming entirely occupied by the positive atmosphere as my jaw begins to ache from the constant laughter. The warmth of the room and the softness of the sofa against my back making me feel safe. For a moment, my thoughts briefly turn to Sienna, and I feel a pang in my chest. I take my phone out of my pocket and check for messages, but still nothing. I toss my phone onto the carpet and allow myself to get lost in the moment once again; to be present.

As the night wears on and the games come to an end, Skylar's dad begins setting up a bed for me in the guest room.

"There you go, mate. I'll get some more pillows down for you tomorrow when I have a moment."

"This is more than fine for me, thank you again."

"No need to thank me. Get some rest."

"Will do." He shuts the door as he leaves the room and I immediately fall backwards onto the bed, staring up to the ceiling and listening to the sounds of the house settling. I hear some footsteps coming up the hallway and a faint knock on the door.

"It's me, the Monopoly champion." Skylar says through the door.

"You can come in." I laugh. The door opens and Skylar bounces in, sucking on a lollipop and flopping down onto the make-shift sofa bed.

"So, talk to me, loser. What's going on with you?" I laugh at the simplicity of her question.

"How much time have you got?"

"Marcus, I don't sleep until at least 3am and It's currently only 10. I have all the time in the world."

"Fair. Well I'll cut it as short as I can." I let out a loud breath before starting. "So, Sienna stayed at mine last night-"

"In your bed?" She interrupts, winking at me.

"Yes Skylar, in my bed."

"Nice." she smirks. Little creep.

"Don't speak too soon."

"What do you mean?"

"Well actually it was going great at first, I made her breakfast and then I took her out on the bike and we ended up at this river in the middle of the countryside."

"Very romantic."

"I thought so too." I start, "Anyway, she saw this rabbit and ended up falling into the river trying to get close to it and I had to go and grab her."

"Oh shit, was she okay?"

"Yeah she was fine. Well, she scraped her leg up but that was about it. And then I um-" I stop myself and laugh, considering if I even want to share what I did.

"Oh no. What did you do?"

"I told her I love her." I can feel Skylar turn her head to look at me. She says nothing.

"She didn't really respond. She didn't say anything, but she was smiling. And the day had been so good and she looked so happy and I just got so caught up in the moment so-" Skylar puts her arm on mine to slow me down.

"It's okay." She says with a comforting look.

"I tried to kiss her, Sky."

"And what? She didn't want to?"

"She was leaning in at first but then she stopped. She pretty much didn't say a word to me the whole way back and then she mentioned that she would text me but I haven't heard anything. Basically I fucked it." I fake stretch and put my arms up, covering my eyes. Trying to hide from the humiliation.

"She loves you."

"I'm not so sure about that."

"She does. You know she does. But she can be... complicated. She's been through a lot."

"Yeah, join the club." She begins to giggle briefly.

"You think too much, Marcus. Just give her some time."

"I know."

"What about your dad?"

"He's just a prick."

"Nothing new there,"

"Yeah, I should've left that house a long time ago. Seeing that file yesterday just pissed me off so I had to let it out."

"You know you can stay here as long as you need."

"I appreciate that, I do, but it's not fair on your family."

"Oh come on. As if they'd ever ask you to leave."

"That's precisely the problem."

"Where you gonna go then?" She says with a pout.

"I'll stay here until I can convince Dean to let me crash with him."

"Ahh, so forever?" We both laugh and Skylar bounces to her feet.

"Well, I'll see you in the morning, loser" She says walking towards the door, but stopping to admire herself in the mirror first. "Ugh, so nobody thought to let me know that I still have mud on my face?"

"Mud?"

"Yeah, mum dragged me outside today to help her with the garden."

"Very exciting."

"I'm glad you think so, because you'll be here tomorrow."

"Fantastic."

"I'll leave you alone now. Oh and if Sienna finally calls you back, you can sneak her through the back door, it's always unlocked, just keep it down." She suggests raising her eyebrows and winking at me playfully. *Like I said, little creep.*

"I don't see that happening, but thanks."

"You never know what's gonna happen. Nobody does. I mean, you could end up a murderer... or a millionaire... or some kind of super secret agent. Or a -"

"You're rambling."

"Yes, I am. Night."

"Night, Sky."

Skylar smiles and holds up her middle finger to me before shutting the door unnecessarily loudly. The room falls silent once more, and I'm left alone with my thoughts. The most dangerous place to be. Sienna's smile when I told her I loved her is etched into my mind, but so is the look in her eyes before she walked away. Those fucking eyes. Fuck. I'm consumed by the thought of her. I'm tormenting myself.

I need to make her mine. To feel her body. I will. I have to. She's a drug. I check my phone again but still no messages. Should I message her? Will that make things even worse? My mind is reeling with so many thoughts that I can feel my head throbbing. What should I have done differently? Has she been playing with me this whole time? It's possible. She's intelligent enough. I feel myself spiralling. The walls of this room are feeling smaller now than before. I send Skylar a text asking if there's any alcohol I can have, to which she responds by letting me know about some whiskey in the cabinet.

I make my way to the cabinet and grab the bottle, my hands shaking slightly. Walking back to the room, I pop the lid off and take a swig. And another. The burn of the whiskey slides down my throat, becoming a momentary distraction. I can feel the alcohol seeping into my system, dulling the edges of my thoughts. The room begins to spin, in a comforting way. As I take another swig, a heaviness settles upon my chest.

I can't shake the image of her; which is something that usually would be a blessing, a hobby, but today is a terrifying reminder of what I may have lost. Clawing at my sanity. I find myself typing and deleting messages, struggling to find words. After today I'm doubting if I've ever known the right words to say. In a bid to numb myself further, I take another swig, feeling the warmth of the alcohol spreading through my veins.

I'm questioning everything now. Dissecting every conversation we've ever had. Considering if this was some kind of game for her. Manipulation of my emotions. The possibility is a twisting knife in my gut. Summoning the liquid courage, I begin typing. Pouring out my anger and emotions. My words spilling like a dam breaching. With trepidation, I press send and immediately shove my phone back into my pocket. Another swig. A very small weight now lifted from my shoulders.

CHAPTER 14:

NOT JUST THUNDER

Marcus

I open my bag to start unpacking and the book immediately greets me at the top, staring me in the face once again. I take it out and throw it onto the bed beside me. I succeed at ignoring it whilst I unpack the rest of the belongings I need, leaving excess clothes at the bottom. I get changed into some tracksuit bottoms and a hoodie and sit back on the edge of the bed, checking my phone once again. Nothing. She has the power. I check the time, 12:27a.m. With nothing to do, I begin staring into the abyss, thinking again. I have to stop it. The only distraction left in the room is the book. Another thing constantly hanging over my head. I pick it up and fiddle with the lock that no longer closes. Why not? There are no pieces missing.

I start reading the story over again in another attempt to distract myself. I read the story a few times over, cringing at my handwriting but also flushed with a wholesome feeling, imagining my younger self sitting at my desk writing. Creating. I don't create anymore. As I read the story through another time I suddenly feel a strange sense of unease. I try to ignore it but I can't. Something feels off. Wrong. A chill runs down my spine and I quickly look straight ahead, trying to steady my mind. I look back at the page and read again. Wait.

'But then, disaster struck, 'Shy spider' stumbled and fell, injuring one of her many legs.'

The line has me thinking of Sienna, falling into the river. Even the character name. Sienna Saunders. It's all corresponding. I sit up straighter and I feel an intensity take over. Coincidence, it has to be. But I can't help but feel like I've discovered something significant here. My mind swirls with thoughts and possibilities as I flick my way back to the beginning.

'The animals were asleep peacefully in the village, when suddenly they were awoken by the sounds of rain and thunder crashing above the houses and a loud ROAR in the distance.'

Holy fuck. The bang. The storm. I've truly lost my fucking mind. My vision becomes blurry as I rush through the words. I look up and blink hard to focus my eyes again. Suddenly everything is correlating. I'm standing now, pacing. I focus on the names of the characters. 'Derpy Dragon', 'Baker Kitty', 'Sakura Fox'. Dean, Birdie and Skylar. They all match. This can't be happening. I shut the book and launch it onto the bed before grabbing my phone. My hands are shaking more than before. I text Skylar and tell her to come down. Waiting for her, I pace and pace, my mind hazy. I hear her footsteps down the hall and I open the door before she can reach it.

"Woah, you okay?"

"No, I'm really not, you have to look at this." Skylar rushes into the room behind me, a concerned look on her face. She picks up the almost empty whiskey bottle.

"Shit Marcus, how much did you drink?"

"It doesn't matter, look." I pick up the book and search for the line I need.

"You brought the book with you?"

"Yes. For fuck sakes will you just look." I point to the line about Sienna and she reads.

"Oh no, the spider broke one of its legs? And I should care because?"

"Sienna scraped up her leg today, remember I told you?"

"I remember Marcus, but Sienna isn't a spider." She says, looking at me like I'm an alien.

"But look, the name. The initials."

"Marcus, I think you need to sleep."

"Sky please, just listen to me."

"Okay, okay. I'm listening, calm down. Please, you're scaring me."

"Now read this." I proceed to show her the opening line of the story.

"You're fucking with me."

"I promise I'm not."

We lock eyes and I can tell we're thinking the same thing. She grabs the book from me and begins reading intensely. Her eyes widen with disbelief as she too starts to realise that the book is becoming a lot more than just pen and paper.

"Oh my go-"

"What?" I interrupt in a panic. She looks at me with eyes filled with a mixture of fear and fascination.

"Read that." She points me to another line of the story.

'Sakura fox' scrambled desperately to protect the nearby flowers,'

"Gardening."

"Marcus, please tell me you're joking."

"Sky, I'm not."

"This can't be real. Things like this don't actually happen."

"You got a better explanation?" She looks into my eyes, her face white and her eyes empty. We stand in silence for a few moments, the weight of what we've just discovered sinking in. The room feels stifling and the air heavy.

"So what do we do?" She asks in a frenzy.

"We have to tell the others surely."

"But how is that gonna help?"

"I don't know, Sky. Believe it or not I've never actually written a magical future-predicting book before this one." Sky sighs and rolls her eyes, pulling out her phone from her back pocket.

"I'll tell them to come here."

CHAPTER 15:

'OKAY, YOU'VE OFFICIALLY LOST IT.'

Marcus

"So let me get this straight. You've dragged us here in the middle of the night to tell us about a 'magical' book? You realise how fucked that is right?" Dean asks with genuine anger exuding from his slouched body.

"Come on man, you can't seriously sit here and tell me that's a coincidence." I argue.

"Yes. I can. You're fucking pissed bro, you're all over the place. You don't know what you're talking about."

"I'm tipsy, yes, but trust me I know what I'm saying."

"And what you're saying is batshit fucking insane." Birdie adds, looking at me like I'm some kind of nutcase. I rub my eyes firmly and pull my hands down my face in frustration, letting out an audible '*Aughh*'.

"It's just too far-fetched, Marcus. We're not living in a book. This is real life." Sienna adds with a discreet sliver of sarcasm. The one person in the room I want to back me up. I look at her, sat on the floor, her legs politely crossed and her hair a little bouncier than usual. A perfect little creation. I want to be angry with her, but I can't be. Not truly. Not seriously. How can I be when she looks like that?

"It is pretty weird though, you have to admit." Delilah says, finally speaking some sense.

"Don't give them pity, baby." Dean says, pulling her into his lap.

"I'm not, I actually think something might be up. How else do you explain the names matching?"

"Because when this loser wrote his stupid little book, we were the only people he knew." I shake my head and begin reading through the book again, trying desperately to find something convincing. Skylar peers over the book and points me to another sentence.

'Baker kitty' immediately got to work, using her magic to whip up medicine potions and remedies to give the animals strength in battle.'

"Birdie, what did you do today?" I ask, hoping for a correlating answer.

"Well, I met up with a load of girls from my college and went for tea, did some shopping, bought *THE* cutest mini skirt ever by the way… uhh … then we just hung out at mine for a while. Oh and one of the girls surprised us with this cute little cocktail making class. It was adorable." Skylar and I look at each other immediately, our eyes piercing and our bottom lips practically on the floor. We soon notice that the rest of the room are looking at us like they're going to have us sectioned. I turn the book to them and point at the sentence.

"Convincing yet?" I ask, smugly, assuming the evidence is now undeniable. Wrong.

"No, Marcus. I made cocktails not magic potions."

"Obviously not, but it's the book equivalent." Idiots. I'm so passionate in my frustration now that I'm using my hands to act out every word I say. I can sense everybody getting fed up with us.

"Okay, you've officially lost it." She states, conclusively. I slam the book shut and throw it onto the bed. I don't know what else I can say. I'm not going crazy. Surely.

"You wanna know what I did today?" Dean says with an arrogant grin. I know the next thing out of his mouth won't be anything serious. "I turned into my dragon form and flew out of the city, on a search for a small village of animals to destroy with my fire breath. *Holy shit. No way. It can't be.* That's exactly what I did in the magical psychic book too! I'm 100% convinced." He stands up, Pulling Delilah up with him. He starts heading to the door and turns to me before making his exit. "Get some sleep, bro." The two of them leave the room, Birdie following after like the faithful minion she is. I turn to Skylar, feeling defeated.

"I'm sorry." She says, with a look of worry as if she'd let me down. "We tried our best. We'll have to work it out on our own." I motion to her for a hug and she burrows herself under my arms. I rub her back in a grateful way and squeeze her briefly.

"I'll leave you two alone. Night guys." Skylar whispers as she shuts the door extremely gently and the room falls completely silent.

Now what the fuck do I say? How do I fix this fuck up? Is this a *'play it cool'* type situation or a *'sit down and talk to me about your feelings for an hour'* situation? Luckily for me I don't have to give it much consideration, because before I can even utter a word, Sienna starts stepping towards me. Her tiny cold hands reach up around my neck and she attempts to pull me forcefully down. I play along, not knowing how this part of her game is going to end.

I crouch down to her level and before I can even take another breath our lips meet. Her kiss is soft and tentative at first, but immediately ignites a fire within me. I feel my confusion melting away as our lips move together in sync. After a few seconds, our lips part but our foreheads stay touching.

"I'm sorry about earlier, I-"

"Shh," I interrupt. "I want more," I grab her chin and pull her back in. I can feel the warmth radiating from her as our bodies press closer together. I walk forward, my lips not leaving hers, and push her hard against the wall. My arm instinctively resting on the wall beside her head, my body surrounding her, conveying my primal instincts to possess and protect. With each passing second, I can feel her surrender, her body melting. My sweet angel. I sense the intensity of my longing coursing through me.

Lowering to her neck, my kisses remain tender, eliciting shivers that traverse her skin. The fragrance of her skin evokes a comforting familiarity, akin to the feeling of a home for me. Returning to her lips briefly, her tiny hand gripping my jaw amplifies my longing. Eventually, I reluctantly draw back, leaving us both enveloped in a hazy, smoky atmosphere.

I look down, smirking; she's looking back up at me, doe-eyed, flustered and giddy but her glare is so soft. Inviting.

"That was more fun than turning me down. Wasn't it, Sweet?"

"I'm just scared." She whispers.

"I'll go at your pace, wait for you as long as you need me to. But know this, sweet, you have nothing to be scared of." I take a deep breath before continuing, "I'd do anything for you, I promise." She smiles softly and I plant a kiss on her forehead.

"I should get home."

"Of course, let's get going."

"Marcus, my house is a few roads away, I don't need you to come." I scowl and laugh at the stupidity of her sentence before I turn around and grab my jacket, making a crystal clear statement. She pretends to be offended but her body language tells me all I need to know. She's welcoming my assertiveness with open arms. Seeking protection and security.

Waking up this morning, I'm on cloud 9. The room is filled with a lingering scent of alcohol and cigarettes, but for once I quite like that. A smile creeps on my face as I replay the moment with my sweet Sienna. Revelling in thoughts of her vulnerability. I thought I craved her before, but this is a new type of hunger. The door knocks.

"Are you up?" Sky asks.

"I am indeed."

"Mum's making sausage sandwiches, do you want an egg in yours?"

"Mm, yes please." My stomach is growling at the thought. I slip on a top and some tracksuit bottoms and make my way to the kitchen. The breakfast-smells of sizzling sausage and egg fill the air, causing my stomach to rumble beyond belief. Skylar's mum stands at the stove, turning the sausages. She looks up and smiles warmly at me.

"Good morning, darling!" she greets me, "Sleep well?" I nod, trying to conceal my excitement.

"Yes, thank you. Breakfast smells amazing." I say with a yawn and stretch.

"Well, I figured you could use a good meal after yesterday." I take a seat on the end of the dining table next to Skylar who's staring at me with a devilish grin.

"What's up with you?" I ask.

"I may have stayed outside the door for a few minutes last night." She whispers.

"You little creep."

"Hey, it's my house."

The rest of her family join us shortly after. A real family breakfast. As I glance around the table, my eyes linger on Skylar's younger brother. His eyes are full of mischief and pure happiness. Good for him. I've always wanted a brother. The closest I have to that is Dean, and well that speaks for itself. I often wonder what it would've been like to at least have one sibling. Somebody to connect with in that way. To explore and banter with. As Skylar's mum refills my glass of water she catches my eye,

"Everything okay? You seem a little spaced out."

"Yeah sorry, everything is fine. I'm just taking in the moment. I'm grateful for you all having me here. "

"You're part of this family, Marcus." I take a bite of my sandwich, savouring the flavours. After last night, the thought of a family of my own one day no longer seems entirely unattainable. We finish up eating and Skylar's dad and brothers start washing up the plates. I get up to help but Skylar's mum stops me in my tracks.

"Nope, I have a different task for you, darling-"

"Gardening?" I assume.

"How did you know that?"

"Sky was telling me all about how she was *forced into the insufferable activity of planting flowers* yesterday."

"Oh, she has such a hard life. The poor thing."

"Hey! It's not nice to gossip guys." Skylar snaps.

The sun is shining brightly, casting a warm glow on the grass and colourful flowers that adorn the garden. She clearly takes a lot of care in maintaining it. She hands me a trowel and points to a patch of soil that needs some attention. I kneel down to start digging. The earth is moist beneath my fingertips; well-nourished. With a determined grip on the trowel, I press its pointed end into the soil, feeling some resistance as I break through the surface.

A rich, dark layer of soil clings to the silver blade. I can't help but notice the intricate network of delicate, thread-like roots, weaving their way through the earth, silently nourishing the plants that call this garden their home. As I continue deeper the soil becomes increasingly loose and granular, easily shifting around my trowel and fingers. With each rhythmic thrust, the sound of the trowel slicing through the earth resonates, as though nature itself is harmonising with my efforts.

The sun casts its golden rays upon my back, warming my shoulders as beads of perspiration glisten on my forehead. As I dig further, the earth reveals small treasures hidden beneath its surface. Pebbles of various sizes and colours, ranging from smooth and round to jagged and angular, emerge from the depths. Clumps of tangled roots, like underwater creatures caught in a dance, arise with each deep excavation. These surprises serve as reminders of the intricate ecosystem that lies beneath the visible layers of this garden, functioning harmoniously to support its vitality and growth.

With each strike into the damp soil, I notice how the rhythm of my digging mirrors the rhythm of my own heartbeat, a steady but quickening pace fueled by anticipation. Suddenly I'm very eerily aware of my body and of every single grain of soil under me. I feel completely overstimulated and tingles flood me. My heart is beating much faster now, causing me to cough. I take a breath and steady myself. *Too much fucking alcohol I assume.*

I finally reach the intended depth. The hole I have excavated appears like a small abyss, awaiting the arrival of new life. With a gentle tap, I release the soil from the trowel's curved edge, allowing it to cascade back into its newfound dwelling. It settles neatly, making a soft thud of finality, ready to embrace the next seed or seedling that will soon inhabit this hallowed ground. Lost in my thoughts, I'm startled when Skylar's mom taps my shoulder gently. She has a mischievous grin on her face, her eyes sparkling with warmth.

"You know, Marcus, plants have a way of teaching us about life," she says, her voice filled with wisdom. "Sometimes they need a little extra care and attention to grow and flourish. And sometimes, we need to do the same with our relationships." Her words strike a chord with me, she's right. That's exactly what Sienna and I need. "You and your dad, you just need to talk things through. Most importantly he needs to get to know you." Of course. She's referring to my dad, not Sienna.

Why the fuck would she be referring to Sienna? You moron.

"You have the right idea, but unfortunately my dad doesn't do conversations."

"I feared that would be the case." She rests her hand on my shoulder and frowns sympathetically. "You know, Marcus, I meant it when I said you're a part of this family. Skylar had mentioned to me that you intend on heading to Dean's to stay. No offence to Dean, dear God the boy has been through hell and back, but I want more for you. This is your home now, and we're in no rush to get you out of here. Okay?"

"Thank you. I am gonna make something of my life you know? I won't be like my dad, no way. And when the day comes I'll repay you, all of you. That's a promise, and I don't break promises."

CHAPTER 16:
BITTERSWEET

Marcus

Skylar and I arrive at the usual hangout spot to meet the others. They acknowledge us with their typical unenthusiastic and definitely high greetings. This place is a shithole, but we love it. A train track surrounded by woods, next to a small graffiti covered tunnel. Our canvas. The track so rusted you would think it's abandoned; well it almost is. A train will pass by once in a blue moon, going who knows where, but that's it. A couple of ugly sofas, probably dragged here by somebody who was more than desperate to remove the disgusting things from their life, flattened beer cans, broken glass shards, discarded joints and cigarettes. All silently bearing witness to the various misdeeds we'd enacted here.

Hm. I must be making her nervous, likely at the thought of being pushed up against a wall again with my tongue down her throat… and maybe something else.

Oh, my sweet.

I take a seat right next to her and place my hand on her thigh, but she brushes me off. *Interesting*. I guess she isn't in the mood for my advancements tonight. Or maybe the others being around is giving her stage-fright. The night progresses and the group falls into their usual state of intoxication, buzzing conversation mixed with laughter and the occasional argument. A single train passes through which adds an extra zap of rare excitement to the night. Four hours pass and our evening comes to an end. The others stumble off into the darkness and I hang back with Sienna. She's barely looked at me and I'm going to find out why. I walk up to her, as close as I can get without our bodies touching.

"So tell me, what's up with you tonight?" I ask.

"I'm just tired."

"Please, don't lie to me, sweet" She lets out a huff and crosses her arms, finally looking up at me. I'm making sure to soak up every drop of this sliver of eye contact. She's so cute when she pretends to be mad.

"I don't want to be with you, Marcus. Okay?" I raise my eyebrow and smirk at her. How pathetic.

"What did I just tell you? Don't lie to me."

"I'm serious. I don't want to be with you. I felt bad last night and I got ahead of myself." I don't say anything, instead my mind begins ticking. What exactly is she trying to do here? My smirk remains firmly glued to my face because no matter what bullshit she tries to blurt out at me, I know I have her now.

"Are you gonna say anything?" She asks. I don't, not yet. I want her to keep talking for a little while longer. "I'm sorry, Marcus. I don't want to hurt your feelings but I don't want any of this. I'm not in love with you and I just want you to be my friend again... and I really fucking wish you wouldn't have told me you loved me. It's stupid, okay? This whole thing is so stupid... I loved how I felt around you, I loved the thought of you but I realise I'm just not in love with you." I chuckle at her frantic rambling and crouch down to her eye level.

"Oh, Sienna. Using book quotes on me now? You must be head over heels." I whisper, my voice husky; dripping with a mix of amusement and faux sympathy.

"H-how did you know that was a quote from a book? You hate books."

"I know, but if you tell me about a book, I will force myself to read it," I pause to admire her angelic little face for a second, "I have to say I'm a little offended that I haven't been asked to recreate some scenes yet." I flash her a cheeky smile. "You must think I'm a fool." A flicker of confusion crosses her face, but it quickly fades, replaced by an adorable little defensive glare.

"What are you talking about? Are you even hearing me?" she retorts, her voice tinged with frustration and defiance. I love the taste of her resistance. It only fuels my desire to unravel her further.

"Loud and clear, sweet. But it's all bullshit." I say, my voice velvety smooth. "You see, I've always known you were playing hard to get, but it's cute how you thought that even after last night you could still toy with me. Make me believe that you're not interested anymore." She gulps and a sly smile curls on my lips. She knows every word out of my mouth is exactly right. I'm reading her like a book, and she's breaking character. This power play between us is intoxicating.

A game of control and manipulation that I'm fucking revelling in.

"Do you really think I'm that naive, sweet? That I wouldn't see through this?" I lean in even closer now, my breath warm against her ear. "You may be trying to push me away, but deep down, I know you want me *almost* as much as I want you." My words hang between us, the charged atmosphere crackling with tension. Sienna's eyes dart around, searching for an escape, for a way to regain control of the situation. But I won't let her. Not again. Never again.

"You're wrong, Marcus," she finally says, her voice trembling. "I don't want you. I never did." A surge of annoyance rises within me at her audacity, at her feeble attempt to deny our undeniable connection. She's merely testing my patience, attempting to gauge my reaction. But I won't let her win this battle. I chuckle softly, the sound dripping with arrogance.

"Sienna," I start, shaking my head. "I'll let you try your best to keep up the act, but we both know the truth. You can have a smart mouth and throw all the insults at me that you want, but unfortunately your body language is giving away all of your secrets." Sienna's eyes narrow, a mix of anger and resignation flashing across her face.

"You think you know me so well, don't you?" she scoffs, her voice laced with bitterness. "Well, let me tell you something, Marcus. You know *nothing* about me." Her words sting, but I refuse to let them derail me.

"You couldn't be more wrong, sweet." I trail my fingers lightly across her hand, relishing in the shiver that courses through her body. She makes no effort to stop me, of course.

"I know you like the back of my hand, and you have me in the palm of yours."

She pulls her hand away feistily and begins walking away in an adorable angry strut, making sure to brush me as she passes. I follow her, of course. I can't let her walk the streets alone, regardless of how much it may frustrate her. I'm certain she's aware of my presence behind her throughout the route, but I don't disturb her. She clearly has some shit to think through. We reach her house eventually and I stand straight outside the gate, lighting a cigarette. As she waits for her mother to open the door she turns around, a grumpy little look on her face.

"I can take it from here." she announces defiantly. I smile.

"I'll wait until you're inside."

CHAPTER 17:
DRAGON

Marcus

I make my way back into Sky's house through the back door. Come to think of it, it's pretty dangerous for them to leave it unlocked like that. I sit down on the bed and roll myself a joint. I deserve one after today. I'll admit, I'm a little surprised that Sienna is still messing me around. But things are different now. I've had a taste of that power and no way in hell am I ever giving it back. She can play her little game all she wants, but I have a new strategy.

Just as I'm about to call it a night, Skylar bursts in the room.

"Hey, I know it's not my house but it would be nice if you would knock first." I burst out like an idiot before noticing that her face is etched with panic. I instantly know something is terribly wrong. I hastily stub out my joint and stand up straight, my heart pounding irregularly in my chest.

"What's wrong?"

"We have to get to Dean's, like now." Her voice is trembling.

"Why, what's happened?"

"His place is on fire."

"On fire? Are you sure?"

"Yes, Birdie just sent me a text. Delilah's there too." I shake my head in disbelief and try to gather myself.

"Are they hurt or?"

"She didn't say, Marcus. We just need to get going."

I don't ask anymore questions and we get straight on the bike. As we speed over there my mind is completely numb. A million different thoughts are banging around in my brain. I'm jumping every red light, swerving around every speed bump. The image of flames engulfing the place, consuming everything in its path. Is Dean okay? Is Delilah alright? I can't bear the thought of them being trapped inside an inferno. Skylar clutches onto me tightly, her nails digging into me, her fear palpable in the tight grip of her fingers. I try to reassure her, telling her that everything will be okay, but even I can't be sure. The panic in her eyes, the way her voice trembles, only adds to the anguish pulsating within me.

As we approach Dean's house, the sight that greets us is heart-wrenching. Flames dancing hungrily from the windows, smoke billowing into the night sky, casting an eerie haze over the street. The sound of sirens are filling my ears, serving as a chilling reminder of the chaos unfolding.

"Holy fuck, Marcus." Skylar yells.

We come to a screeching halt, abandoning the bike on the side of the road. Without a second thought, we sprint towards the blazing building. The heat hitting us like a wall, making it difficult to breathe. Each step forward feels like an eternity, the fear in my chest mounting with each passing moment. The lights from the fire engine are only making this feel more real.

Firefighters in their bulky gear are already on the scene, battling the flames with torrents of water. The sound of crackling wood and glass shattering echoes through the air. I scan the building, desperately searching for any sign of Dean or Delilah. My heart sinks when I see Birdie standing outside, her face overtaken with worry, tears streaming down her cheeks.

"Birdie, are they okay?" I ask, my voice trembling with anxiety. She shakes her head, her eyes filled with anguish.

"I don't know any more than you do. I saw the flames from my window and got here as quickly as I could."

A sickening feeling washes over me, threatening to swallow me whole. I push through the disgusting crowd of people, none of them I've ever seen before, standing around watching Dean's house burning to the ground. I'm desperately calling out their names, hoping for any sign of their survival. My body moves on pure instinct, ignoring the heat and smoke, driven by the need to find them. Suddenly, I hear a familiar voice calling my name. I turn to see Delilah staggering towards me, her clothes soot-covered and her hair tangled. Relief floods every fibre of my being, but my joy is short-lived. She collapses into my arms, her body weak and trembling.

"Marcus," she gasps, her voice barely a whisper. "Dean.. he's still inside."

My heart stops, the world around me fading into a blur. I can't comprehend the words she is saying. This can't be happening right now. Dean, my best friend, my brother, trapped in that burning house. Panic overwhelms me, immobilising me for a moment before my brotherly instincts kick in. Without hesitation, I dash towards the inferno, my mind on complete and utter overdrive. A few firefighters attempt to get in my way, but no force can stop me getting into that building. The heat intensifies with each step, threatening to consume me. The smoke chokes me, making it difficult to see, but I press on, driven by love and desperation. *Fuck, fuck, fuck.*

As I enter the house, the fire envelopes around me, licking at the walls and ceiling. I shout Dean's name over and over again, my voice desperate and pleading. The noise of crackling flames and the falling debris fills my ears, drowning out all other sounds. Time seems to stand still as I push through the flames, my body screaming in protest. But against all odds, I hear a faint cough from upstairs. A glimmer of hope ignites within me as I follow the sound. Through the smoke, I spot Dean, disoriented and struggling to breathe. Adrenaline fuelling my strength as I race towards him, grabbing hold of his arms and dragging him towards the stairs.

In a complete haze, I manage to pull Dean out of the burning house and onto the front drive. His body is limp, his breathing shallow. Panic grips me as I assess his condition. His clothes are charred, his skin scorned; covered in soot and blistered from the intense heat. I frantically search for any signs of life, praying that he's still hanging on. He is, but only by a thread. Tears well up in my eyes as I realise the severity of the situation. I can't lose him. Not now, not like this. I dig deep within myself, finding the strength to keep going. Without another moment's hesitation, I scoop Dean's limp body into my arms and sprint towards the approaching paramedics.

The paramedics rush to Dean's side, their faces filled with concern as they try to stabilise him. The chaos around me fades into the background and I focus solely on Dean's well-being. The sirens wail, the firefighters continue their battle against the raging inferno, but none of it matters as long as Dean makes it through. Minutes pass by like hours. Before I know it Dean is whisked away in an ambulance, and I jump in beside him, refusing to leave his side. My eyes don't leave him. I don't feel myself even blink.

At the hospital, doctors and nurses spring into action, assessing Dean's injuries and working relentlessly. I'm left in the waiting room, my mind in a constant state of turmoil. Guilt gnawing and gnawing at me. If only I had been there sooner. Skylar sends me a text, finally.

Sky: Delilah's at home now. A little groggy but fine. Dean awake?

M: He wasn't awake in the ambulance but I don't know. They haven't told me anything yet.

Sky: I took your bike home. You need me to come get you?

M: Not yet. I'll let you know.

Hours pass, and the waiting becomes unbearable. I pace back and forth, my nerves on edge when finally, a doctor emerges from the double doors, his face a mix of exhaustion and concern. I walk straight at him, desperate for any news about Dean's condition.

"He's stable," the doctor begins, his voice soothing yet laced with caution. "But he's suffered severe smoke inhalation and burns. He's still in a pretty critical condition, and we're going to need to monitor him closely."

"But he's gonna live?"

"It wouldn't be fair for me to say that. We're going to do what we can, okay?" My heart sinks at the doctor's response. "There's nothing you can do for him right now. We have your details and we'll give you updates when we have them. Please, go home and get some sleep." With that, the doctor walks back the way he came and I'm left with no option but to leave.

M: You still up?

Sky: Of course. Should I leave?

M: Yeah. I'll wait out front.

I slowly wander out of the hospital, my mind in a whirlwind as I make my way to the front entrance. I collapse onto the bench and bury my face in my hands. How did it come to this? I replay the events of the night over and over in my head, torturing myself with the thought that I could have done something more to prevent this. The street is eerily quiet, the only sound being the occasional passing car. The only light coming from a single streetlight in the hospital car park. My mind becomes completely silent for a while. And weirdly, I like it, but the peace doesn't last long. *It never fucking does.*

I hear the screeches of my motorbike coming down the road and I stand up sluggishly. The thought of Skylar riding my bike is cringe-worthy, but I'm too exhausted to care. Sky pulls up beside me and parks the bike, her eyes puffy and red from crying. She immediately launches at me for a hug, her presence offering some comfort amidst the chaos of my mind.

"How is he?" She asks, her voice barely a whisper.

"He's still in critical condition. The doctor said they're doing everything they can, but it's too early to tell." She stays in my arms for a few moments, not saying a word, and I can tell she's holding back more tears.

"You too tired to drive back?"

"Nah, I'll be alright, Sky. Come on."

We get back home and lie down on my bed for a long while. Letting everything soak in. My head is completely frazzled, as I'm sure hers is too.

"Marcus…" She says with hesitation, a concerned look on her face. "You don't think what happened tonight had anything to do with the book, do you?" I pause for a moment, the thought of it alone sending a chill down my spine. The book.

"It's just that, Dean's character was a dragon, right?..." I'm not sure I have the energy to handle where I think she's going with this. "Who destroyed the little village with…with fire." She looks at me and I look back. Her stare freakily intense. She's waiting for me to reassure her. I feel sick at the thought that she could be onto something. I start thinking about the events that have happened since opening the book, and now, watching Dean's house engulfed in flames, it's hard to ignore the possibility that the book is involved somehow. I sit up, the weight of the realisation heavy on my shoulders. Skylar watches me intently, waiting for my response, her eyes searching mine for any sign of understanding or confirmation. I take a deep breath, trying to gather my thoughts.

I grab the book and flick past the lines we had previously focused on. Skylar is now sitting up too, peering over my side. I begin reading aloud.

'At last, the Derpy dragon arrived, accompanied by his loyal sidekick who is 'definitely a Froggy'. The chaotic battle began and the village was soon awash with flames as the dragon breathed fire on the homes and shops'

I shake my head in denial.

"This can't be fucking happening." A sense of anger starts peeking through me.

"Keep reading."

'Despite their fear, the animals fought back valiantly, determined to defend their beloved home. All of a sudden, the dragon began losing energy, and fell to the ground, dead.'

"No. No. No." She squeals frantically. "That can't be right. That's not right, surely." She's standing now, holding me for stability and shaking like a leaf. I feel my entire body shut down. My throat dries out intensely. No words can leave my mouth right now. No words are even capable of forming. "Marcus.." A knot tightens in my stomach and I begin seeing stars.

"Fuck. Oh my god. I need to tell Delilah. Holy fuck. Dean is gonna d-."

"He won't, Sky. Not once we get rid of this fucking book."

CHAPTER 18:
DESTROY THE BOOK

Marcus

The moon shines brightly overhead, casting an ethereal glow on the garden. The air is thick with tension and anger as we wait for the flames in the firepit to build. I approach the pit slowly. The weight of the book feels heavy in my hands before I throw it into the rising flames.

As I watch the flames licking at the edges of the book I can't help but feel like it's taking too long. The fire appears to be bending around the pages. We stare at it. Waiting.

"Fucking burn, you piece of shit." I murmur as I grab a stick, confusion painted across my face. I can feel the sweltering heat coming from the pit now. I use the stick to push the book deeper, hoping to progress the consumption. As I push the book deeper into the flames, frustration and desperation well up inside me. The book seems resistant to the fire. It's taunting us, mocking our attempts to destroy it. The pages flicker in the heat, but they refuse to turn to ash. I press the stick harder against the book, determined to force it to succumb to the inferno. But it remains unyielding. A sense of dread begins to creep its way into my heart. Now I'm pissed.

I drench the pit in water and snatch the book, taking it to the kitchen immediately. Skylar follows silently behind me. I rummage through the kitchen drawers to find a knife. And not just any knife. The largest one. The sharpest one. Once I find it I stab and stab at the book with no hesitation. Nothing. Not even a dent.

"How?" Skylar questions under her breath. The frustration and anger within me reach a boiling point as I continue to stab at the book, desperately trying to destroy it.

We move onto hammers, scissors, even attempting to drown the fucker. But no matter what we try, it remains unscathed. Each attempt is met with resistance, as if the book itself is fighting back. Skylar watches in horror, her eyes wide with disbelief and fear.

"I don't understand," she whispers, her voice barely audible. "How is this possible?" I shake my head in disbelief.

"There has to be a way, Sky."

We stay up until the early hours of the morning trying to destroy the book. Nothing works. After all we've put it through there's not so much as a scratch. I open the book again and try to find some answers in the words. Unfortunately for us, there are only a couple of sentences left.

'King 'Mint choc chipper' and Queen 'Milk 'n' cookies, deer?', who had been watching from the safety of their castle, waited for the dragon to die before emerging from the castle to inspect the damage brought by the dragon. Together, they closed the gates once again to protect their village.'

I read it through, studying every word, my exhausted mind ticking and ticking.

*'Together, they closed the gates once again to protect their village.'. 'Together, they closed the gates once again to protect their village.'. **'Together, they closed the gates once again to protect their village.'.***

Close the gates. My focus turns to the now unsealable clasp on the book. I try sealing it, but I know it won't be that easy. *Why the fuck would anything be that easy?*

"What are you thinking?" Sky asks.

"Look here, the very last line. What if the answer isn't destroying the book, but closing it." I suggest.

"Maybe if we find a way to close it before Dean dies we can change the ending of all of this."

"It's worth a try. But look," I flick the lock again. "It's not gonna shut. We're still missing something here." Skylar takes the book from me. Her eyes narrow and she begins biting on her thumb as she focuses on every word.

"Who's '*they*'?" She asks.

"The king and queen."

"*No shit.* I mean are they anybody's initials?"

"Well, the king would definitely be me. The main characters in my books were always based on myself."

"How very humble of you, Marcus." I smirk at her and we let out the first little laugh in a while. "Well, whoever the queen is, we must need her to close the book with you." I take the book back and think hard about the name. It doesn't take too long for me to realise.

"Fuck."

"What?" I look at Skylar before rubbing my hands across my face, knowing things just got a lot more difficult.

"It's Millie. The queen is Millie."

"Oh shit."

I flop back on the bed, head in hand.

"*Yeahh*, that book ain't getting closed anytime soon."

"Marcus, we don't have a choice."

"I know, I know." I sigh loudly. "It's fine, don't worry about it. I'll go and speak to her tomorrow. I need some rest first, it's like 7 a.m. You should sleep too."

"I will. By the way I have to be at Sienna's house at 6 today, you mind dropping me off?" She says with a defeated look. The mere mention of Sienna's name brings a grin to my face. The suspense of not knowing when I'll get to kiss her like that again has been taunting me.

"Yeah 'course. What you going to Sienna's for?"

"She didn't tell you about it?"

"Tell me about what?"

"Marcus, she has a date tonight." I sit up straight and feel my face morphing into a concerned scowl. *A fucking date?*

"What do you mean a date? A date with who?"

"That boy from her science group. I saw you two hanging behind at the tunnel yesterday, did she not mention it?" I stand up slowly.

"Not a word."

Adrenaline begins to rise up through my body. Filling my veins. Every time I think I know how her game works, she throws something else at me. Oh, my sweet angel. So clever. But clearly not clever enough to know that letting another man touch her isn't something I'd ever entertain. The thought of it alone is enough to make me lose my fucking mind. But if she wants to take it here then I'm more than happy to play along. Clearly she needs a reminder of who she belongs to. I chuckle slightly, running my hand across my jaw. How exciting. I just hope my sweet doesn't have her confidence knocked too hard when her date doesn't show tonight. That fucker is going to die instead.

"Marcus I'm sorry. That's awful. I'll let her know I'm not gonna help her get ready-"

"No, no, no. I need you to go. I need you to do me a favour,"

"For fuck sakes, please don't get me involved in this."

"Just one thing,"

"Tell me what it is first."

"I want her phone."

"Okay, no."

"Oh come on,"

"That's too risky, Marcus. We don't need any more trouble right now."

"I'll take all the blame for it, I swear. I just need the phone... please."

"I don't know-"

"I need this, Sky. I really *really* need this... please."

"What are you even gonna do with it?"

"Cancel her date of course." She pauses for a moment, crossing her arms and tapering her stare.

"Marcus, we have bigger things to worry about," I stare at her and say nothing. My eyes pleading for me. She rolls her eyes and sighs dramatically. "Fine. But if she catches me you're taking all of the blame, got it?"

"Got it, pickpocket. Thank you very much."

"Yeah, yeah. Goodnight, loser." She says abruptly shutting the door as she slouches off.

"Night."

I take off my shirt and get into bed, closing my eyes instantly. As I drift off to sleep, Sienna is the only thing occupying my mind. *Nothing new there.* What was she thinking? After all these years I finally get a taste of her and she really believes I'm going to allow her to place her lips on some other man? Possible images enter my thoughts of some prick from her college daring to lay claim to what is rightfully mine. The thought of him looking at her in a class, or his hands on her body infuriates me to no end. A sinister smile takes over my lips. My mind has been shot into a frenzy. It's a possessiveness that scares even me, but I can't help it. She is mine. She belongs to me, body and soul. She knows that. But clearly she's underestimated me. Believed she could challenge me, push me to the very edge. Well then, let the games begin. I'll teach her a lesson she won't soon forget.

It's about to be a big day.

CHAPTER 19:
FINDING MILLIE

Marcus

Waking up I feel incredible. Like an unstoppable force. I check the time. 2:13. With a burst of energy, I practically spring to my feet and put on my classic hoodie and baggy jeans. I grab myself a brand new pack of cigarettes, my bike key and of course, the book, from my bag before leaving the room. *I'm not usually a cigarette kind of guy, I prefer a good joint, but today I think I'm gonna need them.* I shoot a quick "Afternoon" to Skylar's dad and brother who are sitting in the living room, before making my way out. Sitting on my bike, I check my phone before heading off. One text from Delilah.

> **Delilah: I told Dean about the book when he woke up this morning. He left the hospital. The doctors and I begged him not to but he wouldn't listen, he's not doing good Marcus. Please hurry up and sort this book stuff out. My heart is breaking.**

I take a big breath in before replying. I can't even imagine how she's feeling right now.

M: Don't worry. I'm gonna get this book shut, I promise.

It's a perfect day. The sky exactly how I like it, nice and grey. I'm riding smoother today than I have been recently. I'd almost gotten used to rushed, thoughtless driving after this week. It's a nice reset. Riding has always been my way of escaping. It's my graffiti. It's taught me a lot about myself. Patience being the most notable. Not to mention the ability to adapt to various terrains and the unknown. On the road, time seems to slow down, and every passing second becomes a treasure to be cherished.

As I throttle the bike, feeling the raw power pulsating beneath me, I notice all my senses awaken. The rumble of that engine reverberating through my bones. My bike really is a sleek, powerful beast. We both wear our scars proudly. We gained most of them together after all. There are scars etched all across my body that I've collected from my time with this thing. The road has become my sanctuary, my place of solitude. The scent of rain lingering in the air mixed with the faint smell of gasoline fills my nostrils. The hanging grey clouds adding to the atmosphere. Today is going to be perfect. I can feel it. I can taste it.

Arriving at Orchid's, I swiftly navigate into the car park, leaving my bike behind as I vault through the window. No time to explore today; I need that file. Traversing the scattered debris on the floor, I make my way to the office. Pausing briefly, I light up my first cigarette of the day, slowing down for a moment and relishing a few puffs. I open up the cabinet and search through the files. Bingo. Millie Devons.

I had almost wiped her from my memory entirely. From what I *can* remember, she was a posh girl. A quiet girl. It never really seemed like she wanted to be involved with us. I think she looked down on us. She never settled; just woke up everyday waiting for it to be time to go home. Orchid's was like one big waiting room for her. Once her dad's health improved she knew she'd be out of there. I even had a 'backup-crush' on her at one point when I had felt like I had no hope of ever being good enough for my sweet. *Clearly when I had written this shit book.*

That was until my Sienna finally started to give me the time of day. As soon as she settled in her new life with her adoptive mother and started routine therapy sessions, she started to open up to me. Trust me. The greatest thing to ever happen in my life. Discovering my sweet angel. Where would I be without her now? The worst part is that I had found out after I left that Millie had been picking on Sienna. Now I have to go and ask this bully for help. *Kill me now.*

Blackthorn children's shelter. Maybe they'll have some information on where she is now. I make my way outside and start putting the shelter address into my phone. An 18 minute ride. I know nothing about this shelter, apart from the fact that the social workers in Orchid's had moved over there once it shut down. *And that it's probably a lot nicer than our home was.* I put out my cigarette and start making my way over there.

CHILD INFORMATION RECORD
GREAT BRITAIN

NAME: MILLIE DEVONS

DATE OF BIRTH: 03/12/2004

DATE OF ARRIVAL: 23/04/2006

REASON FOR ADMITTANCE:

TEMPORARY CARE

ANY FAMILY STILL IN CONTACT: YES

ELIGIBLE FOR FOSTER/ADOPTION

PROGRAMMES: NO

PERSONAL NOTES:

Millie was admitted at the age of 1 after her father fell sick and had to be hospitalised. Her father remains in contact but is unfit to care for her at this time. Once he recovers he shall once again obtain full custody.

Millie's dad has not yet recovered at the time of Orchid's childrens home closure and therefore she was transferred to Blackthorn childrens shelter on 09/12/2019

Arriving promptly, I park my bike. The area exudes a cosy, homely vibe. The streets are well-kept, and the people I had passed by appeared content and cheerful. As I take my helmet off, a few kids whiz past me on their bicycles, laughing loudly. I watch them whisper to each other and look over at my bike, an awkward, curious look on their faces. I snicker before acknowledging them with a nod of my head.

"You wanna give it a try?" I offer, gesturing towards the bike. Their faces brighten with delight, eagerly nodding in agreement. I hand them the helmet one by one, carefully explaining how to strap it on properly. They take turns sitting on the bike, gripping the handles tightly. I demonstrate how to rev the engine, guiding their hands and teaching them the basics. The thrill in their eyes brings back memories of my own fascination with motorbikes when I was their age. It's a moment of connection, where the boundaries between age and experience fade away, leaving us all united by the simple pleasure of a shared adventure.

We laugh and chat as they ask me questions about my bike and share their dreams of riding one day. It's refreshing to witness their unbridled enthusiasm and optimism, a stark contrast to the darkness and uncertainty that has consumed my life recently. After some time, the kids reluctantly hand back the helmet and bid me farewell, still buzzing with excitement. As I watch them ride off on their bicycles, their laughter echoing, I wonder about their futures.

It makes me think about Sienna and I having kids of our own one day. I fantasise about it a lot. I know she'll be a wonderful mother. I imagine her tenderly cradling our child in her arms, her eyes filled with love and adoration. I envision the laughter and joy that would fill our home, the sound of tiny little footsteps from mini versions of us running through the hallways. Lost in this daydream, I'm brought back to reality by a gentle tap on my shoulder. I turn around to see one of my old social workers.

"Dot," I smile.

"What are you doing here making all this racket, love?" I reach out and give her a hug. I'm towering over her now which is a strange feeling.

"Oh my, you just keep going." She says, laughing and gesturing to my height.

"It's good to see you, Dot."

"It's good to see you too, sweetheart. Though I'm not too happy to see you riding one of these." She points to my bike with a disgusted look on her face.

"What's wrong with the bike?"

"Ooo, I can't stand those things. Much too dangerous. Anyway enough of that, it's far too cold to be talking out here, come inside."

I follow Dot inside the shelter, greeted by a warm and inviting atmosphere. The walls are adorned with colourful artwork, and the sound of laughter and chatter fills the air. We keep walking and arrive at her office, a cosy space with a desk cluttered with paperwork and a worn-out yellow armchair for visitors. As I settle into the armchair, Dot pours us both a cup of steaming hot tea. Taking a sip, I feel a sense of comfort wash over me. Dot's presence has always had that effect on me. She was a subtle pillar of support during my time at Orchid's, always there to offer guidance and a listening ear. Like a grandmother I didn't have.

"So, Marcus," she begins, her tone gentle yet concerned. "What brings you here today? It's been a while since we last saw you. You must be wanting *something* from me." I take a deep breath, trying to gather my thoughts.

"Yes, I need your help, Dot. I've been looking for Millie Devons. Do you have any idea about where I could find her?" Dot places her tea on the desk, her gaze filled with compassion.

"Millie huh," she sighs. "I remember her. With those rather large glasses. She was such a quiet girl, always kept to herself, didn't she?"

"Yeah, I haven't seen her since I left but I really need to speak with her." Dot nods, her wrinkled face creasing a little deeper with the weight of her memories.

"Well, she moved out a few years ago. Managed to find herself a nice little apartment just outside the city. Last I heard, she was doing very well for herself." Relief and anticipation flood over me as Dot's words resonate. Finally, a lead to follow.

"Do you have her address or even a phone number I could grab?" I ask eagerly, my voice betraying my attempt to hide my urgency. Dot reaches into a drawer and pulls out an old notepad, flipping through its worn pages until she finds what she's looking for.

"Here," she says, handing me a slip of paper with her shaky, withered hand. "This is the address I have. Just you be careful, Marcus. She's been through a lot and may not be too thrilled to see you." I take the slip of paper, holding it tightly between my fingers.

"Thank you, Dot," I say sincerely, meeting her gaze. "I appreciate your help. And uh, I'm sorry about the noise outside." Dot smiles warmly, her eyes crinkling at the edges.

"Oh, I understand, love. We all have our hobbies. Just promise me you'll be safe on that thing. I don't want to see you getting hurt."

With a nod of gratitude, I stand up from the armchair, slipping the piece of paper into my pocket.

"I will, Dot. Thank you again. It means a lot."

"And do come and visit more often, won't you? I've missed seeing your face around here."

"Of course."

CHAPTER 20:

A NOT SO WARM WELCOME

Marcus

I linger outside the apartment building, taking a moment to enjoy my cigarette before retrieving the piece of paper to double-check the apartment number. No.2. I ring the buzzer and crack my knuckles while I wait nervously for an answer. I hear a slight crackle followed by a muffled voice,

"Hello." I clear my throat and put on my professional voice.

"Yes, hello. Delivery for Millie Devons." A beep comes from the speakers and the door clicks open. *Nice work, Marcus.* The entrance is perfectly white with beautifully smooth wood floors. The girl has money, that's for sure. Ascending the stairs, I make my way to apartment No. 2 and gently rap my knuckles against the door.

Millie opens the door almost before I can finish knocking and instantly it's fair to say she doesn't look happy to see me.

"Marcus?" She scowls.

"Hey, Millie."

"What the fuck are you doing here?" She snaps, "How did you find my address?" She has a fire in her eyes, burning into me. The conversation is already off to a bad start and I'm only two words in. *Remember, this is all for Dean.*

"I'll explain, can I please come in?" She begrudgingly moves to the side and lets me in. I take a moment to look around, noticing the minimalist decor and the faint smell of vanilla in the air. It's clear that she has made a home for herself in this space. It's so clean that I feel like just breathing in here will make a mess. Millie gestures for me to sit on the sofa, her expression filled with scepticism. I can see the anger brewing beneath the surface, and I brace myself for what is to come. Taking a deep breath, I begin to explain

"Look, I know this is random and I don't want to make you angry, but Dean is in some pretty serious trouble and we're hoping that you can help us fix things." She laughs bitterly at me.

"You're asking for *my* help?"

"Yes, I am."

"The answer is no, now get out." Her words hang in the air and I rub my hand on my forehead briefly, trying to think of how I should navigate this.

"Just give me two minutes."

"I said get out."

"I know what you said, but I can't. Millie, please. We're adults. At least listen to what I have to say first." She sits down on the sofa opposite me, her arms crossed. I start explaining, keeping the story as short as possible. "We went back to Orchid's the other night and started searching through the old bedrooms. I found this book," I pull out the book and place it on her coffee table. "Once we opened it, there was a huge bang and since then the things I had written have been happening in real life,"

"I can't even believe I'm sitting here listening to this." She says, beginning to stand up.

"Look, the book has these characters, okay? And the characters correlate with everybody in the group, including you. Dean is the dragon and he's about to die, Millie."

"This is the dumbest shit I've ever heard-"

"You and I are the King and Queen, and the book ends with us closing the 'gates' after the dragon dies, to end the story. The gates correlate with this lock right here." I point her to the lock on the book and notice that she's looking at me as if I just parked my UFO in her living room or something. "I need you to come to Orchid's and close the lock with me before Dean dies. After that I promise I'll leave you alone."

"You're fucking psychotic. Now get out."

"Dean is gonna die! Don't you get that?"
Millie scoffs, her face contorted with frustration.

"You think 'Dean the dragon' dying is my problem? After everything that happened, I don't owe any of you anything. You all left me behind, and now you expect me to swoop in and save the day? Unfortunately it doesn't work like that." I sit there, the tension between us discernible. Millie's eyes bore into mine, her anger simmering just below the surface. I can feel my frustration mounting, a mixture of confusion and resentment.

"Left you behind? *Oh* you mean we got adopted? I'm so terribly sorry for that, your highness."

"Fuck you, Marcus. While the rest of you were off having a great fucking time with your new families, I was stuck in that shithole all alone. Not a single one of you bothered to send me so much as a text message." I'm standing now. I didn't come to argue but I'm not accepting that bollocks for a second.

"You weren't ever interested in being involved with us anyway. Constantly acting like you were above us, remember? You'll never know what it was like for us, Mill. You had a home waiting for you outside that place, whilst the rest of us sat there wondering if we'd ever even have parents."

"My dad is fucking dead. He's dead, Marcus. But you wouldn't know that because you never bothered to find out."

Ah fuck.

I take a step closer to her, my voice laced with frustration.

"I'm sorry, okay, I'm really sorry. That's terrible and I can't imagine how that felt. But being mad at us isn't fair. We were kids, Millie. We got adopted for fuck sakes. I don't mean to be blunt but you can't seriously have expected us to be thinking about you at that moment."

"You guys were like a family to me. The fact that I wouldn't be on your mind is so fucked up and selfish."

"We had just been adopted, are you insane? The world doesn't fucking revolve around you, you know?"

"You don't understand, Marcus. You never will. You didn't have to watch your father take his last breath, or deal with constant reminders of what you lost. Just because you got your happy ending doesn't mean the rest of us did."

I laugh at her pretentious assumption.

"Of course, you're such a fucking victim. You forget that Sienna had both of her parents killed on the same day? Or is that not important enough because it isn't about you? Newsflash Millie, you're not the only one with fucking problems. "

"You're right, Marcus, I'm not the only one with problems. But I *am* the only one who had to go through it on my own."

"You know you have a phone too right? Why is it our job to reach out to you?"

"So when you guys all left to your new families, I was supposed to sit in that fucking home and message *you*?"

"That's what the rest of us did. What makes you so fucking special?"

"Okay, Marcus. You don't know anything about what I went through. You don't know how it felt to be forgotten and abandoned. While you were off living your perfect little lives, I was just trying to survive."

What a fucking drama queen.

I can feel my blood boiling, frustration seeping into every fibre of my being.

"Survive? You think the rest of us had it easy? You think being adopted meant rainbows and unicorns? I seriously don't know what you expected. Even before we left, you chose to isolate yourself." Millie's eyes blaze with fury, her voice trembling with intensity.

"I isolated myself? No, Marcus, I protected myself. I couldn't trust anyone, couldn't believe that anyone would truly care or be there for me. And you proved me right."
I stop myself from saying anything more. This clearly isn't working. I need to try a new approach. I step closer to her, my voice softer this time and filled with sincerity.

"I'm not here to argue with you. You can hate me and that's fine, but deep down you know we're still a family. Nobody leaves that place without a lifelong connection to each and every other person there and right now this isn't about us. Dean is gonna die and we can't save him without you."

Millie's eyes remain filled with anger, her walls still stubbornly intact. But I can see a flicker of hesitation in her gaze, a sign that maybe, just maybe, she's considering my words. I continue, my voice pleading.

"This isn't about who was right or wrong, who deserved what, or who should have done what. It's about putting aside our differences and being there for Dean, because that's what a family does... Millie, please." She finally looks at me, the look in her eyes slightly less sharp than before. Some emotion pushing its way to the surface.

"I think you should leave." As Millie utters those words, I feel a mix of frustration and disappointment wash over me. Have I just fucked up the last chance to save Dean? *Think, Marcus.* I pull out the paper from my pocket and rip off a piece. I grab a pen that I spot sitting on a counter in her entrance and write down my phone number.

"Here," I drop the piece of paper on top of the book on the coffee table, "It's all up to you. You can stay trapped in your past, holding onto your anger, or you can choose to move forward. We have a real chance here to save Dean, to rewrite the ending to his story and we can't do that without you. You can choose to be a part of something bigger than yourself, or you can continue to sit in your fancy little apartment and wallow in your own self-pity."

Millie stands there, her hands clenched tightly at her sides, her breath coming in shallow gasps. I can see the inner battle raging within her, the conflict between her desire to protect her ego and her grudging recognition of the truth in my words. After what feels like an eternity, she finally speaks, her voice barely above a whisper.

"I'll think about it."

That's good enough for me.

With that, I make my exit, closing the door gently behind. I check my phone. 5:29. Perfect.

Time to deal with Sienna's little date.

CHAPTER 21:
CONSIDER IT CANCELLED

Marcus

7:51. I stop outside Sienna's house once again and wait patiently for Skylar to emerge. *With any luck, she'll have an extra phone in hand.* Another cigarette destroying my lungs in the meantime. At long last the door cracks open and I vaguely hear Sky talking.

"Thank you for having me." Skylar shouts to Sienna's mother. I take a final drag from my cigarette and flick it onto the ground, carefully stomping it out with the toe of my shoe. As she rushes down the front steps I catch Sienna standing in the doorway; our eyes meeting for a brief moment. She's wearing a short, alluring black dress. The outline of her body on display. Emphasising her slender waist. I've never seen her in a dress like that. She notices me ogling her and gifts me with a disobedient little smile. She knows what she's doing. *Very brave, sweet.* Flaunting like that in front of me, knowing she's wearing it for another man.

We'll see if that smile is still there after tonight.

Chapter 21

"I got it." Skylar whispers to me with a proud grin. Those three words are music to my ears. I keep my eyes latched on Sienna's whilst I wait for Skylar to get on the bike. There's a confidence in her eyes that I haven't seen in a while. Who knew she could get more irresistible? I make sure to give her a fake-stern look, just to remind her that she's in trouble, before slipping on my helmet and speeding away.

Once we reach the house, Skylar hands me Sienna's phone. A pretty lilac case on the back and a picture of her cat as her lock screen. I close the door, crack open the window slightly and sit down on the bed. The room dimly lit. I light up another cigarette; the least I can do to calm myself before the night I'm about to have. With a purposeful click, I unlock the phone, directing my attention straight to her messages. At the pinnacle of the list, a contact labelled 'Skinny jeans' catches my eye. This must be it.

S: Are you still on for tonight?

Skinny Jeans: Yeah sure.

'Yeah sure.'. Ungrateful bastard.

S: What's the plan?

Skinny Jeans: I'm down for whatever, just as long as you actually let me kiss you this time.

Excuse me? There's no way this fucker tried to kiss my sweet.

S: How about that little Italian restaurant near college? I heard the food is amazing :)
Skinny Jeans: Cool

S: I'll book for 9?

Skinny Jeans: Alright see you then.

Wow. Mr. 'Skinny Jeans' certainly seems like a bundle of fun. *Not that I would expect anything else from a man who wears skinny jeans of course.* Let's change up this plan a little.

S: Hey. Change of plan, I'm not really feeling like going to a restaurant. How about we keep it more casual instead?

I put the phone down and glance at the window waiting for a reply. Taking a long, deep draw of my cigarette, feeling the heat of the smoke trickling down to my lungs. The phone screen lights up.

Skinny Jeans: Yeah sure, what you wanna do instead?

S: There's this spot I like to go to sometimes to watch the trains go by that I think you'd appreciate

Skinny Jeans: Yeah that's fine, just send me the address.

I send 'Skinny Jeans' the location of the tunnel and tap out my cigarette. I change into my least favourite black hoodie and tracksuit bottoms. *No way am I getting my good clothes dirty for this prick.* Making my way to the kitchen I feel a surge of adrenaline building. Am I actually about to do this? Admittedly, the question doesn't linger for too long in my mind. *Yes, yes I am.*

I instantly grab the knife I had found last night and slip it into my waistband before making my way out to the back garden. Opening the shed door, I flick on the light, scanning every object within. There it is, the shovel. I rush out, hopping onto my bike. My thoughts are too consumed to bother with a helmet. I speed toward the tunnel, the chilly night air whipping past me with a rough, sharp intensity.

I drop my bike just before I reach the tracks and make a pitiful attempt at hiding it behind a couple of trees. 8:58. I pull up my hood and wait. My adrenaline is building in a way I've never experienced. I can feel every single vein in my body. Everything is tingling. My entire vision is static. My body begins breaking into a cold sweat. My heart beating so fast that it can't be healthy. I remain in this state for a while. Waiting… and waiting. The tension in my body begins to settle slightly. I check the time. 9:17. Does this idiot know who he is supposed to be meeting? How dare he leave my sweet waiting in a place like this alone at nighttime. The cold nerves in my body morph into a burning rage.

S: Where are you?

I hold the phone waiting for a reply but keep my stare locked in front of me. *Ping.*

Skinny Jeans: Just left. Won't be long.

Just left? I clench my jaw and shove the phone back into my pocket. If only he knew how much easier he just made this for me. Continuing to stare forward at the opening to the tracks I remain completely patient. My body is frozen entirely. I'm unsure if time is passing by too fast or too slow. Either way, it's passing by, and I'm very aware that every second I wait is a second closer. *Ping.*

Skinny Jeans: Where you at?

Pure excitement floods every inch of my body. A sinister smile carving its way onto my face. My eyes dart around desperately, trying to locate him in the darkness. Found you. He's standing next to our sofas facing away from me. His eyes sealed on his phone screen like a moron. *Ping. Ping.* This is it.

I make my way towards him extremely slowly. My hand steadily making its way to the knife in my waistband. The closer I get the more I understand the nickname. His jeans are so skinny I'm surprised he even has any blood flow to begin with. I'm assessing him. Examining him. Average height with a muscular build. If the jeans weren't bad enough he's wearing a polo shirt at least two sizes too small. The cliché scent of his aftershave is getting stronger and stronger. He's certainly not a man even worthy of breathing near my sweet. *Or breathing at all for that matter.* I make my move.

As I grab his forehead and pull his head back, I feel the heat of his body in the palm of my hand. I quickly pull my knife from my waist and slice the side of his throat. I don't know what I was expecting, he'd just drop dead instantly? *Well it's safe to say that doesn't happen.* He wriggles out of my grasp, holding his neck. I watch the blood pour between his fingers and down his arm while he stares at me. The poor guy, he doesn't even know who his killer is. As I watch the red serpents grow from between his fingers, slithering down his porcelain hand and ever-whitening skin, his eyes become dreary.

Before I even have time to gather my thoughts he lunges at me and goes for my knife, his grip easily escapable thanks to his blood covered hands. He tries swinging at me but barely makes an impact on my chest; merely grasping my hood and falling to the floor.

His face scrunched on the ground, wheezing, choking, drowning in his own blood. I feel sick, but I feel nothing. My hands are dead cold but my heart is beating faster than ever. I step back and watch his ribcage expand and retract with every noisy, bloody curdling, crackling breath he takes, knowing one of them soon will be his last. Not wanting to waste any time I roll that corpse onto his back, his eyes stay fixed onto mine yet his body is completely still. He can speak to me through his eyes, I can see the fear of death, the feeling of utter confusion as to who I am and why I feel the need to execute him this way. Stop. I can't waste any more time.

I walk around his still croaking body, his hands bent inward in impossible positions as his organs begin to fail. I stand directly above his head, his eyes now slightly veering off the right, focussing on nothing but death. Red foam drips from the side of his mouth as I watch his eyes glass over. I crouch down over him and bring my blade to his throat for the second time, look once more in his eyes, and slice. Deeper than before. I seem to bring him back to life for a mere second as he groans and begins to drown in his own blood pouring down his open throat from his arteries.

His body twitches as I bring my blade to his throat again. Slice. And again. Slice. Each time his groans get quieter and quieter. I have never felt this way. The further I go, the more it feels like I'm doing this random, innocent man justice. Putting him out of the painful misery I placed him in. Well, *he* placed himself in. I just keep going. I can't stop myself. I am beginning to feel myself getting more comfortable doing what I'm doing. I take the bloodied blade and raise it to my eye level above him, and smash the knife deep into his spine through his throat. Silence.

Just the sound of blood trickling like that small stream in the countryside. I leave my knife there, stand up, and grab the shovel I had brought along with me.

No kiss for you, *Skinny Jeans.*

I spend the next hour muddying my trainers, digging a shallow grave for the rotting corpse beside me, I walk back over to his body, now grey with death. Dark red blood dried up down the side of his face, his eyes still in that same position when I struck him with the final blow. I take his phone from beside him and use his fingerprint to unlock it. Quickly blocking Sienna before I put it in my back pocket. His contacts littered with other women. *Something my sweet should never have to worry about.*

I unnecessarily take a moment to crouch down next to him and follow his eyes to where he was looking, just to imagine what it would be like to be in his position. To die in a foreign place, alone, with no one but a monster.

I grab his feet and try pulling him over to the eternal hole I dug for him next to the train track. He's too heavy, or maybe I'm just exhausted. Either way, I try a different approach, rolling him over, and over, and over again until I get him exactly where I want. He's trying to piss me off, trying to fuck me over, even in death. Leaving a trail of blood from where he died to where he now lies. *Does he think I'm stupid?*

I grab my shovel and scoop up every speck of blood I can see on the floor to bury it with him. I tip him over the edge of the grave and he lands with a thud. I stare at him for a few minutes while he lay in a position impossible for a conscious person to put themselves into. Knotted limbs covered in blood, his nose pressed against one of the walls of the hole. Cringe. I don't hesitate to throw dirt over the corpse. One after another. Shovel after shovel.

I just fucking killed a man.

And the worst part is I don't seem to feel much.

Maybe I need time to soak it all in. I'm sure that's it. Or maybe *this* is it. It can't be, surely. Is murder just that simple? I keep waiting for my legs to give way or my heart to explode out of my chest. Something. Anything. But I feel pretty fine. I notice a slight tremble through my body but my heart rate seems to have calmed. My vision is clear. I just destroyed every memory this man has ever made and yet right now I'm wondering if I'll even remember doing it one day. I pick the knife up off the ground and slide it back into my waistband.

Do I just leave now?

What else would I do? I'm not sure. But walking away seems.. wrong. I briefly sicken myself as a slight chuckle escapes my lips thinking about it. It's almost awkward. I take a look around, but I'm confused on exactly what for, before I make my way back to the bike. Rain starts pouring from the blackness of the sky above as I ride down to a small pond within the woods a few minutes away. I toss in his now-useless phone, checking the time before I do so. 11:27. Back on the bike. I arrive at Sienna's house and make sure her phone is clear from any blood or dirt before walking silently up to her living room window. Thankfully for me it's still open slightly. I reach my arm through, unintentionally budging the window open an inch more than before, and place the phone behind the sofa cushion. That should be enough to convince my sweet that she had just misplaced it.

After returning the shovel to its home and sneaking in silently through the back door, I get straight to washing the knife. I smother it in bleach, over and over again. The final drops of blood rolling down the plug hole. I've never put so much effort into washing up. *I fucking hate washing up.* Once I'm happy with it I place it back in the drawer and scramble to my room, locking the door behind me. Pulling off my stained clothes and leaving them momentarily on the floor. I put on a pair of clean tracksuit bottoms and pick up the discarded clothes in a bundle. I walk out through the back door to the bins, making sure to shove the clothes deep into the bin bag. Taking a quick deep breath and feeling a huge sense of relief graze over me. Everything is covered. It's done.

Now, I'd better check on my sweet.

CHAPTER 22:
SWEET SURRENDER

Marcus

I sit down on the edge of the bed, leaning forward onto my knees, and roll up a joint. The house is extremely quiet. My room feels tranquil. It's strange to see that life is just continuing as if I didn't slit a man's throat a few hours ago. I pull out my phone and call Sienna. *I know she won't answer, but at least she'll find her phone so I can bother her over text instead.* As expected, the phone rings a few times before she hangs it up. Text it is.

M: How did your little date go, sweet?

She responds much faster than usual.

Sweet: It was amazing. We're gonna get married and have babies.

I smirk at her audacity. I didn't know my sweet was a liar.

M: That's cute. Make sure you invite me to the wedding so I can burn the venue to the fucking ground.

I take a deep drag from the joint, feeling the familiar wave of relaxation wash over me. I exhale the smoke slowly, watching it swirl and dissipate into fumes. The scent of cannabis fills the room, mixing with the faint smell of blood that still lingers in the air. Which I'll admit is creeping me out slightly.

Sweet: How romantic.

M: Drop the act. **We both know you're smirking and giggling at your phone right now.**

Sweet: Attachment - 1 image

I briefly bite my bottom lip and smile as I see the image pop up. A risqué picture of her, still in that tiny black dress, sticking up a middle finger to the camera. *Well...to me.* I crack my neck and readjust myself. I know she's teasing me, and it's working.

M: You couldn't wait to show me that dress again, could you?

Sweet: Don't flatter yourself.

M: Just let me know when you want me to come and rip it off.

Sweet: That would be never. In case I didn't make myself clear, I'm not interested.

M: Prove it. I'll take you on a real date and we'll see if we can keep our hands off each other.

Sweet: You're so fucking arrogant.

I raise an eyebrow and smile. I can see her little character breaking once again. I finish my joint and stub it out, conjuring up my next response. Suddenly the phone rings.

"Are you gonna stop harassing me now and let me get some sleep?" She snaps. I laugh and lean back on the bed.

"You know you don't have to reply, right?" She says nothing in response. She's caught. "So you wanna tell me what this whole date thing was really about? And don't give me some bullshit story about you actually liking anybody else because I know it's a lie."

"You clearly can't take no for an answer so I had to make it crystal clear that I don't want you."

"Sounds like you're doing a very bad job at trying to convince yourself of that." I pause before continuing. "Talk to me. What's really stopping you, sweet?" The conversation falls silent for several seconds and I can almost hear her pretty little mind ticking through the phone.

"I'm in love with you. Like really *really* in love with you." I hear her vaguely whimpering through her words and her voice beginning to tremble.

"I know you are. So what's all this about then?"

"Marcus, I can't be with somebody I truly love. I just can't. I won't. I loved two people in my life and both of them left me on the same fucking day. But I can't escape you. I'm doing everything I can to move on from you. Nothing I try works." My poor angel, now almost sobbing down the phone. Her voice filled with pure pain. I can't bear to hear one more syllable without having her in my arms.

"I'm coming over to listen, okay? Unlock the door for me and I'll be as quick as I can. Please."

"Fine," she whispers before hanging up. I slip into a plain T-shirt and race over to her.

Sienna opens the door, biting her fingers nervously, her face wet with tears. It stings me to see her like this. Without second thought, I scoop her into my arms, her legs wrapping around me. I close the door with my elbow whilst holding her tight, feeling her tension as she sinks herself into me.

"Let it out, sweet. I'm here, I've got you. I've always got you." With that, her soft whimpers turn into hard, deep cries. Her body jolting with every sob. Her tears, relentless, find refuge in the fabric of my t-shirt. I hold her closer, wanting to absorb some of her pain, to bear the burden with her. I cup the back of her head with my hand, her beautiful curls spilling through my fingers, rubbing her back slowly with my other hand. We stand in the doorway for what feels like an eternity, her cries echoing through the silent house.

Slowly, I begin carrying her to the stairs and up to her bedroom, shutting the door carefully behind me. Trying my best not to change her position, I sit down on the edge of the bed. I continue to hold her tight: to let her cry, making sure not to interrupt her. Feeling the warmth of her tears against my chest as she clings to me, seeking shelter from the storm of emotions consuming her.

Her cries gradually begin to subside, replaced by softer sniffles and shaky breaths. I glance down at her, the dim light of the room illuminating the tear stains on her cheeks. I delicately brush away a single soft curl, stuck to her damp face. She remains clinging to me, still seeking solace in the midst of her vulnerability. I hold her close, pressing gentle kisses against her forehead. Her eyes and cheeks now puffy, but still so incredibly beautiful. An entirely flawless being.

"You ready to talk to me?" I ask, caressing her cheek. She nods briefly and takes a breath, followed by a couple of precious little sniffles. Her wide eyes, flushed with tears, looking right up at me.

"I'm terrified of loving you." she whispers, her voice trembling. She searches my face, desperate for reassurance and understanding. My body tightens as I contain my emotions.

"Sienna, I'm never gonna leave you." I assure, a whisper against her skin.

"You can't promise me that. Nobody can. Just look at what's happening with Dean right now." Leaning in closer, I gently press away a tear from her cheek with the back of my hand. Her lip begins to shake and she breathes in hard through her nose. "I miss my parents so much, Marcus. I can't miss anybody like that again." I pause and think carefully about my words.

"You're right, I can't promise you that." I start, looking deeply into her eyes, "But what I can promise, is that every moment I have left of this life will be devoted to loving you." A single tear trickles down her cheek, rolling onto her chin and forming a single gorgeous droplet, as she listens attentively. "Sweet, as long as I have breath in my lungs and a beat in my heart, everything I do is for you. You *are* my life, and I'm not going anywhere."

The air in the room feels heavy with the intensity of the moment, as if time itself has paused to witness this pivotal exchange between us. Without saying a word, Sienna leans in, her trembling lips brushing against mine. It's a gentle, hesitant kiss, filled with both longing and fear. I can taste the saltiness of her tears mixed with the sweet warmth of her breath. At this moment, everything else fades away. All dissipating into nothingness. There is only Sienna, and the overwhelming rush of love and obsession coursing through my veins.

I respond to her kiss with tenderness and passion, pouring every ounce of my devotion into that single, electrifying touch. Our souls are intertwining, finding solace and strength in one another. My entire being and existence depending on the beautiful angel sitting in my lap. Sienna's fingers thread through my hair, pulling me closer, deepening the kiss. It becomes more urgent, more desperate, as if we're trying to consume each other's pain.

In this stolen moment of raw vulnerability, I whisper against her lips, "Is this finally a sweet surrender?" She smiles and rests her forehead on mine before answering.

"I don't know, I quite enjoy playing hard to get." With that, I smile wide and pull both of our bodies back onto the bed, squeezing her tightly and planting hundreds of playful kisses over her body.

We lay together in silence for a while. My fingers tracing every curve.

"You're still in trouble, you know?" I say, breaking the silence and giving her a faux mean glare. Her face drops slightly, a nervous glint in her eyes.

"I lied about the date. I was just trying to find somebody else I could be with and put my focus on. I needed a distraction and I couldn't even get that. The guy fucking stood me up." She looks away from me, almost embarrassed. Her poor little face, sheepish and drained. "He even blocked my number."

Fuck it.

"He didn't stand you up, sweet." She looks back over to me, scrunching her eyebrows.

"What do you mean?" I draw her focus to the dried patches of blood still remaining on my hands, staring intensely at her in anticipation of her reaction. Her eyes widen in shock and disbelief as she looks down. Her mouth opens, intending to say something, but no words come out. Fear and confusion dance across her face, and I can see the wheels turning in her mind as she tries to process the horrors I've just revealed. I watch her body freeze, her breath caught in her throat.

"Fuck Marcus, you ki-"

"Don't think about it, sweet." I interrupt, "You'll make yourself sick."

"That's beyond crazy. You can't just go around killing people! Why would you do that? How?-"

"I told you, I'd do anything for you," I pause, "You're *mine*, sweet. Any man who tries to take you from me is a threat and I will eliminate that threat." Sienna doesn't respond. The look on her face is unreadable. I'm not worried, I know she didn't care about him. I sit back up on the edge of the bed, leaning forward, and place a comforting hand on her thigh. "It was over quickly, I promise."

"Because of a date? Have you lost your mind?" I stand up and face her.

"If I didn't do something, that fucker would've tried to kiss you, sweet ..for the *second* time." I say, raising an eyebrow. *Busted.* She looks up at me, sucking in her bottom lip. Guilt written over her face as though she's being reprimanded.

Which she is.

"I stopped him the first time,"

"There shouldn't have been a fucking first time. What if you couldn't stop him the second time? What if he wanted more than a kiss? Huh?" I challenge. She doesn't reply. "Let's call it even, shall we?" She remains frozen in place, her eyes glaring up at me. A hollow expression on her face. Almost as if she's afraid of me, and if I'm honest I quite like it. I wait a few more seconds for a response that doesn't come, before letting out a big sigh.

With slow, deep footsteps I make my way to her bedside table and open her pyjama drawer. I sift through her collection, picking out a cosy little beige set. The act of carefully selecting her sleepwear feels strangely comforting. Intimate. As if I'm taking a small step towards creating a sense of security and stability for the both of us. I turn around to face Sienna, still sitting on the bed, her eyes locked on me with a mix of confusion, disbelief, and a hint of fear.
Who knew fear would be an expression I'd enjoy seeing on that sweet face?

"Come on," I coax gently, holding the pyjamas in my hand, "Let's get you ready for bed." She hesitates for a moment, her eyes oscillating between the offered garments and I. I can see the internal struggle, weighing her emotions against the grim reality of what I had just revealed. Apprehensively, she climbs up off the bed and stands in front of me, fidgety and timid. As her hand reaches out for the pyjamas, I intercept, placing them beside me on the bed. "Turn around," I instruct. She complies, her back now turned to me.

I carefully lift up her hair and unzip the sexy little black dress. The soft fabric falls to the floor, pooling around her feet, leaving her in nothing but her underwear. My fingers skilfully trace down her body, revealing the vulnerable beauty hidden beneath the fabric. Her body slowly unveiled before me, a canvas of temptation, each layer discarded with reverence as if unwrapping a precious gift. I swallow hard, trying to suppress the rush of torturing desire that threatens to consume me, reminding myself that this moment is about comforting her. Once my hands reach her hips I tighten my grip and spin her back around to face me. I keep my hands lingering on her hips for a moment whilst her beautiful doe eyes glance up uncertainly at me.

Picking up the pyjama top, I gently guide her arms through the sleeves, the soft fabric embracing her delicate frame. Pushing her down onto the bed's edge, I kneel before her, sliding the pyjama bottoms up her legs, cherishing each inch of her body. The fabric, velvety against my touch, reminding me of her innocence I'm slowly beginning to take from her. I look up, meeting her eyes as I pull the bottoms up to her thighs, the boundary of my touch marked by the bed's edge. There's a tangible, sensual tension between us, and for once, I can tell I'm not the sole participant in this unspoken exchange of desires. She lets out a soft sigh, her eyes fluttering closed as she leans back lewdly onto the bed. Her back arched.

Adding to my mental list of reasons why she has me entirely mesmerised.

She raises her hips as I pull at the bottoms once more, knotting the waistband to complete the ensemble. Admiring her in those adorable pyjamas, a surge of protective satisfaction washes over me. Sienna opens her eyes, her gaze filled with a mixture of vulnerability and desire. Without saying a word, I lean over her, my lips hovering just inches away from hers. The anticipation hangs heavy in the air as we both feel the electricity between us.

I press my lips against hers, starting off slowly, savouring the softness and warmth of her mouth. It's a gentle kiss, filled with tenderness and a yearning that only grows stronger with each passing second. As our lips move in sync, I feel her body relax against mine, a whispered moan escaping her mouth. The kiss deepens, becoming more passionate and intense.

My hand explores her body, tracing along her spine and down to the curve of her waist. The fabric of her pyjamas feeling impossibly soft against my fingertips. I can feel the heat radiating from her body, matching the fire that courses through my veins. I stop myself. Nothing more can happen tonight. Not yet.

I don't want it to be that easy.

As I pull away from Sienna's lips, I can see the confusion and desire etched on her face, still sprinkled with a hint of genuine fear for me. I know that she wants more, *bless her heart*, but I can't give her what she's craving just yet. I want to build her up. I sigh and take a moment to be in my thoughts. Looking down at her in this state is forcing me to realise just how terribly twisted I have become, I'm completely relishing in the power I hold over her. Knowing that eliminating that loser has gained me an extra degree of intimidation and control over my sweet is a very dangerous weapon in my arsenal. At long last, this little game she had me playing has been fully turned against her. I have her exactly where I want her now. Vulnerable and afraid, yet still entirely drawn to me. I resist the urge to smirk and instead focus on the task at hand.

I lift the duvet cover, inviting her to slip inside, ensuring it wraps snugly around her. I position myself behind her, spooning her body, and gently wrap my arm around her waist.

"Marcus, what if you get caught?" She whispers suddenly. I pull her body closer to me before responding.

"I don't get caught."

The warmth of our bodies mingling creates a comforting cocoon. Sienna remains silent, her breathing shallow and uneven, as her mind processes the conflicting emotions coursing through her. I nuzzle my face into the crook of her neck, planting soft kisses along her collarbone, savouring the sweet taste of her skin. Every touch and caress is deliberate, calculated to keep her off-balance.

"Sleep tight, sweet" I whisper gently into her ear. Pressing a firm kiss to her temple; relishing in the way she nestles closer to me in response. It doesn't take long for my exhausted little sweet to drift off. I watch over her, my fingers gently stroking her hair as she rests. Her body is entirely peaceful, as it should be.

I close my eyes too and in the quiet darkness of the room, I find myself drifting into a restless sleep. Momentarily, a surge of self-awareness washes over me as I question my motives for the first time. Two foreign sensations that I seldom experience. It's almost as if the line between protector and predator is becoming slightly blurred in my mind. I'm jolted from the precipice of slumber, a cruel reminder that peace eludes me. The image of my violent act replays like a dreadful loop, each detail becoming more vivid with every repetition. I glance down at my blood-stained hands as the weight of what I have done bears down upon me.

But instead of remorse tugging at my conscience, there is an unsettling absence of emotion, a void where regret should reside.

As the night wears on, I find myself trapped in the clutches of insomnia. There is a disturbing calmness that's eating at me.

What does it say about me as a person, as a human being, that I could commit such a horrific act and feel nothing but a sense of satisfaction, tinged with regret over my own naiveté? That I could slice a man's throat several times, watching the blood drain from him and still feel okay. I find myself hoping, praying even, that some semblance of guilt will eventually find its way into my heart. That perhaps there is still some flicker of humanity buried deep within my soul, struggling to surface amidst the darkest recesses of my consciousness. It is an odd desire, to long for the torment of remorse. But in its absence, I am left wondering if I have truly lost myself in the process of this monstrous act.

I feel really fucking good, and there's a lot wrong with that.

CHAPTER 23:

A SLICE TO DIE FOR

Marcus

After an hour or so of successful sleep, I'm awoken by Sienna's disgraceful and frankly terrifying alarm. *I guess 'bad taste in alarm noises' will be the first and only negative I can give her.* I reach over to turn it off before placing a kiss on her forehead.

"Good morning, beautiful." I start, smiling at her with pride "How did you sleep?" She delicately rubs her eyes, with clean hands, before turning to snuggle into me.

"Good actually," she replies, her voice soft and drowsy. "I slept right through." I can't help but chuckle at her response, finding her innocence charming, even in light of my newly shared secret.

"Because I'm here?" She shrugs me off and sits up, yawning and stretching her dainty arms out wide.

"No, because you exhausted me." She retorts with a hint of attitude.

"Well I'm glad you slept well, you always should."

"What about you?" She asks softly, concern lacing her voice. "Did you sleep well?" I offer her a faint smile, masking the internal tumult that has plagued my mind all night.

"I never sleep well." It's a half-truth. Sleep has always eluded me, but last night felt like a punishment rather than a natural state.

As I begin to get out of bed, my phone pings.

Sky: Get here. Right fucking now.

Well, that's not very polite.

I sigh in annoyance as I read Skylar's demanding message. Despite the urgency in her tone, I can't find it in me to muster any enthusiasm for her problems. With minimal effort, I reply with a curt message, 'On my way.' before tossing my phone onto the bed and turning my attention back to Sienna, who is now awake and watching me curiously. I can see the concern in her eyes, but I quickly dismiss it as irrelevant.

"I'm sorry sweet, I have to rush off."

"What's wrong?"

"Nothing," I reassure her. "Sky just needs my help with something. You'll be at Delilah's tonight, right?"

"Yeah of course." I quickly get myself ready and grab my bike key, giving sienna a kiss on the forehead before making my way out.

Opening the door, I'm immediately greeted by Sky's mum and dad decorating. Both with their arms full of vibrant streamers and colourful balloons. A wave of cheerful chatter and the sweet aroma of freshly baked cake catching me by surprise. I think about Sky's text. I must have forgotten somebody's birthday.

148

"Afternoon, darling!" Her mum shrieks, embracing me in a hug. "How does it look?"

"It looks amazing, you guys did a great job."

"Thank you, Marcus. I've got a lovely birthday lunch coming up too, you're going to join us aren't you?"

"Definitely." I flash her a smile before walking through to my room.

As I open the door I'm startled to see Sky sitting on my bed, angry as angry could be. I raise an eyebrow, puzzled by her rage and shut the door behind me.

"Care to explain?" She snaps, holding out her phone. I take Sky's phone from her outstretched hand and glance at the screen. My heart skips a beat as I read the headline:

'Local Man Reported Missing.'

My eyes narrow in disbelief as I scroll through the article, detailing the disappearance of the man I had killed just last night. *Fuck me, that was fast.* A picture of his smug little face staring back at me. I look up from the phone and meet Sky's intense gaze.

"I'm sure I don't need to tell you this, but that's the man Sienna was planning to go out with last night." She continues. I shrug nonchalantly.

"So what?"

"Really, Marcus? That's all you've got?"

"What do you want me to do? Break down in tears?"

"Cut the shit. What did you do?" Sky's accusing eyes bore into mine, demanding an explanation that I'm not ready to give. I meet her gaze, my voice calm and steady,

"I did what I told you I was gonna do, I cancelled the date." I remain impassive, unwilling to give her the satisfaction of seeing me squirm. She scoffs, a bitter laugh escaping her lips.

"Cancelled the date, huh? That's a clever way of putting

it." She sneers, "You killed him. Didn't you?" I take a deep breath and rub my face briefly. The weight of the situation is slowly resting on me.

"Look, I took care of it. That's all you need to know."
I walk over to the window and light up a cigarette, Skylar's eyes burning a hole through the side of me. I take a drag, trying to maintain my composure.

"How could you?" I turn to face her, looking her directly in the eye.

"What did you expect me to do, Sky?" I ask, my voice calm and composed. Her brows furrow in anger and disbelief.

"You don't just get to play God, Marcus," she snaps, her voice filled with frustration. She covers her mouth with her hands as her emotions begin to surface. "How did you do it?"

I blow some smoke slowly from my mouth, observing it closely as it swirls. My mind transported back to the moment the knife pierced through his throat. I can feel it again. Hear it again. Smell it again. The crack of his spine. The blood soaking into my skin; rising up through my nostrils. His contorted corpse on the soil. Feeling his life drain into my hands.

Holy fuck, I wish I could do it again. Over and over.

Isn't that disgusting? Insane? Yes. But it's the truth. I don't like to run from the truth. Most of the time. I fade out of my daydream and catch myself unintentionally smiling.

"You're sick!" Skylar seethes at me. "How did you do it, Marcus?" Her voice is so shrill it's starting to piss me off.

"Do you really wanna know?" I ask with a smirk as I walk up close to her, my cigarette wobbling between my fingers.
"I grabbed his face. I pulled his head back." I pause for dramatic effect, "And I slit his fucking throat."

Skylar's jaw drops to the floor, her face now void of colour. Tears beginning to fall like silent raindrops.

"You won't get away with it."

"Why's that? You gonna turn me in?" I taunt. She won't do anything, I know that. She's not that stupid. I'm met with no response, her eyes now streaming with tears. I meet her gaze with an unsettling calmness, my voice dripping with a detached yet sinister elegance. "Sky, don't worry about it. It's over." I remark coldly, turning away from her to take another drag of the cigarette, the acrid smoke curling around my words. "I did what I needed to do to protect Sienna."

Skylar scoffs incredulously, her voice laced with a mix of bitterness and desperation.

"Protect her? Is that what you call it? Taking matters into your own hands, playing judge, jury, and executioner?" A flicker of pain flits across Skylar's tear-stained face, a reflection of the fracture in our friendship. She takes a step back, her resolve waning in the face of my unwavering conviction. "You're evil, Marcus." she whispers, her voice barely audible through choked sobs.

"And Sienna is innocent, pure," I say, my tone now softening but no less determined. "She needs me, whether she likes it or not, and if I have to become the villain to keep her safe then that's what I'll do." Skylar shakes her head, tears surging down her face as her voice trembles with a mix of anger and hurt.

"You can't just justify your actions like that, Marcus. That was someone's life you took."

"And I'd do it again." I state firmly, my voice devoid of remorse or regret. The room seems to grow colder, as if the weight of my actions are sucking the warmth out of the air.

"Now, if you don't mind, I'm gonna go and enjoy some birthday lunch." I say, leaning in close to her. "Pull yourself together, Sky."

I pass her slowly and leave, slamming the door behind me. abandoning the tension and heavy air from the room.

As I make my way down the corridor, a burst of energy comes charging toward me in the form of Skylar's younger brother. His face lights up with an exuberant smile, proudly sporting a sizable 'Birthday Boy' badge on his jumper. The weight of whatever I had just been absorbed in discussing dissipates instantly as I mimic his infectious grin and crouch down to his level.

His infectious spirit rubbing off on me.

As he reaches me, I catch him in my arms and toss him high in the air. His laughter echoes through the hallway as I spin him around, feeling my smile carving into my cheeks and aching my jaw. Lowering him back down to the ground and setting him back on his feet, he grins up at me, the shadows in his dimpled cheeks bright against his pale skin.

"Look at you, little birthday boy!" I exclaim, my voice filled with genuine happiness. "You're getting bigger by the minute."

"I'm six now!" He announces.

"You know what being six means, right?" I ask, a mischievous grin forming on my face. His eyes widen with anticipation, his voice bubbling with excitement.

"What? What does it mean?"

"Well," I begin, placing a hand on his shoulder. His face lights up with excitement as he remembers an old promise, and he begins to bounce on his feet.

"You're gonna get me a bike just like you?"

"Absolutely," I say, ruffling his hair. "Pick out whatever bike you want and I'll get it for you, yeah?"

"Really? I can pick any bike I want?" he squeals, his voice filled with disbelief and excitement. I can't help but laugh at his enthusiasm, a sound that feels rare and foreign on my own lips.

"Yup. Any one you want, little man."

"I want a black one just like yours!"

"A black one huh? Excellent choice." With a gentle pat on the back, I guide him toward the living room. "Alright, birthday boy, let's go tuck into some birthday lunch." I suggest, winking at him. He nods eagerly and reaches out to grab my hand, his small fingers intertwining with mine.

As we enter the living room, Skylar's parents, adorned with abundant smiles, beckon us to join them at the beautifully decorated dining table. I lead her brother to his designated seat at the head of the table and sit down next to him. The room is filled with the aroma of delicious food, and I can't help but be drawn to the spread in front of me. The table cluttered with various sandwiches, sweet treats and finger food. As I begin to serve myself, Skylar takes a seat opposite me, her face red and blotchy. *This is going to be fun.*

"The roast potatoes are incredible!" I declare, nodding my head in approval to Sky's mother.

"Thank you, darling. They're one of my specialties." Skylar spitefully grabs a roast potato and takes a bite, staring through me.

"Mm!" She exaggerates. "You're right, Marcus. The seasoning is killer." I raise an eyebrow and connect to her gaze.

Safe to say, if looks could kill, I'd be in the ground with Skinny Jeans right about now.

She takes a huge scoop of roast potatoes, her eyes still fiercely fixed on me as if daring me to respond. A smirk plays on my lips as I take a sip of my drink, keeping up with the charade.

"Woah, don't get carried away there, Sky. You wouldn't wanna take on more than you can handle."
Her dad quickly interrupts, laughing. "No need to worry about that son, the girl can eat. There's never food left on her plate."

"Well, dad." She starts, abruptly. "That's because I'm grateful for what I have. I make sure to cherish every single meal I get to enjoy in my life," She looks back at me. "Because you never know when it could be taken away, right Marcus?" A menacing scowl takes over her face and I can feel the tension mounting. Very funny.

"Unfortunately, life isn't fair." I respond with a phoney empathetic look. The room falls silent and Sky's family can almost certainly feel our tension.

Our discreet conversation of digs continues throughout the lunch. Every word we exchange is laced with underlying meaning, a game of cat and mouse that neither of us seems willing to back down from. As the lunch comes to a close, Sky's mother begins to clear the dishes, her eyes darting between us with a mix of suspicion and concern. I can see the wheels turning in her head, trying to decipher the meaning behind our cryptic conversation. She stands up with a small stack of plates.

"Right then," She starts with a smile, "I think it's time for some birthday cake. Marcus, darling, will you come and help me?"

"Of course." I respond, grabbing the rest of the plates on my way.

Sky's mother hands me an old tin full of various, mismatched candles and some matches. I begin placing them around the cake in a strategic pattern, making sure that they're evenly spaced. Some are tall and slender, with long, thin wicks that curl and twist as they burn. Others are short and stout, with thicker wicks. I strike the matches and hold them to the candles, watching as

154

their flames leap up eagerly, casting a warm glow over the room. The scent of burning wax filling my nose, reminding me of childhood birthdays. That's pretty much all we had back at Orchid's. A birthday cake and a gift under £20.

As I step back to admire my handiwork, Sky's mother gasps happily, as if my mediocre candle placement is a work of art.

"Beautiful! Thank you for the help."

"Of course."

She scurries off excitedly to switch off the living room light and returns quickly to begin carrying the cake. As she begins to lift the cake, my attention diverts momentarily to the drawer tucked beneath her. I attempt to hide my creeping, impish smile with my hand, barely able to contain the playful anticipation bubbling within me, as I wait for her to begin walking away. *Let's see if Sky has a snarky remark to make about this.* With a flick of my wrist I grab the knife from the drawer and slip it into my back pocket, before following her lead.

We begin singing in unison.

'Happy birthday to you…happy birthday to you…'

I lock onto Sky with an icy glare. Anger still painted across her face. As we reach the second line of the song, I reach into my back pocket and pull out the knife, twiddling it idly between my fingers. The dim candle light glinting ominously on its surface. A brief moment passes before realisation of my intent dawns on her. Her mouth snaps shut, and the vibrant red hue of her face swiftly drains to a pallid white. The tension in the room is now thick enough to cut with the very knife I'm wielding. As the chorus fills the air, the innocence of the song clashes violently with the dark, twisted dance between her and I. Her chest heaving as she struggles to maintain her composure.

I twirl the knife deftly, a sinister ballet in my fingertips. The movement is deliberate, a silent taunt that only she and I understand. The singing morphs into a haunting symphony in my mind, each note a discordant echo amplifying the silent turmoil between us. It's as if the very air around us is charged with our unspoken confrontation. Sky's facade crumbles slowly. Her attempt at maintaining composure battles against the fear that's etched across her face. Her eyes dart between mine and the knife, an unspoken dialogue of terror and defiance. I hold her gaze, revelling in the fear that courses through her veins. The power shift between us is palpable, a thrilling rush that electrifies the charged atmosphere.

The blade dances on, a macabre conductor orchestrating the sinister duet we perform. The song finally comes to a close, the last note hanging in the air like a lingering echo of the turmoil that just transpired. Sky's breaths are ragged, her facade barely holding up against the sheer weight of our unspoken confrontation. I meet her gaze one last time, a silent promise of more to come, before turning away and seamlessly joining the applause for the birthday boy as he blows out the candles, my expression a mask of casual indifference.

As the chatter and laughter crescendo, I take a step toward the table where the birthday cake awaits, an innocent smile playing on my lips.

"Who wants the first slice?" I announce cheerfully, my voice cutting through the jovial atmosphere. Sky's eyes widen with a mixture of dread and disbelief as she watches me approach the cake, her unease blatant.

"Sky?" I offer with a deceptive charm, my tone laced with an undercurrent of menace that only she can detect. Her breath catches in her throat, her eyes fixated on the glinting blade. A sudden wave of obvious nausea washes over her.

"I-I'm fine, thanks." She manages to stutter. Ignoring her refusal, I move closer, the knife glinting under the ambient light. The room seems to hold its breath, the festive air tainted by an unspoken tension. I begin to slice. And slice again. The piece falling softly from the knife and onto the paper plate. I extend my hand towards her and place the plate at her fingertips.

Sky's face fills with pure disgust.

"Sky, are you alright, darling?" Her mother questions. Without a word, she pushes back from the table, the chair scraping against the floor in her haste. She staggers to her feet, her hand clasped over her mouth as she rushes out of the room, a torrent of emotions evident in her hurried departure. The room falls into an uncomfortable silence, the cheerful ambiance shattered by her abrupt exit. Murmurs of concern and confusion ripple through her family, but I maintain a facade of nonchalance, carefully concealing the thrill that pulses beneath the surface.

With a casual shrug, I set the knife down beside the cake, effortlessly blending back into the facade of normalcy.

"Guess she's not feeling well," I remark, my voice carrying an air of faux concern. The room attempts to return to its previous state of celebration, but an unspoken tension lingers, a reminder of the chilling exchange that just unfolded. I continue to play my part, engaging in small talk and laughter, effortlessly slipping back into the role of the affable guest. But beneath the facade, a sense of exhilaration thrums within me, a rush fuelled by the power I wielded in that fleeting moment.

Checkmate.

CHAPTER 24:
BIKER'S DELIGHT
Marcus

I lightly knock on the front door, the sound echoing faintly in the hallway, while I patiently await Delilah's answer. She soon greets me in the doorway, her hair messy and exhaustion written all over her tiny face. She barely mutters a word and walks straight into the living room. Closing the front door I plod in behind her, the echo of my entry lost in the palpable fatigue that hangs heavy in the air. My friends, usually high and bubbly, are instead worn-out and worn-down. Scattered around like fallen soldiers in a battle they never signed up for. Dean, our unfortunate general, looks like he's gone ten rounds with a tornado and lost.

"Where's Skylar?" Birdie asks.

"She wasn't feeling too good." I respond, taking a seat on the arm of the sofa.

"Join the club." Dean snaps, rightfully so.

"Why didn't you stay in the hospital?"

"If I'm gonna die, I'm not dying in a hospital." He states; I can see the fury and impatience building up inside him. The room seems to hold its breath, each of us lost in our thoughts, silently grappling with the weight of the situation. The fatigue is a tangible entity, wrapping itself around us like a heavy shroud. Delilah sinks into the armchair, exhaustion etched into every line on her face.

"Any progress?" she asks, her voice barely audible.

"A little," I respond, almost scared of the building reaction to whatever will come out of my mouth. "I went to see Millie." The room once again falls into a silence at my revelation. It's as if I've dropped a bombshell, one that no one expected, especially considering our collective uncertainty towards Millie. I can feel their eyes on me, questioning and confused. Dean's brow furrows in disbelief.

"Why the fuck would you wanna go and talk to that snob?"

"You think she has something to do with all of this?" Delilah asks.

"She's the answer to all of this, I'm sure of it. We can't close the book without her."

"Are you sure?" Birdie questions, "We haven't heard from her in years." At this point I can feel the scepticism in the room cutting into my flesh.

"I know, but unfortunately for us she's the queen in the story." All of their doubt is weighing down on me and I feel as though I'm disappointing them more and more with every word leaving my lips.

"Well, what did she say?" Delilah asks with concern. I take a sharp breath before answering honestly.

"She was pretty pissed and uh, she basically told me to get out."

Fuck I wish the ground would just swallow me.

"Well that's fantastic. I'm *so* glad to hear that my life is in her hands." Dean says, now standing agitatedly.

"I get it, I get it." I try to reassure, rubbing my face with my hands. "You guys just have to trust me."

"Incase you haven't noticed, I'm running out of time here. I'm sick and tired of sitting around and talking about this bullshit." He states, shaking his head, "Get the book out right now and we'll glue the fucker shut." I can sense the room's temperature dropping as Dean's frustration soars to new heights. His demand for the book making my heart pound a little faster. Their anger is warranted, but what I have to reveal might just push them over the edge.

"I don't have it." I mumble. I look into Dean's eyes and can see he's about to explode. *If he was feeling better I'd likely have a fist in my face right about now.*

"You what?" He asks. I don't repeat myself. He doesn't actually want me to. Instead, I swallow hard, the weight of his glare suffocating. I can practically feel the heat radiating from him. I know he feels like I'm letting him down, but I know what I'm doing. I know his words are fuelled by fear, by desperation. The weight of his expectations bears down on me, each syllable heavy with disappointment and anger. A raw intensity flickers in Dean's eyes.

"What do you mean you don't have it?" His voice rises, the anger simmering beneath the surface.

"I left it with Millie."

"You're a fucking idiot."

"She needs to read it." I assert, holding onto my certainty that this is the only way forward, even if it feels like I'm standing against a hurricane.

"You have no idea what she's gonna do with that book." Dean counters, his voice a tumultuous clash echoing off the walls.

"She'll read it, man. Trust me. I've got this."

"You're full of shit."
"I know what I'm doing."

"We can't afford to take those kinds of risks." Delilah interrupts.

"We don't have a choice. We can't do this without her." I reiterate. With that, Sienna readjusts her seating position with a frustrated sigh.

"Oh my God, Marcus. We get it. *Queen Millie's gonna save the day, blah blah blah.*"

Damn, there's my angry little sweet.

Her hostility at my mention of Millie is stirring a mix of emotions inside of me. It's a nice change to see my Sienna getting a little possessive, but I'll have to make sure she learns quickly that talking to me like that is going to get her in trouble.

"I'm very sorry, sweet." I say with a smirk. Sienna's crossed arms and narrowed eyes tell me she's not having any of it. I get it; she's protective, and bringing up Millie might have struck a nerve.

That's okay, I'll make it up to her.

Dean walks up closer to me, his stance is angry but I can tell from his eyes he's pleading.

"Do me a favour, fuck off and go get the book back."
I look around the room in search of some support, which of course doesn't come.

"Fine."
I walk out, leaving the heat and tension behind me, the front door closing with a firm thud. The warm night air outside is a welcomed relief, a balm to my frayed nerves. I make my way out of the front garden and lean against the brick wall in wait of my sweet Sienna, who I know will be foolishly assuming she can

make her way home alone. Watching the stars speckling the sky is a peaceful contrast to the chaos inside. I reach for a cigarette, but the allure of a joint tucked in my pocket calls to me instead. A sigh escapes as I light it, the flame casting fleeting shadows that dance around my form. A sense of calmness settles within me, amplified by the soft rustling of the leaves in the gentle breeze. Minutes pass, marked by the rhythmic puffs of smoke that dissipate into the velvety night.

As I hear the door opening I crush the spent joint against the ground. The soft shuffle of steps approaches, and in the dimly lit night, Birdie and Sienna emerge, their attempt to disregard me palpable as they stride toward the front gate. Without hesitation, I reach out, seizing Sienna's wrist in a firm grip, halting her retreat. The subtle resistance she offers does nothing to deter my determined pull, drawing her back into my orbit. I wait for Birdie to walk away before turning to face Sienna with a stern scowl.

"Where do you think you're going?"

"Home." She replies sarcastically.

"On your own? Not happening." I state firmly, my tone leaving no room for negotiation.

"I can handle myself."

"I'm sure you can, but I'm not willing to test it out."

"You're not my boyfriend, Marcus." she snaps. I laugh.

"You may not be my girlfriend, *Sienna*, but you are mine. In every sense of the word," I sneer. She tugs feebly at her hand, 'attempting' to free herself from my grip, but I don't let go. Instead, I take a step closer, our bodies almost touching, and lower my voice to a whisper. "You think I'm just going to let you walk away from me like that?" I challenge, my eyes locked with hers.

Holy fuck, she's so beautiful.

"What do you want?" She sighs.

"Right now, I want you to show me some respect," I start, "Or this attitude is going to get you into trouble." She tries to maintain her defiance, but her voice wavers slightly as she responds,

"I don't appreciate being treated like a possession."

"It's not possession, sweet. It's an addiction." A shiver runs down her spine, and I can see the internal battle raging within her. The desire to resist, to maintain control, warms with her desperate need to surrender. With a final surge of determination, she pushes me away, her hands finding their way to my chest.

"I won't be controlled, Marcus," she says, her voice steady, but her eyes smouldering with a fiery intensity. I chuckle softly, the challenge in her eyes only fuelling my desire.

"Who said anything about control? I don't want to control you, sweet. I want to worship you. To explore every inch of your body until you're begging me for release. I want to give you pleasure like you've never experienced before."

With a newfound hunger, I press my lips against hers, claiming her in a searing kiss. Our bodies meld together, each touch and caress a testament to our shared need, our shared addiction. Her resistance falters further, a breathless sigh escaping her lips. I take the opportunity to press my body against hers, allowing her to feel the undeniable evidence of my own yearning. The tension between us crackles in the air, the world fading away until it's just the two of us once again, caught in a web of desire and power.

Sienna's eyes flutter closed, surrendering to the intoxicating pull we share. I release her wrists, my hands now free to roam over her body, memorising every curve and dip. I pause to whisper in her ear.

"You think you can resist me, but I can feel how your body betrays you, how your pulse quickens beneath my touch." I say, my voice dripping with smug satisfaction. "I killed for you and you still have no idea what I'm capable of. If you want to be disobedient, my sweet, I can make you forget your own name. You'll forget every reason why you tried to fight me in the first place." Sienna's lips part, a soft whimper escaping as my thumb brushes against her inner thigh, edging closer to the heat between her legs. Her eyes darken with a mix of anticipation and surrender.

In one smooth motion, I sweep my 5-foot-nothing angel off her feet and carry her over to my motorbike, sitting her sideways on the seat, my body still pressed against hers.

"Marcus, what are you doin-" she says softly.

"Open." I command. She doesn't respond, and instead meets me with a bewildered look.

"Your legs, sweet. Open your legs." She hesitates for a moment, a beautiful hint of fear in her eyes, but begins slowly parting her legs. *Too slow for my liking*. I grip her thighs and forcefully spread her legs open, exposing her further.

Without wasting another second, I keep one hand tightly holding open her thigh and begin tracing underneath her skirt with the other. My fingers reach her underwear and slowly hook into them, shifting them to the side; remaining eye contact. Teasing her entrance with a featherlight touch. Her face flustered. Sienna's breath hitches, her eyes widening with a mix of excitement and vulnerability.

The thrill of the forbidden fills the air as I continue to touch her, my movements deliberate and calculated. I run a finger upwards and stop once I reach her clit, pulsing it lightly. She begins to whimper and her arms reach down to grab my hand. I hold her arms firmly, refusing to let her take control of the situation.

"No, sweet. You're not allowed to touch," I growl, my voice laced with authority. Sienna's eyes widen even more, a delicious mix of arousal and uncertainty swimming within them. I can feel her body trembling beneath my touch, the anticipation building with each passing second. Without warning, I slide a finger inside her, feeling her wetness coating me. She gasps, her back arching involuntarily against the bike. I move my finger slowly, teasingly, relishing in the way her breath becomes ragged as her pleasure intensifies.

She becomes more flustered and begins looking to her side, afraid of being caught. I firmly grab her chin and turn her back to face me.

"Eyes on me, Sienna."
Her gasps turn into whimpers as I find her sweet spot, my fingers skillfully working their magic.

"*Fuck,* you're so tight." I smirk at her moans of pleasure and decide to push her further. With a devilish glint in my eyes, I add another finger, stretching her slightly to accommodate the new sensation. Sienna's eyes widen in surprise as I continue to pump my fingers inside her, matching the rhythm of her moans. Each stroke sends waves of pleasure coursing through her body, her grip on the bike tightening. I lean in closer, kissing and nibbling at her neck as I whisper,

"You like that, don't you, sweet?" She can only nod, her words lost in a whirlwind of pleasure and desire. My fingers explore her folds, parting them gently to delve deeper. She continues to moan softly, her hips instinctively shifting against my hand, seeking more contact. "You look so pretty like this."
I pick up the pace, my fingers dancing over her sensitive clit, applying just the right amount of pressure to drive her wild. Sienna's moans grow louder, her breathing ragged. Her hands now gripping deep into the seat of the bike. I can feel her walls

contracting around my fingers, a sign that she's getting closer to the edge.

But just as she's about to tip over into ecstasy, I withdraw my fingers, leaving her panting and unsatisfied. Her eyes shoot open, a mixture of confusion and frustration in her gaze. I give her an indulgent smile, knowing exactly what I'm doing to her.

"Did you think it would be that easy, sweet?" I tease, my voice dripping with lust. I lean back and take in the sight before me. Sienna, flushed and panting, her eyes filled with a mixture of anticipation and frustration, aching for the pleasure I can provide. My hold on her thighs tightens, another silent reminder of my control.

"Now, sweet, I want to hear you beg for me." I demand.

I eagerly await her response, my gaze locked on her tight. The silence that follows is heavy with tension, each passing second amplifying the anticipation in the air. Her chest rises and falls rapidly, her lips trembling as she tries to find the right words. Finally, she takes a deep breath, her voice quivering as she speaks.

"Marcus-"

"Beg."

"Please," she whispers, her voice filled with need. A wicked grin spreads across my face, an intoxicating combination of triumph and desire. My thumb caresses her inner thigh, the touch light yet tantalising, as I lean in closer to her ear.

"Good girl," I growl, my breath hot against her skin. I reach between her legs once again, my fingers eagerly finding their way inside of her. This time, I don't hold back. I delve deep into her, my fingers moving with a hunger that matches her own. The sound of her moans fills the night air, mingling with the soft rustle of leaves and the distant hum of passing cars.

As I pleasure her, I study her every reaction, taking note of what drives her wild. I devour her gasps and moans, savouring the taste of her pleasure mingling with the night. With each stroke and curl of my fingers, I can feel her walls tightening around me, her body teetering on the edge of release. I lovingly stroke her cheek, the cruel smirk on my face contrasting with the tenderness in my touch.

"I want to hear you beg a little more."

Sienna's eyes lock with mine, her desire burning brighter than ever. With a pleading look, she whispers,

"Please,"

"Please?" I raise an eyebrow at her.

"Please let me come."

The desperation in her voice is like music to my ears. It fuels my arousal, making me more determined to push her to her limits. My fingers return to her core, expertly working their magic. I alternate between gentle caresses and firm strokes, bringing her closer and closer to the edge with each passing moment.

Her moans become louder, she's on the precipice of climax, her muscles tensing as she fights against the overwhelming pleasure coursing through her veins. Sensing her imminent release, I lean in close, my lips grazing her ear.

"There you go," I whisper. With those words, Sienna's resistance shatters. Her body convulses with euphoria as her orgasm crashes over her, wave after wave of pleasure coursing through her body. I release Sienna from my grip, allowing her to recover from the intense pleasure that just washed over her. As her breathing slows and her body relaxes, I lean in closer.

"Now I get to taste you, right sweet?"

Without waiting for a response, I crouch down in front of her, my hands still firmly gripping her thighs. her eyes widen with a mix of shock and anticipation as she realises what I have in mind. The crisp night air adds an extra thrill to the moment as I slide her skirt up, revealing her pussy. Seeing it for the first time feels indescribably rewarding.

I bury my face between her legs, inhaling her intoxicating sweet scent before flicking my tongue lightly against her clit. She gasps, her hands instinctively reaching for my hair, but I grab her wrists and pull them away, maintaining control. I want to show her that this pleasure is all about me, that she is at my mercy. I continue to tease her, alternating between gentle licks and firm sucks, relishing in the way her moans grow louder and her hips instinctively grind against my mouth. The taste of her arousal is addictive, driving me to explore every inch of her with my tongue.

With each flick and swirl of my tongue, her body trembles, her pleasure building with a ferocious intensity. She tugs and scratches at the seat, craving the release that only I can give her. I tighten my grip on her thighs, holding her firmly in place, denying her the freedom she so desperately seeks.

As I continue to devour her, my own arousal intensifies, evident by the bulge pressing against my tracksuit bottoms. I release one of my hands from her thigh, reaching down to free my erect length from its confines and returning my hand instantly. My body aches with the desperate need for release; the craving to bend her over this bike and fuck her from behind. To fill her and watch her drip. But I resist the urge to give in to my own desires. Right now, it's all about Sienna. I focus solely on giving her pleasure, my tongue working fervently against her sensitive bundle of nerves. Her moans grow louder, more desperate, as I bring her closer to the edge once again. The vibration of her pleas sends shivers down my spine, and I can feel myself throbbing with need. But I remind myself to stay patient, to savour this moment of control.

Her body tenses beneath me, her breathing becoming erratic as she nears her second climax. I can sense it, the way her muscles tighten, the way her hips grind against my mouth. She's on the precipice, just a few more flicks of my tongue and she will fall into bliss. With one final lick, my tongue flat, I push her over the edge, her body convulsing as waves of pleasure crash over her.

I continue to lap up her sweet essence, savouring every drop as she rides out her orgasm. The taste of her on my tongue is intoxicating, driving me to a new level of insanity. As her moans fade into soft gasps of satisfaction, I place a kiss on her swollen clit and release her thighs before standing back up to look down at her flushed and needy state. I chuckle softly, relishing in the power I hold over her. I lean in close, my lips brushing against her ear as I ask,

"You want me to fuck you, sweet? You want me to prove that you're mine?" She nods, her breathing rapid and shallow. "Then beg for it. Beg me to fuck you."

"Please-" I grab her throat, tight enough that she should be seeing some stars, and force her to look deep into my eyes. *She fucking smiles. Holy shit.*

"Please, what? Tell me what I want to hear."

"Fuck me." *This can't be real. Is this real? I hope so.*

"Who do you belong to?" I ask.

She hesitates for a moment and attempts to gulp through her restricted throat.

"You."

I smirk proudly and shake my head.

"I'm not gonna fuck you yet." I step back, a triumphant smile on my face as I deny her request. She looks up at me confused. "Not tonight. I want to take my time with you." She attempts to hide the smile creeping onto her face by sucking in her bottom lip. I crouch down to her eye level and brush my hand across her cheek. "I've got you for life, Sienna. I don't wanna rush a single thing." I kiss her forehead and stand back up straight, my eyes not leaving hers.

"Come on, sweet. Let's get you home."

CHAPTER 25:
TRY AGAIN

Marcus

11:00 a.m. Back to apartment No.2 I go. I ring the buzzer. No need to lie about who I am this time. Millie's rapid response to let me in surprises me, almost as though she's been anticipating my arrival. That can't be good. I reach the top of the stairs and I'm immediately met by Millie's viscous gaze as she stands in the doorway, book in hand. Neither of us speak, and the absence of words feels unsettling, amplifying the strained atmosphere that suffuses the space.

Little bit awkward, Millie.

Millie remains steadfast, her silence cutting deeper than any words could. Instead, she slowly extends the book towards me, a deliberate movement. I accept the book with a hesitant nod, meeting Millie's unyielding gaze. The exchange lingers. It's not often people make me feel uncomfortable, but she's an enigmatic figure.

"So uh, did you read it?" I manage to force out, a feeble attempt to ease the observable discomfort. A beat passes, the air laden with anticipation, until, unexpectedly, Millie's response is stark and unembellished.

"Yes." The simplicity of her reply in the midst of this surreal moment strikes a chord that teeters on the edge of comical and absurd. In the midst of this bizarre exchange, I can't help but stifle a nervous chuckle, the tension momentarily broken by the sheer peculiarity of it all. Millie's stern expression doesn't waver.

"So what are you thinking?" I venture cautiously, hoping to prod some rationale from the enigma that is Millie Devons.

"The answer is no." Her reply, devoid of any embellishment or explanation, cuts through the tension like a blade. The abruptness of her refusal stuns me momentarily. The absurdity of the situation, coupled with the gravity of what's at stake, threatens to tip the scales between irritation and amusement.

"You can't seriously be that childish."

"You claim to have brought me a magical book, and *I'm* childish?" She scoffs. Millie's retort hits a nerve, her sarcasm twisting the situation into an absurd tangle of frustration and disbelief. I chuckle slightly in anger.

"You're impossible. Dean's life is on the line and you're acting like this?" The exasperation in my voice is tangible, a mixture of anger and desperation bubbling beneath the surface.

"Go ask Sienna for help."

This fucking bitch.

The mere mention of Sienna's name from her pretentious mouth is like a lit match in a room drenched in gasoline.

"How dare you even say her name."

"Does she know that I'm the queen in your little book?" Millie's spiteful words cut through the air, a venomous arrow aimed at distorting reality. I scoff at the absurdity of her claim. The audacity of her implication catches me off guard, the insinuation so far from the truth that it's almost laughable.

"You're nothing to me-"

"There's always a hint of truth in story books," she interrupts, her words dripping with condescension. I can't help but laugh out loud.

"Millie. You're the queen in the book because 11 year old me was in his feelings over the fact that Sienna didn't want me." She has the audacity to look hurt. So I continue, "I would wipe you off the face of the earth in a heartbeat for her. Is that clear?"

"You're really still that obsessed with her after all these years?"

"You seem pretty obsessed with her yourself." I counter. Millie's face contorts with anger and frustration.

"I don't care about Sienna." She hisses.

"You've always been jealous of Sienna, ever since we were kids, that's why you fucking picked on her."

She rolls her eyes and cackles spitefully which sends me into a frenzy.

"Oh please, I never picked on her. I went through hell in that home. You have no idea what you're talking abou-"

"I'm not doing this, Millie." I interrupt, shaking my head. "I didn't come here to listen to your shitty little sob stories. This is about Dean." Millie's face softens momentarily, a flicker of concern crossing her features before returning to her usual stoic expression. She says nothing and I allow the silence to linger for a moment, hoping it will cool things down.

"Is he in a bad way?" She finally mumbles, a sliver of humanity actually peeking through. Images of Dean's wilting face from last night flash into my mind. I feel a lump form in my throat, swallowing hard before responding.

"Yeah." My voice cracks slightly as I speak through the emotions. "And he's just getting worse." Each word seems to carve a deeper groove of concern into my heart, mirroring the gravity of Dean's deteriorating state. The weight of Dean's condition finally seems to be reaching Millie. Her gaze falls to the book in my hands, a hint of guilt shadowing her features. The tension in the room shifts as a shared concern for Dean's well-being seems to unite us briefly.

"Did you read the last line of the book carefully, Marcus?" I look at her in a confused scowl.

"Close the gates." I quote.

"To protect the village." She counters. "You haven't stopped to think about the fact that Dean is the villain in this story? A threat to the rest of us. The village." I stop to think about her words, goosebumps running up my arms. I shake the suggestion away and bring myself back to my goal.

"It's a possibility," I admit, "But it's a risk I'm willing to take. He's my brother, Millie, and I need him alive. Villain or not."

As her eyes meet mine again, a rare glimpse of genuine emotion flickers within them, softening the edges of her guarded demeanour.

"I'm sorry," She murmurs, shaking her head. "I have to go." Before I can process her words, she starts to retreat, backing away into her apartment. Confusion and frustration surge within me, an urgent plea rising in my throat.

"Wait." I quickly jam my foot in the crack of the door and look intensely at her. One last attempt, Marcus.

"Look, I don't care what you think about me. This isn't about us. Millie, If Dean doesn't make it, his blood is on your hands. You can't just walk away from this."

I remove my foot and stand back, hoping for a response. Instead, the door inches closed, the barrier between hope and hopelessness now shut. The definitive click of the door echoing through my ears. I stand alone in the corridor, the book in my hand feeling heavier than before. A knot of despair constricts my chest, every breath a struggle against the invisible shackles of powerlessness. Tears well up, a silent testament to the maelstrom of emotions raging within, but they refuse to spill, trapped behind a dam of frustration and anguish. The knowledge that Dean's lifeline may have just slipped away leaves me hollow, my spirit crumbling under the weight of my inadequacy.

Dean's gaunt face, etched with suffering, haunts my thoughts, each fading memory another lash upon my soul. The weight of responsibility presses down, heavier than I've ever known, the realisation that I failed to secure the help Dean so desperately needs clawing at my conscience. But there's nothing more I can do. I can do nothing but wait, and hope.

The short journey to my bike feels like a trail through a desolate wasteland. Each step is heavy, burdened not just by the physical weight of my body but by the weight of my failure. I can't shake the exhaustion settling in, not just from the encounter but from the entirety of this futile quest for help. It's like shouting into a void and receiving only echoes in return. I'm fed up with this relentless cycle of trying and failing, and each step back to my bike adds another layer of disillusionment.

I slide my hand into my pocket to grab my bike key. The familiar cool metal meeting my fingertips, grounding me in a reality I'm not entirely ready to confront. A long, weary sigh escapes my lips, a mix of frustration and resignation. It's as if I can taste their metallic tang against my tongue as I pull them out.

With a jaded flick of my wrist, I insert the key into the ignition, the soft click ironically signalling readiness. The engine's growl is a comforting reminder in a world that feels increasingly foreign. With a subtle nudge, I shift the bike into gear, feeling the subtle resistance beneath my boot. My bike hums in anticipation, a faithful steed awaiting its rider's command.

The wind greets me, ruffling my clothes and tousling my hair, as if encouraging me to leave everything behind. The weight of responsibility, the day's stresses, they all begin to fade into my mirrors. Each bend in the road demands my attention, and I respond, leaning into the curves with a fluidity that comes from years of riding. There's a rhythm to the ride, a synergy between man and machine that's more than just a dance; it's an understanding, an unspoken language where the bike becomes an extension of my being.

For me, riding isn't just a hobby. It's a way of life, a passion that courses through my veins. The ride becomes more than a means of transport; it's a sanctuary where I find solace, rejuvenation, and a sense of belonging. And I need all of the above right now.

CHAPTER 26:
BOOK MAIL

Marcus

I coast along the urban arteries, the wind weaving through my hair. Stopped in traffic, my eye is suddenly drawn to the bookstore across the street. Sienna loves going there. It's then that I remember that I had taken a sneaky picture of her book wishlist she'd scribbled down a few weeks ago. Maybe today, amidst the chaos, grabbing my sweet some gifts could be my flicker of light.

After all, she was a very good girl for me last night.

I pull up outside the shop entrance, enjoying a cigarette as I dig through my phone for the image. It doesn't take long to locate the list since I don't have much saved on my phone. Just sneaky pictures I had taken of my beautiful Sienna and a shitload of bike videos. There are eleven books on the list. Easy. With the image in hand, I flick the cigarette to the ground and pocket my phone.

Stepping into the store, the familiar scent of paper and ink envelops me. It's actually a comforting embrace amid the city's hustle. My gaze sweeps the shelves, scanning titles and sections.

I'm fumbling through this place, surrounded by rows upon rows of books that might as well be written in some ancient language. Sienna's wishlist, the crumpled photo on my shattered phone screen, is my only guide in this sea of words and covers. Classics, poetry, fiction, non-fiction, authors I've never heard of; my knowledge barely scratches the surface. Sienna deserves more than my cluelessness, but fuck, I'm trying. I clutch the list, scanning titles as if I might just magically stumble upon exactly what she wants.

In the end, I admit defeat. I approach the cashier, pulling out my phone with her scrawled wishlist.

"Hey, just wondering if you could help me find these books." With a mix of resignation and hope, I hand it over, silently pleading for assistance. She grabs the phone and begins reading the list, a smile creeping on her face.

"So you're a romance book kinda-guy, huh?" She says playfully.

"They're not for me." I clarify, rubbing my neck.

"Yeah, that's what they all say. Follow me." she beckons, leading the way. Her willingness to assist turns this daunting task into a delightful adventure. Together, we navigate the shelves, her expertise guiding me through the literary cosmos to find the treasures on Sienna's list. With each book found, I can't help but feel a surge of gratitude toward this stranger aiding me on my quest to spoil my angel.

She stops at one book on the list,

"This one is part of a series, are you looking for just the one or the whole set?" she asks. Leisurely I reply,

"If you have the whole series that'd be great."

Would it, Marcus? What if she has the rest of the set already?

As we continue searching I stop to look at the size of the mounting pile of books in our hands and I can't help but wonder about the expanding hole in my wallet. Books aren't that expensive, right? I continue to glance at them in an attempt to mentally calculate just how much this random adventure is going to cost me. After what feels like hours, it seems this treasure hunt is nearing its end. The cashier glances at our increasingly hefty bundle of books and chuckles softly.

"That's a full house, what a lucky girl." she says, gleaming.

But Sienna isn't lucky. This is nothing. She deserves the world.

The cashier scans each book, the beeps marking the countdown of my recklessness. With every beep, I'm watching the total add up on the screen. It's more than I anticipated. A lot more.

"That'll be £178.84"

Nearly £200 on books. Have I lost my mind? I stand there, and my mind drifts back to the countless mornings I've spent on construction sites for some extra cash. The backbreaking labour, the sweat, and the occasional cursing at a stubborn nail or an uncooperative piece of wood, surrounded by loudmouths I can't stand. Things like this are what it's all for. Hearing Sienna's laughter, watching her eyes light up when she talks about her favourite stories. That's what I'm working for.

Your money is there to spoil Sienna with, Marcus.

I grit my teeth and hand over my card, plastering a smile on my face that I hope looks confident and unfazed by the cost. The cashier hands back my card along with a mighty stack of books wrapped in a store-branded bag, giving me a knowing nod as if she understands my plight.

I make my way onto Sienna's doorstep, holding the bag of books I had carefully picked for her. My heartbeat seems to synchronise with the knocking rhythm. A second passes, and then the door creaks open, revealing Sienna's adorable curious face.

"What are you doing here?" she asks, trying to hide her pretty little smile. I hold out the bag of books for her to take. "What's that?" I nod down at the bag slightly as a gesture for her to take it.

"I bought you some gifts." I say, a faint smile tugging at the corners of my lips. She looks at me in awe and attempts to grab the bag, the weight of it pulling her arms down.

"Marcus, you didn't have to-"

"You deserve it, sweet."

She vaguely rummages through the bag, her fingers tracing the book spines. Her doe eyes alighting with delight as she recognizes familiar titles among the mix. A grateful smile brightens her face, and for a moment, the air feels lighter, as if the tension I carried in my chest has dissolved.

"How did you know which books to get?" she asks, bewildered.

"That's for me to know." I tease. We pause momentarily, soaking up each other's eye contact and grinning from ear to ear.

Fuck I'm so in love.

"What have you been up to today then?" I ask, rolling up a blunt in the meantime.

"I went on a date." She jokes bravely.

"Oh yeah?" I raise an eyebrow, feigning surprise. "Who do I have to kill this time?" I ask with a devilish grin. Utter shock takes over her face for a brief moment, as if she had forgotten my heinous act, committed in her honour. She swallows her shock and smiles timidly.

"He was very charming. He bought me a bag of books."
Nice recovery, sweet.

"Ah, now he sounds like a real catch." I wink, finishing up the blunt and lighting it. The pungent scent fills the cool air, and I'm momentarily lost in the familiar ritual. Sienna's expression shifts, her amusement replaced with a much more serious look.

"Marcus, you know that stuff isn't good for you, right?" I exhale a plume of smoke, considering her question.

"And going on dates with men who wear skinny jeans is any better?" I challenge. Sienna sighs, shaking her head. "It helps me unwind, sweet." She crosses her arms, her gaze unyielding.

"There are better ways to unwind, Marcus. Healthier ways." I chuckle.

"You sound like my conscience." Her eyes soften as she regards me, a subtle understanding passing between us.

"You need a new hobby. Something that won't slowly kill you." I smile and nod slowly.

"I'll think about it."

"Not good enough." She remains locked in her grumpy face, her arms firmly crossed, so I crouch down to her eye level. I take another drag and turn my head to the side to exhale away from her face.

"Sweet, if you're gonna be naughty, I'll take those books back and give you something else instead." I threaten playfully, raising my eyebrows. Her beautiful big eyes widen and I watch her pupils dilate. With that I place a kiss on her forehead and stand back up straight. She sucks in her bottom lip and starts backing into the entryway.

"Thank you for the books." She says softly.

"You're welcome, sweet. I'll see you soon."

CHAPTER 27:
FUGITIVE FRIENDS

Marcus

7:20p.m. Getting back after a long joy ride, I lie down on my bed, permitting my mind to be clear for a change. This room has definitely become a small haven for me, an oasis from the storm of obligations outside.

As usual, my peace is destroyed rather quickly.

The door slams open, hitting the wall behind, and Skylar charges in; her voice a tempest in the calm. I had been successful at avoiding her after the birthday lunch but clearly there's no option now. Her eyes pierce through me, harbouring an anger I recognize too well. But she started it. How could I resist? Knowing her hands were tied, locked in a vault with my darkest secret.

"You feeling better?" I dare to ask, an arrogant smile breaking out.

"Fuck you, Marcus! What the hell was that all about?" Her words seethe with indignation, her eyes ablaze.

"Just a bit of banter, Sky. Relax." I say, my tone far too casual, trying to dismiss the gravity of my actions.

"Banter?" Her voice begins to rise in an ear-splitting screech. It's like nails on a chalkboard.

"You can't tell me you didn't find it a little funny. And anyway, you started it."

"Funny? Marcus, this is serious." I adjust my pillow, unfazed.

"What's done is done, Sky. You pushed me to tell you my little secret and so now you're as trapped as I am. Get over it,"

Skylar's frustration intensifies at my dismissive attitude. She paces the room, her anger tangible.

"Do you even care? I mean, I didn't even kill anybody and yet this whole thing is eating me alive. But you're so, so-" She pauses and looks at me, flustered and struggling to find any words. I vaguely lift my head off my pillow and look back at her, expressionless. "So calm."

"What do you want me to do, Sky? Curl up in a ball and cry? Pace back and forth like a lunatic? Because that *really* seems to be working for you."

"Do you not feel anything? Any remorse?" She questions.

"Look, you've got your own way of dealing with things. I've got mine. Can you leave me alone now?"

With that, she shakes her head and leaves, slamming the door on the way out of course. In the midst of this chaos, an unexpected calmness once again descends, a rare occurrence that leaves me bewildered. Relaxation is a foreign notion to an insomniac like me, yet an unexplained tranquillity invites me to succumb to sleep.

Am I actually about to have a nap?

The concept is alien to me. As my eyelids yield to the weight, the world fades into the distance, and I surrender to the rare allure. Sleep envelopes me, and there are no vivid dreams, no surreal landscapes, just a void. A vacuum. My mind simply floating in an empty expanse of darkness. It's a peculiar sensation, devoid of the usual rush of thoughts and images that frequent my mind. This absence of dreams feels almost deafening in its silence. No subconscious narratives or fragmented whispers traversing my slumbering mind. No fantasies of having my way with Sienna. Literally nothing but blackness. It's as if time has paused, leaving me adrift in an abyss of nothingness, disconnected from the usual currents of consciousness.

As moments pass, though in the realm of sleep, time feels elusive. I hover on the edge of awareness, suspended in a state of rest that feels both unfamiliar and oddly serene. A strange comfort within the void.

Eventually, consciousness tiptoes back, gently nudging me from the abyss of dreamless sleep. I emerge, somewhat disoriented yet strangely refreshed, as if the emptiness within had briefly found solace in the absence of thoughts. Opening my eyes, I find the room unchanged, the echoes of the confrontation with Skylar lingering in the air. My fingers stretch out, navigating through the sheets to reach my phone. As the screen illuminates at my touch, revealing the time in its glowing digits, I notice a map etched upon my arm in the form of deep sleep lines, like delicate rivers marking their way along the terrain of my skin. I can't even remember the last time I had them. The significance of these imprints looms large, an enigmatic reminder of a sleep so peaceful it feels almost mythical. The memory of such undisturbed repose feels elusive, distant; like an echo from a forgotten melody, faint yet resonant.

10:14p.m. Three texts from Dean. Strange.

> **Dean: Bro, we need to talk.**
> **Dean: Yo.**
> **Dean: You there?**

Dean hasn't ever been the type to text more than once. A sense of unease gnaws at me, a small pit settling in my stomach, signalling that something isn't quite right.

> **M: Sorry mate I was asleep. Everything good?**

Dean reads my message immediately and begins typing. I'm now sitting upright in full anticipation.

> **Dean: I need to see you. Meet me at the end of Delilah's road by the alley?**

> **M: On my way.**

I rub my eyes in an attempt to wake myself up and swiftly grab my bike key as I head out. My mind is a whirlpool of thoughts once again.

I soon reach the alley and catch sight of Dean, resting against the railing with a large, black duffel bag at his feet. His face looks grey and lifeless, like some kind of zombie. He's running out of time. I remove my helmet and approach him slowly.

"You alright?" I ask with concern. He doesn't respond, instead he picks up the bag at his feet and passes it to me. A pause lingers as I grasp the bag, a silent plea for any semblance of an explanation.

"You're gonna need that." He states, breaking the silence. I crouch down eagerly and unzip the bag, revealing a handgun nestled on top of a shitload of cash. At least ten grand.

What the fuck is going on.

I glance up at him, searching his face for clues, but his expression remains inscrutable.

"They dug up a body at the tunnel today." His words send a jolt of shock through me, my mind racing to comprehend the situation. "I don't really care what happened," he continues, "All I know, is that you've gotta get out of here, and luckily for you, so do I." I stare at Dean, dumbfounded by his words. The weight of his revelation sinks in, the gravity of the situation hitting me like a ton of bricks.

"What do you mean-" I manage to mumble out as I stand back up.

"I've been dealing for a long time, and I've got myself into some serious trouble with some serious people." Dean confesses, his words heavy with the burden of truth. "If I make it out of this book bullshit alive, I'm leaving, and you're coming with me." I stop for a while to gather my thoughts.

"Leave where?" My voice cracks, the enormity of his proposal hitting me with a force that leaves me reeling.

"A little bit of everywhere," He chuckles, "We're on the run. We can't hang around anywhere for too long."

"But we have a life here."

"Neither of us will once all these fuckers figure out where we are. I'm not asking. I'm telling you, we're leaving." The bag in my hands suddenly feels like a ticket to an uncertain future, a future I never thought I'd face.

A murderer on the run with his drug dealer friend.
It's like something out of a movie. A bad movie.

"I found a B&B a few hours away in the middle of nowhere that I think is a good place to start." I shake my head, hoping to shake away all of my new responsibilities along with it.

"How did you hide all of this?"

"Marcus, we've been hiding forever. Hiding from our childhood, hiding from our futures, hiding from ourselves And after seeing those files and dealing with this fucking book, I think its time we stopped."

With a mix of fear and resignation, I nod, acknowledging the reality of the situation.

"What about Delilah?" I ask. Dean's face desaturates even further and he scratches nervously at his jaw.

"She wants to stay." He states.

"She can't stay here, she'll be a target."

"I know," He admits, his voice filled with stress and worry. "But her family is here. I can't pull her from them."

"Fuck."

"I know, man. I'm shitting myself about it. I gave her a gun and convinced her to install a load of security cameras." He pauses, "You're gonna have to do the same for Sienna."

I think the fuck not.

I laugh,

"Sienna will be coming with me, whether she likes it or not." I declare firmly, leaving no room for debate in my words.

"She'll be distraught."

"Maybe," I concede. "But she'll be safe." Dean nods slowly, understanding the weight of the responsibility we both carry.

"Are you gonna sort this book out?" He asks, desperately.

"Of course. Dean, I'm not gonna let you die." I promise, "Millie's gonna come around, I know it. I'm just waiting for her to text me." He nods his head again and briefly places his hand on my shoulder.

"As soon as it's shut, we leave. Got it?"

"Got it."

With that, Dean texts me the address of the B&B, runs me through a few of his plans and takes off back to Delilah's house. I feel the weight of his words crushing down on me, heavier than the duffel bag in my hands. The night air feels charged with uncertainty as I contemplate the sudden turn our lives have taken. How did we end up in this mess?

Now alone in the alley, I lean against the cold metal railing, the dimly lit street casting elongated shadows around me. I light a cigarette, the ember casting an intermittent glow against the night, and for the first time in a long while, fear clenches at my insides. Not only are the police after me, and closing in quickly, but now Dean's secret enemies will be hot on my tail too. A bone-deep chill sets in, amplified by the swirling mist of the night. The smoke spirals up, dissipating into the inky sky, disappearing like my chances of staying here unscathed.

The duffel bag at my feet feels like an anchor, grounding me in this unexpected turmoil. A gun and cash, a testament to a life I thought I'd be able to just leave behind. Thought I'd gotten away with. But now, it's resurfaced, like all problems in my life, they creep back in; nightmares knocking on the door.

This time, I have no choice but to answer.

CHAPTER 28:

SOUR

Marcus

I stumble into my bedroom, shutting the door behind me, and unceremoniously toss the bag onto the floor. Without warning, my legs give way and I can no longer stand, dropping to a crouch as the gravity of it all hits me. My vision becomes speckled, and the room begins to spin. This is it. The mirror I've avoided, the reflection of the monster I've become, the monster I never wanted to face. My hands begin to tingle, and I place one firmly on the floor in an attempt to steady myself.

Guilt begins to claw at my chest, a crushing weight that suffocates, a raw, searing pain that rips through my being. Killing is one sin, but tearing Sienna from her mother, thrusting her into a storm she didn't ask for is a cold, despicable evil that I'll never forgive myself for. It sears at my soul. A sob escapes me, the first crack in the fortress of indifference I'd spent my entire life carefully constructing.

I'm in an awakening, a reckoning, a gut-wrenching realisation that I've become the very nightmare I always feared. And I have no choice but to confront it head-on, to bear the burden of my actions and the inevitable fall out they bring. Each breath feels like a stab, each sob a rending of my heart. The walls I've erected around my emotions, the barriers that shielded me from the world's cruelty, crumble like sandcastles against an incoming tide. Now I am that cruelty. A fortress of indifference, now in ruins, revealing the wicked, heinous man I've become. Inhuman.

I lift the gun from the bag and hold it in my trembling, blood-soaked hands. Knowing this gun can only symbolise that there is more to come. I'm forced to confront the atrocities I've committed, and I'm fine with them. I'll kill anyone. Fuck it. But now I must face the consequences of much bigger crimes that will engulf Sienna, the innocent soul I've unwittingly pulled into my darkened existence. She, my sweet angel, who already bore the scars of losing her parents, now faces the agony of separation from her adoptive mother. And it's my doing. The anguish tears through me like a hurricane, ripping apart the fabric of my being. The tears flow freely now, cascading down my cheeks in a torrent, mirroring the flood of despair and self-reproach drowning my conscience.

Although I'm painfully aware this upheaval is for her safety, there's no way she'll ever comprehend that. The thought tightens a vice around my heart. The thought of bringing my sweet back to a place of such familiar pain is a concept so sickening. How could I? How could I possibly look into those beautiful eyes, those eyes that have finally sought refuge in mine, now bound to see a tormentor instead of a protector? How do I make her understand that I've become a monster, a villain in her story, all for the sake of keeping her safe? My heart shatters at the thought of betraying the trust she'd placed in me, tarnishing the fragile sanctuary I'd worked to build for her.

I yearn for absolution, a sliver of hope in this abyss I've descended into. But the truth remains; the monster within me is the monster Sienna now faces, and I'm powerless to change that reality.

I'll make things right for her. One day. It's a promise I make to myself, and I don't break promises. Ever. I'll kill every fucker on this planet to fulfil my promise if that's what it takes. I'll slit every throat. She *will* have a good life. I will change things for her. I'll make sure of it. I've made my peace with the atrocities I've committed, but for Sienna, I'll fight tooth and nail to ensure her innocence remains untouched.

My sweet's innocence is my responsibility; her happiness and safety too. And I'll do what's necessary to ensure her sanctuary, even if it means embracing the shadows once more, or a thousand times more. The thought of sacrificing everything to protect her, including my own humanity, sears through me.

Fucking pull yourself together, Marcus.

With a firm resolve and one large sharp breath, the emotional turmoil dissipates, replaced by an eerie cruelness. The fortress of indifference begins to rebuild, layer by layer, obscuring the fractures of empathy that briefly cracked its surface. I stand, the room still spinning but my mind resolute. The vulnerability, the anguish, I shove them deep into the recesses of my being, locking them away. The monster reclaims its dominion, a cold, calculated protector emerging once again.

The tears that had once cascaded freely, now a distant memory as I wipe away the remnants of any weakness. The reflection in that mirror morphs from that of a tormented soul to a steely-eyed harbinger of my own salvation, and Sienna's. I crack my neck and square my shoulders, as a smirk grows on my lips. The familiar chill seeping back into my veins, numbing the raw ache within. I'm back.

Alone in the stillness of my room, I raise the gun, its weight a sinister reassurance in my grip. I don't flinch. Instead, I embrace the chilling certainty that I am no longer the man I once pretended to be. The gun, an extension of my will, whispers promises of power, of control over a world that dared to challenge me for my entire life. My finger hovers over the trigger, a moment frozen in time, where the past and the present collide in a fucked up embrace. The man I was fades into obscurity, a figment of a distant memory. I've willingly surrendered to the allure of this newfound malevolence.

In this room, where the air hangs heavy with my decisions, I make peace with the monster I've become. I embrace him. I am the architect of my own damnation, a maestro orchestrating the symphony of my own malevolent destiny. The monster within is no longer a foe to be fought; it's a companion I've chosen to accept, a relentless shadow that cloaks me in its perverse clutch. The gun doesn't shake in my hand. Instead, it becomes an instrument of my will, a tool to carve out my new path.

Suddenly, a vibration in my pocket jolts me out of the trance-like state I'd sunk into. Finally, the text from an unknown number I've been waiting for.

Unknown: It's Millie. I'm going to close the book, for Dean. I'll be at Orchid's ASAP. Don't make me wait.

The room feels foreign, almost surreal, as I stand in its midst, surrounded by the fragments of a life I'm about to abandon. The black duffel bag, my new faithful companion, lays open, its yawning mouth waiting to swallow the remnants of my existence. Each item I pack, the clothes hastily folded, the stacks of cash neatly aligned, and the gun cold and unforgiving, feels like a shard of the life I'm leaving behind. There's an unsettling finality to the act of packing, as if each piece I place within the confines of the bag seals a chapter of my life. The book resting on top, the source of all of this bullshit.

The sense of unreality thickens the air around me. Here I am, leaving behind the familiar, a semblance of normalcy; all for a world of uncertainty, a life of crime. It's a dizzying juxtaposition. As I zip the bag shut, the sound echoes with a hollow finality, a closure to the life that Skylar's family had offered me. My heart pounds against the cage of my chest, a cacophony of emotions. A tinge of remorse for the life I'm willingly discarding. Each fold of fabric, each touch of the gun's steel against my palm; these actions carry a weight that transcends the physical.

I pause, taking a final sweeping glance around the room, trying to imprint every detail into my memory. Procrastinating my departure from the familiar. I almost feel a little ungrateful. Staring down at my new makeshift bed that Skylar's father had put up for me. With a deep breath that quivers in my chest, I sling the bag over my shoulder. The strap digs deep into my skin, a constant reminder that within its confines lies not just my belongings, but the fragments of a past life I've willingly surrendered.

As I walk, the hallway seems to warp, the walls closing in on me, suffocatingly close yet infinitely distant. My mind teeters on the edge of acceptance and denial, wavering between the surrealness of this departure and the undeniable truth that I've chosen this path willingly. Leaving behind a home, a life, a family. All the things I spent my entire childhood longing for. They're at my fingertips and I'm pulling away.

But if it means Sienna will be safe, and mine, I'll give up anything.

I make my way to Skylar's room and knock on the door, tapping a message into the group chat amidst the anticipation of Sky's response. She opens the door and is less than pleased to see me.

"What the fuck do you want?" she snaps.

"We're closing the book. Right now." Skylar's eyes narrow, suspicion laced with excitement.

"For real?" She asks

"Yeah, for real," I reply, my voice carrying the weight of determination and urgency. "It's time."

"Oh my god." She flusters, grabbing her phone from her bed. "Okay, okay," Skylar mutters nervously, "Let's do this."

"I need you to get a car." I instruct.

"A car?"

"Yes. If this doesn't work we're gonna need to get him to the hospital." She nods, the urgency in my voice resonating with her innate understanding of our covert world.

"Got it. I'll be as quick as I can."

CHAPTER 29:
LOCK FIX

Marcus

I bolt out of the house, urgency propelling me as I rush towards Orchid's. With no time for a helmet, I race through the streets, my hair whipping in the wind. The roads become a blur, the city lights streaking past as if in a hurry to escape the night. The urgency of our situation eclipses all other concerns. The roar of passing cars, the blaring horns; they all fade into insignificance against the gravity of what we're about to undertake. I weave through the traffic, my movements fluid and calculated, each turn a well-practised manoeuvre honed by necessity.

The roads, once familiar, now seem like an obstacle course, every bend a hurdle to overcome in this race against time. My mind races faster than my bike, a cacophony of thoughts urging me forward. Every passing second feels like an eternity, the moments stretching and compressing in an erratic dance with my pounding heartbeats.

The screech of my bike as I skid into the car park punctuates the silent tension of the group, who are standing tensely in a circle. Dean barely keeping himself standing. Adrenaline courses through me as I leap off the bike, urgency propelling my every movement. Millie, standing at a cautious distance from the others, casts a wary glance in my direction, a silent acknowledgment laden with uncertainty. The air hangs heavy with anticipation, the collective tension notable as I head join the circle, their faces etched with a mix of apprehension and resolve. I throw the bag to the floor and pull out the book with purpose. I lock eyes with Millie, a silent nod between us affirming our shared resolve. She walks timidly towards me and grabs the other half of the book.

Millie and I stand opposite one another, gripping the book tight, our gazes pinned onto the stubborn lock. As our fingers edge closer, a subtle resistance emerges, a minuscule defiance that echoes the colossal power imprisoned within the pages. It's as though the lock itself hesitates, whispering reminders of the untamed forces. I push Millie on with my determined gaze, forcing her to mirror me. With a shared glance that speaks volumes, we lean forward, fingers hovering over the lock. It resists, fighting against our unified effort, a silent protest against the impending culmination of this journey. But we persist, applying as much pressure as we can. It begins to progress and I feel the closure beneath my fingertips looming closer.

The resistance intensifies, the lock pushing back against our insistence. Each push, each attempt to snap it shut feels like a battle against an unyielding force. But with an unspoken pact, a fusion of resolve, we push harder, gritting our teeth against the resistance, our knuckles turning white with exertion. The others stand around with faces of hope and pleading. The lock begrudgingly begins to relent, its rigid defiance giving way to the persistent pressure we apply.

The moment of truth dawns upon us, a crescendo in the symphony of our combined efforts. With one final surge of resilient determination, the lock yields. It clicks into place with a resounding finality, as if acquiescing to the force of our collective resolve.

An abrupt explosion of radiant light erupts from the book, a coruscating beam that pierces the night sky, illuminating the world in a breathtaking display of otherworldly splendour. The air crackles with raw, unrestrained magic, an ethereal shockwave reverberating outward from the epicentre of our unified action. The luminous cascade engulfs us, bathing the surroundings in an incandescent glow that dances and weaves through the night. The sheer brilliance blinds our senses momentarily, yet we remain holding the book tight, permitting the magical light show to play around us.

All of a sudden, a thunderous, resonating boom echoes across the vast expanse of the car park, a deep and sonorous sound that seems to reverberate through the very fabric of existence. Far more intense than the first explosion we had felt. The ground quivers beneath our feet, an imperceptible tremor echoing the magnitude of the magical release. It's a sound that seems to carry the weight of a thousand destinies shifting, a testament to the monumental shift occurring in this space. Amidst the cacophony of sound and light, our senses momentarily overwhelmed, a profound sense of fulfilment washes over us.

I turn my head to face Dean who has his eyes tightly shut, with Delilah held tightly in his arms. Tears of relief and desperation streaming down her face, glistening in the brilliant radiance that envelops the air. It's a moment that transcends the mundane, an extraordinary convergence of forces that binds our fates together.

Time seems to stretch and fold in on itself, a poignant pause in the midst of the chaos that had unfurled in our lives. As the iridescent glow slowly recedes, casting a serene blanket over the car park, the edges of my vision clear. The thrum of magic that had enveloped us begins to ebb, leaving behind a sense of serenity and fulfilment.

The radiance dims, revealing Dean's face fully. His once pallid complexion slowly breathes with life, each inhalation filling his lungs with newfound strength. I observe, a quiet spectator in this surreal moment, as Dean's eyelids flutter open. His irises glisten with a rekindled light, carrying the weight of emotions known only to those who've tiptoed along the precipice of loss. Delilah remains cradled in his arms, her teary gaze meeting his, an unspoken conversation passing between them. It's a shared relief, a silent understanding of the edge they nearly slipped from.

A soft smile graces Dean's lips, a gentle acknowledgment of the tumultuous journey they've just weathered. The weight lifts off my chest, replaced by a swell of relief. It's as though fate rewound its threads, granting him a second chance, one we have fought relentlessly to secure. Delilah's eyes shimmer with tears, a testament to the cascade of emotions surging within her. Joy, relief, and a profound love intermingle, weaving an intricate tapestry of emotions. Her fingers tighten around Dean, anchoring herself in the reality of his living, breathing presence.

My gaze shifts across the group, noting the shared sense of accomplishment etched into their expressions. Millie stands beside me, her shoulders easing, the tension of the moment dissipating. The car park holds witness to an otherworldly tableau; a victory shining amidst the mundane backdrop of concrete. Dean's eyes find mine as he keeps Delilah held tight, a silent bridge forming between us. Gratitude shimmers in his gaze, an unspoken depth that transcends words. His lips part, a silent 'thank you,' though no sound carries in the serene aftermath of the magical burst. Yet, in that wordless exchange, our mutual understanding resonates. A smile tugs at my lips, mirroring the shared triumph binding us. It's a smile speaking volumes, a testament to the unbreakable bonds in this circle.

My family.

I turn to face my beautiful little Sienna, her face drowned in unconcealable happiness. I drop the book to the floor and charge to her, lifting her effortlessly into my arms, her legs wrapping instinctively around me. Her sweet scent breaks into my nostrils as I bury my face into her neck. My hand firmly gripping her hair in a celebratory embrace. As she giggles and squirms in my arms, her joy reverberates through me. It's an unadulterated happiness, a feeling so pure that it momentarily erases the weight of the trials we've weathered. Her laughter dances on the edges of the car park, a triumphant melody. The vibrant spectrum of emotions spreads like wildfire, engulfing us all in a radiant moment of unfiltered elation. It's the melody of victory serenading us, painting the night with hues of hope, relief, and unabashed happiness. I cherish this instant, embracing Sienna like she's the very embodiment of the world's newfound harmony.

Soon enough the others pile onto our embrace. Enfolding us all in a warm, collective squeeze. Arms wrap around shoulders, and bodies meld together in a cascade of emotions; a symphony of relief, joy, and undiluted love. We tighten and tighten together, as if trying to etch this monumental moment into our memories forever. As the embrace gradually loosens, the shared sense of camaraderie lingers in the air like a gentle breeze. It's the kind of unity that cements bonds and fortifies spirits.

A reminder that amidst the chaos, we stand united, a family forged not by blood, but by the trials we've endured together.

CHAPTER 30:
TIME TO GO

Marcus

As the group disentangles from the embrace, a shadow falls over our collective joy. Millie stands apart, her silhouette etched in seclusion, her face etched in a tapestry of bitterness and betrayal. The accusatory silence she exudes cuts through the elation, leaving a disquieting hush in its wake. Sensing the sudden shift, I glance around, and the tendrils of unease tighten within me. Millie, the linchpin of our journey, now appears distant, alienated amidst our celebration. She stands, a lone sentinel of resentment amidst our jubilant tableau. Her eyes bore into us with a mix of anger and hurt, her for-once-warm demeanour cloaked in the frigid chill of betrayal.

We stand almost in a line against her, as if we're ready for some kind of battle.

"So that's it?" She starts, "Now that you got what you wanted from me, I'm thrown to the side?" We look at one another in complete confusion. All beyond fed up with her negative attitude.

"What are you talking about?" Birdie snaps back.

Fire vs Fire.

"You think we pre-scheduled our group hug or something? Just join in if you want to, don't try to make this about you, Millie."

"Shut up Birdie! None of this would have happened without me. Where's my credit? Huh?" She squeals like a lunatic.

"You're a psycho." Birdie continues. The air crackles with emotions as Millie's frustration ignites like a wildfire, engulfing the fragile peace we had just tasted. Birdie's retort, fuelled by the same intensity, only adds fuel to the fire, a clash of wills in a moment of escalating turmoil.

"Alright, alright. Enough, both of you." Dean interrupts in an attempt to bring back the celebratory atmosphere.

But the flames of conflict are already ablaze.

"You can't just blow up on us, Millie!" Delilah's voice quivers, her eyes brimming with unshed tears, a reflection of the hurt and confusion that has unexpectedly swept through our group. Sienna grips my hand tightly, her wide eyes darting between each person in the tense standoff. She hates conflict, my innocent angel.

"Stop it, please!" Her voice, small yet filled with genuine distress, cuts through the escalating argument. Her plea seems to echo in the car park, a poignant reminder of the ripple effects of our discord. I envelop her in a tight embrace and gently guide her towards my bag, hoping to divert her attention from the escalating argument.

I zip up the bag and sling it over my shoulder once again, Sienna's gaze suddenly filled with concern.

"What was that in your bag?"

Uh oh.

"Don't worry about it, sweet-"

"Was that a gun?" She asks, her eyes widening. Her voice trembles with a mix of alarm and uncertainty. The innocent honesty in her question feels like a sharp pin prick against my knowledge of what happens next.

"It's nothing, okay? I'll explain later. I promise"

The situation's escalating gravity sets in as Sienna's grip tightens around my hand. Her eyes, wide with a mix of fear and confusion, search for reassurance in my gaze. My attention snaps back to the group, the turmoil between Birdie and Millie still flaring. Their heated exchange seems to have reached a point of no return, caught in a vicious cycle of accusations and frustration.

Suddenly, an unsettling chill courses through me as, through the argument, I hear the faint sound of sirens in the distance. Am I paranoid? Maybe. But where else are they going in this small residential area at this time? I look to Dean and attempt to draw his attention to the distant echo of sirens.

The sirens, faint at first, now grow louder, punctuating the silence like an ominous drumbeat. My heart races, the adrenaline-fueled urgency heightening my senses. Dean, his eyes mirroring my concern, nods in silent acknowledgment. There's no need for further explanation; the threat of the approaching sirens speaks volumes. I turn my attention back to her, crouching to meet her gaze, trying to paint a reassuring smile on my face despite the unrest brewing within.

"Sweet, we have to go." I tell her softly.

"Go where?"

"You just have to trust me."

"Marcus, I don't understand." Her eyes now frantically scanning my face for answers. The sirens grow louder and louder and I feel the clock ticking against me. I begin to feel my heartbeat take over my entire body.

The dissonance of sirens swells like a relentless symphony in my mind, each wail slicing through my brain and ringing in my ears. What was once a distant echo now feels like an ominous, impending doom, closing in with a relentless intensity. Every nerve in my body tingles with an urgent alarm, the growing intensity of the sirens reverberating through the very core of my being. My thoughts scramble, a rush of disjointed fragments that struggle to form a coherent plan amidst this noise. Each siren feels like a countdown, a merciless metronome ticking away the moments we have left before something cataclysmic unfolds.

"Sweet, please. Get on the bike." I plead.

"You have to tell me what's going on."

"I'm not gonna ask you again. Get on the bike or I'm putting you on it myself. Please, sweet. Please. For once in your life stop fighting me." She stands still, staring through my eyes, longing for an explanation I don't have time to give. With no more time to waste, I scoop Sienna into my arms, her small frame fitting perfectly against my chest.

"Fuck off, Millie. Nobody gives a shit! You're nothing but a pretentious bully!" Birdie shouts in the background. I glance over briefly to catch sight of Millie turning and beginning to walk away.

"I love you, sweet. I'm doing this for you. Everything is for you, my angel." I whisper to Sienna, the urgency in my voice unmissable. Without listening for a response, I sprint toward the bike, my heart pounding in rhythm with the blaring sirens that have still continued to grow impossibly louder. I sit her on the bike, placing a reassuring kiss on her forehead before mounting on infront of her.

"Hold on to me tight, sweet." Her tiny arms grip tight around my waist and I rev the engine. The tense atmosphere around us feels charged with impending chaos, the sirens now roaring with an alarming proximity. My focus narrows solely on Sienna's safety, an urgency that eclipses everything else.

A sudden intrusion sends shockwaves through the air, disrupting the charged atmosphere of tension and escalating emotions. It happens in the blink of an eye; a car swerves into the car park. An ear-splitting screech of tires pierces the air, followed by an ominous thud that plunges us into a sudden, eerie silence. Dust and dirt erupt in a frenzied whirlwind, enveloping the immediate space in a shroud of debris. The sound of the collision lingers. A tense stillness blankets the car park, an unexpected interlude. Dust motes hang suspended in the air, caught in the fading echoes of the abrupt impact.

The cloud of debris eventually disperses, unveiling the scene beneath its transient veil. A haunting sight comes into view in the form of Millie lying motionless on the ground.

"Oh my God." Sienna whispers behind me. I instinctively shield Sienna's view, my fingers tightening around her hand in an effort to shield her from the distressing sight.

"Don't look, sweet. turn around." I order, in all attempts to protect her innocence from the jarring scene in front of us. The car, an ominous harbinger of catastrophe, stands sentinel in the midst of the chaos, a chilling reminder of the unforeseen. Its metal frame, now an instrument of terror. Dean, his once-confident demeanour now stripped bare, steps forward hesitantly, his eyes fixated on the motionless figure.

"Is she... is she alive?" His voice, a mere whisper.

Time slows down momentarily and suddenly blue lights from a trailing police car fill the car park in front of me. The light spills across the dirt, a sinister glow outlining the unmoving silhouette of Millie on the ground. The flashes illuminate the significant puddle of blood now pooling on the floor around her head. The life knocked out of her entirely. She lies dead. But I've seen much worse now. My mind briefly flickers back to the image of Skinny Jeans' blood trickling down my arm. I have to get used to death. To murder. After all, it seems I'm going to be doing a lot more of it.

I turn to make sure Sienna isn't looking and tighten my grip on her hand, rubbing my thumb back and forth in a soothing motion. We have to get out of here. I rev my bike again and scan the escape gaps in the crime scene now settling in front of me.

"Skylar?" Birdie's voice suddenly wavers, with a mix of disbelief and dread. Her abrupt exclamation shatters the eerie silence that envelops us, her hands instinctively rising to cover her gaping mouth. I turn to her, the confusion etched across my face. Following her gaze, my eyes fall upon the killer-car, now a haunting monument to the chaos that has unfurled. There, behind the wheel, sits Skylar. Her eyes wide with shock, a visage of terror etched across her face as though she's trapped in a nightmare from which she cannot wake.

A sinister smirk, filled with satisfaction, takes over my lips.

Well, Sky.. *I guess that makes two of us.*

PART TWO:

SAVING SWEET SIENNA

CHAPTER 1:
QUICK ESCAPE

Marcus

Fuck. That's about the only thought my mind can articulate right now. The red and blue lights relentlessly flash across the car park, stabbing at my eyes like shards of urgency. I take a quick breath, glancing around to assess the scene. The eerie puddle of blood spreading beneath Millie's head, a dark pool illuminated by the harsh lights. I watch as a police officer pulls Skylar from the mangled wreckage, her complexion drained to a deathly, pallid white.

As he shoves a now-handcuffed Skylar into the back of a police car and slams the door shut, her eyes meet mine. Her gaze, once fiery and defiant, now holds a cold, haunting depth. I smirk at her. I must admit it feels pretty good to not be the only one in the 'murderer-club' anymore.

211

The other police officers begin striding towards our group, their authoritative presence sending tension rippling through the air. Dean and I exchange a quick, concerned look as the sirens continue to wail through the car park; a tormenting reminder of the night's chaos. At that moment, my eyes are lured back to a narrow gap between the police cars. It's a risky proposition, the passage so small that doubt creeps in. But I have no other option. I briefly turn my head to instruct Sienna.

"Hold onto me really tight, sweet." With that, my sweet squeezes her little arms tighter around my waist and leans her head against my back. My motorbike rumbles beneath us as I rev the engine, its power ready to surge at my command.

With a resolute nod to Dean, I break away from the group, my eyes fixed on that narrow escape route. The concrete walls of the car park seem to close in as I approach the gap, the challenge ahead magnifying with every inch. The pulsating lights and sirens create a surreal soundtrack to my escape, the world around me warping into a high-stakes battleground. As I navigate through the perilously tight gap, the wind howls in my ears, and time itself seems to slow. The narrowing passage becomes a needle's eye, and every calculated manoeuvre is a dance with fate. Adrenaline courses through my veins, heightening my senses as the blurred scenery becomes a kaleidoscope.

I grit my teeth as we somehow successfully slice through the space, the narrow gap grazing the sides of my legs and bike mirrors. The world beyond the car park unfolds before us, the city's streets a familiar canvas. Behind, the coppers shout, the echoes of their voices mixed with the sirens as yet another chase begins.

They're almost getting boring at this point.

A grin creeps across my face as I surge ahead. My bike responding to my every command, weaving through the labyrinth of city streets. With every twist and turn, the "fuck" on my lips is both a curse and a celebration, a raw expression of defiance against the encroaching forces of capture. I'm fucking untouchable. This chase is not a pursuit; it's a celebration of my prowess, a reminder that I am the architect of my escape. That I'm simply too fucking good for them. They don't realise that this is the easy part for me. The thrill courses through my veins like a drug. I've already escaped.

Catch me if you can, dickheads.

As the sirens wane in the distance, a triumphant laughter escapes my lips. I'm leagues ahead. A vanishing phantom in the city's nocturnal embrace. Sienna loosens her grip slightly and leans away from my back. It's subtle, but I notice. It brings me a surge of arrogant satisfaction. It's like she's acknowledging that I've got everything under control, that she can relax because I'm here.

And damn, does it feel good.

"You okay, sweet?" I ask. Sienna huffs out a single sarcastic laugh.

"Never been better."

"Hey, we're alive, aren't we?" I counter.

"Well, Millie isn't." Her cold, honest response catches me off guard. I can hear a tinge of guilt in her voice. The scene was truly horrific, and Sienna shouldn't have been subjected to such a distressing sight.

"It was a terrible accident, there was nothing we could've done."

"That doesn't change the fact that she's dead because of us. We made her come, Marcus."

"She chose to be here, Sienna. Yes, we needed her help, but it was her decision to give it to us." I say, my voice firm but empathetic. "If she didn't show up it would've been Dean instead."

The truth of my words and the unsettling reality of life's demand for sacrifice, hangs between us. Sienna's eyes wander off to the side.

"I know," she admits, a resigned acknowledgement in her voice. "But it doesn't make it any easier, does it?"

"No, it doesn't," I concede, understanding the complexity of emotions that must be swirling around in her pretty little head.

As we approach the outside of the city, I reduce my speed, allowing the rhythm of the night to soothe the edges of tension.

"Where are we going anyway?" Sienna asks. The dreadful question I was hoping to somehow avoid for the rest of my life. The truth hovers on the tip of my tongue, but the fear of her reaction holds it back. Instead, I choose my words carefully, for now.

"Somewhere safe, sweet."

CHAPTER 2:

OPERATION SKYLAR

Dean

How did I end up in this fucking mess?

I scan my eyes across the shitshow unfolding around me; a dead girl just casually bleeding out on my right, Birdie and Delilah crying to my left, coppers surrounding us. The scene could be lifted straight from a bad movie. I stand there, momentarily frozen, watching Marcus tear away on his bike, Sienna gripping onto him for dear life. A dynamic duo attempting a Houdini-like escape.

"Nice one, Marcus." I mutter sarcastically under my breath, my lips curling into a dry smirk as his audacious manoeuvre includes an unexpected scrape between the police car and his bike mirror. As he disappears into the night, I shake my head in disbelief.

I'm about to be on the run with this guy?

Chapter 2

Turning back to Delilah, I realise the clock is ticking, and I've got a decision to make. The sirens grow louder, the flashing lights more insistent, and as one of the police cars races off behind Marcus, I'm urged to act. It's time to go. I look down at Delilah, tears and concern welling in her gorgeous, moss-green eyes as she glares back up at me.

"Are you sure you don't want to change your mind?" I ask, trying to convince her to come with me. She nods her head subtly as her bottom lip begins to quiver. "You'll be safer with me." I continue as I rub my thumb lightly across her cheek.

"My family is here." she whimpers. I give a silent nod, grasping the reasoning behind her words, and then plant a firm kiss on her forehead.

"I'll be back soon to check on you, okay? I promise."

"Be safe."

"Always, my darling."

I pivot away from Delilah, moving with purpose towards the police car where Skylar sits defiantly in the back seat; the unwilling star of this twisted performance. A wry grin etches its way onto my face as I approach. The absurdity of the situation isn't lost on me.

Her pastel pink hair glows through the window, a bizarre contrast against the stark, monochromatic backdrop of the crime scene. I chuckle to myself with an odd sense of amusement. Skylar, usually the wildcard in our escapades, has now become an unexpected protagonist.

Approaching the police car with a calculated nonchalance, I consider the best way to execute the upcoming rescue mission. A quick scan of the surroundings reveals the focus of the police officers elsewhere. Perfect. With a creak, I swing the door open, revealing Skylar's defiant gaze. Tears stream down her face in unbridled hysteria, leaving trails of smeared makeup in their wake.

"Fucking hell, you look a mess." I laugh.

"Maybe we should've let you die, prick." She snaps with a cold glare.

A little harsh.

"So, you just felt like running someone over tonight?" I tease, gripping her arm to pull her out. She reluctantly swings her legs around to step out of the car, rolling her eyes in the meantime.

"What can I say? I like to make an entrance."

The night wraps around us like a shroud as Skylar and I slip away from the tumult, our hurried footsteps echoing through the deserted alleys. We quickly begin to sprint with unbridled urgency, our legs pumping relentlessly against the pavement. The cityscape blurs around us as we cover ground with a desperate determination to put distance between us and the scene. The rhythmic pounding of our steps harmonising with the adrenaline coursing through our veins.

We need to find a car.

Now.

As we sprint through the alleys I notice Skylar starting to lag behind.

"A little bit of urgency would be nice!" I taunt.

"Yeah, okay. You try to run with your hands cuffed behind your back! It's not as easy as it looks, knobhead!"

"I have, many times!"

Finally, I spot a car parked along the curb. Relief floods through me as I approach our ticket to escape. I pull on the handle, hoping for an easy steal. No luck. Skylar eventually catches up, positioning herself on the passenger side, as I focus on the task of prying the door open. Which is pretty much impossible considering I have no fucking tools with me.

"A little bit of urgency would be nice." Skylar mocks with an arrogant smile.

"Fair play, cunt." I concede with a nod as I continue to pry at the door for a while longer, but to no avail. The urgency of the situation reverberates in my mind, a relentless reminder that time is slipping away.

"Ah, fuck it." I mutter through gritted teeth, my frustration and pressure mounting, as I smash through the window in a single punch; blood instantly spilling from my knuckles.

"Dean!" Skylar shrieks.

"You got a better idea? Huh?" I question, my voice raising "Yeah, didn't think so." I slide into the car and ping open the passenger door. "Get in the fucking car."

Without a moment's hesitation, I ignite the engine, and the vehicle surges forward onto the road, the tyres screeching as they skid against the asphalt. Skylar, still nursing her bound wrists, shoots me a sceptical glance, her eyes a cocktail of disbelief and exhilaration. The city lights streak past like shooting stars, and I begin to relax as a small weight lifts from my shoulders; alive with the thrill of escape once again.

As for Sky, well she doesn't look so relaxed. A mischievous smirk graces my lips as I crank up the car radio, filling the vehicle with a pulsating wave of sound. Her eyes burn into me as she scrunches her face in unmistakable anger.

"Turn it off!"

"Sorry, can't hear you!" I shrug. Skylar's scowl deepens, and she struggles against her restraints.

"Ugh! I'm serious! Dean, turn it off!" A devilish glint dances in my eyes as, instead, I proceed to raise the volume to the max. As the music reaches its zenith, Skylar leans closer, her voice now a determined whisper.

"Dean Douglas, if you don't turn it off right now I swear to God I'll-"

The threat remains unfinished as the road ahead suddenly transforms into a wash of blinding headlights. My reflexes kick in, and I swerve violently to avoid a head-on collision. The tyres screech in protest, and for a brief, heart-stopping moment, it feels like we're right back on the edge of disaster. Skylar's scream mingles with the abrupt silence as the near-miss unfolds.

The car narrowly avoids collision, and I exhale a breath I didn't realise I was holding.

"Fuck me, that was close." I admit with a chuckle as I turn off the radio.

"Are you fucking serious?"

"It was an accident, chill."

"Chill? You almost got us killed and you want me to fucking chill?"

"I'll gladly take you back to the police car if that's what you'd prefer?" I raise my eyebrows and look over at her.

Death glare.
She's giving me the Skylar-death-glare.
I lean back in my seat with a sigh before backing down, "Alright, alright. My bad."

"So what's your plan exactly?" Skylar asks, breaking a few minutes of silence.

"Marcus is gonna meet us at a B&B a couple hours away and we're checked in there for a few weeks."

"A few weeks?"

"Yeah, Marcus and I have some people on our backs."

"Ahh, I always knew you were a scammy dealer. That's why I never bought from you."

"How do you know I've been dealing?" Skylar rolls her eyes, a playful smirk dancing on her lips.

"Are you really asking me that? You're like the most stereotypical looking drug dealer I've ever seen."

"Ouch."

"It's the truth."

"And I'm not scammy. I'm.. strategic."

"Whatever you wanna call it.

"Back on topic," she continues, "what happens after these few weeks?"

"Yeah, our plan hasn't really gone any further than that."

"Wonderful." she says, rolling her eyes.

"We're gonna figure it out, just roll with it, Sky."

"Yeah, yeah. You're paying for my room."

CHAPTER 3:
FAR FROM HOME

Sienna

I often wonder, what cruel logic, if any, governs the arbitrary distribution of life's suffering and serenity? What cosmic lottery decides who gets calm and who gets chaos? I mean, genuinely, what on earth did I ever do to deserve all the things I have to deal with? I'm beginning to suspect that my past-life self might have been a *little* bit of a twat.

After a couple of annoyingly-secretive hours of riding, we finally arrive at a small B&B situated in the midst of nowhere. I swing my leg over and hop off the bike, determined to absorb the surroundings despite the shroud of darkness enveloping the night sky above. The only illumination emanates from the warm glow spilling through the windows of the rural building before me.
What in the world is going on?

Chapter 3

I turn to face Marcus, fully intending to sternly demand some answers, but the moment my eyes catch him dismounting the bike, my resolve shatters. My thoughts scatter like leaves in the wind as I get lost in the details that make him, well.. him.

His dark brown hair, charmingly tousled, framing his face perfectly; while the play of shadows highlights every contour of his tall, toned body. His light, rugged facial hair outlining his jaw. The deep dimple that forms on his left cheek when he flashes me that beautiful, sick smirk.

He's the kind of man who knows how to take exactly what he wants. Which should make me nervous, of course.

Yet as his piercing hazel eyes lock onto mine and that crooked smirk plays on his lips, I instead become acutely aware of the throbbing between my legs.

He's a walking contradiction and, despite the warning bells, I can't deny the thrill that comes with the realisation that he's exactly the kind of bad, evil man that I shouldn't want. But I do.

As he steps closer, I open my mouth to speak but my words get caught in my throat as the subtle intensity in his eyes locks me into place. The curl of his lips deepening as though he's aware of the effect he has on me.

"Got something to say, sweet?" Marcus' voice, low and gravelly, sends a shiver down my spine. I swallow hard, attempting to gather my thoughts.

"Where are we?" I manage, my voice confident and triumphing over the nervous flutter in my chest.

"That's for me to know." He says, leaning in with a wink before walking past me and towards the building. "You coming?" he asks, holding the door open for me.

I take a deep breath, my mind still racing with questions, but the allure of the unknown draws me forward. With a reluctant nod, I follow him into the cosy B&B, the door closing behind us with a soft click. The interior is exactly as you'd expect from a random bed and breakfast out in the countryside; quaint, with rustic furniture and dim lighting. Marcus approaches the small front desk, its surface adorned with a weathered bell that hints at years of stories and arrivals.

He presses the bell and stares down at me as we wait for a response. His eye contact is intense. He's not looking at me, but rather he's looking into me. The intensity of his focus is both intimidating and strangely affectionate, a paradoxical mix that leaves me entranced. In those moments, he's not just staring; it's as if he's unravelling me with his eyes.

And as the seconds tick by, one single thought occupies my mind..

I want to kiss him.

Yes, I want to kiss a murderer.
Suddenly an unexpected creaking sound steals my attention. Descending a set of stairs, an elderly man in a dressing gown appears. His eyes, gentle yet perceptive, meet ours as he reaches the bottom step, and a warm smile graces his weathered face.

"Sorry for the delay. We don't usually have people arrive this late in the night." He begins. I manage a small smile, feeling a mixture of relief and embarrassment for being caught in such an obviously intimate moment.

"All good, man." Marcus responds. "I've got a booking for the next few weeks."

Weeks?

"Lovely, what name is the booking under?"

"Dean."

Dean?

My mind rolls back to the gun laying in Marcus' bag and suddenly fear overtakes my body again. My heart starts to beat harder through my chest and my vision becomes unsteady. I try to slow my breathing, my mind racing through the fragments of information Marcus has just casually shared. He notices my anxiety rising and reaches out to touch my arm, causing a conflict to erupt within me.

Despite my rising fear, part of me still craves the false-safety of the familiar. Still craves the man I grew up with, and I'm worried I always will. Somehow, even after all that he's done, he makes me feel safe.

The elderly man retrieves a set of glasses resting on the desk and gracefully slides them onto the bridge of his nose. He settles into the chair, the rhythm of clicking keys and the soft hum of his computer filling the air as he adeptly works on the keyboard.

"Okay, looks like you've got a booking for two double rooms?"

"Yeah, that's the one." Marcus confirms.

Though it irks me to admit it, my heart faintly aches at the revelation that Marcus had booked us separate rooms. Surely he would want to be in bed with me, right?

Not that I want that, of course.

"Great, follow me." With a friendly smile, he briskly escorts us back outside, making his way across a small dirt path, toward a line of five twee cottage-style outbuildings. He gestures towards the two buildings at the end of the line before handing

Marcus two sets of keys. With a few parting words, the man strolls away, leaving Marcus and I alone once more.

Marcus smirks as he unlocks the door, breaking the silence settling between us.

"Come on in, beautiful." I love it when he calls me beautiful. Growing up, I never obsessed over my appearance. Never really even thought about it; there were far weightier matters to contend with, like navigating life without my parents. Sure, I knew I wasn't unattractive, but I also never considered myself particularly beautiful.

But his words, delivered with such sincerity, made me think about it more. And as I did, I began to see it too. His focus on my beauty served as a gentle mirror, revealing facets of myself I had overlooked or simply never cared to think about. I began to enjoy my beauty. And while I still don't like to dwell much on aesthetics, there's an undeniable sweetness in knowing that in his eyes, I'm the most beautiful thing in the world.

I follow him inside, the sudden warmth enveloping us. The room is surprisingly nice. Almost homely. Marcus locks the door behind us, the twist of the lock echoing through the room. Rather than placing the keys on the side, he discreetly tucks them into his back pocket, arousing my suspicion and fear once again.

As my uncertainty rises I take a few steps back, creating some distance between us. We lock eyes, both hesitant to break the silence by speaking first.

Come on Sienna, don't be such a wimp.

"You need to tell me what's going on. Right now." I assert, irritatingly-weakly.

"Curiosity killed the cat, sweet," he teases, his voice low and dripping with a seductive edge. My heartbeat quickens, partly from frustration and partly from an unsettling allure.

"I'm serious, Marcus. Tell me what's happening or I'm leaving." He leans against a rustic dresser, the subtle play of shadows accentuating the contours of his rugged features.

"But where's the fun in that?" he replies cryptically.

"Fun? You think I'm interested in having fun right now? First you confess to me that you're some kind of psycho killer, then I watch Millie die right in front of me and suddenly you're whisking me away to a cottage in the middle of nowhere and you think I care about having fun?"

The silence continues as I watch Marcus carefully consider his next words. I pose another question, aiming to simplify the clearly very complicated situation.

"Why is it booked in Dean's name?"

"Because Dean is on his way. The second room is his."

"So we're not in separate rooms?" I accidentally say out loud, far too quickly, causing Marcus to smirk even more smugly than usual.

Sienna, you absolute idiot.

He laughs softly as he takes a few steps towards me.

"No, sweet. We're not in separate rooms. I wouldn't torture you like that." I roll my eyes and cross my arms, failing to let his cocky demeanour crack me.

"Marcus, please. Just tell me what's going on."

"We're on the run, sweet. Dean's been dealing and got some dangerous people on his back. Plus the police found your little boyfriend 'Skinny Jeans' body."

Marcus sighs at my silence, his eyes searching for the right words. "Look, I didn't wanna get you tangled up in this mess. But circumstances changed, and I had to act fast."

"I'm not staying here." I scoff.

"You don't have a choice."

"Excuse me?"

"You're safe here, Sienna."

"Oh great, I'm so glad the murderer is here to teach me a lesson about safety."

"You're very cute when you're mad, my love." he says with a soft laugh.

"I'm not even your girlfriend."

"We've been over this, sweet. Put whatever label on it you want, It doesn't matter. You're mine, and I'm gonna make sure I keep you safe. Whether you like it or not."

I clench my jaw in frustration and attempt to barge past him towards the door but he softly and effortlessly pushes me back.

"I'm leaving. I mean it." I state firmly.

"Oh yeah?"

"Yes." With that, he crouches to my eye level, his gaze now stern.

"You step foot out of this room without my permission and there will be consequences. Is that clear?" Before I can formulate a response, Marcus closes the remaining distance. Our faces are inches apart, the fucked up sexual tension between us impossible to ignore.

Just as the intensity peaks, a sudden knock on the door startles us both. Marcus maintains eye contact, his authoritative expression turning into a knowing smile before he heads towards the door.

CHAPTER 4:

A SKYLAR SURPRISE

Marcus

As I swing open the door, I'm greeted with one extra pink-haired, handcuffed person than expected.

"What the fuck is she doing here?"

"Ah yes, hello to you too, Marcus." Skylar chips in sarcastically, receiving no reply. "Well, fuck you all then. I'm going to my room. Twats." With that kind comment, Skylar walks off down the dirt path and up to her room, tripping over a stone on the way.

"It's a long story." Dean mumbles, shaking his head.

"We need to talk," I start, "In your room, not here." I can't let Sienna listen, no way. It'll freak her out far too much knowing how serious this situation really is.

My sweet angel doesn't need that.

I'm painfully aware of how much I'm fucking with her anxiety just by bringing her here and it's killing me. But I have no choice. Her safety remains my top priority, no matter the circumstances.

I take a seat in Dean's room and we each roll up a joint. The smoke gradually filling the air around us.

"What on earth were you thinking bringing Sky here?" I question, entirely perplexed.

"Yeah, I'm not sure I made the right call on that one."

"You don't say." We exchange a muffled laugh. "So, what's your plan from here?"

"Lay low." Dean replies with a puff of smoke.

"That's it? Just sit still and wait? Let these cunts slowly hunt us down?"

"I don't see what else we can do?"

"Fight back. When have we ever allowed people to walk over us? We can't just sit here like pussies."

"Bro, it's not just some random kid from the estate we're fucking with. These are dangerous people, far more dangerous than us."

"Why are you even on their radar to begin with?"

Dean releases a protracted, tension-laden sigh. The palpable burden upon his shoulders becomes increasingly evident. The weight, both metaphorical and tangible, pressing down on him like an unwelcome companion, leaving an indelible mark on his posture and expression.

"That's the weirdest part." he reluctantly begins, "I'm not exactly sure. Don't get me wrong, I owe a lot of fuckers money. But these guys, not a penny."

"That makes no sense." I blurt out, scrunching up my face in total confusion. "Who are they?"

"They're all working for the same guy. Calls himself 'Grizzly'."

"Real intimidating," I chuckle sarcastically, "And you have no idea what he wants from you?"
Dean shakes his head and shrugs defeatedly.

"I can only assume they want money. We deal in the same areas but I don't see how I could possibly be any threat to their business."

We sit in speechless thought for a few moments, grappling with the situation. The hushed atmosphere is occasionally punctuated by the rhythmic sound of inhalation and exhalation as we each take deliberate puffs on our joints.

In this chill silence, our blunts aren't just rolled-up temporary escapes; they're like conversation pieces passing between us. Each puff feels like a nod of understanding, a quiet acknowledgment that we're both trying to make sense of everything being thrown our way.

"Let's find him." I eagerly suggest.

"Are you mad?"

"I mean it." Dean looks at me with a mixture of disbelief and concern, his eyes searching mine for any sign that I might be joking. "We can't just sit here and wait for trouble to arrive," I declare, exhaling a plume of smoke. "We need to take control of the situation. Find these guys before they find us."

Dean leans back in his chair, a thoughtful expression on his face. The room is filled with the pungent aroma of cannabis as our joints burn slowly, the smoke swirling around us like a protective haze.

"I get your point, bro, but these people are organised, and they've got something bigger at play. Going after them blindly could make this shit a whole lot worse," Dean warns.
Ignoring the scepticism in Dean's eyes, I lean forward, determined to drive my point home.

"Waiting around is a death sentence, man. We need to at least figure out what we're up against" Dean takes a thoughtful drag from his joint, considering my words.

"Alright, let's say we find them. What's the plan then? We can't just barge in and demand answers. It's not that simple." he rambles, "And how would we find them anyway?"

"That's where Skylar comes in," I suggest. "She's got connections. She knows just as many dealers as we do, and she's close with them. If anyone can help us navigate this mess without drawing attention, it's her." Dean raises an eyebrow, a sceptical look returning to his face.

"You trust her that much?"
I shrug.

"Not necessarily, but she's our best bet." After a brief moment of contemplation, Dean nods in agreement.

"Alright, I'll talk to Skylar." Dean begins to stand up and finishes his blunt. "We have to be careful here, bro." He warns, his face serious. "We're stepping into some deep shit, and it's not just *our* lives on the line." He tilts his head subtly in the direction of my room, a silent indication to Sienna that instantly sends a shiver down my spine.

I give a clear, understanding nod as I take a final puff. His insinuation lands like a leaden weight in my chest, stifling any words that dare to rise. Instead it creates a tangible lump in my throat. Realising that Dean believes my plan could jeopardise Sienna's safety hits me like a sledgehammer to the heart. Words fail me in this moment, not for lack of understanding, but because the depth of my sudden emotions transcends mere language.

Are we doing the right thing here?

CHAPTER 5:
HUNT FOR GRIZZLY

Dean

"I'm asleep!" Sky shouts as I knock on the door.

"For real, Skylar, I need to talk to you."

The door flings open, revealing a definitely-not-asleep Skylar with a hint of annoyance in her eyes.

"This better be good." she mutters, stepping aside to let me in.

"Oh you're gonna love it. The topic is drug dealers, your favourite."

"I fucked two drug dealers, okay? Can we just let it die?" As Skylar sits down I lean against the wall in front of her, head in hand.

"As much as I would *love* to, no. They might be able to help us out with something."

"No, no, no." Skylar begins, shaking her head and arms dramatically. "I'm sick and tired of trying to help you morons. Look at what just happened. Marcus, oh-so-simply suggests '*hey*

Sky, it would be really helpful if you would go get us a car' next thing you know I've splattered Millie across the car park."

"To be fair, I don't think getting chased by feds and killing Millie was mentioned in his instructions."

Probably not the wisest response from me.

Skylar shoots me a glare that could freeze lava.

"I mean, I did pay for your room so you kinda owe me." I continue, stupidly trying my luck.

"Dean, shut the fuck up." I slowly retrieve a paperclip I had snagged from the front desk and start twirling it between my fingers.

"I guess you don't mind keeping those handcuffs on then?" I suggest with a dramatic huff. Skylar's eyes narrow at my attempt to blackmail her.

"Unlock them. Now."

"Help me. Now." There's a long pause as Skylar's eyes burn through my skin.

"Fine. What do you want?"

"I want you to message your little fuckbuddy drug dealers and ask them for some info."

"What *kind* of info?"

"Anything and everything they know about a guy who goes by Grizzly."

"Grizzly? All this chaos and we're running from a guy called Grizzly?" Skylar bursts into genuine laughter. "Is he friends with the big bad wolf or some shit?"

"Hilarious.. So, are you gonna help?"

Skylar's laughter gradually subsides as she regains her composure, blinking away a tear from her eye.

"Okay, okay. I'll message them and see what I can dig up. Just please, for the love of all that's holy, unlock me now."

With steady hands, I carefully insert the paperclip into the lock, recalling the lessons I learned from watching Skylar do the same countless times before. The mechanism clicks softly as I apply gentle pressure, and with a sense of triumph, the handcuffs spring open. Skylar rubs her wrists with a sigh of relief, the tension in the room easing as the metal restraints fall away. There's actually a moment of quiet gratitude between us.

Wholesome friendship.

"Thanks, twat."

Nevermind.

As Skylar picks up her phone to send the messages, I take a step back, giving her some space to work her magic.

"Do they usually reply fast?" I ask.

"Depends. Sometimes they answer straight away, sometimes they leave me hanging."

"You know, Sky, at this hour? They'll probably reply instantly in hopes they're gonna get a little more than just a sale."

"Very funny."

"I'm serious."

"We don't just hook up, okay? We have a good relationship." She insists, trying to convince herself.

"Aww, do they bring you flowers when they come to rail you and drop off your drugs?" Skylar rolls her eyes as she tries to hold in her escaping laughter.

"Sadly not everyone can have what you and Delilah have."

"You deserve more though." As Skylar shoots me a sidelong glance, there's a flicker of vulnerability in her expression, a hint of longing hidden beneath her tough exterior. It's a rare glimpse into the softer side of her, a side that she guards fiercely.

"But the kind of love you and Delilah share.. It's like something out of a fairy tale. It's rare, Dean. It's not the kind of love most people get to experience. Definitely not somebody like me. I'm too broken. No normal, good guy is ever gonna deal with my baggage."

"Then that's not a *good* guy." I reply, my voice firm and resolute. "No good guy would see your past as 'baggage'. It's not baggage, Sky, it's your story. Don't ever let what we went through make you question your ability to be loved."

Skylar's glare meets mine and a begrudged smile flickers across her lips. Behind that forced smile lies an obvious shadow of doubt that tugs at my heartstrings a little. It's as if she doesn't believe me, doesn't believe that she deserves the kind of love I'm talking about. As strange as it is for me to say, I actually feel bad for her.

As I begin to make my way to the door, I offer Skylar a reassuring smile, my hand reaching out to grasp the handle.

"Let me know if you hear anything, yeah?"

"Will do." With a nod, I slowly step out, gently closing the door behind me.

The cool night air greets me, and I fish out a cigarette, lighting it with practised ease before embarking on a leisurely stroll toward my own cottage situated at the end of the row. Each step is deliberate, allowing me to mull over the evening's events as the smoke curls lazily around me. The night is quiet, except for the occasional rustle of leaves and distant hoot of an owl.

As I reach my room, lost in thought, a sudden crack splits the silence, followed by the sound of splintering wood. My instincts kick in, and I barely have time to react before a massive tree limb crashes down from above, landing with a deafening thud just a few feet away from me.

235

What the fuck just happened?
I can't help but gape at the sight of the fallen limb, utterly dumbfounded. The night was calm, no hint of any strong wind, yet here I am, staring at a tree branch that decided to take a nosedive out of nowhere. I scratch my head, trying to wrap my mind around the bizarre occurrence. It's like the universe decided to play a prank on me, except this isn't the kind of joke I find funny.

Glancing around, I half-expect to see hidden cameras, waiting for my reaction. But there's nothing. Just the usual quiet of the night, broken only by the rustle of leaves in the gentle breeze. It's as if the world is shrugging its shoulders, just as clueless about what just happened as I am.

With a furrowed brow, I turn my attention back to the fallen limb, its presence casting a long shadow across the ground. I crouch down beside it, running my fingers along its rough surface, trying to glean some insight into its sudden descent.

But the limb remains stubbornly silent, offering no answers. I stub out my cigarette, the ember fizzling out in the darkness, and I make my way back inside, leaving the fallen limb behind me. Whatever caused it to fall, I'm not in the mood to figure it out tonight.

CHAPTER 6:
WHO'S IN CHARGE?

Sienna

Marcus re-enters the room; the unmistakable scent of marijuana following him. He immediately buries the keys in his pocket and confronts me with that sick, tempting smile.

Remember, you're angry Sienna! You're really really angry.

I stand up off the bed and face him, arms folded tightly across my chest.

"Why are you still awake, beautiful? You must be exhausted." he begins, his words laced with a charm that threatens to disarm my anger.

"Take me home."

"I am your home." he counters softly.

"Marcus, you can't keep me here. This is like.. kidnapping." He chuckles darkly, taking a deliberate step closer.

"Kidnapping implies you're not here willingly, sweet. And we both know that's not the case." His words are like a punch to the gut, leaving me breathless and uncertain. I know he's right in a twisted sort of way. My pulse quickens at the reminder of just how deeply entangled I've become in his web.

He strides towards me, his presence commanding and dominating, until he stands towering over me, casting a shadow that seems to engulf my entire being.

"I'm trying to keep you safe."

"Keep me safe? Really? By trapping me here against my will?" I question, "Give me the keys, Marcus. Now." His gaze hardens, his eyes flashing with possessive determination.

"You want the keys?" He taunts with a smirk, his voice laced with amusement as he takes a seat on the edge of the bed. With a brazen display of confidence, he slips them down into the front of his pants, his eyes never leaving mine. "Take 'em."

A rush of conflicting emotions washes over me; anger, frustration, and a hint of something else which I dare not acknowledge.

"I'm not playing games. I want to go home."

"You're making this so much worse for yourself."

"Do you seriously think you can just keep me here?"

"I can and I will." He asserts, his tone laced with a chilling certainty. "I'm doing what I need to do to keep you safe. You have no choice in this."

"I'll find a way out, sooner or later."

"Oh yeah?" He raises an eyebrow, "Then what? You don't even know where we are, sweet."

"I'll figure it out." Marcus' smirk widens, his amusement evident as he leans back against the bed, his posture relaxed yet oozing with dominance.

"You're pushing your luck now." Marcus starts after a short silence, "Please, let's just get some sleep." he suggests, before standing up and pulling back the duvet for me with a gentle tug.

"Fine, but don't expect me to still be here when you wake up." I threaten with venom, and almost instantly regret.

His jaw tightens, and his eyes narrow with a predatory focus I've never seen before. He immediately paces towards me, closing the distance until we're face to face; his eyes ablaze with fury as he crouches down to my eye level, our gazes locked in a tense standoff.

"I fucking dare you." For a moment, silence reigns, broken only by the sound of our shallow breaths filling the space between us. "Try to sneak out and watch what happens."

"What are you gonna do? You gonna kill me too?" I challenge, trying to keep my voice steady despite the tremble in my limbs. "I'm not scared of you."

"I don't want you to be scared of me. I want you to respect my orders."

"Or what?" I ask spitefully, as I push my face even closer to his, daring him to respond.

Bad idea.

In one sharp motion he grabs me by the throat and forcefully pins me against the wall. His mixed scent of aftershave and weed overtaking my senses.

"Let me make myself fucking clear, sweet. You leave this room and you'll be punished until I think you've learnt your lesson."

"Punished?" I manage to choke out, my voice strained under his relentless grip.

"Yes, pretty. Punished." Marcus' grip tightens, his fingers digging into my flesh with cruel intensity. "I'll have my way with you until you're crying out for mercy. Begging me to stop."

I know, I know. I should be terrified. But right now looking up into those hazel-green eyes, *all* I want is whatever he's thinking about doing to me. Every single dirty, twisted, painful fantasy he has going on in that insane mind. I want it all.

"You're a sick, sadistic-." My sentence is cut off by his grip somehow still tightening around my throat.

"Are you sure you want to continue that sentence?" he asks in a deep whisper.

Tears prickle at the corners of my eyes as I struggle to breathe, the world spinning around me. With all the strength I can muster, I somehow manage to shake my head. Marcus' grip tightens for a moment longer before, with a sudden jolt, he releases me. I stagger backward, my legs giving way beneath me, and I collapse to my knees, gasping for air.

Marcus slowly crouches down in front of me, his gorgeous, vein covered hand firm as it grips my chin, forcing me to look at him.

"Look at me, sweet." he commands calmly, "As much as I'd enjoy disciplining you, I'd prefer you didn't give me a reason to." His grip on my chin tightens, his fingers pressing into my skin with an uncomfortable force leaving bruises blossoming beneath his touch. "Have I made myself clear?"

"I don't even have any clothes here," the words escape me in a feeble attempt to divert the conversation, to cling to some semblance of normalcy. But even as the words leave my lips, I know they're futile. His gaze narrows, and for a moment, I catch a flicker of something unreadable in his expression before it softens, just barely. It's a small reprieve, a fleeting moment of tenderness.

"I'll take care of that." He promises, his voice a low rumble.

As he reaches out to touch my cheek, a shiver runs down my spine, a chill that cuts through the warmth of his touch. I know I should pull away, should resist the temptation of his embrace, but I find myself leaning into his touch. Marcus rises to his feet and begins looking through his bag as I stay frozen on the floor. He pulls out one of his black t-shirts and returns to where I'm kneeling, gently crouching down to offer it to me.

"Wear this for tonight." he says softly, his voice barely above a whisper, yet it resonates with an undeniable authority. It's a command disguised as a suggestion, leaving me with little choice but to comply.

I take off my top to change, revealing my bare chest. As Marcus watches me, I can see the hint of a smile playing at the corners of his lips, a subtle satisfaction in knowing that he has me under his control. It's both infuriating and extremely fucking attractive, a constant tug-of-war.

"So pretty." he states, his eyes devouring me hungrily.

I slide his t-shirt over my head and enjoy the feeling of his aroma engulfing me. It's like I'm wrapping myself in him.

"There you go. Good girl." he murmurs, his voice laced with approval.

I sit in his oversized t-shirt, as he watches me intently, his eyes lingering on every movement as if he's savouring the moment.

"Are you happy now?" I snap, with a smirk of my own. Marcus' expression remains unreadable for a moment before a thick smile curls his lips.

"You have no idea how happy I am, seeing you in that."

I begin to stand up but before I can even reach my feet, Marcus moves with lightning speed, effortlessly scooping me up over his shoulder.

"Marcus, put me down!" I protest, my fists pounding against his back in a pathetic 'attempt' to break free. But Marcus pays no heed, his grip firm as he carries me towards the bed.

Just as I'm about to unleash another barrage of complaints, I feel a hard, sharp smack to my ass that sends a jolt of surprise and pain coursing through me.

"Hey!" I start, indignation rising in my throat, but Marcus cuts me off with a playful chuckle.

"Consider that another reminder of who's in charge."

In one swift motion, he slams me onto the mattress, the force of it knocking the wind out of me. Before I can even gather my wits, he's straddling me, pinning me down; one hand still lingering on my now tingling backside. Despite myself, a blush creeps across my cheeks.

"I love when you give me attitude, sweet. It really fucking turns me on. But sometimes you have to relax and stop fighting me." he chides, his fingers tracing lazy circles on my skin. Despite my best efforts to resist, a shiver runs down my spine at his touch.

It's not fair for him to be this hot.

Before I can faux-protest and further, his fingers dig into my sides, eliciting a squeal of laughter as he tickles me mercilessly. I squirm and wriggle beneath him, unable to contain the infectious giggles that bubble up from deep within me.

Just as quickly as it began, Marcus relents, his touch softening into gentle caresses as he peppers slow, firm kisses all over my body. I catch my breath, my laughter fading into contented sighs and whimpers. It's a dizzying whirlwind of sensations, leaving me breathless and disoriented.

"Now," he starts, whispering in between kisses, "are you gonna get some sleep?"

I nod, my eyelids heavy with the promise of much-needed rest. Marcus's lips trail down my neck, leaving a tingling sensation in their wake as he murmurs, "Very smart."

"Sleep tight, sweet."

CHAPTER 7:
ONE STEP CLOSER

Dean

I bang on Marcus' door as I start rolling my first joint of the day. the crinkling sound of the paper and the sweet aroma of freshly ground cannabis waft up. The door swings open, and Marcus emerges with a brisk step, swiftly slamming it shut behind him. He takes one look at me and my blunt and lets out a huff.

"What's the issue?" I ask, knowing exactly what the issue is.

"It's not even 10 a.m."

"I deserve an early joint after gathering info all night."

"Sure, keep telling yourself that." We both settle into my stolen car and I start the engine with a loud rumble.

"So, what have you got for me?" he asks,

"I had Sky message her little druggy friends and they actually had some info on one of Grizzly's runners." I say,

244

handing him the joint. Marcus takes a long drag, his eyes squinting against the smoke.

"Nice, do share." he says, passing the joint back to me.

"This guy goes by the name of Razor. Apparently, he's been moving some serious weight lately, and he's got ties to Grizzly. If we can track him down, we might get some leads on where he's been hiding." Marcus nods, his mind already churning.

"So where do we find this guy?"

"There's a rundown warehouse about an hour away. Word is, that's where he operates out of. I figure we pay him a visit, see if he's willing to talk."

"Sounds like a plan," Marcus says, a glint of determination in his eyes. "Let's go pay Razor a visit."

As we approach, the areas become increasingly gloomy, graffiti-covered walls and broken windows decorating the landscape. Feels just like home.

I fucking love it.

"Shit." Marcus mutters under his breath as he stares at his phone screen.

"What's up?"

"They're expanding the search for the murder." he explains. I shrug.

"So? They're not gonna find you where we're staying."

"I hope you're right." he sighs, rubbing his head.

As we pull up to the warehouse, I reach behind me, my hand finding the familiar bulk of the bag nestled in the backseat. With practised ease, I withdraw my gun, it's cold steel fitting snugly into my palm like a well-worn glove. A quick glance at Marcus confirms his readiness, his nod signalling the presence of his own weapon, snug in his waistband. A grin spreads across his face, reminiscent of the mischief we used to get up to as kids, and for a moment, the tension of the impending confrontation is broken by a shared memory of simpler times.

"Remember the time we broke into that abandoned factory and got into a fight?" I ask with a smile. Marcus's expression falters, and for a moment, I can almost see the memory unfold in his mind.

"How could I forget? We were lucky to make it out alive." he says, a low laugh rumbling up.

"Yeah, we had a few bruises to explain to the home staff." Marcus nods, a wistful look creeping over his face.

"Those were the days."

"We were trouble."

"Some things never change." With that we turn to each other, sharing a knowing glance. I slide my gun into my waistband, feeling its weight against my hip.

"You ready?" He asks.

"Let's fucking go." With a shared nod, we simultaneously open the car doors and step out.

Razor doesn't know what's coming.

The gravel crunches beneath us as we approach the worn, corrugated steel door. The faded sign creaks in the gentle breeze, reading 'Industrial Warehouse' in rusty letters. We exchange a look, and then, together, we push the creaking door open, revealing the musty interior. The silence is a palpable thing, punctuated only by the hollow echo of our footsteps as we step into the cavernous space.

Adrenaline courses through my veins as we venture deeper into the heart of the building, every sense heightened, every nerve on edge. The only sounds are the faint echoes of our footsteps, resonating off the walls in a rhythmic cadence, punctuated by the occasional drop of water from a leaking pipe. Then, without warning, a voice pierces the silence, sharp and commanding, making me jump slightly.

"Who the fuck is in here?"

We press on, moving deeper into the labyrinthine space. As we round a corner we come face to face with what has to be Razor, considering the large tattoo of a razor blade across his throat, and two other guys; a motley assortment of rough-looking characters. Razor himself stands at the forefront, a short but menacing figure.

"Well, well, well. Who do we have here?" Razor sneers, his voice dripping with contempt. "Mr. Dean Douglas, huh? What the fuck do you want?"

"We're looking for Grizzly." I start.

"And he's looking for you. Word on the street is, he's not too happy. There's a big reward out for whoever brings you to him." As Razor's smirk widens, it becomes evident that he's not about to make this easy for us.

"Where is he?" Marcus asks.

"You two think you can waltz in here and make demands?" He takes another step closer, his hand tightening into a fist. "You got balls, I'll give you that."

Marcus tenses beside me, his hand inching closer to his gun. I shoot him a warning glance, silently urging him to hold back for now.

"We're not here to start trouble," I say, keeping my tone even despite the adrenaline coursing through me. "But we need to find Grizzly. Help us, and maybe we can all walk away from this in one piece."

Razor's lips curl into a sneer, his eyes narrowing as he considers our proposal. For a moment, the only sound in the warehouse is the distant hum of traffic outside. Finally, Razor breaks the silence with a derisive laugh.

"Oh don't worry. I'll take you to Grizzly." he starts, "In a fucking bodybag. Do you know how much money I'm about to make for this?"

"It doesn't have to be like this, man. Let's talk it out." I suggest.

Suddenly, one of Razor's cronies makes a move, reaching for his gun with lightning speed. Instinct kicks in, and Marcus and I draw our weapons in unison, the sharp crack of gunfire echoing through the warehouse. In the moments that follow, bullets fly and bodies fall, the air thick with the acrid scent of gunpowder. Adrenaline courses through my veins as I take aim, my focus laser-sharp despite the chaos unfolding around me.

When the gunfire finally ceases, the warehouse is eerily silent once more, the only sound the ragged tone of our breaths. Marcus and I exchange a grim glance, our hearts pounding in our chests as we take in the aftermath of the confrontation. Razor lies on the ground, clutching a wound in his shoulder, his eyes wide with shock and pain. His two companions are sprawled motionless nearby.

With a deep breath, I crouch and hold my gun to Razor's tiny, square head.

"You've got one more fucking chance," I say, my voice low and dangerous. "Tell us where he is, or you'll end up like your friends here."

"I-I don't know where he is, okay? We're not allowed to know his location."

"Bullshit." Marcus adds.

"I'm not lying, man. I can g-give you money instead?" I push the gun harder against his temple.

"We don't want your mon-"

"How much?" I interject. Marcus gives me a confused look but I keep my eyes on Razor.

"I got a couple bags in the safe back there."

"What's the code?"

"1403." I tilt my head slightly, prompting Marcus to check the safe.

Marcus wastes no time, swiftly moving towards the safe with a sense of urgency. He punches in the code, 1403, and with a satisfying click the safe door swings open. Marcus grabs a few handfuls of cash, stuffing them into his waistband. Meanwhile, I keep my gun trained on Razor, my finger twitching on the trigger.

I stand up over him, my gun frozen in place.

"Appreciate the money, but we have a little problem, Razor." I start with a grin, "I have a terrible feeling that you're fucking lying to me." Razor's eyes widen in panic as he realises that his attempt to buy his way out of trouble has failed. Sweat beads on his forehead, and his breath comes in short, ragged gasps as he struggles to come up with a response.

"Fuck, man. I swear."

But I'm not convinced.

With a cold glint in my eyes, I press the gun harder against his temple, the metal biting into his skin.

"You expect us to believe this bullshit?" I growl, my voice low and dangerous. "You expect us to believe that Grizzly doesn't trust his own men with his location? That he doesn't have someone like you keeping tabs on his operations?"

Razor's eyes dart between us, his breathing growing more frantic with each passing second. It's clear that he's caught between a rock and a hard place, torn between the fear of crossing Grizzly and the fear of what we might do to him if he doesn't cooperate.

"I don't know where he is, I swear."

"Then you know somebody who does." Marcus adds. Razor's eyes widen in fear at my words, and I can see the wheels turning in his head as he weighs his options. He knows that we're not messing around, but he's also smart enough to know that crossing Grizzly is a death sentence.

"Fuck, fuck okay. Fine." he strains, "I-I know someone who might know. But you didn't hear it from me." I nod, satisfied that we're finally getting somewhere.

"Who is it?" I demand, my voice hard and uncompromising.

"His name's Moth."

"Where do we find him?"

"He's in London."

"Home shit home." Marcus inserts. Razor then reluctantly reveals Moth's exact whereabouts. I exchange a glance with Marcus and we share a brief, unspoken understanding that our mission is done, and it's time to exit this precarious situation.

Or so I thought.

Slowly, I take a step back, allowing Razor to untense. I tuck my gun away, ready to turn around and leave the warehouse's dark recesses behind. Marcus, however, seems to have other plans.

As I turn to make my exit, I hear a sudden gunshot ring out and Razor's skull hitting the ground. I whirl my gaze back and forth between Razor's lifeless body and Marcus, dumbfounded, trying to process what just happened.

"What the fuck was that for?" I ask. Marcus shrugs nonchalantly, as if he didn't just murder someone.

"I didn't like him."

I shake my head, trying to wrap my mind around Marcus's bizarre logic and find some words.

"I- Seriously?"

"What? He got on my nerves. You gonna miss him or something?"

I can't help but chuckle, despite the absurdity of the situation. "I'm not saying that. But did you have to shoot him right when we were about to leave?"

"Eh, it felt like the right moment."

"You know, most people just say goodbye or something." Marcus gives me a lopsided grin.

"Yeah, well, I've never been one for formalities."

"So is murder just your thing now?"

"Keeping things interesting." I rub my forehead and sigh. "Well, we've got what we came for. Let's get out of here."

"Hold on." I make my way towards a sleek black M4 parked in the corner of the warehouse.

"Nice." Marcus remarks.

"Fuck our car, I'm having this." I check the trolley next to the car and find the keys nestled on top.

Fucking morons.

"Okay, *now* let's get out of here."

CHAPTER 8:
A FRIENDLY BREAK-IN

Marcus

We get back into the car and start heading back to our rooms, but I'm not ready to go back quite yet.

"I need to make a little stop." I declare.

"Oh yeah? Where you wanna go?"

"Sienna's. I wanna grab some of her stuff."

"You got a key?" He asks.

"Nah. Smart girl knows if she ever gave me a key, I would've been barging in on her every chance I got." With a shared laugh, Dean veers towards Sienna's place.

"How you planning on doing this then?" Dean asks, curiosity gleaming in his eyes.

"I've gone in through her bedroom window before," I explain. "I'm just gonna climb in and fill a bag."

"Well, good luck with that. Since we're here, I may as well go give Delilah a visit, right?"

We pull up to the house and I hop out of the car, snatching a duffel bag from the back seat. With an obnoxious rev and wheel spin Dean shoots off into the late afternoon sunlight, leaving me to tackle my mission alone. The late afternoon sun casts a warm glow over the street, bathing the scene in a kaleidoscope of pink and orange hues. The branches of the trees stretch towards the sky, their leaves filtering the sunlight and casting intricate patterns of golden light across the pavement as I approach Sienna's window.

I glance vaguely up to the window, taking in the height as I mentally calculate the distance. With a swift burst of energy, I take a small run up and sprint towards the wall, my hands already grasping for the rough bricks as I launch myself up. The abrasive texture of the masonry scrapes against my palms as I climb.

With a grunt of effort, I reach the window ledge, fingers locking onto the frame with a vice-like grip. I continue to hold on with one arm and pry the window open with the other, the hinges protesting with a faint squeal. In a calculated motion, I propel myself upwards and into the room, landing with a purposely soft thud on the floor below.

Once inside, I take a moment to let the familiar surroundings sink in. Sienna's room is a haven of comfort, a reflection of her sweetness. Everywhere I look, there are touches of her warmth and affection. A riot of neutral and pastel colours, an abundance of teddies, plants galore and a fluffy pink cat tree. Blankets are strewn haphazardly across the bed, inviting and comforting in their disarray. The walls adorned with photographs, suncatchers casting rainbows across the room, and shelves overflowing with books; the very essence of her passions.

Her scent lingers in the air, a delicate mix of vanilla and sandalwood, calming me instantly.

I begin grabbing her clothes from the wardrobe and drawers. Every piece of clothing I handle is immaculately kept, carrying the scent of freshly laundered fabric softener. I marvel at the dainty size of each item in my hands, except for her adorably oversized jumpers that even I could practically swim in.

God, she looks so fucking sexy in those.

They make her seem so innocent, so pure, but I know better. I know the secret fire that burns beneath that soft exterior. The way she smiled as I gripped her throat on that motorbike.

Those damn jumpers, they fuck with my head, just like she does. So fucking adorable. But they hide her, and all I want to do is strip them off and show her she can't fucking hide from me. Show her just how much she drives me crazy. I imagine running my hands over her body, feeling the tremble of anticipation beneath my fingertips as she fights me verbally, yet arches against me, hungry for more. It's a fantasy I've played out a thousand times, each time more vivid than the last.

With deliberate care, I fold the clothes, taking pains to preserve them. As I finish packing, my eyes drift to the untouched bag of books in the corner; the ones I gave her just days ago. Untouched. The unopened pages seem to mock me, a tangible reminder of my haste and disregard. I curse under my breath, feeling a pang of regret for upending her life like this. Before I made the decision to change our lives.

I grab the bag of books with determination. Those books were meant for her, and she fucking deserves them, even if everything else has gone to shit. It's a small gesture, hopefully a reminder that I'm not a complete monster, despite what she might think at the moment.

As I sling the bag over my shoulder alongside the duffel, a sense of remorse washes over me. It's not often that I find myself second-guessing my actions, but at this moment, I can't shake the feeling that I've fucked her up too much. Maybe it's the way her room feels so empty without her, or maybe it's just the realisation of what I'm doing sinking in. Either way, it's not a feeling I'm used to, and it's one I'd rather not linger on.

I slip back out the window and tread down the familiar road, which is when it actually dawns on me that Dean has gone to see Delilah.

I'm gonna be waiting here for a long fucking time.

CHAPTER 9:
ALONE TIME

Dean

As my gorgeous Delilah opens the door, her lips part in a soft gasp. I'm sure she wasn't expecting to see me so soon.

"What are you doing here?" She asks with a squeal and a beaming smile.

"I'm here to see my girl, of course." I start, lifting her up. "We had some shit we needed to do a few roads up so I thought I'd pay you a visit." I carry her into the living room, planting kisses on her cheeks and forehead.

As our lips connect, there's an intense urgency in the way our hands clutch each other. Our hands begin to roam each other naturally, and fingers dig into skin. Our kisses are fierce, hungry, as if we're trying to devour each other whole. There's no room for softness here, no matter how delicate she is.

Just as things start to heat up, and our hands start exploring more daring territories, there's a sudden interruption. From the doorway comes an audible gag, followed by Birdie's unmistakable voice.

"Ew, get a room." To which I respond plainly.

"Actually, this is a room, that had a door, that was closed."

"So sorry, Dean. I wasn't aware that I was entering your love nest, I must've mistaken it for the living room." I roll my eyes at Birdie before turning my attention back to Delilah, who is trying her best to stifle her laughter.

"I'm guessing you've filled her in on everything." I start, but before Delilah has the time to reply, Birdie answers for me.

"Yes, Dean. I know all about it. I'm glad Sky warned me never to buy from you."

"Hold on-"

"Always knew you were a dodgy dealer."

"I'm not a dodgy dealer-"

"So can I watch TV or are you guys still planning on fondling each other in here?"

With a playful glint in her eyes, Delilah takes my hand and leads me towards the staircase.

"Let's go upstairs," she suggests, her voice dropping to a sultry whisper.

As we reach her bedroom our kisses continue, intensifying by the second. I grip and caress her body with eager hands, feeling the heat radiating off her skin as she pulls me closer, her nails digging into my back. But just as things start to escalate, Delilah suddenly pulls back, her breath coming in ragged gasps.

"Wait," she murmurs, her voice husky with desire. "I almost forgot." I watch, slightly dazed, as she reaches over to her dresser, retrieving a burner phone. With a swift motion, she places it in my hand, her fingers lingering against mine for a moment longer than necessary. "Here," she says, her eyes wide and loving, "So you can stay in contact, okay?"

I nod, barely able to form coherent words as the heat between us intensifies.

"Good idea, baby." Without wasting another moment, our lips crash together once more, hungry and insatiable.

I sit on the edge of the bed and pull her straddled onto my lap. She grinds slowly against me as I suck and nibble on her neck, my hands pressed against the small of her back.

"So fucking sexy." I whisper into her ear. I tug gently on her top and continue, "Take this off for me." Delilah complies, her movements fluid and graceful as she reveals her body for me.

I drink in the sight of her, utterly captivated by her beauty. I rub my face, attempting to conceal the elated smile that threatens to escape, and my eyes linger on hers.

"Fuck. I'm a lucky man, Delilah." Leaning in, I gently take one of her nipples into my mouth, sucking and nibbling on it lightly. Delilah lets out a soft moan, her hands coming up to run through my hair, guiding me. As I move from one breast to the other, I leave a trail of hickeys across her delicate skin. I can feel her heart pounding from beneath as I claim her.

With a breathless sigh, Delilah breaks away, her eyes dark with desire as she meets my gaze.

"Your turn," she whispers with a giggle, tugging on my shirt.

She's the cutest fucking thing on the planet.
I smirk as I discard my own shirt with a swift motion, revealing the contours of my chest and my awful self-drawn tattoos hiding

beneath the fabric. Delilah's eyes widen with appreciation as she takes in the sight before her, her fingers tracing the lines of my muscles with gentle reverence.

Unable to resist any longer, I darken my eyes.

"On your knees, baby." I instruct, my voice low and commanding. Delilah's eyes sparkle with a mix of desire and anticipation as she obeys my command, her body gracefully lowering to the ground. Just the sight of her on her knees is enough to finish me off. Her eyes travel down my body, taking in the sight of me, and I can see the hunger in her eyes. I grip her chin and pull her gaze up to meet mine.

"Show me how bad you want it." I demand. Delilah's hands shake slightly as she takes me out, her eyes never leaving mine. After a few moments, she reveals the full extent of my desire for her, my arousal standing proud.

"Such a good girl." She leans forward, her tongue darting out to trace the outline of my length. With a soft moan, she takes me into her mouth, her lips wrapped around me, her tongue swirling around my shaft. I grasp her hair, my fingers gently guiding her movements, my breath hitching as she takes me deeper.

"That's it, baby. Just like that." I encourage. Delilah's response is to redouble her efforts, her tongue flicking against my most sensitive spots as her lips move in rhythm.

Every sensation becomes magnified, sending waves of pleasure coursing through my body. Her tongue dances along my length with a skill that drives me wild, her mouth a haven of ecstasy as she takes me deeper, her lips tight around me. I can feel the tension coiling within me, the anticipation of release growing stronger with each passing moment.

"Fuck."

Feeling the time is right, I gently release her from her position on her knees, guiding her to stand. As she does, I take a moment to appreciate the sight of her body before me. She's a work of fucking art.

"You've earned this, my darling." I whisper. I lay her down on the bed, positioning myself between her legs. Swiftly, her shorts and knickers are removed, and I drop them to the floor beside me.

Leaning in, I gently pin her arms above her head as I enter her.

"God, Delilah. You're so wet."

"I know." She moans softly beneath me as she bites her lip. Her hips bucking slightly as I begin to move within her. Delilah's moans grow louder, more fervent, her breaths coming in short, sharp gasps. Her body undulates, her breasts bouncing with each thrust, her nipples hardening into small, erect peaks.

"Harder." She whimpers. With a growl, I oblige to my girl's demands, thrusting deeper into her pussy, our bodies now moving in perfect harmony; every muscle, every nerve, every fibre.

"Holy fuck-" she cries out, her nails digging into my back.

"You like that, baby? You like the way I fuck that little pussy? Tell me how much you fucking like it."
I feel her walls clenching around me, urging me on, pushing me to the brink of madness. With each thrust, I can sense her release drawing nearer, and it ignites a fierce hunger within me. I drive into her relentlessly, the sound of our bodies colliding fills the room. Her eyes roll back in her head, pleasure coursing through her veins like wildfire.

"Use your words."

"Dean, I'm gonna-" she pants, her words barely coherent amidst her pleasure.

"Good. Come for me." Delilah's body tenses beneath me, her nails digging into my back as she rides the waves of pleasure crashing over her. Her moans grow louder, more urgent, as she approaches the peak of ecstasy.

"You're taking it so well, baby." I whisper with a smirk. With a primal cry, she shatters, her release cascading. I feel her walls pulsating around me, draining me for all I'm worth. "Fuck, Delilah."

As I feel Delilah's climax enveloping her, I surrender to the mounting pressure within me. With a primal roar, I spill into her, our essences mingling in a frenzy of lust.

As our panting breaths begin to slow, I kiss and caress her body, a smirk stuck arrogantly on my lips. Delilah lies there, with the body of a goddess; her skin glistening with sweat.

"I'm so proud of you." I whisper, my voice low and gravelly in her ear. "I could live inside that fucking pussy." I press a lingering kiss to her neck, my hands roaming over her trembling form. With a playful grin, I continue, "I bet you could take more too, couldn't you? My dirty little girl." She nods subtly, her eyes heavy.

"I love you." she whispers. I place a firm kiss on her temple before standing up.

"I love you more." Her eyes flutter shut and a cheesy smile takes over my face. "Looks like somebody's tired." I play.

With delicate care, I clean Delilah up, my fingertips tracing the contours of her skin with tender precision. As I dress her in a soft, buttery yellow nightgown, the fabric whispers sweet nothings against her curves, moulding itself to her form like a gentle lover as I slide it over her body.

Once she's freshened up, I move to the window and draw the curtains closed, dimming the room to create a tranquil atmosphere. The soft, diffused light casts a warm glow over Delilah's form as I turn my attention back to her.

As I step back to survey my handiwork, the room now cloaked in darkness, I notice her childhood teddy bear sitting on the bedside table. Her Grandmother had bought it for her as a kid. I remember it being practically glued to her hand when we were in the home. With a warm smile, I pick him up and place him gently in Delilah's arms.

"Our old friend." I say softly, a tender smile gracing my lips. "He'll watch over you while I'm gone. Isn't that right mate?" I pretend to ask her little friend. She laughs sleepily as I brush a stray lock of hair away from her face, tucking it behind her ear.

Before I leave, I pull a fluffy blanket from the foot of the bed and carefully drape it over her. I take a moment to ensure it's positioned just right; cocooning her properly.

"Be safe." she murmurs.

"Always." With a final tender kiss pressed to her forehead, I watch over her for a moment longer. Then, with a lingering glance, I quietly slip out of the room, leaving Delilah to drift off into dreams, knowing she's safe, satisfied and cherished.

As she *always* fucking should be.

CHAPTER 10:
SWEETS

Sienna

The door pounds open, which means that Marcus is finally back. I quickly turn away from the door to fix my hair and reapply a subtle layer of lip gloss.

God he makes me so nervous.

How do I handle myself? Attitude? Silent treatment? Kiss him? *No Sienna, you idiot.*

"Where have you been?" I snap. He doesn't respond, instead he shoots me a cold glare and a faint smile, dropping several bags in front of his feet, unzipping the big black duffel that was previously holding a gun.

"Take a guess." he says calmly, his tone betraying nothing.

My eyes flicker down to the bags, and I notice with a mixture of surprise and confusion that the duffel is filled with my clothes, neatly folded; while beside it sits the bag of books he had bought for me. The unexpected sight strikes me dumb, my ire momentarily tempered by a mix of fascination and a flicker of appreciation, as if my anger's fiery passion has been doused by the cool waters of curiosity.

"You went to get my stuff?" I ask softly.

"I told you I'd take care of it, didn't I?" he responds, his words laced with a hint of arrogance. I bristle at his tone, torn between gratitude and resentment at his control over me. Despite the gesture, I can't forget the truth of our situation. Yes, Marcus may have brought me my belongings, but I'm still his captive.

"You could have just let me leave, you know. It would've been a lot easier for both of us." I fire back, a trace of defiance seeping into my tone, and Marcus' laughter follows, a low, husky sound that sends a thrill coursing through me as he steps to the side. His eyes flicker between the door and I, a calculating glint in their depths, before settling back on me with a subtle intensity.

"The door's unlocked right now, sweet. Go ahead and leave," he challenges, his eyes locking onto mine with an intensity that makes my heart race. I hesitate, the weight of his words pressing down on me. Despite the opportunity before me, a part of me is reluctant to seize it. Deep down, I know that I'm drawn to him in ways I can't explain.

So I stand there. I just stand there.

"Changed your mind, huh?" he taunts, raising an eyebrow knowingly. I say nothing. What is there to say? He has me exactly where he wants me and honestly, I'm more than happy to be here.

Before I can respond, he locks the door behind him with a deliberate slowness. I watch him warily as he reaches into one of the bags, withdrawing a small packet of love heart sweets. His actions are calculated and the truth is I'm struggling to keep up.

With a playful grin, Marcus takes a few more steps toward me, the distance between us narrowing with each deliberate stride. He opens the bag of sweets and shakes them lightly.

"Come here," he commands, his tone firm yet strangely enticing. I obey with little hesitation, drawn to him like a moth to a flame. As I stand before him, my pulse racing madly, Marcus reaches out to take hold of my chin, tilting my head back slightly.

"Now, open your mouth," he instructs, his voice a terrifying whisper. I hesitate once more, gulping nervously as I look up at him.

"Open, Sienna. Tongue out." I comply, parting my lips as Marcus places a single sweet on my tongue. I hold my breath, waiting for his next move. My heart is racing so swiftly that I can barely catch my breath. It's as though it's attempting to break free of its confines entirely.

"You feel that?" he asks, his voice vibrating in my ears. "That instinct to swallow as the sweetness lingers on the tip of your tongue," He pauses and breathes in passionately through his nose. "But you resist. You keep it in place no matter how tempting." he continues, "Well that's my fucking life, Sienna. Constantly resisting the urge to consume you entirely."

"And yet, regardless of how much it fights against you, against all your instincts," he adds, a hint of a smirk playing on his lips, "letting this sweet fall off that pretty little tongue is something you haven't even considered, right?"
I shake my head, the motion so subtle it's almost imperceptible. I'm unsure if I even moved at all.

"Sweet," he sneers, his tone laced with venom, "you can fight against me until the day you die, but the thought of letting you go, of losing you, has never once crossed my mind. You're stuck with me, whether you like it or not," he smiles, "and we both know you fucking love it."

Marcus watches me closely, his eyes dark with desire and something else I can't quite place. Riskily, I give in to the sweetness on my tongue and swallow, feeling his intense stare like a heated touch against my skin. Now I consider taking another risk, a big one. The thought lingers in my mind for a few moments as I consider my choices.

Fuck it.

"Then do it." I suggest softly but with confidence. "Consume me."

His eyes widen slightly, caught off guard by my boldness. A slow, predatory smile spreads across his lips as he closes the distance between us, his presence overwhelming. A primal hunger flashes in his eyes, and before I can even react, he's upon me. With a swift, almost feral movement, he grabs me and throws me onto the bed, his strength overpowering. I gasp in surprise, the air knocked out of me as I find myself pinned beneath him.

"Remember, you asked for this." he warns.

Before I can protest or even catch my breath, he's tearing at my clothing with a raw urgency, stripping away the barriers between us. His touch is rough, almost bruising, as he exposes my lower half to him. And then, without a word, he descends upon me with a ferocity that steals my breath away. Gripping to the flesh on my thighs and spreading my legs, his mouth finds me hungrily; his movements unyielding and demanding as he does

267

exactly as I asked. He consumes me. Consumes me with an intensity that leaves me trembling in his grasp.

His tongue darts and thrusts, exploring every inch of me with a fervour that leaves me breathless. Each suck and pull sends shockwaves of pleasure coursing through my body, making my back arch involuntarily. The sound of his lips smacking against my skin fills the room, punctuated by the occasional soft growl escaping his lips.

His hands grip my thighs tightly. Very tightly. Pinching me. Holding me in place as he ravages me with unabashed desire. I can feel his beard stubble against my sensitive skin, adding another layer of slightly painful sensation. His name escapes my lips, a plea for him to stop. *Or to continue.* That part, I haven't quite decided. I feel his hot breath against my skin as he pulls away, a sly smile playing on his lips. Without warning, he spits. His eyes bore into mine, a silent challenge in his gaze as he watches for my reaction.

I have no reaction except to lay my head back onto the bed. I can't comprehend anything happening to me right now. I can't comprehend how one man can be so disrespectful and so rough yet so fucking sexy.

Just as I think it's over, he slaps my inner thigh, hard, causing a squeal to leave my lips. His hand leaving a stinging mark on my skin.

He slowly rubs his hand against my swollen clit, hard and demanding. Suddenly he slides two fingers inside, immediately pumping deeply into me. My nails claw into the sheets and an uncontrollable moan leaves my lips.

"Oh, sweet." he smiles, "You're soaked. You like this, don't you?" His words are barely comprehensible in my mind as fingers continue ramming into me. "Who knew my precious angel would enjoy being used like a dirty little slut?" I can only nod, my body trembling with pleasure as he continues to degrade me.

He grips me roughly once more, pinning my legs up by my side, higher than I even thought they could go. His fingers digging into my flesh as he positions himself over me once again. He drives his tongue into me with a force that borders on painful. But it's a good pain. The kind of pain you miss when it leaves.

And then, without warning, he spits on me once again, aiming purposely for my clit; the act rough and demeaning, but causing a surge of desire to flood through me. He licks up the saliva, his tongue flicking against me as I cry out in pleasure. He replaces his tongue with his fingers once more, as he bites down hard on my inner thigh, his teeth leaving a mark instantly.

He moves to the side of me now, towering over my exposed body. Marcus's fingers bury deep inside me, his other hand gripping my hip as he pumps in and out with aggressive, relentless movements. As he continues to dominate me, he grabs my hair, pulling my head back to expose my neck to him.

"That's it, sweet," he growls, his voice filled with desire and malice. "Come for me. Come hard while I finger-fuck you like the dirty little girl you really are." My pussy clenches around his fingers, desperate for more, desperate for him to ruin me completely.

He pushes into me once more. This time, it's slow, hard and out of pattern. His fingers lingering and vibrating deep inside. I cry out for him as I reach my release, my body convulsing as pleasure engulfs me. The room seems to spin as I reach the pinnacle. As I orgasm, feeling the wetness spread between my

Chapter 10

legs, he's watching me like a hawk. With a satisfied look, he adjusts himself, witnessing me unravel before him.

Finally, he slides his fingers out of me, but before I can catch my breath he grabs my face, squeezing my cheeks, forcing my mouth open. He leans down, his lips brushing against my ear as he shoves his fingers deep down my throat.

"Suck on them. Taste yourself." I struggle against him, but he holds my head in place, his fingers thrusting in and out of my mouth, choking me slightly as he does so. I obey him and begin to suck. "There you go, good girl." His fingers thrust deeper, his thumb rubbing against my cheek. My eyes water from the force he uses to hold my head but, enjoying the praise, I continue to do as he told me, swallowing my own essence.

He stops, pulling his fingers out of my mouth and wiping a tear from the corner of my eye as I sit up; finally taking in a good deep breath.

"Aww," he taunts with a smirk. "How pathetic, sweet." He steps back, his smirk growing as he studies my reaction before continuing to tease me. "If you can't even handle my fingers, how do you expect to take my dick?" I don't respond, but the thought of it makes me throb with need.

He removes his shirt and crouches in front of me.

"Don't worry, sweet. When I decide to fuck you I'll make sure you handle my cock. I'll make sure you take every fucking inch."
As the filth leaves his mouth all I can do is stare in awe. I gulp and nod like an idiot, not even sure if I'm fully listening. Staring into those gorgeous eyes, seeing the sweat glisten on his perfect face, I'm not certain that he's even real. I'm not certain that *I'm* even real.

"That's it," he continues, "Imagine it. Think about me thrusting deep inside you, stretching you beyond your limits."
Oh, don't worry. I'm imagining it.

"I'm gonna take what I fucking want from you, Sienna. I'll make sure of it. I won't stop until those pretty little tears are streaming down your face."

I believe him, and though I'd never admit it, I can't fucking wait. He stands again, his 6ft4 shirtless body towering over me. The room falls to silence, and he doesn't take his eyes off me, not once, despite the fact that I'm not looking back. I'm looking at his body. It's no secret that Marcus is sexy. I've always known that. But right now, in this moment, it's like I'm seeing him for the first time all over again.

My eyes trace the lines of his chest, where beads of sweat cling to the taut muscles, highlighting every ripple and ridge. His abs are a work of art, sculpted and defined. As his chest rises and falls, his dark hair lies tousled and damp from the effort he just exerted into pleasing me.

He chuckles lightly as he watches me ogling him, the dimple on his cheek sitting deep.
"What you thinking about?"
"I don't think I've ever noticed that tattoo," I blurt out. He's covered in them, and I pay attention to them; or so I thought, "Is it new?" I ask, finally looking back up at him.
"I did it myself a few nights ago." he replies calmly.

"It's a spider."
"Correct," he laughs. "A shy one."
Marcus winks at me, his smile intimate and genuine. I try to hide my grin by biting my lip, but it's no use. I'm too flattered. He really is obsessed with me. The mere consideration of having my

character from his book permanently inked onto his skin is so incredibly beautiful.

"I like it." I whisper.

"Sorry, you *like* one of my tattoos?"

"Just that one."

"Well, I guess I'll have to consider keeping that one then."

"Funny," I say, my eyes roaming his body once again. "You genuinely don't have room for any more. Well, unless you plan on getting one down there." I add with a mischievous grin, gesturing subtly to the bulge in his grey tracksuit bottoms.

"I think 'Choking Hazard' would be quite fitting."

"Gross."

My eyes linger on Marcus's chest, tracing the lines of his muscles as he chuckles, the sound like music to my ears. His dimple deepens, a crease of pleasure etching itself on his face, and I'm caught in the undertow of his charm, my heart swelling with a warmth that's hard to ignore. He leans in, pressing a gentle kiss to my forehead, his lips warm against my skin.

"You're fucking adorable, sweet." he murmurs, his voice low and affectionate. I smile up at him, my heart fluttering in my chest at his words.

I watch as Marcus reaches for a joint, deft fingers rolling it with practised ease. As he lights it, the room is filled with the earthy scent of cannabis. Taking a puff, he exhales slowly, the smoke curling around him like a wisp of temptation. His eyes meet mine, a glimmer of mischief dancing within them as he speaks.

"Now, naughty girl." he mumbles, the joint held between his teeth "Get some sleep," he says, his voice low and teasing, a hint of authority underlying his words.

"Okay."

CHAPTER 11:
TRACKER TROUBLE

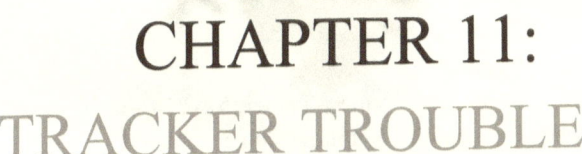

Skylar walks out of her room and, as usual, she immediately begins to verbally assault me.

"What the fuck are you doing?"

I shimmy myself out from underneath the car to respond, as this pink-haired dictator looks down at me; a very scary iced coffee in her hand.

"Ice skating." I respond sarcastically.

"Dickhead." she scowls. "For real though, what are you doing?"

"Thank you so much for that completely unnecessary insult." she doesn't respond and instead just scrunches her nose up at me, "I'm making sure there isn't a tracker." Skylar's eyebrows shoot up in surprise, followed by a burst of laughter.

"A tracker? Who do you think you are, James Bond?" she mocks, taking a sip of her iced coffee, causing me to wonder where the fuck she got an iced coffee from and why she didn't

273

get one for me. I sigh and continue inspecting the underside of the car.

"I took it from Razor's warehouse." I explain.

"So? They're not the Mafia."

My God, she gets more insufferable by the minute.

"That's not the point. He works for Grizzly, that's nothing to scoff at."

"Paranoid much? Maybe it's the shitty weed you smoke."

"Could you do me a favour, Sky?" I ask in an attempt to set her up; intending to follow with a 'fuck off'.

"No." she replies bluntly, completely slaughtering my joke. I slide out from under the car with a dramatic huff, standing up and brushing off imaginary dirt like a failed car mechanic wannabe.

"Look, I don't have time for your babbling."

"You know, if these guys do catch you, can I have your gun collection?"

"Sure, I'll put it in my will."

I get back to business, poking and prodding around the engine components. There's no way Grizzly's men haven't slapped trackers on their vehicles; and I'm not about to be caught off guard. As I delve deeper into the engine bay, my fingers graze something metallic. With a careless flick of my wrist, I reach for what seems like an innocent wire, only to be met with a surge of electricity that shoots all the way up my arm.

"Fuck!" I shout, as my body is thrown backwards.

The pain is unbearable, like a thousand needles stabbing me all at once. My muscles seize up, and I swear I'm staring down the Grim Reaper himself. Sparks fly, and for a moment, all I can see is blinding white light. The smell of burnt flesh fills the air, and my heart feels like it's about to leap out of my chest. Skylar, startled by my very embarrassing electrocution, rushes over, her eyes wide with panic.

"Dean! Oh my God, are you okay?" I can barely form words, still reeling from the shock, instead I nod, catching my breath.

Skylar's face pales as she looks down at my hand and realises the severity of the situation. My skin instantly blistered and my hand trembling beyond description.

"Shit, we need to get you to a hospital."

"No," I insist snappily, "I'm fine, honestly. Just give me a minute."

I sit there, shock still coursing through me. I begin to think and dwell on the series of near misses I've encountered recently. The incident in the car, the tree falling out of nowhere, now this? It's like I'm constantly dancing on the edge of a blade, tempting fate with every step.

Skylar's concerned voice cuts through my thoughts, pulling me back to the present.

"Dean? You okay?" I blink, realising I've been lost in my own head for God knows how long.

"Yeah, I'm fine," I mutter as I pull myself up onto my feet, trying to push aside the mounting nerves gnawing at my insides. But deep down, I know I'm not fooling anyone; least of all Skylar.

She raises an eyebrow, clearly not buying my feeble reassurance.

"You sure? You look a little fucked up." I hesitate, unsure how to put my sudden existential crisis into words. But as I look into Skylar's eyes, so full of genuine concern, I know I shouldn't keep it bottled.

"It's just, this is the third time after leaving London that I've almost been killed. I nearly crashed the car on the way down here; and when that tree fell down," I explain pointing at the tree next to my room, "it was as if it was aiming right at me." Sky listens intently, as she quickly pans her eyes to the fallen tree. "I don't know, Sky. I'm sure I'm overthinking, but after this it feels like I may be tempting fate."

Skylar bites her nail and scrunches her face, which suggests to me that something is concerning her.

"What?" I ask softly.

"I probably shouldn't bring it up, but do you think it could be related to the book in some way?" I shake my head adamantly, the idea of the book having anything to do with anything else in our lives isn't something I even want to entertain.

"Nah." I reply, dismissing the notion outright, "We sealed it tight. The book is dead and buried."

Skylar nods, a smile gracing her face. But it's weak, and it doesn't quite reach her eyes.

"Yeah, you're right." she says, though her voice lacks conviction. "It's probably just your karma for dealing dodgy drugs." I muster the energy to grin at Skylar's quip, enjoying the banter.

I feign a cough, my hands settling lightly on my knees as I pretend to double over, a ruse designed to unnerve Skylar. Her eyes dart towards me, and she startles, her hand shooting out to settle on my back in a gesture of concern.

"You good?" she asks.

"Yeah fine," I say, purposefully straining my voice "Can you just do me a favour?"

"Yeah, of course-" Skylar begins, but I cut her off abruptly with a forceful push, shoving her onto the grass beside us.

"Fuck off." I retort, the words laced with playful aggression.

"Dean!"

CHAPTER 12:
BREAKING THE RULE
Sienna

ONE WEEK LATER.

It's 6:24p.m.

Marcus left the room to go and talk to Dean about an hour ago.

He forgot to lock the door.

I've spent the last hour thinking. My mind keeps circling back through the same mismatched thoughts, like a record stuck on repeat. I don't particularly care about escaping this place. Sure, I miss my mother, but the truth is I would miss Marcus a whole lot more. I want to be here with him. Yet, there's an undeniable urge within me to get out, to see the countryside, to know where I am exactly, to just breathe some fresh air.

Be a little rebellious.
Prove a point.

My brain is entirely split, torn between conflicting desires. So many thoughts running through me that my mind is eerily silent. I need a break from this room. But Marcus made it clear that if I left, he would punish me.

And the unsettling part is, I think I want him to punish me.

But it's not right, is it? Marcus keeping me here like this. I should be screaming for freedom, for the autonomy to make my own choices. But what if I enjoy being treated like this? Is that so wrong? That I enjoy the way he controls me, protects me.

I've been trying to figure out why he hasn't gone the full way with me, despite me finally admitting that I wanted it. It's a persistent itch I can't scratch.

But I'm sure this would push him there.

The question is can I handle it? Is he bluffing, using fear to keep me tethered to his side? To keep me safe. Or does he truly intend to push me to my limits? Break me entirely. I'm battling with my morality but deep down I know exactly what I want. All I want right now is to be at his mercy, to feel the weight of his control bearing down on me. I want to be degraded, humiliated, ruined beyond recognition. It's a twisted desire, one that I can hardly bring myself to admit, even to myself.

But it's the truth.

With it settled in my mind, I bite the bullet. I head towards the door and make my way outside. The warm evening air kisses my skin as I take a deep dramatic breath. A soft glow over the landscape illuminates my path as I cautiously sneak my way past the cottage where Marcus is undoubtedly preoccupied.

Every rustle of the bushes and crunch of gravel beneath my feet feels amplified in the stillness of the evening, heightening my awareness of the risk I'm taking. The urge to glance back, to ensure I haven't been detected, tugs at the corners of my mind, but I resist. The countryside stretches out before me, vast and inviting, with fields of verdant green rolling gently into the horizon.

I wander aimlessly, revelling in the sensation of grass beneath my feet and the whisper of the wind in my ears. Every step feels like a tiny victory for me. Like I'm getting back that teasing sliver of control I used to have over him. I drink in the beauty of the landscape, letting the sights and sounds fill me. It's peaceful. So peaceful, and I wish Marcus was here to see it with me.

As I perch against a weathered fence, watching the sun sink below the horizon, a sense of tranquillity washes over me. The sky transforms into a canvas of fiery hues, casting a warm, aureate glow over the landscape. The distant chirping of crickets and the gentle rustle of leaves in the breeze form a comforting backdrop, lulling me into a momentary state of peace and reverie.

For a while, I allow myself to simply exist in this serene setting, letting the beauty of the evening envelop me. The colours of the sky deepen, painting streaks of orange and pink across the heavens, and I find myself mesmerised by the dance of light and shadow.

But amidst the breathtaking beauty of the sunset, memories of my parents begin to seep into my thoughts like gentle whispers. I close my eyes, allowing their faces to materialise in my mind's eye. I miss them so much. The pain of their absence is like a wound that never fully heals, a constant ache that's always there, lingering beneath the surface. They were good people. Pure. Quiet. Tears prick at the corners of my eyes as I remember them; my father's warm smile, my mother's gentle touch. I recall the small, everyday moments we shared. But the memories are tainted by the pain of their loss, their sudden and brutal deaths.

I'll never forget the day they were taken from me. The visions I have about their final moments. It must have been terrifying for them.

I recall the way my father's eyes would light up when he spoke of the kind of love I deserve; the kind that would cradle, cherish and shield me, that would accept me without condition. He'd whisper stories of the person who would one day make my heart sing, who would love me with an unwavering devotion.

Marcus is that person.

Sure, he's not a perfect person. Far from it. In fact, he's a very bad person, evil even. But he's good to me. There's a fierceness in him; a pure and obsessive determination to love me and keep me safe at all costs, that I know my father would appreciate. He looks at me the same way my dad used to look at my mum. As if she was the centre of his entire universe.

With a heavy heart, I watch as the last traces of daylight fade into darkness. Each flicker of light extinguished feels like a small farewell.

Hours slip by unnoticed as I sit there, under the stars, alone with my thoughts. And then, as if from out of the darkness itself, I'm startled by the sound of gravel crunching. A car approaches. A black car with tinted windows, its engine purring softly as it slows almost to a stop behind me. Its presence is ominous and creepy. Cold, paralysing fear grips my heart. The hairs on the back of my neck stand on end as a shiver runs down my spine.

Instinctively, I rise to my feet, my heart pounding in my chest as I watch the car slowly pass me. On autopilot, I rise to my feet, my eyes fixed on the receding brake lights. I think it's time to leave.

As I approach the cottage, my paranoia begins to seep into my bones like a chill. Every flicker of movement, every creak of a branch, seems to take on a menacing quality. I'm convinced that the shadows themselves are closing in on me. But as I pause, my breath fogging in the misty air, I begin to realise I'm probably being overly dramatic. My imagination is running riot, conjuring up monsters from every tree and rock. Maybe Marcus was right. I shouldn't have wandered out here on my own.

I walk back past Dean's cottage and notice the lights off. Marcus must have gone back. Standing at the door, I feel a wild mix of nerves and, dare I say it, excitement. I know he'll be furious that I left and I don't know what insane punishment he's planning on giving me, yet here I stand, holding in my squeals of excitement over the thought of it. I hover there, hand trembling over the door handle, battling with myself. Should I go in? Or should I wait, relish in this moment of defiance a little longer?

But as the door swings open and I'm yanked into the room by my hair, it's safe to say the decision is made on my behalf.

CHAPTER 13:
CONSEQUENCES

Marcus

As I sit on the edge of the bed, I'm well aware that one of two things have happened here. Either Sienna is genuinely attempting to get away from me and therefore I'm about to spend my night riding around until I find her; or she's about to walk back in here and realise just how serious my threats are.

Though she'd never give me the credit, I know Sienna now. I know exactly how she works. Exactly what she's thinking. She wouldn't leave. She's testing me. She wants me to crack. She's desperate for it. I see the hunger in her eyes. She wants more, and maybe I should've already given it to her. I was trying not to push her too far, but clearly I didn't push her far enough; and that's about to change.

Then it happens. I hear Sienna's footsteps approaching on the gravel outside. I rise from the bed with a controlled grace and crack my neck. I approach the door, shifting all my weight with each slow, calculated step. A predator stalking its prey, my senses sharp and attuned to every sound and movement.

As the door handle twitches under her hesitant touch, a smirk twists my lips into a smug grin. The poor thing. So fucking cute. She's second-guessing herself, debating whether she should face the storm she's unleashed. The thought elicits another low laugh, a primal sound that reverberates with a promise of impending retribution.

In one swift motion, I yank open the door, the wood slamming against the wall with a satisfying thud. Before Sienna can react, I grab a fistful of her hair, and pull her into the room with a forceful tug, shutting the door instantly behind us. She stumbles forward, caught off guard by my sudden aggression, but I show no mercy. With one hand tangled in her hair, I pull her close, feeling the heat radiating off her skin. My other hand finds her wrists, twisting them behind her back, pinning her against me.

"Look who decided to come back."

"I can explain-" I give her no time to even think of an explanation before I snatch her, lifting her off her feet and carrying her towards the dining table. The moment we reach it, I slam her down onto the wooden surface, her back meeting the cold, hard material with a thud. Her eyes widen further as she struggles to catch her breath, her body arching slightly under the sudden impact.

Quickly, I position myself above her, pinning her arms above her head with one hand, my other hand resting on the table next to her face.

"If I knew you were this desperate to take my fucking cock, I would've given it to you sooner." I say before I rip off her shorts and throw them to the ground.

Pulling out my butterfly knife from my pocket, I watch her pupils dilate.

"I don't want-" she lies.

"Then why did you come back? Huh?"

I grip the handle of the knife, my fingers tightening around it, feeling the cold steel beneath my touch. With a stern face, I slide the knife's blade under the fabric of her top, cutting through it with a rough, unyielding motion. The material parts like a curtain, revealing her bare skin.

Her eyes, filled with a mixture of fear and desire, meet mine as I continue to cut, the knife dancing over her skin, leaving a trail of goosebumps in its wake. The knife glides through her knickers next, tearing the fabric away from her body, leaving her exposed and vulnerable.

"Marcus, please-"

"Then fight, sweet. Show me what you've got." I growl, my voice dripping with menace as I press the tip of the knife against her skin, tracing lazy circles along her beautiful body.

She hesitates for a moment, her body tense with anticipation. And then, with a sudden burst of strength, she obeys. She kicks out at me, her movements frantic but not entirely serious. There's no conviction. It's a feeble attempt to fight me off. She wants this and I'm more than happy to oblige.

But hey, at least she's learning to follow orders.

As much as I'd love to kiss that gorgeous fucking body and hold her close, I don't waste time on pleasantries or pretences. This is punishment, and I intend to make it crystal clear. I spit on her pretty little pussy, the saliva landing with a small splatter on her sensitive skin. A weak attempt to lubricate her. Then, without any hesitation, I thrust my fingers into her, not caring if it hurts. Hoping it hurts.

As I finger fuck her roughly, I can feel her muscles clenching around my fingers, her body trying to find some semblance of pleasure amidst the pain. Her body continues to tremble and she tries to catch her breath, but the sensation from my fingers still inside her persists.

"Marcus, stop." she whines pathetically. I smirk, enjoying the sight of her vulnerability.

"Stop? I'm just getting started, sweet." I reply, my fingers still thrusting inside her, my grip on her wrists tightening. I'm not stopping. She doesn't want that. I'm going to make her come, over and over again. I want her arousal dripping down my fingers.

I increase the pace, enjoying the sight of her struggling against my invasion. I twist my fingers, exploring her depths, making sure she knows I'm in control. Her body responds to my touch, her hips bucking against my hand, but I hold her in place, her legs spread wide, her body at my mercy.

The minutes pass, and her moans become more frenzied, her body trembling with anticipation. I can feel her tight walls clenching around my fingers, and I know she's close.

Then, without warning, she cries out in pleasure as she comes against her will. Her body convulses, her eyes wide with a mix of shock, pain, and the raw intensity of her unwanted orgasm.

"Did I tell you to fucking come? Huh?" I ask. As she shakes her head, I deliver a sharp slap to her swollen clit, causing her to squeal in pain. I force her legs apart even wider, spreading her come-soaked pussy with my fingers, making sure they're covered.

As I stand over her trembling body, I hold my fingers up.

"Look at the mess you've made." I say, my voice dripping with disdain. I slowly spread her come across my fingers, making sure she can see. I watch her eyes widen, a mix of shame and arousal still present.

I know she's caught between wanting more and hating me for it. But that's exactly what her punishment is.

I slowly bring my fingers to my mouth, savouring the taste of her. No drop going to waste. The act intended to degrade her further, to show her that, at this moment, she's nothing more than a fucktoy for my pleasure. And it's all her fault.

I drag her from the table and position her over my knee as I sit on the edge of the bed. I hold her securely, her hands bound behind her back as I trace my fingers slowly down her body, each touch a teasing promise of the pain to come.

"Why did you leave, Sienna?" I ask calmly.

"I'm sorry." I spank her ass hard, my hand connecting with her flesh in a rough, deliberate motion.

"That's not an answer."

"I-I don't know." In response, I deliver another swat to her ass, this time harder and more forceful. My hand leaving a burning sensation that she can't ignore.

"Don't lie to me." I pull firmer on her restrained wrists and a whimper leaves her lips. "You wanted me to fucking punish you. Right?" I taunt, my voice dripping with malice before I strike her again. She manages a faint "Yes," her voice shaking with emotion.

I dig my nails into her skin and scratch up the back of her thigh, followed by one more smack to her ass, causing her to cry out even louder; her body trembling under the force of my hand. As a tear rolls down her cheek, I taunt her.

"It's okay to cry, little one. I enjoy seeing you weep for me." I wet two fingers with spit and push them back inside her cunt. Pumping slowly.

"*This* time, sweet, you have my permission. I'll give you thirty seconds, and you better fucking come." I have no intention of timing her. My angel can take as long as she wants, but I don't want her knowing that. Her moans fill the otherwise-silent room as I twist and drive my fingers deep inside her. My rhythm is steady.

"Time is ticking, pretty." I taunt. I feel her inner walls clenching around my fingers, a desperate grip of submission pulling me deeper into her abyss. Each quake that racks her body sending vibrations of primal satisfaction coursing through me. Her ass bouncing with every jolt of my fingers. I press closer, my breath a searing brand against her ear

"Are you learning your lesson?" She doesn't respond, I don't expect her to. And then, with a final, guttural wail, she capitulates utterly, her body a vessel for the overwhelming sensations crashing over her.

She collapses against me, spent and trembling; the dripping evidence of her obedience covering my fingers. I don't stop. With a predatory grin, I continue to ravish her relentlessly. I increase the pressure of my fingers, pushing her past the point of pleasure into a realm of pure agony. She's already broken. She's mine, completely and utterly, to use and abuse as I please. And I'll make sure she never forgets it.

I stare down at her, bruised and crying, and whisper close to her body.

"You think you can take more, sweet?" Reluctantly, and to my genuine surprise, she nods her head, a silent agreement to endure more of my cruelty.

"Are you sure?" I confirm, raising an eyebrow.

"Yes, I'm sure."

"That's it, sweet. Take every fucking inch. My dirty little slut." I slam into her, my body moving with a ferocity that leaves her breathless.

Her cries grow louder, her body arching to meet mine, her submission evident in every movement. As I notice a tiny drop of blood I'm like a fucking shark. The sight of her torn cunt being assaulted by my cock only fueling my aggression further.

"You're doing so well, beautiful. Such a brave girl." I grip her throat, my fingers digging into her delicate skin. She tries to struggle, but I hold her in place, my eyes locked onto her.

"Remember, you deserve this. I warned you. I'm gonna have my fucking way with you until *I* decide you've had enough."

I can feel my release drawing near and the thought of filling her with my come isn't even a debate. I smack her ass and grab her hair again, using it to control her movements.

"Are you ready to take my come, sweet?"
She doesn't reply. I pull out slightly, my cock glistening with her arousal, I look down at her and issue my command.

"Beg for my come. Beg me to fill that tight little pussy." She doesn't. Instead she continues to whimper and cry. Not good enough. Seeing her faux-reluctance, I decide to force it out of her. I press the tip of my thumb against her asshole, causing her to flinch and cry out in pain. Her body tenses, but I don't relent.

"Now, Sienna. Beg."

"Fuck-" she mumbles, "Please." I press harder.

"Please what?"

"Please.. fill me." Hearing her beg, I remove my thumb.

"Good girl, there you go. I'll make sure I give you every last fucking drop." With that, I push my cock back into her, feeling her pussy clench around me in response. I pull her hair even tighter, forcing her to arch her back and take my dick deeper than ever before. "Fuck, Sienna. You feel so good."

As I reach my release, I continue to fuck her with reckless abandon, my dick sliding in and out of her wet pussy with a lewd slapping sound. With a final, powerful thrust, I release my come into her, as deep as possible, filling her with the evidence of her degradation. I can feel the warm liquid spilling inside her, coating her walls. I stay buried inside her for a few moments, making sure she takes all of me. I pull out slowly, my cock glistening with fluid, feeling her pussy grip me.

As I step back, I spit on her one last time, a final act of degradation before I leave her there, lying in the aftermath of our encounter. My come leaking from her hole. Her panting, spent body trembling. I've claimed her now. Taken her in the most brutal way possible.

"God, look at you. You're so fucking beautiful."

I pull up my joggers and approach her slowly, my steps deliberate and purposeful, until I'm standing right beside her, looking down at her trembling form. With a predatory gleam in my eyes, I crouch down to her eye level, my glare piercing through her.

"Sweet," I growl, my voice low and commanding. "Don't you ever leave this fucking room again." I reach out and grab her chin, forcing her to look at me. Tears still filling her eyes. "Do you understand?" She nods weakly. She knows better than to disobey me now.

CHAPTER 14:
BUTTER

Marcus

I wake up my sleeping angel with a rough shake, my hand gripping her delicate shoulder.

"Wake up, sweet," I growl, my voice low and commanding. She stirs, blinking sleepily as she tries to focus on me.

"What's.. what's going on?" she mumbles, her voice groggy. I can't help but admire the way her hair tumbles across her pillow, her tousled curls framing her face in a way that makes my heart skip a beat. But I push those thoughts aside, focusing on the matter at hand. Ignoring her question, I press on.

"What sandwiches do you like the most?" I demand, my tone brooking no argument. She blinks, taken aback by the abruptness of my random question.

"Um, I don't know," she stammers, her confusion evident. I grit my teeth, playful frustration simmering beneath the surface.

"Well, figure it out," I snap, "I'm not asking again." With a sigh, she nods, understanding the urgency in my tone.

"Okay, okay," she says, scrambling to gather her thoughts. She bites her bottom lip briefly and a tiny 'hm' comes from her mouth.

She's perfect. She really is fucking perfect.
I can't take my eyes off her.

Finally, she speaks, her voice hesitant.

"Ham and cheese?" she says, her words tentative. I nod, a small smile tugging at the corners of my lips.

"Good choice," I say, my tone softer now. "Now hurry up and get ready. We're going out."

A little while later, Sienna finally saunters out of the bedroom. My eyes roam over her, taking in every inch of her beauty, and for a moment, I forget how to fucking breathe. She's wearing a short white dress with a corset top that accentuates her curves and a puffy out skirt that sways with each step she takes. My eyes practically devour her as she approaches.

"Jesus Christ." I say, licking my lips; my hand rising to cover my smirk. Sienna grins at my words, a playful glint dancing in her eyes. She knows she's got me twisted around her little finger, and she's loving every second.
Without another word, I hold the door open for her, nodding my head for her to walk out. She struts slowly past me, her eyes deliberately never leaving mine, like she's daring me to make a move.

Little fucking tease.
Her perfume punches me and my jaw clenches as I fight the urge to grab and fuck her right then and there.
I lead her outside to where my bike waits, its sleek black frame gleaming in the morning light. I step closer to Sienna, my fingers

lingering as I lift the helmet from where it rests. With a deliberate slowness, I lower it over her head, the straps cinching tight as our eyes meet.

"There you go, sweet. Can't have you getting hurt now can we?" I say with a wink, alluding to last night's events. I bring her hand to my lips, pressing a tender kiss to her skin before helping her onto the bike. As Sienna adjusts herself on the seat, I slide my hand across her waist, resting it there for longer than necessary. My thumb gliding back and forth.

I ride her out for around half an hour, speeding the entirety of the way, until I park up at a field. The engine's roar fading away as I kill it. The field is reminiscent of the one I had taken her to before. Except this one is covered in a dreamy array of flowers. I lift off Sienna's helmet with a flourish, revealing her blooming hair and those honey brown eyes. The sunlight painting golden hues across her; a vision of ethereal beauty.

I hold out my hand for her to grab onto and instead she grabs onto just my outer two fingers, and I can't help but chuckle. It might be the cutest fucking thing I've ever seen.

Together, we stroll through the field, the flowers swaying in the gentle zephyr like they're putting on a show just for us. I lead her to a shadier spot beneath the sprawling branches of a large tree, where the sunlight filters through the leaves in dappled patterns. With a quick search in my bag, I retrieve the blanket and sandwiches I had tucked away earlier.

"Isn't this...?" she starts, trailing off as realisation dawns on her face. I give a low chuckle,

"Yes, it's the blanket from your bed," I reply, my tone casual. "I hope you don't mind that I borrowed it for our little date."

Sienna smiles and scrunches her nose.

"A date, huh?" she asks, amusement evident in her voice. I nod, not bothering to elaborate.

"Of course."

We settle on the blanket, the air heavy with the scent of flowers and the warmth of the sun. I nod towards the sandwiches.

"Eat." I say, my tone gruff but not unkind. She takes a bite.

"Mm, very nice." she says, a genuine smile on her lips.

"What can I say? I pride myself on my culinary skills." I joke, knowing full well all I did was slap some ham and cheese between two slices of bread. She laughs, her eyes sparkling.

"You're quite the chef," she teases, her tone playful. I raise an eyebrow, a grin spreading across my face.

"Oh, you haven't seen anything yet, sweet." I reply, leaning in closer. "I make a mean bacon sandwich that you'll have to try." Her laughter fills the air, the sound like music to my ears. She bites her bottom lip and looks down briefly before her eye contact intensifies; those beautiful eyes twinkling with mischief.

"There's something else of yours I'd like to taste."

What the fuck.

My heart skips a beat, her boldness catching me completely off guard. I swallow hard and clear my throat, my mind racing as I try to regain my composure.

"Excuse me?" I ask. But Sienna's expression instantly morphs back into one of oblivious curiosity as she meets my gaze. Then, with a playful glint in her eyes, she simply says,

"Nothing," her tone innocent but loaded with suggestive undertones.

I shift discreetly, trying to hide the growing bulge in my pants. Did that really just happen?

Fucking hell, Sienna.

I guess this is what I get when I try to be romantic. Her eyes flicker down for a moment, and then a proud smile tugs at the corner of her lips. Oh God, she's noticed. But instead of commenting or making a fuss, she just gives me this sly look, like she's silently congratulating herself on getting under my skin. Lucky for me, Sienna's attention is suddenly diverted by something in front of us.

"Ooh, look!" she exclaims, her voice bubbling with excitement.

I follow her eye-line to see a butterfly fluttering nearby, its delicate yellow wings catching the sunlight. Relief floods through me, grateful for the timely distraction.

"Yeah, wow. Look at that." I reply, doing my best to sound enthusiastic.

I watch in awe as Sienna's eyes light up with childlike wonder as she follows the delicate movements of the butterfly. She reaches out a hand, her fingers trembling with anticipation, as if she's afraid the slightest movement might scare it away.

"Isn't it just the most beautiful thing?" she asks. I nod, my gaze fixed not on the butterfly, but on her.

"Yeah, it really is," I reply, my voice barely audible over the soft rustle of the leaves.

As Sienna reaches out to touch the butterfly, a gentle breeze sweeps through the field, causing her hair to dance around her face like golden threads in the sunlight. The butterfly lands gracefully on her outstretched hand, its delicate wings quivering against her skin. She gasps softly, her eyes widening in amazement as she holds her breath, afraid to disturb the fragile creature. And in this instant, she's the most enchanting sight I've ever beheld. She's like a dream made flesh.

Sienna's fingers trace the delicate, iridescent patterns on the butterfly's wings, her touch gentle and reverent. The butterfly seems to respond to her, its movements growing even more graceful as if in acknowledgment of her tender care. After a moment, she reluctantly tries to release the butterfly, her hand opening slowly as she lets it go. But instead of flying away, the butterfly hovers nearby, as if reluctant to leave her side. Sienna's ebullient laughter fills the air.

"It wants to stay." she exclaims, her eyes sparkling with excitement.

"Looks like you've made a new friend, sweet." I tease, unable to hide my awe at the magical moment.

Sienna's smile still lingers on her face as she settles back onto the blanket beside me, the butterfly's delicate wings still dancing against her hand. She scoots closer, her radiant warmth seeping into my side as she leans into me, her soft breath a gentle caress against my skin.

Just as we melt into the peaceful moment, a large black car rumbles by on the road where we parked the bike. Sienna's expression tightens, her eyebrows scrunching together as she watches the car pass by.

"What's wrong?" I ask. Sienna hesitates before answering, her eyes still fixed on the retreating car.

"Nothing," she says, but I can tell by the tension in her voice that she's hiding something.

"Sure?"

"Yes, I'm sure."

She shakes her head and proceeds to hold out her hand towards me, her eyes alight with anticipation.

"Your turn, tough guy," she says, her voice filled with excitement. I grin as I hold out my hand for the butterfly to walk onto. To my surprise, the tiny creature flutters over and lands gently on my outstretched palm, its delicate legs tickling my skin. Sienna's smile widens as she watches. "See, it likes you too," she says, her voice filled with affection.

I raise an eyebrow.

"You should give it a name." I suggest, passing back our new little buddy. Sienna doesn't miss a beat.

"Butter," she declares, a pure smile playing on her lips. I can't help but chuckle at the simplicity of her choice.

"Butter it is." I reply, feeling a strange sense of fondness for the little creature.

After spending some time basking in the tranquillity of the field, Sienna and I reluctantly rise to our feet, ready to make our way back to the bike. But as we start to gather our things, Sienna hesitates, her eyes fixed on Butter, who is now sitting leisurely on her shoulder.

"I don't want to leave Butter here." she says, her voice filled with concern as she pouts her bottom lip. I glance down at the butterfly, understanding her reluctance.

"We can't exactly take it with us, sweet." I reply, feeling a pang of guilt at the thought of leaving her beloved Butter behind.

She doesn't reply, instead just stares up at me with the saddest, most guilt-tripping eyes I've ever seen.

I sigh, knowing there's no arguing with her when she gets like this. I rummage through my bag, coming up with her small Tupperware container I had brought for the sandwiches. Without a word, I reach for my butterfly knife, flipping it open with practised ease. Sienna's eyes widen in surprise as I press the tip of the blade against the lid of the container.

"What are you doing?" she asks. But I simply shake my head, a small smile playing on my lips.

"Trust me," I reply, as I stab several holes in the lid of the Tupperware. Sienna watches in silence, her eyes fixed on my hands as I work. And as I finish, I hold up the container for her to see, a satisfied grin on my face.

"There," I say, "now Butter can breathe."

Sienna's face breaks into a relieved smile as she gazes at the container in her hands. She delicately places Butter into the container and shuts the lid before looking back up to me.

"Thank you."

"You're welcome." I reply, kissing her forehead before grabbing her bike helmet. As I hand it to her, she looks up at me with a teasing glint in her eyes.

"You really need to stop stabbing things though." I breathe out a soft laugh.

"I'll think about it." I reply with a playful wink.

300

CHAPTER 15:
THE BARN

Dean

"You know, when you mentioned 'exploring'," Skylar starts in her usual sarcastic tone, "I assumed maybe a nice stroll in the woods, find some animals, maybe a little cafe somewhere. But no, apparently Dean Douglas' idea of 'exploring' means walking at 50 miles an hour down dead-end country lanes!" My patience wears thin as I glance at Skylar.

"Genuinely, do you ever shut the fuck up?" I hear Skylar's laboured breaths as she struggles to keep up, her words coming out in gasps.

"I will if you slow the fuck down!"

"That's a lie."

"You know, Sky, maybe if you focused on actually leaving your bedroom once in a while instead of yapping, you wouldn't be struggling to keep up." Skylar's glare intensifies, but she doesn't miss a beat.

"If you weren't such an impatient asshole I wouldn't *need* to keep up." I let out a bark of laughter, unable to resist the opportunity to annoy her further.

"It's hard to have patience when you're forced to babysit her royal highness all the fucking time."

"I swear, if I collapse from exhaustion it's on you."

"Oh, and what a tragedy that would be." I reply, my voice laced with faux concern.

"You're a cunt."

"Guilty as charged."

We keep walking, and Skylar just won't quit her griping. I figured a bit of wandering would be a nice distraction while Marcus and Sienna are off fucking or whatever it is they do; but it seems Skylar can't muster up a positive thought to save her life.

But then, out of the corner of my eye, I spot a big, old, empty-looking barn looming in the distance, its weathered wood and rusty roof standing out against the landscape like a sore thumb. I grunt in acknowledgment, feeling a flicker of curiosity despite Skylar's sour mood.

"That's pretty cool." I remark, nodding towards the barn, my tone tinged with genuine interest.

"Dean, it's a fucking barn."

"Wow, you're a genius."

Drawing nearer, I'm struck by the sheer size of the barn. It looms over us like a behemoth, its weathered facade whispering tales of years gone by. It's not just big, it's massive; a towering monument to the past.

"Holy shit," I mutter under my breath, taking in the barn's impressive stature. "This thing's huge." Skylar, still lagging behind, lets out an evil giggle.

"Bet you've never heard that before."

Ignoring her jibe, I push open the barn door and step inside, the musty scent of hay and dust hitting me like a wave. As we step into the barn, our eyes immediately fixate on the towering presence of a massive combine harvester. Its sheer size and mechanical complexity stand out amidst the dusty interior, a testament to a bygone era of farming.

"Sick," I breathe, my voice hushed with awe as I take in the sight of the imposing machine. To my surprise, Skylar's usual attitude gives way to genuine interest as she steps closer to the combine harvester, her eyes scanning its intricate details with fascination.

"That *is* pretty cool." I nod in agreement, a smile tugging at the corners of my lips as I watch Skylar's unexpected enthusiasm.

While Skylar climbs up into the driver's seat of the combine harvester, eager to explore its inner workings, I continue to wander through the barn, my curiosity leading me to other relics scattered throughout the space. I find myself drawn to a collection of old farming tools lining the walls; rusted ploughs, weathered pitchforks, and battered scythes.

I'm definitely taking some of this shit.

"Dean, check this out!" she calls, her voice echoing through the barn. As I make my way over to the combine harvester, Skylar's fingers dance across the control panel, her grin widening with each button she presses. With a mischievous grin, Skylar points to the control panel. "Watch this," she says, her fingers dancing across the switches and buttons. With a flick of her wrist, she activates the lights, illuminating the interior of the barn with a powerful glow. "Pretty cool, huh?" she says, her eyes shining with pride. I nod, impressed by her discovery.

"Yeah, not bad."

Chapter 15

As I run my fingers over the sea of blades I can't help but feel a sense of wonder at the machinery before me. It's not every day you get to explore something like this. It's the same rush I get doing graffiti and working on cars; tinkering with engines and machinery. There's something about the raw power and precision that gets my adrenaline pumping. I can't help but be drawn in, my mind racing as I try to figure out how the whole thing works.

Lost in my own exploration, I barely register Skylar's next move.

"Woah, Skylar! Wait-" I start to protest, but it's too late.

With a deafening roar, the combine harvester awakes, its blades whirring to life with deadly precision. Before I can react, my hand is caught in the mechanism, the sharp edges slicing through skin and bone with terrifying speed.

Pain shoots through my hand like a bolt of lightning, and I let out a cry of agony as blood gushes from the wound. Skylar's eyes widen in horror as she realises what she's done, shutting it off immediately; her hands flying to her mouth in shock.

"Dean, oh my God, I'm so sorry!" she cries, her voice trembling with guilt.

Gritting my teeth against the pain, I manage to pry my mangled hand free from the machine's grasp. Blood drips onto the barn floor in a steady rhythm, pooling at my feet as I struggle to regain my composure. The reality of the situation sinks in quickly. I've lost the tops of two fingers, and the pain is excruciating.

I watch, my vision swimming, as Skylar jumps down and hurries to my side.

"Fuck, fuck, fuck!" she panics, looking around. My heart pounds in my chest as I watch her frantically rummaging through dusty crates and old machinery, her movements swift and determined. With trembling hands, she reaches for some old cloth, tearing it into makeshift bandages. "Here," she says, her voice trembling slightly as she kneels beside me and begins wrapping the cloth around my injured fingers; her hands are surprisingly steady. I clench my jaw against the pain as Skylar ties off the makeshift tourniquet, her expression tight with worry.

After Skylar wraps the cloth around my injured fingers, she sits back on her heels, her expression heavy with guilt. I can see the tears welling up in her eyes, threatening to spill over.

"Hey," I say softly, reaching out to gently touch her arm. "It's okay. It was an accident." She sniffles, wiping away a stray tear with the back of her hand.

"But Dean, I have this terrible feeling that.. all of these things *aren't* accidents."

Her words send a chill down my spine, a nagging suspicion clawing its way to the surface of my mind. I swallow hard, trying to ignore the sinking feeling in the pit of my stomach. To push aside the nagging doubt, the creeping sense of unease that threatens to consume me; but sadly, I can't say I disagree with her.

"Come on," I say, forcing a note of false cheer into my voice. "Let's get back so I can wash this out."

CHAPTER 16:

WINGS & WOODWORK

Sienna

Since we got back from the field, Marcus has been up to something outside. I keep hearing all sorts of thumps and bangs, and honestly, I'm too curious for my own good. Yet meanwhile, here I am, snuggled on the bed with my new butterfly buddy on my chest, admiring Butter's beautiful wings; totally mesmerised by her adorable little antics.

As I watch Butter flit around, I can't help but giggle at her playful movements. It's like she knows exactly how to brighten my day with her whimsical, fluttery charm. With each graceful loop and gentle landing, I feel my heart warming to this tiny creature. Her delicate yellow wings shimmer in the soft daylight, casting colourful patterns across the room that match the joy bubbling up inside me.

"You're so pretty, Miss. Butter," I whisper, reaching out a finger for her to perch on. And just like that, she obliges, her tiny feet tickling my skin as she settles in.

Lost in Butter's enchanting dance, I'm startled when the door creaks open, and Marcus strides in, his chest glistening with sweat, his eyes aglow with triumph. He's shirtless, and his rugged physique is accentuated by the effort he's clearly exerted. There's a triumphant grin on his face and he's carrying something wooden.

"Surprise, beautiful." he says softly as he walks closer. I can't help but beam as Marcus sets down a handmade wooden enclosure with mesh walls on the bedside table. It's even filled with plants and a few rocks sitting on the bottom.

"You made this?" I ask delicately. He nods briefly and wipes the glistening sweat from his brow. "It's amazing. I love it." I exclaim, my eyes sparkling with joy as I admire the wooden enclosure. It's clear that he poured his heart and soul into crafting it, and the thoughtfulness behind his gesture warms me to my core.

With a smile, I gently coax Butter onto my finger and guide her into her new home. She flutters around for a moment before settling on a small, wonky perch, her wings beating softly as she explores her new surroundings. Marcus chuckles softly, his eyes glowing with affection as he watches my reaction.

"I'm glad you like it, sweet." he says, his voice tender. Without a word, I jump to my feet, wrapping my arms around his neck and pulling him into a passionate kiss. Marcus freezes for a moment, clearly caught off guard by my sudden display of affection, but soon melts into the embrace, his arms wrapping around my neck and cheek as he returns the kiss with equal fervour.

Our lips move together in a sweet symphony of love and longing, each kiss filled with the unspoken promise of a future together; Butter fluttering happily in her enclosure next to us. And at this moment, I know I'm exactly where I'm meant to be.

With a soft moan, I pull Marcus closer, my fingers tangling in his hair as I lose myself in the sensation of his lips on mine. His touch sets my skin ablaze, sending shivers of pleasure racing down my spine. I arch into him, craving more of his touch, more of his love.

Marcus' response is fervent, his lips burning with an intensity that leaves me gasping as he maps every curve of my body. His lips trail down my neck, marking me. As he trails his lips along the curve of my throat, I tilt my head back, offering him access to my neck; my breath quickening.

His hand moves slowly, purposefully up my thigh. The fabric of my dress whispering against my skin as he inches closer to my core. With a gentle touch, he teases the soft skin of my inner thigh, lightly tracing patterns. As I gasp in pleasure, my body responding to his every touch, Marcus continues his sweet torture, slowly inching his hand closer and closer to my pulsating heat. I bite my lip, feeling the dampness between my thighs grow as he continues to tease me through my knickers.
His fingers play with the fabric as he whispers in my ear.

"*Fuck*, sweet. You're so wet already. You want it badly, huh?" I look up at him, my eyes wide and needy, as I give a subtle nod. He kisses my forehead before continuing his whispers into my temple. "Not yet, I want you to ache for me." My breath hitches as his fingers graze the sensitive skin of my inner thigh once again, torturously light and deliberate.

I arch my back, pushing my hips towards his hand, silently begging for his touch to move higher. But Marcus doesn't give in to my silent begging. Instead, he continues to draw out the sweet torture. With a whimper of frustration, I cling to him, my body trembling with need. Marcus leans in, his breath hot against my ear as he murmurs.

"Good girl, so patient."

Just as I think I can't take it anymore, he finally gives in to my silent plea, his fingers slipping past the fabric of my knickers and finding the wet heat waiting for him. Marcus continues to torment me, his fingers expertly teasing my clit with devilish precision. He slides his fingers down from my swollen clit and pushes the tip of his finger into me, slowly stretching and filling me with his touch. I gasp at the sensation, the feeling of him penetrating me so intimately. But before I can fully revel in the pleasure, he cruelly withdraws his finger.

"Marcus, please." I plead, to which he chuckles darkly in response.

"*God.* I love hearing you fucking beg for me." Marcus finally stops his teasing and gives in to his own desire, plunging his fingers deep inside me, causing a squeal to leave my lips. He looks at me with a hungry glare, a predatory glint in his eyes that both thrills and terrifies me.

"Is that what you wanted, sweet?" I nod, unable to form words as his fingers continue their aggressive exploration. I cling to him, my nails digging into his back as I lose myself in the carnal pleasure he's providing.

I feel Marcus's hand tighten around my waist with a possessive grip, as his fingers delve deeper. Pushing firmer. Then he switches; his eyes darken suddenly. Without a word, he flips me over onto my stomach, his strong hands holding me firmly in place as he positions himself behind me. His hands move with purpose, sliding down my spine with a steady pressure that makes me arch my back in response.

He holds me down firmly, his touch demanding as he enters me with a rough thrust. I grip the sheets tightly, my knuckles stretching as I brace myself. Each thrust is deep. He's making the most of me. As Marcus' thrusts grow more intense, I can't help but cry out. I bury my face into the pillow, muffling my moans as he uses me relentlessly.

I swallow hard, my heart pounding in my chest as I feel his dominance enveloping me like a thick fog. I know I should push him away, reclaim control over my own body, but something inside me yearns to surrender; to let him take me completely. With each punishing thrust, he drives me closer to the edge, his fingers digging deep into my skin. I gasp for air, my chest heaving with each ragged breath. Suddenly, his hand wraps around my throat, his grip tight and unyielding.

I choke back a gasp as his fingers tighten, cutting off my air supply.

"You're mine, you hear me?" he growls, his voice rough and commanding. "Mine to fuck, mine to use. Say it." I nod, but that's not what he wanted. With his other hand he sends a punishing smack to my ass. The crack of skin meeting skin reverberating through the room. The pain, sharp and immediate. "Say it. Use your fucking words, Sienna."

"I'm yours," I manage to cry out, my body trembling. A cruel smirk twists at his lips.

"There you fucking go."

He continues to thrust deep into me, hitting every sweet spot there is. I writhe and whimper beneath him, lost in a whirlwind of pleasure and pain. Marcus's voice cuts through the haze once again.

"You want me to fill your mouth or your cunt, sweet?" Before I can answer, he thrusts into me with a brutal force that steals my breath and mind entirely.

"Marcus, please," I manage to whimper, the words barely escaping my lips.

"Fucking pick one," he snarls, his voice dripping with contempt and impatience. With a trembling breath, I manage to rasp out,

"My mouth.. "

"Dirty little girl," he taunts in my ear. "Get on your fucking knees."

Tears sting at the corners of my eyes as I comply, kneeling to the floor beside him, but he walks further away and sits at the dining chair. He pats his leg twice to summon me over.

"Crawl." he commands, "Eyes on me."

Excuse me, sir?

I crawl towards him on my hands and knees, the cold, hard floor scraping against my skin as I move closer; the anticipation and fear building in my chest with every inch I cover. His presence looms over me, casting a dark shadow that engulfs me in a mix of nerves and arousal. My eyes glued up at him. His smile grows with every movement.

"*Fuck*, look at those pretty eyes."

When I finally reach him, he grabs a handful of my hair in a tight grip, pulling me closer to him. His other hand forces his throbbing cock into my unsuspecting mouth, the taste of him overpowering my senses. I gag and choke, the pressure in my chest building as he holds my nose, controlling my breathing with cold calculation. His movements are quick and unforgiving as he uses me for his own pleasure. His grip on my hair tightens, guiding me as I struggle to accommodate his length.

"Take all of it, sweet. Remember, you asked for this." he growls, "Now open nice and wide and choke on my fucking cock." The desire is evident in his voice as he plunges deep down my throat. Each thrust pushes me further into a state of helpless submission. I can only whimper around him, unable to respond as he dominates me completely. The taste of him mingling on my tongue.

With a sudden slap to my face, Marcus' command cuts through the haze of sensation. "I don't want to feel your fucking teeth," he barks, his voice harsh "Suck on it. I want it deep down that little throat." I comply, focusing on relaxing my jaw and throat as I take him as deep as I can, trying to please him just as he demands. The tears streaming down my face mix with the saliva dripping down my chin as he continues to thrust forcefully, using my mouth as his personal playground.

I eagerly obey his command, taking his throbbing cock as deep as I can as he nears his climax. With a primal groan, Marcus' hips jerk forward, and he spills himself into my mouth, filling me with come. Before I can catch my breath, Marcus' hand reaches out, gripping my nose tightly and cutting off my oxygen once again.

"Come on, sweet. Make me proud." he purrs, "swallow every last fucking drop." The taste of him lingers in my mouth, the sensation overwhelming as I struggle to swallow without being able to draw in a breath through my nose. With every ounce of my being, I force myself to swallow, the sensation of his release beginning to slide down my throat.

"That's it," he praises, "Keep going. You're doing so well for me."

As I finally manage to swallow every last drop, a sense of relief washes over me. Taking in a deep breath as Marcus releases his grip on my nose, I gasp for air, feeling his pleasure at my compliance radiating through the room. He pulls up his tracksuit bottoms and settles again onto the edge of the dining chair.

As Marcus leans forwards, he holds my chin in a firm grip, his eyes bore into mine with ferocious intensity. A smirk plays on his lips as he takes in the dishevelled state I'm in; flushed cheeks, heavy breaths, and a wanton look in my eyes.

"Look at the mess I've got you in." He husks, his tone smouldering with desire. "You're dripping for me, aren't you?" I don't reply. He already knows the answer.

"Spread your legs wide, sweet. Let me see you."
As I spread my legs in front of him, Marcus' eyes narrow with a predatory glint. He smirks at the sight of me, exposed and wet.

"Touch yourself, beautiful." he orders, his voice filled with a softer yet commanding authority. Reluctantly, I slowly lower my hand towards the sensitive flesh between my legs, my movements hesitant and uncertain; maintaining eye contact with him as he towers over me.

His eyes narrow with a cruel intensity, a smirk playing on his lips as he takes in the sight of my rising vulnerability. I begin to circle my clit slowly, feeling my wetness on my fingertips; soft whimpers leaving my mouth. His gaze is a piercing force, relentless and unyielding as it rakes over my exposed skin with a primal, hunger-driven intensity that makes my skin prickle with awareness.

"Spread that pussy wider. I wanna see everything." Marcus growls. I comply with Marcus' commands, my legs trembling as I spread myself open for his inspection. My breath hitches at the intimacy of his gaze, his eyes never leaving mine as he takes in the display of my submission. His enjoyment is palpable, his arousal evident in the way his cock strains against the fabric of his joggers.

"Good girl," he murmurs, his voice low and husky with arousal. "Now, put two fingers deep inside for me." I pause, my stare imploring him as I consider whether or not to obey, my fingers trembling with anticipation. But then I surrender, my body responding to the unspoken command as I ease two fingers in, feeling the velvet tightness enveloping them; a soft moan escaping my lips.

"*Fuck.* So pretty when you obey me. All filled and stretched." he murmurs, his voice low and husky with arousal. "Deeper." he commands, his eyes blazing with desire as he watches me comply, sinking my fingers as far as they'll go, seeking out that elusive spot of pleasure deep within me. I gasp at the overwhelming sensation, pleasure coursing through my veins like wildfire. His hands clench, trying to suppress his bulge.

"Soak your clit, now. Let me see how wet you are." He instructs, his voice a husky whisper, flustering me entirely. I slide up my fingers and begin to circle my swollen clit, coating it in my own slick arousal. Marcus watches with hungry eyes, a smirk playing on his lips.

"Such a good girl," he murmurs, his voice laced with approval. "You know just how to please me now, don't you, sweet? How to make yourself all wet and needy." I moan at his words, feeling a rush of heat pooling between my legs at the praise and the degradation mingling together.

"You have my permission, sweet. Now, come for me." With his permission ringing in my ears, I allow myself to succumb fully to the building ecstasy. My movements become more frantic, more desperate as I chase the release he's granted me. Each deep stroke, each touch sends shockwaves of pleasure through me, driving me closer and closer to the edge.
His eyes gleam with primal hunger as I writhe and moan under his command.

"That's it, beautiful. Let me hear you whimper as you fall apart for me." he taunts, his voice thick. The slick sounds of my wetness mixing with the heavy breathing fill the room. My movements become erratic, desperate as I feel the pressure building, the tension coiling tighter and tighter within me. With one final, desperate push, I shatter into million pieces, waves of pleasure crashing over me like a tsunami. I cry out, lost in the overwhelming sensation of release.

Marcus' dark eyes become even more predatory, a low growl slipping from his lips as he watches me fall apart for him. As I collapse in a trembling heap before him, Marcus leans down, his lips brushing against my ear as he whispers,

"Such a good girl. Look at you, all used up and desperate for more."

With a gentle touch, Marcus lifts me from the floor, cradling me in his strong arms as if I were his most precious treasure.

Well, In the most humble way possible, I think I am.

I nestle against his chest, feeling the steady rhythm of his heartbeat beneath my ear, a comforting reassurance of his presence. He holds me close, his warmth enveloping me like a protective shield. His hand strokes my back in soothing circles.

You did so well, sweet" he whispers, his voice soft and filled with tenderness. "I'm so proud of you." I snuggle closer to him, feeling his warmth seeping into my skin.

He suddenly squeezes me extra tightly, spinning me around in his arms before pressing firm, eager kisses to my neck. I gasp in surprise, laughter bubbling up.

"What's with all the excitement?" I ask, trying to sound nonchalant despite the flutter in my chest. He pulls back just enough to lock eyes with me, a mischievous grin spreading across his face like a sunrise.

"Nothing, it's just.. If my younger self could be here now, he wouldn't fucking believe what he's seeing." I blink, struck by the sincerity in his words.

315

"What do you mean?" I whisper, feeling a lump form in my throat. I can't help but beam from ear to ear, my face aching with the force of my smile. Marcus' chuckle is a low, gentle hum, his eyes sparkling with love and adoration as they drink in the sight of me.

"Sienna, I don't think you realise. You're literally all I've ever wanted."

I meet his stare, feeling a rush of warmth spread through me at the depth of his words. My heart flutters in my chest as I listen, unable to tear my eyes away from him. He brushes his thumb against my cheek,

"You're the only person I can soften up around, sweet. You're a constant." he says, his voice filled with a quiet sincerity. "When everything in my life is continuously changing, you're the one thing that remains the same." I find myself at a loss for words, my heart overflowing with emotions. Unable to find the right words to express how I feel, I simply gaze into Marcus' eyes, my own eyes welling up with tears.

"I'd do anything to spend the rest of my life just curled up with you in your little bubble," he continues, his voice soft yet strong with conviction. "Where regardless of everything you're put through, you act like the world is full of rainbows and unicorns, and everything tastes like strawberries."

I can't help but smile, a soft, gentle curve of my lips, as I bask in the glow of his love and devotion. A rush of warmth floods through my veins, leaving me tingling from head to toe.

It's like I'm floating on a cloud.

"You know what's funny?" I reply, timidly "I love that you remind me that the world isn't all rainbows and unicorns."

Marcus chuckles, the sound vibrating against my skin as he continues to hold me close. His laughter is infectious. Wrapping my arms around him, I bury my face in his chest, feeling his warmth envelop me like a cocoon.

And In this moment, I know that I'm exactly where I belong

CHAPTER 17:
LOST LEADS

Dean

Marcus and I bundle into the car, the engine growling to life as we set our sights on Moth. Marcus' eyes flick to my hand, his brow furrowing in concern.

"What's up with your hand?" he asks. I let out a defeated sigh, my grip on the wheel tightening.

"It doesn't matter." I mutter, lacking the energy to explain. "So, Moth," I grunt, "you think he's gonna play nice?" Marcus smirks, his eyes scanning the passing scenery with a steely gaze.

"I doubt it."
He reaches into his pocket and pulls out a joint.

"You want a hit?" he offers casually. I hesitate for a moment before taking the joint from him, indulging in a quick drag. As I exhale, I glance at Marcus.

"You think we smoke too much?" I ask in a half-serious tone. Marcus chuckles, exhaling a cloud of smoke.

318

"For the shit we've been through, I don't think we smoke enough." I smirk at Marcus's response, shaking my head in amusement.

"Fair point," I concede. Marcus takes another long drag, his expression thoughtful as he exhales a plume of smoke out the window.

I glance over at Marcus, noticing the relaxed demeanour he's sporting.

"You don't seem too worried about these guys," I remark, raising an eyebrow. Marcus lets out a low chuckle, a smirk playing on his lips.

"Dean, you gave me a fucking gun. You realise I'm like invincible now," he says with mock seriousness, his ego seemingly inflated. I know he's always been into weapons. Far more than I am. His collection of knives is ever-growing and I suppose I should've guessed that giving him a gun was quite the step up.

"It'd be great if it worked like that, huh?"

As we pull up to the location, I spot a very large, muscular figure standing outside, puffing away at a cigarette. Tattoos cover his body and face; but not the cool kind of tattoos, the really shitty kind of tattoos. He looks like the type of person you wouldn't fuck with. Instinct tells me it's Moth. We exchange a glance, and without a word, Marcus and I decide to observe from the other side of the street through our tinted windows. We sit and we watch.

But before we can make a move, his sharp glare catches sight of our car, and he immediately senses something's amiss. With a quick pivot, he strides purposefully a few paces down an alleyway, disappearing and reappearing in a car. I gun the engine, peeling out from our hiding spot and tearing after him.

As we chase him through the labyrinth of streets, the car's tires screech against the asphalt. Marcus grips the grab handle, his knuckles white with tension, while I focus on keeping us on his tail.

Just as we start to gain ground, I can't help but notice the number plate on the car, 'M0TH M4N' The arrogance of it makes me smirk. Marcus catches my eye, a silent acknowledgment passing between us. I'll give it to him, It's a bold move, broadcasting your identity like that when there's probably a lot of fuckers wanting him dead.

As the pursuit intensifies, Moth leads us into a part of town we know all too well from our upbringing. The streets grow narrower, the buildings taller and more dilapidated. It's the kind of place where trouble lurks around every corner.

Suddenly, Moth's car cuts sharply into a narrow alley, and we follow, adrenaline pumping. But as we emerge on the other side, his vehicle suddenly screeches to a halt, wedging us in place. The abrupt halt leaves us momentarily disoriented.

Before we can react, the sound of unanticipated gunfire fills the air, bullets raining down on us from Moth's car. Marcus and I duck for cover, the car's windows shattering under the onslaught. We grit our teeth, scrambling for our weapons as we desperately return fire. But as we exchange shots, it becomes painfully clear that Moth's not alone. Shadows move in the back of his car, indicating he's got backup.

"Bro, we've got no fucking chance!" Marcus shouts, his voice strained with urgency as he squeezes off a few rounds in Moth's direction.

My mind races as I weigh our options. We're outnumbered and outgunned, and staying put is a death sentence.

"Stay down!" I bark, my voice strained with determination; barely audible over the chaos. Bullets whiz past us, kicking up puffs of dust as we move, the adrenaline coursing through our veins.

I slam the gear into reverse, the tires screeching as we peel out of the alley, narrowly avoiding another barrage of bullets. As we speed away, I spare a glance at Marcus. His jaw is set in a grim line.

"Fucking bastards," he growls, his voice low and menacing. I nod in agreement, my own anger bubbling to the surface.

"Oh, don't worry. If they wanna play fucking dirty, we will too."

CHAPTER 18:

TAKEN

Sienna

7:43 p.m. Marcus has been gone for a while, but thankfully, the gentle presence of Butter has stopped the boredom. Her wings flutter softly, dancing around me; a vibrant splash of colour against the dimly lit room.

With a soft giggle, I lift my head from the pillow and reach for the slice of juicy orange that sits on my bedside table, holding it out like a precious gift. Butter lands on my finger with the grace of a ballerina, her tiny legs brushing against my skin as she nibbles on the sweet treat.

"Do you like oranges, Miss. Butter?" I whisper, my heart swelling with love as she dances around in delight.

As Butter continues to flit around me, her movements grow increasingly erratic, and a sense of unease creeps over me.

322

"What's wrong, Butter?" I ask softly, my voice tinged with concern as I watch her fluttering about in a frenzy. But before I can register what's happening, the peaceful serenity of the moment shatters into chaos as the door bursts open with a deafening crash. Four menacing figures, clad in black hoodies and masks, storm into the room and straight at me with ruthless efficiency.

My heart pounds in my chest as fear grips me, paralysing me for a moment. But instinct kicks in, and I let out a piercing scream, my voice echoing off the walls as I fight against the hands that grab at me. With desperate strength, I struggle against my assailants, clawing and kicking in a frantic bid for freedom.

"Let me go! Please!" I plead. But their grip is unyielding, and a sharp blow sends searing pain coursing through me, causing stars to dance before my eyes.

"Shut the fuck up." one of them laughs, his voice cold and menacing.

Blood spurts from my lip and I'm greeted by the bitter taste of iron, but I refuse to give in, fighting with every fibre of my being. Through the haze of pain and panic, I catch a glimpse of Butter, fluttering in confusion as she lands in a pool of crimson. As I'm dragged away, my fingernails scrape against the floor, my desperate fingers flailing wildly in a futile attempt to grasp hold of anything that might grant me a fleeting chance of freedom. The sound of my own ragged breathing echoes through my mind as I'm pulled inexorably towards the door.

Salt-stung tears stream down my face, blurring my vision and rendering the world around me a hazy, indistinct mess. I let out a raw, anguished cry, my desperation echoing through the air.

"Marcus!" But my cries fall on deaf ears, drowned out by the cruel laughter and taunts of my captors.

"Your little boyfriend can't save you now, sweetheart," one of them sneers.

How dare the word 'sweet' even leave his ugly fucking mouth.

Then the tallest one chimes in, his words laced with venom.

"Your friends should have known better than to mess with us, princess. Now you're gonna pay the fucking price." *The price for what?* Amidst the chaos, I glance around and notice the others looking to him, as if seeking approval or direction. Each word cuts deeper than the last, a cruel reminder of the danger I'm in. But even as fear grips me, I refuse to give up hope.

Another voice joins in, equally sinister.

"She's putting up quite the fight, boss," he chuckles, addressing the tallest man with a tone of reverence. I watch him survey me with a cold gaze. His eyes eerily the same colour as Marcus'.

"Yeah, she's a feisty one, that's for sure," he replies, his voice carrying a dangerous edge.

With every ounce of strength I have left, I continue to struggle against my captors, my cries of defiance echoing through the night. But as they drag me further and further away from safety, the darkness closes in around me. My struggles grow more frantic, but the iron grasp of my captors holds firm, inexorably propelling me towards the sinister silhouette of a black car, its very presence seeming to draw all lingering moonlight out of the air. I pay attention to the number plate, not that I even know how it will possibly help me now; 'M0TH M4N'

I prefer butterflies, fuckface.

As I'm bundled into the boot, the same sense of dread washes over me, the memory of this same black car following me days before flooding back with chilling clarity. It's a grim realisation that crashes down on me like a hammer blow; I've been caught in the snare of those who have been stalking me, and now I'm trapped, at their mercy.

The boot lid crashes down, a metallic slap that reverberates through my eardrums, like a guillotine blade falling. The sound waves resonate through my body, sending a shiver of dread coursing down my spine, as I'm trapped in the dark, airless tomb of the car. The metal presses against my skin, cold and unforgiving, as if it's trying to crush the life out of me.

We speed off into the unknown, and my mind races with a million thoughts and fears. What do they want with me? Where are they taking me? And most importantly, is Marcus okay?

As the engine dies, the silence is oppressive, my heart racing in tandem; uncertain of what's waiting for me outside this car. The boot suddenly swings open, and I'm roughly pulled out of the car, my feet stumbling on the ground as they cover my mouth and drag me towards a looming house. I find myself in the middle of nowhere, surrounded by darkness that stretches as far as the eye can see. The house before us seems out of place in this desolate landscape, its silhouette stark against the night sky.

As the men force me inside, I realise the interior of the house is not what I had expected. It's messy, cluttered with the detritus of daily life, but there's an eerie sense of emptiness to it, as if no one truly lives here except for the occasional visitor.

Down we go, deeper into the bowels of the house until we reach a basement. It's dank and musty, the air heavy with the scent of neglect. The walls seem to be slowly surrendering to the relentless creep of dampness; the floor littered with discarded items. There are two rooms down here. One door is locked tight, its presence ominous.

My captors push me into the other room, the darkness swallowing me whole. There are no windows, no lights, just a bed in the centre of the room. Thrown onto the cold, hard ground, I gasp for air as they yank off their masks and pull down their hoods. My eyes dart wildly around the room, trying to commit each face to memory. But it's like trying to grasp a handful of sand; the features blur together as I struggle to process the horror before me. I focus. I focus *hard*.

The first man is a behemoth, his massive muscles bulging beneath his hoodie like a grotesque parody of human form. A tattoo slashes across his cheek, a cruel smile twisting his lips as he leers at me with a calculating gaze.

The second man is a scrawny figure, his face contorted in a sadistic grin as he watches my struggles with an air of morbid fascination. His eyes seem to gleam with an unholy excitement.

The third man stands tall and imposing, his features obscured in darkness. The only noticeable feature being his large, black beard, like a shadowy halo. Exuding an air of authority, his presence commanding respect from the others.

And then there's *him*, the tallest one, his presence looming over me like a dark storm cloud. There's something about him that makes my skin crawl.

He's handsome.
I think it's his smile.

Charming, with deeply sunk dimples on both of his cheeks.

No, it's his eyes; cold and calculating, but the same fucking hazel colour as Marcus'.

I hate him instantly.

He takes a deliberate step forward, his movements calculated and menacing, as he drops to one knee in front of me. his glare locks on mine as he reaches out to caress my cheek with a chilling familiarity.

"Pretty little thing, aren't you, princess?" I recoil from his touch, his resemblance to Marcus sending waves of disgust through my body.

As he turns to the others, his voice cold and commanding, I know what's coming next.

"Strip her." he orders, his gaze never leaving mine as the others move to obey his command. And in that moment, as their hands reach for me,

I know that my nightmare has only just begun.

CHAPTER 19:
THE WORST THING POSSIBLE

Marcus

After a few hours of joyriding, in an attempt to clear our heads, Dean eases the car to a stop outside the cottage; a small sense of contentment washing over us. But as he kills the engine and I glance towards the cottage, that contentment evaporates in an instant.

"Hold on," I mutter, my eyes scanning the surroundings with a sense of unease.

The door, usually sturdy and secure, is now hanging off its hinges, splintered wood scattered across the ground. My heart lurches into my throat, and a cold sweat breaks out on the back of my neck.

"Oh, fuck," I whisper under my breath, my pulse quickening and dread settling like a heavy weight in my gut.

Without waiting for a second thought, I'm out of the car and charging towards the cottage, my footsteps heavy and urgent. Every worst-case scenario unfolds in vivid detail in my mind's eye as I step inside, Dean following close behind. As Dean mutters, "Shit." under his breath, a sinking feeling settles in the pit of my stomach. The sight of blood staining the floor sends a wave of visceral horror and anguish crashing over me, threatening to drown out all rational thought.

My heart clenches painfully in my chest, each beat echoing like a drum of despair. "No," I whisper, the word barely audible over the pounding in my ears. The realisation hits me like a freight train and the guilt is suffocating, choking me with a relentless grip.

My legs tremble beneath me, unable to support my weight; my knees buckling beneath the crushing weight of despair as I crouch to the floor. The sight of crimson staining the floor is like a knife to the heart; each drop a painful poke in my side, tormenting me with thoughts of the danger she's in. But then, I catch sight of Butter, her delicate wings now smeared with the same red hue. The memory of Sienna's warm laughter and gentle touch as she played with Butter flashes before me, filling the room with a sense of warmth and light.

The thought of her, so innocent and sweet, torn from us in such a brutal way is almost too much to bear. Where could she be? What unspeakable horrors are being inflicted upon her? My thoughts spin into a maddening vortex. A complete frenzy.

With a guttural growl, I rise to my feet, the sight of Butter triggering a torrent of rage. My hand lashes out, striking the wall with a resounding thud as I curse under my breath. The wall folding around my cut knuckles.

"Fuck!" I roar, the sound echoing around the room like thunder. Without another word, I storm out of the room. "Go check on Sky, now!" I order.

"Bro, wait, we need to think this through-" Dean's voice cuts through the haze of my anger, but I don't stop.

"Now!" I bark, my tone laced with a lethal edge. "I'm not fucking around." There's a tiny moment of hesitation in Dean's eyes, a flicker of uncertainty. But then he nods, the gravity of the situation dawning on him. "Okay, okay," he says, his voice firm. "I'll go get her. Just breathe, man. Please." I turn away, my mind consumed by a single, burning thought.

I won't rest until every single cunt who laid a hand on her is dead.

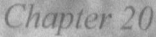

CHAPTER 20:
HELP

Sienna

My heart races as the men advance, their movements predatory, like wolves closing in on their prey. I scramble backward, my hands searching desperately for something, anything to defend myself with, but finding nothing but empty space.

The first man grabs at my shirt, ripping it open with a forceful tug. I feel a surge of panic, a primal instinct to fight back rising within me, but I know deep down that resistance would be futile against their overwhelming strength. Tears sting my eyes as they strip away my dignity along with my clothes. I close my eyes, trying to block out the horror unfolding around me, but their taunts and jeers seep through, haunting me like a nightmare from which I cannot wake.

I try to scream, but my voice catches in my throat, choked off by fear and disgust. I can feel their eyes on me, leering with a

332

sickening hunger that makes my skin crawl. Panic grips me as they pin me down on my back. The hard, unforgiving surface of this sad excuse for a bed, pushing into my spine; their weight crushing me beneath them.

With rough hands, they pin my legs up by my side, exposing me completely to their depraved eyes. A wave of loathing and desperation crashes over me as they loom closer, their malevolent intent palpable in the air.

"Shit, look at that," one man grunts, his voice thick with malice, his calloused hand grabbing at my ass, squeezing it roughly.

"Yeah, we're gonna have fun with this one."

"Please," I whimper, the word barely more than a whisper as tears stream down my face, mingling with the sweat that coats my skin. But they pay no heed to my pleas, their hands roaming over my body with greedy anticipation.

"You scared, princess?" The tall one taunts. I remain frozen, staring into him with sick intensity. "Don't worry, you'll learn to love it." He states as he touches me; colder and more calculated than the others. He watches me with a predatory gleam in his eyes, his fingers trailing lightly over my skin as if savouring the sensation of my helplessness. Their laughter filling the room like a noxious gas.

I feel a sickening knot form in the pit of my stomach as one of them takes out his penis, the sight of it making me want to retch. Before plunging into me, he utters,

"Let's see how much fight you've got, sweetheart." Every fibre of my being screams in protest as he moves closer, his eyes gleaming with malicious intent. I struggle against their grasp, but it's futile. They overpower me easily, their strength too much for me to overcome.

Marcus. All I want is Marcus.
…Unaware that I had even closed them, I open my eyes. Fuck, I must have passed out. Pain radiates through me as I hit the floor, the cold surface biting into my skin like icy tendrils of despair. I whimper in agony, my senses overwhelmed by the sheer brutality of their actions.

The men crouch down, their hands reaching out to deliver one last punishment. Some of them slap my ass while one slices my thighs with brutal force; another holding me down by my hair. The sting of their blows is like a physical manifestation of their contempt, branding me. And then, one by one, they add insult to injury by spitting on my spent body with contemptuous disdain. Each glob of saliva lands with a sickening splatter.

I lie there, despondent and broken, as they continue their assault, their laughter cutting through me worse than the knife. The room spins with a nauseating haze of pain, each moment stretching into an eternity of suffering. I don't even possess the energy to scream.

"Now, make sure you remember this feeling next time you wanna fucking fight us."

With a glance over their shoulders, they unleash one last volley of contemptuous laughter, the sound reverberating in the confines of the room like a haunting melody of despair. And then, in one swift motion, the leader reaches for the door handle, his fingers curling around it.

The door swings open, flooding the room with harsh, unforgiving light from the corridor beyond. For a moment, I'm blinded by its intensity, entirely disorientated. And then, with a deafening slam, the door is closed, sealing me in darkness once more. I can hear the click of the lock, a final nail in the coffin.

Alone in the mirk, surrounded by the wreckage of their cruelty, I lie there in a tangled mess. Tears stream down my cheeks, mingling with the filth that now stains my skin. I am broken, discarded, left to wallow in the aftermath of their depravity.

Marcus, where are you?

CHAPTER 21:
FIND HER

Dean

"So you're telling me you didn't hear or see anything?" Marcus's voice cuts through the tension in the car, his frustration palpable. Skylar's response is quiet, drowned out by the weight of guilt hanging heavy in the air.

"I had my headphones in," she mumbles, her eyes fixed on the back of the passenger seat.

The admission lands like a punch to the gut, and I feel my own frustration bubbling to the surface. I'm happy she's okay but she was right fucking there, lost in her own world. She missed the whole thing, and now she's useless in helping us find Sienna. I clench my jaw, struggling to contain the irritation.

"Fuck's sake, Sky." I growl, my voice rough with emotion. "How could you be that fucking oblivious? You're lucky they didn't grab you too."

337

"I'm sorry, okay! Do you not think I feel bad enough without both of you lecturing me?" Her outburst catches me off guard, the raw emotion in her voice momentarily silencing my anger. I exchange a glance with Marcus, seeing the conflict mirrored in his eyes. We're all on edge, emotions running high in the tense atmosphere of the car.

Marcus's silence speaks volumes, the disappointment thick in his eyes. We all know Skylar fucked us up here, and the thought makes my blood boil, but now's not the time to tear each other apart. I let out a heavy sigh, my shoulders slumping with resignation.

"We can't change what's been done," I mutter, my voice heavy with regret. "Let's just focus on finding her, alright?"

With a nod from Marcus, I turn my attention to the road ahead. But as I glance past him, I notice his knuckles white from gripping the steering wheel so tightly. His jaw is clenched, his eyes locked in place, focused on the dark road like a hawk zeroing in on its prey.

He's driving like a man possessed, his anger and determination fueling every reckless move. The car lurches around corners, accelerates with a roar, and Skylar and I shoot each other a quick, worried glance; I can practically feel Skylar's fear radiating off her as she grips the door handle tight enough to leave marks. We're all tense, but with Marcus in this state, nobody dares speak up.

Don't poke the Bear.

As we pull up in a screech at the place where we first spotted Moth, the tension in the car reaches a notable peak. Marcus doesn't waste a moment. With a sense of urgency that borders on desperation, he reaches for his gun, readying it with efficiency. The click of the magazine being loaded echoes in the tense silence of the car.

Skylar's hand hovers over the door handle, her expression a map of uncertainty and concern. Her eyes, a deep well of worry, plead for Marcus to slow down and think things through. But Marcus seems oblivious to her silent protest, his focus singular and unwavering. Marcus opens the door and stands up, his movements quick and decisive. I start to speak, wanting to urge caution,

"Bro, just wait a minute-" but before I can finish, he cuts me off with a sharp slam of the door.

As Marcus practically runs towards the warehouse, my heart sinks like a stone in my chest. I let out a heavy sigh, frustration and worry mingling in the pit of my stomach. With a shake of my head, I reach for my gun. Skylar shoots me a look of concern, her gaze darting to the weapon in my hand as if it's a harbinger of doom. I nod at her once, a brief, reassuring motion

"You stay in here, alright? Call me if you see anything dodgy." She nods.

"Okay," she says softly, her voice wavering slightly. "Be safe."

My mind instantly pans to thoughts of my Delilah as I reply,

"Always."

With a muttered curse under my breath, I follow Marcus, my senses on high alert as we approach the dark alley. Every step feels like walking towards the edge of a cliff, teetering on the brink of disaster. I quicken my pace to catch up to Marcus, who's already swinging open a door down the side of the alley.

My grip tightens around the handle of my gun as we cautiously move forward, our footsteps echoing against the concrete floor. The darkness inside the warehouse swallows us up as we step inside, the air thick with the smell of weed and motor oil. The dim street lights filter through the dusty windows and cast long shadows across the floor.

Rows of shelves line the walls, stacked high with boxes and crates; full to the brim with packaged drugs. And as my gaze lands on the rows of expensive cars parked neatly on the far side of the room, I understand that this isn't just a simple warehouse; it's a base of operations, a hub for Moth and his cronies.

I exchange a tense glance with Marcus, the weight of our mission bearing down on us like a heavy burden. We need to find Sienna, and fast. But as we move deeper into the warehouse, it becomes increasingly clear that Moth and his crew are nowhere to be found. Our frustration boils over, the anger and stress mingling into a potent cocktail of emotions. We came here for answers, for revenge, but all we're left with is an empty warehouse and more questions than ever.

Without a word, Marcus lets out a built up force of anger, his fists swinging wildly as he starts wrecking boxes, his movements fueled by raw fury. I stand frozen, my jaw dropped in stunned silence, as he swings the butt of his gun with reckless abandon, smashing the car windows into a kaleidoscope of shattered glass and twisted metal. The sound of shattering glass and his screams of frustration echo through the empty space, tearing at my soul like claws. Each blow is a release of pent-up frustration. He's in so much pain, and all I can do is watch him fall apart.

But as the reality sinks in that time is ticking, and we're no closer to Sienna, Marcus's rage turns into something darker. He collapses to his knees, a primal sound escaping his throat, raw and gut-wrenching. It's as if he's been torn apart from the inside. I stumble to his side, my heart shattering into a million pieces at the sight of his devastation.

"Bro," I choke out, my voice cracking with emotion. "We're gonna find her, I know we are." But he doesn't respond, his whole being consumed by a darkness so profound it's suffocating. It's like he's been stripped to the bone by the cruel hand of fate.

Marcus mutters under his breath,

"*God*, what are they doing to her?" I can see the torment etched on his face, the fear and anguish twisting his features as he imagines the worst possible scenarios for Sienna. It's like he's being cursed by his own nightmares, unable to escape the incessant grip of his own imagination.

I glance at Marcus, and the agony etched on his face cuts me deeper than any blade ever could. His eyes are haunted, filled with tears he refuses to shed.

"Don't," I rasp, "Don't you dare even think about it." But Marcus's empty leer betrays the depths of his torment, his mind a battleground of horrors too terrible to contemplate.

It's as if he's already lost her.

As the weight of our failure presses down on us like a suffocating shroud, we resign ourselves to the bitter truth; tonight, there's nothing left for us to do.

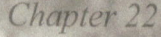

CHAPTER 22: NOAH

Sienna

As I lie there on the cold floor, still reeling from the agony of the assault, the passage of time blurs into a painful haze; and as early morning rays of sunlight creep through the cracks, I soon realise it's the next day.

The oppressive silence is shattered by the faint creak of the door hinges, and a sliver of light spills into the room. My heart pounds in my chest as I watch the leader step inside, a plate of food in hand. He doesn't speak, doesn't offer any words of comfort or remorse. Instead, he simply sits on the edge of the bed, his presence a menacing shadow.

With a callous disregard for my suffering, he places the plate of food on the floor before me, his gaze cold and indifferent.

"Eat," he commands, his voice devoid of any warmth. It's a command, plain and simple. But I can't bring myself to comply, not after everything they've done to me.

"I don't trust it," I whisper, the words barely escaping my trembling lips. Every fibre of my being screams at me to resist, to reject whatever he's presenting me with. But the hunger beginning to poke at my insides threatens to override my instincts, reminding me of my desperate need for sustenance. He chuckles darkly, a cold smile twisting his lips.

"I've killed a lot of people, princess." His tone is icy, like death itself. "And I'll have you know, poisoning is by far the most boring method there is," he continues, his voice lowering to a sinister whisper. "If I wanted you dead, I would've slit your fucking throat. Eat."

The words hit me like a physical blow, knocking the breath from my lungs. The sheer brutality of his statement leaves me reeling, my mind struggling to process the horror of what he's just said. I stare at the food, my stomach churning with revulsion.

How can I even think about eating?

But a deep-seated instinct for survival urges me to obey, to consume whatever morsel of sustenance I can find in this place. With trembling hands, I reach for the plate, my fingers brushing against the hot surface. As I lift the first mouthful of food to my lips, I can feel his eyes boring into me. Each movement feels like a betrayal of everything I stand for, but in this hellhole, defiance only leads to more pain.

Despite my initial hesitation, I tentatively take a bite of the food, expecting the worst. But to my surprise, it's not the tasteless gruel I anticipated. It's warm, comforting even. But beneath its soothing heat, a cold dread simmers, a creeping sense of unease that refuses to be stilled. It's as if the warmth is a fragile truce, one that can't begin to dispel the dark suspicions that gnaw at my gut. This kindness feels like a cruel trick, a prelude to more suffering.

But as I take another bite, I push those thoughts aside, if only for a moment, allowing myself to savour this small semblance of normalcy.

As I finish the last bite of the surprisingly palatable meal, the leader's voice cuts through once again.

"How was it?" His tone is deceptively casual, almost conversational. I hesitate, unsure of how to respond to his unexpected inquiry.

"It was.. fine." I finally manage to choke out. He chuckles darkly,

"Good, good. I'm glad you enjoyed it."

For a moment, we're locked in a tense silence, each of us sizing the other up, trying to gauge the other's intentions. As we lock eyes, a strange sense of curiosity washes over me. I can't help but notice how handsome he is, how clean, how.. normal; his features chiselled and sharp. He couldn't be much older than me, I realise, a fact that only adds to the mystery surrounding him. As his eyes wander, I'm suddenly acutely aware of my vulnerable state that I had almost forgotten, entirely naked in front of him.

"What's your name, princess?" I hesitate for a moment, my mind racing. Should I tell him? Does it even matter?

"Sienna,"

He nods, as if filing away the information for future use. "What's yours?" I find myself asking, unable to stop the words from escaping my lips. He smiles genuinely, his dimples deep; as if he'd never been asked a question before.

"Noah." he replies simply. He looks at me with purpose, his eyes locked in place.

"So, *Sienna*, what's your favourite meal? I'll make it for you later." I should probably be feeling more disturbed about my captor's sudden interest in my favourite food, but I'm honestly more taken aback by the fact that he took the time to cook the meal himself.

"You cooked this?" The words escape my lips in a hushed whisper; disbelief mingling with a tinge of curiosity as I glance at the plate before me. Noah's lips curve into a faint smirk, a glint of pride dancing in his eyes.

"Yes, princess. Surprised?" His tone holds a hint of mockery, as though my astonishment amuses him. I nod slowly, unable to tear my focus away from him, still trying to process. "My mother taught me how to cook." Noah continues, his voice softening slightly as he speaks of his mother.

For an instant, the mask of indifference cracks. There's a flicker of humanity in his eyes, a glimpse of the person he might have been before whatever the fuck happened to lead him here.

"She sounds nice," I offer tentatively. A shadow passes over Noah's features, his gaze distant.

"She was," he murmurs, his voice tinged with melancholy. "She's dead." The silence that follows is heavy with unspoken pain, and I can feel the weight of my own grief settling in my chest.

"I understand." I offer softly, my throat tight with emotion. He raises an eyebrow, urging me to elaborate. "Both of my parents are dead too," I confess, the words spilling forth before I can stop them.

For a moment, a flicker of understanding passes between us, a shared sorrow that transcends the boundaries of the situation. In that instant, the walls that separate us seem to crumble; a strange kinship in our shared loss. Noah's expression softens with genuine empathy.

"I'm sorry, Sienna." he says, his voice carrying a weight of sincerity that catches me off guard.

"It's okay."

I find myself unable to tear my eyes away from him, captivated by the terrifying intensity of his stare. In his eyes, I see a reflection of my own insecurities.

"Why am I here?" I ask, avoiding any continuation of the current topic. Noah gives a sinister grin.

"Your little friend, Dean. And his mates," he starts, "they've got you into quite a bit of trouble."

"What did he do?"

"I wish I knew exactly," he says, "Despite what people think, Grizzly doesn't tell me everything. "

I struggle to find the strength to understand or even process his words. My mind races with questions, but the exhaustion weighs heavy on my limbs, leaving me unable to even muster the energy to ask who Grizzly is.

"Anyway, how are you feeling, princess? Did we rough you up too much?" he asks, his tone strangely calm. I swallow hard, my throat dry and constricted.

"I'm fine." It's a lie, of course, but admitting weakness feels like surrendering.

Without warning, Noah's fingers dig into my arms, his grip like a vice as he hauls me onto my feet. I can't suppress the sharp intake of breath that escapes me.

"I'll be the judge of that." I stagger slightly, my legs threatening to give way beneath me. Noah pays no mind to my struggle, his attention focused solely on my injuries. He runs his hands over my bruised and battered flesh, his touch cold and clinical. But also, strangely gentle.

I flinch as his touch lingers on the most intimate parts of my body, his fingers tracing over the bruises, cuts and marks left behind by their relentless assault.

"Was there much blood when we finished with you?" he asks, his tone disturbingly casual.

"Uh, I don't remember." I mumble, my eyebrows scrunched in confusion.

"It's okay, princess," he says with a straight face, his fingers trailing lightly along the jagged edges of a particularly nasty bruise. "I don't expect you to remember everything."

His words stun me, the contradiction between his gentle and callous words leaving me utterly bewildered. I struggle to comprehend the situation. I struggle to work him out. Why is he even in here doing this? Noah's actions, his alternating between cruel indifference and unsettling care, leave me disorientated and reeling with so many questions.

Then, his hand comes down lightly on my bruised and tender behind; the impact sending a jolt of pain coursing through my body. I gasp, taken aback by the suddenness of the gesture, my muscles tensing in response. My eyes widen in surprise as I process what just happened. It wasn't a harsh or brutal smack, but rather almost casual, as if it were an everyday occurrence.

He chuckles lightly at my reaction.

"You'll live." he jokes with a wink, and in a relaxed yet deliberate motion, he gently shoves me back onto the floor. Though the action isn't rough, the underlying threat lingers in the air, a constant reminder of the power he holds here.

"Hey, what was that for?" I question with a scowl. Noah floods the room with genuine laughter and presenting a charming smile he replies.

"Careful, princess." he taunts, "You're getting too brave."

Noah grabs the plate and stands, his imposing figure casting a shadow over me as he makes a show of straightening his shirt. As he walks and reaches for the door handle, I speak, my voice gentle.

"You're a bad person."

He pauses, his hand hovering over the handle, before slowly turning to face me. A curious glint in his eyes.

"Correct. I am." he admits, his voice low and menacing. "But at least I'm honest about it. Can you say the same about your little friends? After all, they're the reason you're here in the first place, right?"

My breath catches in my throat, a surge of anger rising within me at his cruel insinuation.

"They're nothing like you."

"If that was the case, they wouldn't even be on our radar." he laughs, "And where are they now, princess? Huh? Whilst you're here with me. Lying naked, on the floor. Where are they?" Noah's smirk twists into a sadistic grin as he watches a small hint of doubt dawn on me. "Get some more sleep while you can."

With that, he turns on his heel and strides out of the room,

leaving   me   alone   with   my   thoughts.

CHAPTER 23:
WHERE IS SHE?

Marcus

The morning light filters through the curtains. I sit at the dining table in Dean's room, my mind racing with a thousand thoughts, yet I feel numb, disconnected from reality. Sienna's absence hangs in the air like a heavy cloud, suffocating me with each passing moment.

I haven't slept at all; the events of last night replaying in my mind like a broken record, each moment etched into my memory with painful clarity.

I can hear the soft sounds of breathing from Dean, a stark contrast to the turmoil raging within me. I feel like a caged animal, restless and on edge, desperate for some semblance of control in a situation spiralling out of hand.

I can't bring myself to move, rooted to the spot. Paralyzed.

I close my eyes, trying to push back the overwhelming tide threatening to drown me. But even in the darkness behind my eyelids, I can still see her face, haunted by a pain I couldn't protect her from. Where the fuck have they taken her? What have they done to her? The thoughts fill me with a cold dread that I can't ignore.

Several more hours pass as I sit there, lost in my thoughts. The minutes crawl by, each one more painful than the last.

When Dean finally stirs around 11 a.m., I'm snapped out of my reverie. His voice drifts from the other room, muted yet comforting in familiarity.

"You up?" he asks through the door.

"Of course I am." Dean enters the room, his expression sombre as he takes in the scene before him. He can see the exhaustion etched into every line of my face, offering me a sympathetic glance before taking a seat opposite me at the table.

"How'd you sleep?" he asks, his voice gentle yet tinged with concern. I meet his gaze, unable to mask the weariness that weighs me down.

"Didn't. Personally I don't know how you could." I snap through gritted teeth. I mean what I say. I feel like I'm on another planet. How any of us could sleep through this is beyond me.

"If we get no sleep we're useless, man."

After a moment of silence, Dean begins to get changed.

"How was Sky?" I ask. He hesitates for a moment, his expression guarded.

"Fine," he says tersely, his voice tight with emotion. "I made sure she blocked her door."

"Good."

As Dean finishes getting changed, I straighten up in my seat, steeling myself for the conversation that I know needs to happen.

"We need to go back to the warehouse," I say, my voice low but determined. "I can't sit around any longer."

"Of course," he replies, his voice heavy, "but we need to take our time, bro. The way you walked in there last night would've gotten us killed, we were *so* unprepared." I feel a surge of frustration at his words, knowing that he's right but hating the feeling in my stomach.

"We don't have time!" I snap, through gritted teeth. "Sienna's out there, God knows where, and we're sitting here twiddling our fucking thumbs! Sleeping!" But Dean doesn't back down.

"I get it, man," he says, his voice steady despite my agitation. "But this is a serious organisation, we can't pile in without some kind of plan. If we get ourselves killed what fucking good are we to Sienna?" I scoff, the sound bitter and mocking.

"A plan?" I repeat incredulously. "And what good has all this cautious planning done so far? Huh?" I retort, my voice tinged with annoyance and worry. "We've been tiptoeing around, playing it safe in these shitty cottages in the middle of nowhere, and where has it gotten us?"

Dean meets my gaze, his expression a mixture of understanding and concern.

"I know you're worried, bro. We all are." he says, his voice calm but tinged with caution. "But we need to think this through." I shake my head, my frustration reaching its peak.

"I've been thinking all fucking night!" I snap, the words bursting from me like a dam breaking under pressure. "Trust me, bro. I've thought of everything."

There's a heavy weight in my chest as I say the words, the reality of what Sienna might be enduring as we speak. I can't bear to think about it, can't bear to imagine the pain and terror she might be experiencing. But I can't ignore it either, not when her life hangs in the balance.

Without another word, I rise from my seat, the chair scraping against the floor as I push it back with more force than necessary.

"Fuck this." I mutter under my breath, my hand instinctively reaching for my gun. I can't stand the thought of waiting any longer, of letting Sienna suffer while we sit idly by. Dean's eyes widen in alarm as he watches me, sensing the shift in my demeanour; but I've already made up my mind.

"I'll wait in the car for five minutes," I declare, my voice firm and unwavering. "If you're not there, I'm going on my own."

I stride out of the room, my footsteps heavy with the weight of our situation. Each step feels like an eternity as I make my way to the car, my mind racing with thoughts of Sienna and what those bastards might be doing to her. Is she even alive?

Fuck, Marcus. What have you done?

Settling into the driver's seat, I clench the steering wheel tightly, trying to quell the storm of emotions raging inside me. I watch the clock on the dashboard change.

11:32. 11:33. 11:34. Those agonising minutes pass before the passenger door creaks open, and Dean slides into the seat beside me; his expression hardened, gun in hand. We share a tense glance, before Dean's voice breaks the silence.

"Let's kill some people." he says, his words finally laced with a fierce resolve.

I meet Dean's gaze with a surge of adrenaline coursing through me, and a genuinely proud smile spreads across my face.

"That's more fucking like it."

As we reach the warehouse once again, I can feel the tension thickening in the air. Dean's plan to wait outside this time feels like the right call, a contrast to my reckless charge in last night. We slip into a hidden parking spot, obscured from view but offering a perfect vantage point to survey the warehouse entrance.

The minutes tick by like grains of sand in an hourglass, each one an excruciating reminder of the waiting game we're forced to play. Hours dissolve into an endless expanse of silence, punctuated only by the occasional flicker of a passing car or the distant hum of machinery. Every second feels like an eternity, each tick of the clock a slow, agonizing torture as we remain fixed, our eyes riveted on the building before us.

But finally, our patience pays off. A buff figure emerges and heads towards the warehouse entrance. My heart jumps into my throat as I recognize him. It's Moth.

Dean and I share a knowing look. This is it, our chance to fight back and bring Sienna home.

With a silent agreement, we slip out of the car and move stealthily towards the warehouse, our senses sharp and our movements calculated. We reach the door, and as Dean and I meet each other's gaze, the past unfurls before us like a tapestry. The countless moments of laughter, of danger, of sacrifice; all the memories we've shared flash through our minds in a single, electric moment. It's as if we're speaking a language that transcends words, our eyes conveying a depth of understanding and connection that can only be forged through shared experiences. And now, facing this together, guns in hand, our bond feels stronger than ever.

We know what needs to be done, and we're in this together.

With that, I boot the door open; our hearts beating as one. As we storm into the warehouse, Moth stands there, examining the wreckage of the cars. His eyes blaze with fury as he takes in the sight of us, both armed. I waste no time, my voice dripping with disdain as I taunt him.

"Sorry about the cars, mate." Moth's face twists into an immediate mask of rage, his fists clenched at his sides.

"You will be, you little shits." Moth sneers, his voice dripping with venom. "Come back for more, have ya?" My grip tightens on my gun, my jaw set in determination.

"Absolutely." Moth's lips curl into a smirk, his eyes glinting with malice.

"Why are you doing all the talking, ay?" he taunts. "You're not exactly our top priority here. The Boss wants the blondie." he nods towards Dean.

"I don't give a fuck about any of that," I start as I stride closer, my eyes locked onto my target, "Where's Sienna?" Moth's laughter cuts through the tension, purposefully loud and mocking.

"Ahh, Sienna," he taunts, his voice dripping with derision. "What do you care? She's nothing to you now. In fact, she's been quite entertaining while you've been busy with your little heroics."

My jaw clenches with fury.

"What the fuck are you talking about?" I growl, my voice barely contained. Moth's smirk widens into a cruel teeth-baring grin as he continues to provoke me.

"You know exactly what I'm talking about," he jeers, his tone filled with malicious glee. "Let's just say, our little Sienna's been keeping us quite satisfied in your absence."

Oh yeah, he's about to fucking die.

My vision blurs with rage, the urge to lash out nearly overwhelming. But I reign in my anger until I can find out exactly where they're holding her.

"You have no idea the things we did to her, brother." he sneers, relishing in his adversary's torment. "We showed her a whole new world." I stride forward until we're face to face, my gun held firmly into his side.

"Tell me where she is." I repeat, my voice edged with a lethal threat.

"Drop the gun and I might, pretty boy."

For a tense moment, nobody moves, the air thick with anticipation. Then, with a reluctant nod, I release my grip on the weapon, allowing it to clatter to the ground. Fuck the gun. Once I know where my sweet is, I'll kill this cunt regardless.

"Where is she?" I state, my patience wearing thin. But instead of answering, the prick's grin widens, a dark glint in his eyes.

"Oh, man," he purrs, his voice laced with cruelty. "She felt so fucking good."

With each vile utterance that drips from his lips, my rage ignites like a wildfire, quickly burning away all reason and restraint. My muscles tense with the effort to contain the torrent of emotions coursing through me; my jaw clenched so tight it feels as if it might shatter. He dares to speak again, each word laced with sadistic pleasure.

"Oh brother, you have no idea the pain we put her through. The way her body trembled as we took her, one by one. *Corr.* We passed her around like a fuckin' blunt."

I never truly understood the concept of 'seeing red'.

Until now.

Now I understand.

I'm seeing fucking red. Drowning in it. Every breath tastes like his blood. As I'm staring into his eyes, he's not a man standing before me. He's a walking corpse, a soul already damned. I can smell the stench of death radiating from him. He takes another step closer to me.

"From the moment she stepped foot into our hellhole, we made damn sure she knew who was in charge. We toyed with her head 'till she didn't know which way was up, just so we could watch the hope drain from her eyes when she realised she was fucked."

"I won't fucking ask you again. Where. Is. She?"

No answer.

"We pinned her down like animals, held her helpless beneath us as we ravaged her little body in ways you can't even begin to imagine. Left her raw and bleeding. We made her beg, made her scream for mercy, knowing damn well we weren't gonna give her none. And she screamed, *God*, did she scream."

Fuck red. I'm seeing black. I'm seeing him in a bloodbath so gruesome, it'll make your stomach churn.

"You wanna know the worst part? She screamed out for *you*, brother. Cried out for you to come and save her. And where were you, ay?"

I charge at him, my fists swinging like hammers. I can feel the satisfying crunch of bone beneath my knuckles, the sickening squelch of flesh. Every blow is a release, a cathartic purge of all the anger and frustration that's been building inside me since they took her. I want to see him suffer.

Moth's cries of pain are drowned out by the sounds of my blood pumping in my ears and the echoes of Sienna's screams in my mind, a symphony of vengeance unleashed upon the vile creature before me. Blood sprays across my face, hot and sticky against my skin. I taste it on my lips, fuelling my rage; driving me to new heights of brutality.

Moth lies battered on the ground before me, but I'm not done. I grab him by the collar, pulling him up so I can look him in the eyes. I want him to see the fury burning within me, to know that he brought this upon himself. He's about to pay for his sins in blood.

"I'm gonna ask you one more fucking time. Where is she?"

"Okay, okay, fuck! I'll tell you." he stammers, his voice trembling with pain.

"Now!" His eyes dart around the room before they land on a workbench at the back.

"She's in a house just a few streets up," he blurts out, desperation evident in his voice. "The address is written on a piece of paper over there."

I narrow my eyes, studying Moth's expression for any signs of deception. But there's no denying the raw terror in his eyes, the desperation of a man who knows he's on the brink of his own demise. I turn to Dean.

"Check it," I bark, my voice sharp and commanding. "Make sure he's not lying." Dean nods, his jaw set with determination as he strolls leisurely towards the workbench. Meanwhile, I fix my focus on Moth, my eyes boring into his.

"I'm telling the truth, brother. C'mon.." I don't respond, instead choosing to remain a steady gaze on the vermin in my hand.

Finally, Dean makes his way back over, standing in front of me, a triumphant grin plastered across his face.

"He's telling the truth," he announces, holding up a piece of paper with an address scrawled on it.

"See, I told ya." he has the audacity to murmur.

"I'm glad." I start, "but unfortunately for you, it doesn't matter."

"Please, man!" he pleads *oh-so* satisfyingly.

"And you wanna know the worst part?"
"I apologise, man! C'mon!"

"We just toyed with your head until you didn't know which way was up, just so we could watch the hope drain from your eyes when you realise that you're fucked."

I don't hesitate. With a swift motion, I draw my knife, the blade's deadly edge glinting with an ominous light in the dimly lit room. Without a shred of pity or mercy, I press the razor-sharp edge against Moth's throat, savouring the stark terror that wells up in his eyes like a dark, icy pool.

"This is for Sienna."

With deliberate slowness, I begin to draw the blade across Moth's throat, savouring every agonised whimper that escapes his lips. The crimson torrent erupts, painting his clothes and the floor with a macabre canvas of crimson, as his life force bleeds out in a slow, agonising trickle. I carve him like a fucking pumpkin.

Moth thrashes and struggles, but I hold him firm, my grip unyielding as I continue to slice deeper and deeper. Dean aids me, stepping firmly on his forehead to keep him steady. The metallic tang of blood fills the air.

But I don't stop there. No, I keep going, driven by a primal urge for vengeance that consumes me from within. I stab, and I stab, and I stab. With each stab of the knife, I feel the weight of my torment and anger lifting from my shoulders, replaced by a savage satisfaction that's almost intoxicating. I stab until every feature on his face blurs into one mushy pile of flesh and bone.

Moth's head hangs from his neck, almost as if it's barely tethered to his body. Hanging by threads. The muscles inside his neck twitch chaotically, giving me goosebumps as I watch the life drain from his eyes. There's a sickening gurgle as blood continues to spurt from the gaping wound in his throat, the crimson liquid pooling on the floor beneath him in a gushing puddle.

Despite the horror unfolding before me, I feel good. Really, really fucking good. So good you wouldn't believe.

Finally, with one last gurgling gasp, Moth falls silent, his lifeblood spilling out onto the floor in a gruesome tableau of death. I watch impassively as the light fades from his eyes, knowing that *some* justice has been served.

As I finally stand up, my muscles still trembling with the remnants of adrenaline, I look down on Moth's lifeless body. With a mixture of satisfaction and disgust, I raise my foot and deliver a hard kick to his side, the impact eliciting a dull thud; before spitting on his motionless form.

But before I can turn away, Dean steps forward, a glint of malice in his eyes.

"And just for good luck," he says, his voice dripping with contempt.

Without hesitation, he raises his weapon and unleashes a barrage of bullets into Moth's already mangled head. The sound of gunfire reverberating through the room, each shot a final punctuation mark on the gruesome scene before us.

As the echoes of the shots fade away, I feel a sense of closure wash over me. Moth may have been an architect of torment, but now he's nothing more than a bloody corpse, his reign of terror extinguished for good.

"Let's go get my girl."

CHAPTER 24:
CHARLOTTE

Sienna

I sit on the edge of the bed, my mind swirling with a mix of boredom and desperation. The silence in the room is suffocating, weighing heavy on my chest like a leaden blanket. It must've been hours since Noah left me here, alone and isolated, with nothing but my thoughts for company; drifting into unsettling territory.

I've started to notice the little things, the subtle changes in my surroundings. I find myself watching my own bruises, tracing the patterns with my fingertips and studying them with a morbid fascination. I wonder if they'll change, if they'll somehow fade away as I stare. I listen to the sound of my own heartbeat, the steady rhythm echoing in the silence like a drumbeat of despair. Each thud is a reminder that I am still alive.
My eyes glue to the darkened stains that mar the floor and soak into the bedding.

361

Is this where I'm going to die?

I used to think that the way my parents went was a horrible way to die, to be snatched away so suddenly, with no warning. But now, as I sit here in this dark, forsaken place, I can't help but wonder if their fate was a mercy compared to mine. I'm certain that looking down on me in this room, they would be praying for me to meet death the way they did. It'd be a privilege.

At least they were spared the agony of knowing what was coming, the slow, agonising descent into darkness. At least they were spared the torment of being violated, of having their bodies defiled by those who would seek to break them.

Suddenly the door bursts open, flooding the room with blinding light that leaves me disoriented and blinking furiously. For a moment, I can't make sense of what I'm seeing, my mind struggling to process the sudden intrusion. But as my eyes adjust to the harsh glare, the scene before me comes into focus with chilling clarity. My heart lurches in my chest as one of the men barges in, tossing a woman onto the floor with a cruel disregard, before locking the door once again. The sound of her body hitting the ground echoes in the silence.

I sit in shock, as I watch her crumple to the ground in a heap. She's naked, just like me, her body covered in bruises and cuts that mirror my own. I'm frozen, unable to tear my eyes away from her broken form. Fear and shock grip me like icy tendrils, rendering me speechless and immobile.

Every fibre of my being screams at me to do something, to reach out and offer comfort to this stranger who shares my torment. But I'm paralyzed, trapped in a suffocating bubble of terror that squeezes the breath from my lungs.

And then, almost imperceptibly, she tilts her head upward, and our eyes meet fully for the first time.

It's as if the darkness itself has come to life, two piercing orbs locking onto mine with an unblinking intensity that sears my soul. I find myself unable to tear my eyes away from hers. I feel a lump form in my throat as I struggle to find my voice.

"Hello," I manage to whisper, my voice barely audible above the pounding of my heart.

"Hello?" she murmurs, clearly in shock.

"Hi." It feels strange to speak, as if the sound of my own voice is foreign to me.

"How long have you been here?" she asks, her tone filled with disbelief.

"I.. I'm not sure," I stammer, taken aback by the intensity of her gaze. "I think about a day." Her confusion seems palpable as she fires off questions.

"What's your name?" she asks, her voice trembling with a mixture of fear and uncertainty.

"Sienna," I reply, as I struggle to make sense of the situation. "What's *your* name?"

"Charlotte." she snaps out, "Why are you here?" she demands, her voice growing more urgent with each passing moment.

"I don't know," I admit, my voice choked with emotion. Her brow furrows in confusion.

"But you must know something," she insists, her voice rising with frustration as she moves closer to me. "You must remember something about how you ended up here. You.. you must have some idea. This room is empty, it's always empty." Her words are flustered and frantic and I'm struggling to keep up.

"Then what is this room for?" She seems to be frustrated everytime I ask her a question, as though she's running out of time.

"I get thrown in here for a few minutes every now and then while they 'clean' the room next door." she tells me in a rush, "The man who just threw me in, did he bring you here?"

I close my eyes, trying to block out the flood of memories that threaten to overwhelm me. I nod my head quickly.

"Yes, and three others."

"*Four* men brought you here? Are you sure? I've only ever met three men here aside from Grizzly." she stammers disorderly and in complete and utter disbelief. I nod, my eyes widening with confusion and a sliver of fear.

"I'm sure."

"Four men?" she mumbles to herself, "I don't mean to pry, it's just.." she continues, her voice growing more frantic with each word, "I must've been down here for almost 20 years now and.. and there's never been anybody else brought here."

Charlotte's words hit me like a ton of bricks.

Twenty years?

The realisation sinks in slowly, seeping into the recesses of my mind like a spreading stain. I feel a cold sweat break out across my skin. The thought of spending the next two decades trapped in this hellish prison fills me with a bone-deep dread. Twenty years of torment, rape, loneliness. Twenty years of pain and suffering. Twenty years of endless nights spent lying awake, counting the minutes until morning comes and the cycle begins anew.

"We have to get out of here." I declare, my voice trembling with newfound determination. Charlotte's eyes widen with alarm, her lips parting in disbelief.

"Oh, honey," she murmurs, her voice thick with emotion As she places a quick, comforting hand on mine. "There's no getting out." Her words hit me like a physical blow. For a moment, I'm speechless, her blunt answer crashing down on me with brutal force.

"No," I finally whisper, shaking my head in denial. "There has to be a way. If we work together!" A surge of anger rises within me, hot and fierce, burning away the numbness that has enveloped me like a shroud.

I can't just sit here and accept this fate. Not after what happened last night. Not after the way they violated me, their hands rough and cruel as they roamed my body. The tiny glimpse I've had of this life is enough for me. I refuse to let that be my reality.

"We have to fight back." I spit out the words, my voice cracking. Charlotte's eyes stretch wide in shock, her fingers digging into my hand as if she's desperate to anchor herself to me.

"Don't be ridiculous," she scoffs, her voice tinged with resignation. "Look at me, Sienna. I'm skin and bones. How do you expect me to fight back? You fight at all and you'll be punished for it."

The door explodes open, slamming shut behind the pair of men who storm in, their faces illuminated by the harsh light. The skinny man who had brought Charlotte in earlier returns alongside the bearded man I also met yesterday, their faces twisted into scowls of anger.

"Hey! We didn't put you in here so you bitches could chit chat." one of them barks, his voice thick with menace. Their eyes lock on Charlotte and I, sitting together on the bed, and their expressions darken with fury. It's clear that they're not pleased to find us conversing.

Without a word, the bearded man strides forward, his hand darting out like a snake to snatch Charlotte up by the arm. She cries out in pain as he yanks her roughly to her feet, his grip like a vice around her slender wrist.

In a moment of blind rage and desperation, I find myself rising to my feet, my body moving on instinct alone.

"Get off of her!" I shout, my voice cracking with emotion as I reach out to grab the man's arm. Before I can even register what I'm doing, I sink my teeth into his flesh, biting down hard with all the force I can muster. He recoils with a yelp of pain, his grip on Charlotte loosening just enough for her to break free.

As I sink my teeth into the man's arm, a surge of pain shoots through my own body as his free hand lashes out, punching me with a force that sends me sprawling to the ground. The impact jolts me, knocking the breath from my lungs as I land with a sickening thud.

Stars dance before my eyes as I struggle to push myself back up, my head spinning with dizziness. Through the haze of pain, I can hear Charlotte's cries growing louder, mingling with the shouts of the men as they punish her for my actions. Trembling with a mixture of fear and anger, I force myself to my feet, my muscles screaming in protest. Blood drips from the corner of my mouth, but I ignore the pain, my focus fixed solely on Charlotte.

But as I stagger forward, my legs feeling like lead weights beneath me, I realise with a sinking feeling that it's too late. The other man has already seized her, his grip like iron as he drags her back into the room next door.

As the men loom over me, their eyes gleaming with malice, I steel myself for the onslaught to come. But nothing could prepare me for the violation that follows.

"So you wanna bite, huh?" He yells. "You think you're fucking tough?"

"Clearly she didn't learn her fucking lesson." Their hands roam my body, groping and grabbing with a sickening sense of entitlement. I recoil in horror, my skin crawling with revulsion as his touch sears into my flesh like a branding iron.

One of them pins me down on my back, his weight crushing me as he presses against me; restraining my arms above my head. I struggle beneath him, but he only laughs, his grip unyielding. His breath is hot against my skin, his foul words like a poison in my ears.

Meanwhile, the other man circles around me, a sick grin on his face. He spits on his fingers before forcing my legs apart, his intentions clear. Time seems to slow to a crawl as I watch in horror, every movement drawn out in agonising detail. His fingers inch closer to my most intimate parts, a slow-motion nightmare unfolding before my eyes.

The world narrows down to a singular focus: the impending violation, the violation I cannot allow to happen.

'Then fight, sweet.'

With a surge of adrenaline, I try to summon all of my remaining strength and drive my knee into his tiny little balls with all the force I can muster. He doubles over with a grunt of pain, causing the other man's hold on me to loosen momentarily. Seizing the opportunity, I break free and scramble to my feet, my heart pounding in my chest as I make a desperate bid for freedom.

'Show me what you've got.'

With every ounce of strength I possess, I fight back, lashing out with all the fury of a cornered animal. I claw at their faces, rake my nails down their arms, bite, hit, kick, anything to make it stop.

The fight rages on but despite my best efforts, I'm outnumbered, outmatched, and outgunned. Their fists rain down on me with merciless force, each strike sending shockwaves of pain rippling through my battered body.

"Come on little girl. Just give up and get it over with." the bearded man laughs. I grit my teeth, my fists flying in a desperate bid to fend them off.

"Fuck you!" I shout, my voice raw with defiance.
But it's like trying to hold back a tidal wave with my bare hands. I can't win.

With a final, brutal blow, I'm sent crashing to the ground, the impact jolting the breath from my lungs. I lie there, gasping for air, as they descend upon me like vultures, their hands tearing at my skin, their vile laughter ringing in my ears. Their fingers ram inside me as I scream out in rage and the most intense frustration I've ever experienced.

"That's better." one of them taunts, his voice a sickening whisper in my ear. "Pathetic bitch." Before I can react, he slices through my thighs again, leaving behind a searing trail of pain. I bite back a scream, my body convulsing with agony.

But even as I lie there, bleeding, I refuse to give them the satisfaction of seeing me cry. I grit my teeth, fighting back the tears, as they walk away.

They turn to close the door, leaving me alone in the suffocating darkness of the room, when I catch sight of their bleeding arms and a deep scratch on one of their faces.

As the door slams shut behind them, the room descends once more into suffocating blackness. But I'm not sad. Believe it or not, I feel powerful. The satisfaction that surges through me is electric. A feral grin creeping onto my face, raw and untamed.

I drew blood.

CHAPTER 25:
GET READY

Dean

As we step out of the warehouse, the chill of the air hits me like a slap in the face, jolting me back to reality. My mind is a whirlwind of chaos, trying to process everything that just happened. It's like a bad dream that I can't shake off. I glance over at Marcus, his expression stoic as ever.. somehow.

Don't get me wrong, I've seen and done a lot of shit. Foul, violent, evil shit. But nothing like what just went on in that warehouse. The casual taunts of Sienna's abuse, the blood, the bones, the hanging-off head. It's too graphic to comprehend. Marcus seems to be desensitised. But me? I'm shaken up.

Just as I'm about to join Marcus in the car, my phone rings. It's Delilah. I answer quickly, trying to keep the tremor out of my voice.

"Yo, baby." I say, my voice sounding hollow and distant even to my own ears.

"Dean, where are you? I've been calling all morning." she says, her voice filled with concern.

"I'm sorry I've just been.. Uh-" I reply, struggling to find the right words as my mouth begins watering with nausea. "We've been working on some stuff."

There's a pause on the other end of the line, and I can feel Delilah's worry through the phone.

"Are you okay?" she asks softly, her voice tinged with anxiety. I take a deep breath, feeling a rush of gratitude for Delilah's presence and care. Just the sound of her voice makes me feel calmer.

"Honestly baby, it's been a rough couple days." I admit, my voice cracking with emotion. "Sienna was taken from her room and we've been trying to track her down." There's a long silence before Delilah speaks again.

"Oh dear God, is she okay?"

"We don't know. Marcus just uh.. Just killed one of the guys who grabbed her and we're heading to the address he gave us now. I'm so sorry baby but I have to go."

I can hear my darling Delilah holding her tears back through the phone.

"Please, please be safe, okay?"

"Always. I love you." I reply, feeling a lump form in my throat.

With that, I hang up the phone and slide into the driver's seat, the leather cool against my skin. As Marcus sits calmly in the passenger seat beside me, I start the engine.

"You good?" he asks, his voice low and measured. I force a tight smile and nod.

"Yeah, bro, I'm fine. I'm glad you did that." I grip the steering wheel tightly. I'm not fine, not even close. But I can't let Marcus see that. Can't let him see the cracks in my facade.

"Me too."

"Are you ready to see her? You know, after what he told us." Marcus studies me for a moment, but quickly shrugs and looks away.

"I don't even know if what he said was true, man. I just need to bring her home."

As we near the house, tension coils in my chest like a spring, every nerve on high alert. Marcus's glare sweeps the surroundings, his face a mask of concentration. I'm drawn to the imposing edifice looming before us, its massive walls rising like a monolith from the earth. It's a large home, surrounded by a high black gate that looms like a fortress wall. Several sleek cars are parked in the driveway, their polished surfaces glinting.

The house itself is grand and imposing, exuding an aura of wealth and privilege, a stark contrast to the darkness that we know lurks within. Marcus' jaw is clenched tight, his eyes fixed on the house with laser-like focus. I can tell he's assessing the situation, weighing our options with precision. I swallow hard, trying to quell the rising sense of unease in my gut.

Sienna could be right there, trapped behind those imposing walls, and time is running out.

But then, just as we're about to pull up to the curb, three men emerge from the house. My heart leaps into my throat, and I instinctively slam on the brakes, swerving sharply to the side and ducking out of sight. The car jerks to a halt, the engine still running as we sit in silence, hidden from their view.

I steal a glance at Marcus, his features tight with tension. His eyes are fixed on the men outside, tracking their movements with hawk-like precision. We hold our breath, the seconds stretching into eternity as the men drive off. Only when they're out of sight do we release the breath we've been holding, a collective sigh of relief. My hands tremble slightly as I wipe the sweat from my brow.

"Holy fuck." I mutter.

"Three less cunts to worry about, right?" I nod with a slight chuckle, my own pulse still racing from the close call.

"But how many more inside?"

Marcus' expression darkens at the reminder, his jaw clenched tight with determination. I can see the gears turning in his mind as he calculates our next move, weighing the risks.

"I can't wait any longer," he says, his voice low and urgent. "Let's fucking go." I nod in agreement, a surge of adrenaline coursing through my veins at the prospect of finally confronting the monsters who took Sienna from us. It's time to bring her home.

CHAPTER 26:
SAVING SWEET SIENNA

Sienna

I can't get Charlotte out of my mind.
I can't unsee her.
I can't unhear her.
Her presence lingers in this room like a ghost.

Minutes are blending into hours.
Hours are feeling like days.

The pain is a constant companion. It's no longer a sensation; it's a living, breathing entity that coils around my limbs, gnawing at my flesh. Every movement is agony, a symphony of torment that plays out in every fibre of my being.

I can't escape it. It's everywhere.
Like a suffocating shroud that clings to me, refusing to let go. I run my hands over my body, searching for any patch of unharmed skin, but there's none to be found. Bruises bloom like

374

grotesque flowers across my flesh, their colours shifting from sickly purples to angry reds.

I've learned to navigate the pain, in a twisted sort of way. I have discovered that hurting one part of my body can distract from the unrelenting pain of another.

A sharp pinch to my arm momentarily dulls the ache in my side. A hard stub of my toe removes the pain from my temples.

But it's still a cycle.

I think over Charlotte's words. Twenty years. I can't fathom it. The prospect of spending the next twenty years locked away in this bleak, soul-sucking hellhole fills me with a creeping bone-deep dread. How could I possibly survive another day, let alone twenty years? I can lie to myself all I want. Pretend all I want. The truth is, I'm not strong enough. I'm not strong enough to endure twenty years of this relentless torture, to face each day with the knowledge that there may never be an escape. The thought alone terrifies me.

How is it possible that I've met more people in a single day than Charlotte has in twenty years? *Aside from 'Grizzly' of course.* I'm yet to have that encounter.

And they were together. She was fucking dating the guy! The thought is incomprehensible. This whole thing is like trying to fit a square peg into a round hole. How did she get herself tangled up with someone so fucked up he would lock her in a basement for twenty years?

Says the girl happily in love with a murderer.

But then a tiny voice in the back of my mind whispers some truth; maybe it does make some twisted sort of sense. They knew each other, they had some kind of history. At least there's a thread, no matter how thin.. right?

But what about Dean? Me?

I lie down on the rough, hard bed, the bare mattress biting into my skin like a thousand tiny needles. I close my eyes, hoping that sleep will eventually come. But it doesn't.

I never realised just how many noises the human body makes.

In the dead silence I become acutely aware of the sound of my own breath, a rasping wheeze that fills the air with each inhalation and exhalation. The sound of my own blood pumping around my body. The gurgles in my stomach.

Although, those sounds are tolerable. They're Understandable. Expected.

It's the stranger noises that keep me awake.

There's the soft click of my eyelids closing, the flutter of my eyelashes on my skin. There's the unsettling squelch of my organs shifting inside me, the wet, slurping noise that seems to echo in the hollow cavity of my chest; the creak of my joints as I switch position.

There's the soft, wet sound of my tongue clicking against the roof of my mouth, the rustle of an endless stream of saliva that I keep needing to swallow.

But it's not just the sounds of my internal organs that distract me. There are other, more disturbing noises; the strange clicking and popping sounds that seem to come from within my own head.

A squelching sound emanating from between my legs. A perverse echo reverberating off the walls and crawling beneath my skin.

Then, a sudden break in the monotony; a faint flicker of light seeps through the bottom of the door, casting a feeble glow into the darkness. My heart lurches at the sight, my mind racing with possibilities. Not yet has this particular light shone through.

As a soft shuffle of footsteps descends the staircase, every nerve in my body is on edge. Each creak of wood reverberates through the silence like a gunshot. They're coming back. Panic sets in, and I scramble to hide beneath the bed.

But then the muffle of a voice breaks through.
It sounds like Marcus, my mind whispers.

It's a cruel lie. My hopeful brain playing tricks on me. I'm beginning to hallucinate.

Yet, the voice persists, growing louder and more insistent with each passing moment.

"Bro, check this out," it says.

Holy fuck. It *is* him.

Without a second thought, I launch myself towards the door, my heart pounding like a jackhammer in my chest. Every muscle in my body screams with exertion as I sprint across the room, my feet pounding against the cold, hard floor. I feel like I'm flying. Panic and desperation drive me forward, fueling my pained movements as I reach the door and unleash a barrage of fists upon its splintered surface.

"Marcus!" I scream, my voice raw with emotion. "Marcus, I'm here!"
Tears blur my vision as I pound on the door with all my strength, each blow reverberating through the room like a thunderclap.
"Sienna?!" he shouts back, his footsteps quickly descending closer.

With every passing second, the walls behind me feel like they're closing in, the space around me shrinking; as if the darkness itself is chasing me down. But I refuse to be swallowed by the void.

With every ounce of strength I possess, I continue to hammer away at the door, my cries growing louder and more frantic with each passing second.
"I'm in here, Marcus! Please!"

Marcus

I cannot fucking breathe.

Sienna's piercing screams and cries are breaking right through me.
I've never heard a scream like that before.

My heart thumps like a drum on steroids, pounding out a rhythm of stress and desperation as I fuck up almost every single lock first time, my fingers shaking so hard I can barely get a grip. With each clunk of metal, my chest tightens like a vice.

Each tortured cry is a stab to my heart, a reminder of the nightmare she's living while I stand here fumbling with the disgusting amount of locks on this fucking door.

With a final, desperate twist, the last lock gives way, and the door flies open, flooding the dark room holding her with a blinding light.
As I take in the sight of Sienna, my heart constricts with a visceral agony.
Nothing, absolutely nothing, could've prepared me for what I see before me.

She's a shadow of my sweet. Beaten, battered, bleeding, dirty.. Naked. Her body a canvas of cuts and bruises. Every tear in her flesh is a searing indictment of my failure to protect her. Dark thoughts swarm through my mind like a plague of locusts, each one more sinister than the last. As I take in every mark on her body I imagine how it came to be.

How could I have let this happen?

Without hesitation, I launch myself at her, my arms wrapping around her trembling little body. I hold her as tight as I possibly can, trying to shield her from the horrors that surround us; as if by sheer force of will I can erase the pain and anguish etched into every line of her battered face. Her sobs and guttural screams echo in my ears.

"*Oh God*, sweet." I whisper to her, my voice entirely shaky. "I'm so sorry."
Tears blur my vision as I press my lips to her forehead, murmuring words of comfort and solace against her skin.

"I'm here, okay? I'm here, I've got you. Nobody's gonna hurt you, sweet. I promise." I don't know if she can hear me, if she can even comprehend.

I've failed her.

As I cradle her in my arms, her sobs reverberating against my chest, I cast my gaze around the room.

Bloodstains mar the cold, hard floor.

My eyes catch on to the only piece of furniture in the room. A metal double bed, its frame devoid of any bedding save for a bare mattress. It looms in the dim light like a sacrificial altar, a grotesque symbol of the sickening depths of moral turpitude to which humanity can sink.

As I stare at the bed, Moth's words spiral around my mind.

'We pinned her down like animals, held her helpless beneath us as we ravaged her little body in ways you can't even begin to imagine.'

Believe me, I'm doing far more than imagining it.

I can see it.

I can see her on that bed.

'We made her beg, made her scream for mercy, knowing damn well we weren't gonna give her none. And she screamed, God, did she scream.'

The agonising screams coming from her right now are confirmation.

The cunt wasn't lying.

'You wanna know the worst part? She screamed out for you, brother. Cried out for you to come and save her. And where were you, ay?'

He wasn't. Fucking. Lying.

I promised that I would protect her.
Told her she was safe with me.
Earned her trust.
And then I put her here.

I put her on that fucking bed.
My hands tremble as I hold her close, feeling her shivering against me, her frail form seeming so small and fragile in my arms. She feels smaller than usual. More fragile.

"I'm sorry, sweet. I'm so sorry."
But apologies are meaningless now, mere whispers.

As Sienna slowly pulls away from the embrace, her tear-streaked face turns up to meet mine. Her eyes, once vibrant and full of life, now seem dull and haunted.

"You came." she whimpers. Her words are like a knife to the heart. Tears well up in my eyes as I nod, unable to find the words to express the overwhelming flood of emotions. The disbelief in her voice, the faint tremor of uncertainty, it tears me apart inside.

How could she even question whether I'd come for her? As if there was ever a choice.

All I can do is reach out and gently cup her cheek, tracing the lines of her face with trembling fingers.

"Sienna," I choke out, my voice breaking. "Of course, I came. I'd have watched the world burn around me to find you. I'd have let everything else fade to ashes. "

Dean steps into the room, his footsteps hesitant, his eyes widening in shock as they take in the scene before him. His focus flits from the bloodstains on the floor to Sienna's battered form, his breath catching in his throat at the sight.

"Jesus Christ," he murmurs, the words escaping him in a hoarse whisper. Shock and horror ripple across his features, his hands instinctively reaching out to steady himself against the doorframe.

Dean and I share a look, our eyes locking in a silent exchange that screams volumes. I see the raw emotion etched on his face, a mirror of my own turmoil, and for a moment, we're frozen in mutual disbelief at the depths of depravity we've stumbled upon. Sienna's voice breaks through the heavy silence.

"Marcus? Can we please get out of this room?"

I feel a lump form in my throat at the sound of her voice. Her plea hits me like a punch to the gut, the raw innocence in her voice tearing at my heartstrings. She's just a scared, broken girl, pleading for escape from the nightmare that's consumed her. Without hesitation, I reach out and take her hand, squeezing it and kissing it gently in reassurance. Tears sting my eyes as I reach out to her.

"Of course, beautiful.

"Thank you. I love you."

"I love you too, sweet."

CHAPTER 27:
MEETING GRIZZLY

Marcus

"Let's get you out of here, sweet." As I stand, Sienna sits before me, her body shivering with exhaustion and vulnerability. I reach out instinctively, my fingers finding hers as I lift her gently onto her feet.

My eyes trace the outline of Sienna's naked body, protectiveness washing over me. I refuse to leave her exposed, even for a moment longer. Without a second thought, I shed my hoodie, the fabric heavy with my own warmth and the weight of my determination to shield her from harm.

I step closer, my fingers trembling slightly as I pull the hoodie over her head and arms. The gesture more intimate than any words could convey. It's not just about keeping her warm; it's about giving her back a piece of the dignity and safety that's been stolen from her.

For a moment, there's just the sound of her breath catching in her throat, and then she looks up at me; Her eyes dark, filled with tears and something else I can't quite name. Gratitude, maybe. Relief. Whatever it is, it's enough to make the ache in my chest ease just a little.

As we start our ascent up the stairs, Sienna suddenly yells, catching me off guard.

"Wait!" Before I can even process her words, she releases my hand and rushes back down the stairs, her urgency palpable in every hurried little step. I watch intently, my curiosity piqued, as she reaches the bottom.

With nimble fingers, she begins to unlock the door to the room next to hers. Her fingers deftly find the sliding locks; there's a determined glint in her eye. Her actions deliberate. With one final motion the last lock clicks, echoing off the walls. As the door pops open, she pauses for a moment on the threshold, her breath catching in her throat.

When Sienna returns to us on the stairs, I don't hesitate to gather her into my arms, her body fitting perfectly against mine, as if belongs there.

Because it does.

We inch our way towards the front door, our hearts pounding. Each step feels like a victory. But that changes when we reach the front door.

It's locked.
Locked by a key that we don't have.

I turn to Sienna, trying to give her some kind of reassurance, but all I see is the same fear and confusion mirrored in her eyes. It's like a punch to the gut, the realisation sinking in that our escape might not be as simple as I made her believe.

Desperate for answers, I turn to Dean, but his gaze is fixed elsewhere, his expression pale and drawn. Following his line of sight into the living room, my stomach twists with dread. Something's not right.
And then, as if on cue, a familiar voice slices through the silence like a blade.

"Goin' somewhere?" I whirl around, my breath catching in my throat, to see a figure seated on the sofa.

My heart stops dead in my chest.
It's my dad.

My eyes lock onto the face, and my mind reels in denial as I try to reconcile the reality before me. Shock freezes me in place, a surge of disbelief coursing through my veins like ice water. My breath catches in my throat, my pulse pounding in my ears as I struggle to comprehend what I'm seeing.
"What's wrong, boy?" he asks "Look like you've seen a ghost."

This can't be happening. It can't be real. But as I meet his gaze, the hard lines etched into his face, I know with a sinking certainty that it is. As I lay eyes on my father, a surge of raw emotion courses through me; anger, resentment, and a deep-seated fear.
My father's presence in a place like this can't mean anything good.
"Dad.. what's going on?"

"I'll ask the fuckin' questions," he says, immediately raising his voice, "and it ain't dad right now, boy. You'll call me fuckin' Grizzly."

The revelation hits me like a freight train, the weight of it crashing down on me with a force I can scarcely comprehend. My dad? My fucking dad? The epitome of evil incarnate. And he's sitting right here, in front of me, as if it's the most natural thing in the world.

"I'm disappointed, Marcus," he continues, his tone now chillingly calm. "You were so fuckin' easy to lure. So pathetically predictable. I thought I raised you better than that."

A bitter laugh escapes me; a sharp, mirthless sound that cuts through the tension like a knife.

"Raised me?" I chuckle. "You didn't fucking raise me." Grizzly's lips curl into a twisted grin, his eyes gleaming with a sinister glint.

"Maybe I should've," he sneers, his voice dripping with sarcasm. "Then you would've been a bit fuckin' smarter." I square my shoulders, refusing to let his intimidation get the better of me.

"What the fuck do you want from *me*?" Dean questions, his voice stern. Grizzly's leer shifts towards Dean, his expression morphing into one of disdain.

"Oh, I don't want anythin' from *you*, mate. I just got lucky since my people 'ave already been after you for some drug business." He replies, "I wanted something from my boy after he left and needed a way to track him down. I knew if we increased the pressure, Marcus would follow you 'ere like a little fuckin' puppy."

My blood runs cold at his words, the realisation sinking in like a heavy weight in the pit of my stomach. My dad had orchestrated this entire situation, pulling the strings behind the scenes.

"Ahh, okay. So let me get this straight." I begin, my voice laced with sarcasm as I take a step closer to him. "You wanted something from me and you couldn't track me down? You needed me, so you waited for me to come home and I never did?"

The air crackles with tension as Grizzly's expression darkens, his jaw clenched with suppressed rage. We stare at each other, locked in a silent battle of wills, the weight of years of resentment and unanswered questions hanging between us.

"And how did that make you feel, dad?" I ask, my words cutting through the air. "Angry? Frustrated? Stressed?"

I hold his stare, unflinching, determined to make him understand the impact of his absence on my life. Every forgotten birthday, every unanswered call, every broken vow; all the moments he was absent from my life, all the memories we never made together. I pour them into that stare, a silent rebuke to the years he spent away from me.

The silence stretches on, thick and suffocating, as Grizzly meets my gaze with a steely resolve. His lips remain sealed.

"It's funny, because I can remember feeling that too.. Dad." The tense silence stretches on, my mind swirling with a whirlwind of emotions as I grapple with the anger and resentment that has simmered beneath the surface for so long.

"I didn't bring you 'ere to talk about this bollocks." he sneers, his tone dripping with disdain. My jaw clenches in frustration, the anger boiling within me threatening to spill over.

"Then why *did* you bring me here?" I demand, my voice trembling with barely contained fury. "Why did you put us through all of this? What the fuck do you want?"

"Where's the fuckin' book, boy?"
The room falls into an absolute stunned silence. Sienna, Dean, and I exchange incredulous glances, our confusion mirrored in each other's eyes. It's so absurd, so utterly unexpected, that for a moment, it's almost comical.

"Wait, what?" I blurt out, my mind struggling to process the sudden shift in conversation. "*Book?* What book?"

Don't get me wrong. We all know exactly what book he has to be talking about, but the revelation that my dad not only knows about the book's existence but is also demanding its whereabouts has completely thrown me off.

"Don't play dumb with me. You know what I'm talking about."

"What the fuck does that book have to do with you?" I demand, my voice rising with indignation.

"Just give me the Goddamn book!" Grizzly growls, his tone dripping with impatience and barely contained anger.

"I don't have it," I reply firmly, "And even if I did, why would I give it to you?" Grizzly's nostrils flare, his fists clenching at his sides.

"It's not up for discussion, boy. Hand it over now."

"I said I don't have it!" I snap back, my voice echoing off the walls of the room.

As Grizzly's rage boils over, his face contorts into a mask of fury, veins bulging in his forehead and neck like taut cables.

"You ungrateful little shit," he snarls, taking another step closer, the classic scent of his whiskey-breath now moving towards my face.

"You owe me!"

"I owe you nothing." I spit back.

Grizzly's fury ignites, his face contorted with rage as he stands before me. All of a sudden, the ominous click of a gun being cocked echoes in the tense silence.

My heart lurches in my chest as I feel the cold, hard steel of his gun pressing against my forehead.

CHAPTER 28:
AH FUCK

Marcus

At that moment, time seems to freeze. The world narrows down to the barrel of the gun, a metal extension of my father's wrath aimed directly at me. Disbelief, anger, and a bone-deep revulsion churn within me.

It really is my father that I'm looking at.

The man who was supposed to cherish and nurture me. The man who abandoned me. The man who walked away when I needed him the most. Even when I offered him chances to make things right, he couldn't find it in himself to do so. And now, instead of seeking redemption, he's here, pointing a gun at me.

"You're pathetic." I spit out, my bottom lip quivering with anger. "You think you can make up for all those years of neglect with a gun to my head? You really think you have any power over me after everything you've done?"

But even as I speak, there's a part of me that's screaming, begging him to stop, to be the father I always needed him to be. But it's useless. He'll never change, never admit to his mistakes, never take responsibility for the pain he's caused.

"I don't wanna have to do this, son." he says, his voice strained with a twisted kind of faux-concern. "Just tell me where the book is. We can end this right now."

"I'd rather fucking die." I reply, my voice steady somehow. "I'd rather die by your hands than give you *anything* you want from me."

As I stare into his eyes, a surge of memories flood my mind. The birthdays spent alone, the nights filled with tears, the constant ache of longing for a love that was never there. A childhood he robbed from me.

At this moment, I realise that I don't owe him anything. Not obedience, not loyalty, not even a fucking book. Because he lost the right to demand anything from me the day he walked out of my life. And so, as the gun presses harder against my skin, I meet his gaze with a steely resolve.

"Do it." I say, my voice steady despite the fear clawing at my insides. "Do it! Because getting rid of me doesn't erase what you've fucking done." I declare. "You'll never erase the scars you've left behind." Time slows to a crawl as my father's hand begins to shake around the gun, his face contorting with a mix of anger and frustration.

"Do it, you fucking pussy!" I shout, the words erupting from me with a force I didn't know I possessed.

His eyes flicker with something unreadable, and then, in a sickening twist, he turns the gun towards Sienna.

"No!" I yell, my voice raw with shock as I watch in horror. The word tears from my lips, raw with alarm and desperation, but it feels small and insignificant against the impending threat. In that split second, the world narrows down to the trajectory of the bullet, my heart pounding so loudly I can barely hear anything else. It's as if time itself has ground to a halt, each passing moment stretching out into an endless, oppressive expanse..

Miraculously, the bullet misses Sienna by mere inches as she instinctively crouches to the floor, crying out in terror; her arms covering her face in a desperate attempt to shield herself. I step to the side, deliberately positioning myself between her and Grizzly. Every fibre of my being is focused on protecting her. His hand trembles around the gun, his face contorted with rage.

"You spineless cunt." I snarl, venom dripping from every word. "That make you feel tough, huh?"

"I'll pick you off one by one until I find out where that fucking book is, believe me!"

"I already told you, we don't even have the book! Get that through your fucking head!"

Grizzly's lips curl into a twisted sneer, his features contorted with malice.

"You're just like your mother," he spits, "both got a smart fuckin' mouth."

"I wouldn't know." I state, my voice carrying the weight of a lifetime of absence and neglect. I can see the flicker of something in his eyes, a brief glimpse of recognition, perhaps even remorse, but it's quickly overshadowed by the usual emotion of rage.

"You don't know what it was like, boy," he growls, his grip on the gun tightening. "You don't know what I've had to do to survive!"

"That's on you. Not me, dad." I retort, my voice steady somehow. "You made your choices, and now you have to live with them."

"You think you're any better than me, boy?" he snarls, the gun shaking like a leaf in his hand. "You think you're some kinda saint 'cause you've got all these morals and principles, ay? Well, lemme tell you something, son. In this world, those don't mean shit. It's survival of the fittest, and if you're not willing to do what it takes, you'll end up dead in a ditch somewhere." I meet his gaze with a steely resolve, unflinching.

"Then put me in the ditch," I retort, my voice dripping with defiance. "Buried six feet under, I'll still be standing taller than you ever fucking could."

He fills the room with a deep laughter, a bone-chilling sound that seems to reverberate off the walls. It's a sound I've heard too many times before.

"You think you're tough, don't ya?" he sneers, a cruel smile playing at the corners of his lips. "Well, let's see how tough you are when I put a bullet in your skull."

As his laughter fills the room, a bitter taste floods my mouth, a seeping sourness, but I refuse to let it shake my resolve. Suddenly, Dean steps forward, placing himself directly in front of me, his eyes locked onto Grizzly's with an intensity that sends a chill down my spine.

"What the fuck are you doing?" I hiss, trying to push him back, but he stands firm, his stare unwavering.

"Focus on Sienna." He says, his voice low but filled with conviction.

Grizzly's laughter cuts through the tension like a knife, his eyes gleaming with malice as he watches our exchange.

"Well, ain't that touchin'," he sneers, his voice dripping with sarcasm. "What a little hero." He steps forward, his gaze and gun shifting from me to Dean, his lips curling into a twisted smile.

"Dean, move." I protest, my voice breaking with emotion. "Please."

But Dean just shakes his head, his expression resolute, as he takes a step closer to my father.

"You need to protect Sienna," he insists.

Tears prickle at the corners of my eyes as I stare at him, overwhelmed by the depth of his sacrifice. In this moment, I understand what true bravery looks like; not the reckless bravado of 'Grizzly', but the quiet, selfless courage of Dean willing to lay down his life.

Protect Sienna. Protect Dean.
My entire life summed up in four words.

Grizzly tightens his grip on the gun, his finger poised on the trigger, and I feel the world around me slow to a crawl. Then, I catch a whimper from Sienna. I glance down at her, and my heart shatters at the sight of her beautiful wide eyes filled with tears and horror, taking in the scene unfolding before her.
Without a second thought, I drop to my knees, pulling her into my arms to shield her from watching any longer.

"It's okay, sweet." I whisper, my voice trembling with emotion as I press her face against my chest. "Close your eyes. I'm here, okay? I've got you." She clings to me, her small frame shaking with fear, and I hold her close, my own heart pounding in my chest as I try to comfort her.

Sienna's cries echo in the room, her tears soaking my shirt as she holds onto me. The sobs fill my ears, tearing at my heart as I rock her gently, whispering words of comfort. I press my lips against her cheek, tasting the salt of her tears, as I will away the world to disappear. With a shudder, I close my eyes, burying my head into her hair, seeking solace in the scent of her.

And then, like a bolt from the blue, the deafening crack of a gunshot shatters the fragile bubble of our sanctuary, sending shockwaves reverberating through the room; followed by the thud of a body hitting the ground. Sienna gasps, her grip on me tightening with a vice-like intensity, as if she could hold onto me forever.

And though I can't bear to look, a sickening ball lurches in the pit of my stomach; the realisation hitting me like a physical blow,

Dean's been shot.

Sienna's cries reach a crescendo, a heartbreaking symphony of fear and despair that threatens to consume us both. I hold her even closer, if that's possible. A single thought echoes in the recesses of my mind; a name, a face, a presence so integral in my life that the mere thought of this actually happening is simply incomprehensible.

But just as I'm about to succumb to the suffocating weight of uncertainty, a sudden, shocking shout pierces the silence;

a voice so familiar, so unmistakably.. Dean.

CHAPTER 29:

DELILAH

Dean

"That's my fucking girl!" I shout. The words, raw with emotion, rip from my throat as I turn, my heart pounding; to see Delilah standing there in the hallway between the living room and the kitchen. My mind struggles to comprehend the scene before me as I take her in; the gun in her hand aimed at Grizzly, who now lies lifeless on the ground. Everything else fades away; all I see is her, my saviour, my love, my everything.

My heart swells with a mixture of awe and disbelief. Without thinking, without hesitating, I charge towards her, my legs feeling like they're made of lead and feathers at the same time. My blood thrumming in my veins. I close the distance between us in a heartbeat, and before I know it, I'm sweeping her off her feet, pulling her into a desperate, frantic embrace.

"*God*, Delilah," I growl, my voice rough with emotion, as I hold her tighter. "You are amazing."

She clasps onto me just as fiercely, her nails digging into my back, her breath coming in ragged gasps. And in this embrace, in this desperate, frantic tangle of limbs and hearts, I find everything I ever knew I needed. Home.

I glimpse briefly to Marcus and Sienna, who are slowly rising to their feet behind me. Locking eyes with Marcus, I offer him a subtle nod, a silent promise that I'm still here, still standing. His eyes, brimming with tears, meet with mine, and in that raw, unfiltered moment, it's like our souls are having a conversation; saying everything we can't put into words.

As I spin Delilah around in my arms, the rush of emotions threatens to overwhelm me. She laughs, the sound like music to my ears, as I finally place her back on her feet, holding her face tight between my hands.

"How the fuck did you get here?" I ask, my voice tinged with incredulity and relief. Delilah looks up at me, her eyes sparkling with mischief and affection.

"Well, you know that phone I gave you?" she says, her tone playful and lighthearted. "I might have kinda used it to check your location." I can't help but chuckle at her admission.

"Ah, so you're a little stalker, huh?"

"Hey, desperate times call for desperate measures," she quips, her tone playful yet sincere. I can't help but shake my head in mock disapproval, though my heart swells with affection for her, entirely unable to contain the grin spreading across my face.

"Thank you for saving me, my darling." She smiles softly, her hand coming up to cup my cheek.

"Always."

As I reluctantly pull away from Delilah, a heavy feeling settles in the pit of my stomach. Turning around, I'm met with a scene that couldn't be more different from the warmth and relief I just experienced.

Marcus stands over his dead father's body, his gaze fixed steadily on the lifeless form on the ground. There's a haunting stillness. My heart aches for him, for the pain and the trauma and the confused blend of emotions he must be feeling.

The grief of losing a parent he waited so long for, the relief of being freed from a lifetime of abuse, the guilt of feeling relieved, the anger at the injustice of it all. He stands at the crossroads of conflicting emotions, grappling with the aftermath of a lifetime of abuse and the sudden, stark finality of death.

As I look at Marcus I don't ever see a grown man standing at 6 foot 5. A man covered in tattoos, old enough to have a child of his own if he wanted. I see the little boy I once knew. The boy I grew up with. The boy who, like me, dreamed of a life beyond the confines of that shitty children's shelter; a life filled with love and laughter, a life that always seemed just out of reach.

Now, all he ever wanted lies dead on the floor.

He mourns not only the physical loss of his father but the shattered illusions of what could have been. He'd always craved parental love; the warmth of a real family. Birthday parties, pets,

holidays; a christmas morning with a tree and a stocking. The simple things that most people take for granted.
We never did.
It's all we ever longed for.

I always saw it in Marcus' eyes. The silent plea for something he'd never received. He'd given his dad endless chances to step up, to be the father figure he desperately needed. Yet, time and time again, his pleas fell on deaf ears, drowned out by the deafening silence of indifference or punctuated by the searing sting of betrayal.

I know that feeling all too well. It's an excrutiating punch to the gut, beginning to realise and understand that the people who are supposed to love you the most couldn't care less.
Coming to terms with that. Ignoring that. Living with that. Acting like that's okay, like *you're* okay. Pretend it doesn't eat away at you every single fucking day.

   "I'm fine," you say, over and over, until the words lose their meaning, until they become a mantra, a shield against the pain. They become hollow. *"I don't care,"* you repeat, like a broken record, hoping that if you say it enough times, you might actually start to believe it. But deep down, you know the truth; it's not okay, and you're not okay.

Yet you grow and you mature and eventually it genuinely does become *almost* okay. It becomes bearable. Tolerable. Forgettable. Ignorable.

Then you realise one day *you* will be a father to somebody. *You'll* be the one to make sure a child doesn't feel the way you did. That's what drives you forwards.

And that's where it ends.

The past loses its grip on you, its relevance fading into obscurity as you focus solely on building a future. Healing.

Approaching Marcus, I grip his shoulder, feeling the tension in his muscles like coiled springs.

"I'm sorry." I offer.

Scrunching his eyebrows, he points to the blood pooling on the ground.

"See that?" he says, his voice raw with emotion. "We share that." I follow his focus, feeling a lump form in my throat. He looks back to me and meets my gaze with purpose, a haunted look in his eyes. "And *we* don't," he continues, his voice heavy with regret. I offer a faint smile and airy chuckle in return.

"Fucked up, huh?"

As Marcus and I exchange tense glances, the room is suddenly rocked by a cacophony of crashing and banging against the front door. Marcus and I exchange puzzled glances as the noise grows louder, the door now shaking with each feeble impact.

With a final, desperate strike, the door gives way, folding open in a grandiose display of splintered wood and dramatic flair. And lo and behold, through the now-gaping entrance stumbles none other than Birdie and Skylar, their entrance more reminiscent of a slapstick comedy than a break-in. Birdie clutches a comically undersized 'battering ram' -a tiny, old hammer repurposed for the occasion- while Skylar follows close behind, her expression a pathetic mix of triumph and amusement.

"She wouldn't let me pick the lock." Skylar states ridiculously blunt and casual.

"Holy shit, is that a dead guy?" Birdie blurts out. The room falls into silence as we all try not to laugh, the only sound is the collective intake of breath as we process the sheer ludicrousness of the situation. Skylar's eyes widen in realisation as she takes in the scene, her expression a mix of shock and disbelief. She nudges Birdie with her elbow before attempting to whisper,

"Oh my God, Birdie! Shh, that's his dad!"

Marcus stares at them, his expression a masterclass in incredulity, with a dash of amusement and exasperation.

"Yup, that's my dad," he deadpans, his tone laced with sarcasm as he tries to keep a stern face. Following this, as if a switch had been flipped, the tension dissolves into uproarious laughter.

As the laughter fills the room, an odd mix of catharsis and absurdity. It's a strange sound, given the grim scene before us, but it's also a release. A needed release. There's a sense of unity again. We've been through so fucking much, and somehow, we always find a way to come out on the other side.

Alive and more connected than ever before.

CHAPTER 30:
A BOMBSHELL

Marcus

As my father lies dead on the floor in front of me, I feel everything all at once. Anger mostly. Lots of deep-rooted, passionate anger. He's taken the easy way out. Death has absolved him of all responsibility, leaving me to grapple with the wreckage he left behind. The fact that he's gone now feels like the ultimate betrayal, the final abandonment in a lifetime filled with them.

But he doesn't deserve my rage. I've wasted enough energy on him, and he's not worth another second of my life. I refuse to let his death define me as much as his life did.

Instead, I turn my thoughts and energy towards Sienna. My sweet Sienna, my future. She represents everything my father never was; loving, supportive, hopeful. Present. She is the light that guides me. Her body is a mosaic of bruises and cuts, her eyes haunted yet resilient.

For a moment, we just stand there.

I take a tentative step towards her, my heart aching at the sight of her pain.

"How you holding up, sweet?" I whisper, my voice cracking. She looks up at me, tears streaming down her face.

"I didn't think I'd ever get out of there, Marcus." She trembles, "I didn't think I'd ever see you again."

"I'm so sorry, sweet." I say, "I should've protected you." Sienna lifts her head, her eyes locking with mine.

"This wasn't your fault."

"But it was." I confirm, guilt gnawing at my insides. "It was all my fault. I'm supposed to keep you safe."

"You can't carry that weight, Marcus." She insists, her eyes pleading with me to see reason. "All I wanted was to see you walk through that door, and that's exactly what you did. You saved me."

You might look at somebody like me and pity the life I've been given. You might think I'm a failure. You might even feel sorry for me.

But as I look down at her right now, my entire world in my hands; those big, beautiful honey-brown eyes staring back at me, I know I'm in fact the luckiest man alive.

I pull her into a hug, laying her head against my chest. I can feel the tremors coursing through her body, matching the erratic beat of my own heart.

"I love you, Marcus." she breathes against my chest. I hold her even tighter, if that's even possible.

"I love you too, sweet." I reply, my voice thick with emotion. "More than anything." And then, as if on cue, we both break into a bittersweet smile, the weight of the world momentarily lifted from our shoulders. I squeeze and I squeeze her tighter, rocking her in a silent rhythm that speaks volumes without the need for words. Planting tender kisses upon her cheeks, I shower her with affection, each touch a testament to the depth of my adoration.

We reluctantly untangle ourselves, but our eyes stay locked. I squat down to her level, a grin spreading across my face as I take her hand in mine, pressing a kiss on her knuckles. We smile at each other. We just smile. Stare and smile. It's one of those rare moments where everything else fades away, leaving only the two of us in our own little bubble.

"You know, sweet. There is one brightside to this whole thing." I start, a hint of arrogance laced with affection in my voice.

"Do tell." she replies in a feminine tone.

"Maybe this will teach you to follow my orders in future." I smirk.

As we stand there, lost in our shared moment, a sudden interruption breaks the spell. An unfamiliar female voice echoes from behind me, jolting me out of my reverie.

"Sweet?"

As I Turn my head slowly, I'm met by a small, battered woman standing at the top of the basement stairs, wearing only a bed sheet wrapped around her. Her form is hunched, her frame fragile and worn, like a delicate porcelain doll weathered by time and circumstance.

My heart drops like a stone in my chest, a heavy weight that threatens to crush me beneath its burden. A thunderous drumbeat echoes in my ears, drowning out the sounds of the world around me. A cold sweat breaks out on my forehead as I lay eyes on the figure standing in front of me.

In an instant, the world tilts on its axis, spinning wildly out of control as the pieces of the puzzle fall into place.

The photograph from my childhood that I had tucked away in the back of the pile, in the back of my mind, races to the forefront. In a millisecond, I analyse every feature of her, a game of spot the difference playing out in my head. But there are no differences to be found, no discrepancies to reconcile.

Recognition crashes over me like a tidal wave, leaving me breathless and dizzy.

It can't be... But it is.

"Mum?"

The woman whose face has haunted my dreams, whose absence has left an ache in my heart that I couldn't name until this moment. She stands before me, a living, breathing enigma, and I'm frozen in place, unable to tear my gaze away from her.

"Yes, sweet. Yes, it's Mum!" she confirms, her voice trembling with emotion as she nods eagerly, tears streaming from her eyes.

My mind reels, struggling to process the enormity of what I'm living through. Mum? Just saying it felt so unnatural. The word echoes in my head. A distant echo, foreign and yet achingly familiar all at once. Without hesitation, she speeds towards me, her movements desperate and urgent. As she rushes towards me, her movements fuelled by a desperation I can't begin to fathom, I'm rooted to the spot, unable to move, unable to speak.

I barely have time to react before she falls into my arms, her body trembling with the weight of years of longing and separation. In that moment, time stands still, suspended in the delicate balance between what was and what could have been.

"Oh God!" She sobs.

I struggle to make sense of it all. This woman, her scent, her touch; it's all so overwhelming, so disorienting. My dad was the parent who came back for me. My mother left the both of us. Left without a trace. He was the 'better' one. The best of the worst, right? And yet, here she is, in the flesh, her warmth seeping into my bones.

I find myself hesitating as I begin to hug her too, unsure of how to react.
I've never done the whole 'mum' thing before.

Glancing over her shoulder, I'm met with a tableau of stunned faces, each mirroring my own shock and disbelief. They too are grappling with the surrealness of this moment, their eyes wide with astonishment, their mouths agape in silent wonderment as they bear witness to the unfolding scene before them.

As she frantically pulls away, her trembling hands delicately stroke through my hair, her touch a tender caress laden with years of longing and regret. Tears stream down her cheeks, mingling with my own, as she steps back slightly to glare into my eyes, her expression a tumult of disbelief and overwhelming emotion.

"Oh, Marcus," she whispers, her voice trembling as she gently caresses my cheek. "I can't.. I can't believe this is really happening. You're really here."

I stand frozen in place, like a statue carved from stone, unable to tear my eyes away from her. As she continues to speak, I'm lost in a whirlwind of thoughts and emotions. I find myself lost in the labyrinth of my own thoughts, navigating through my memories. Memories long buried resurface, fragments of a past I've struggled to make sense of.

But amidst the overwhelming flood of her emotions, there's a sudden urgency in her face, a desperate plea masked by the veil of tears.

"Sweet," she continues, her voice trembling with apprehension, like a delicate leaf caught in the breeze of uncertainty. "Where's your brother? Is he okay?"

The question doesn't even compute in my brain. To say I'm overwhelmed would be an absolute understatement. The world around me blurs as my mind races to grasp the enormity of what has been asked of me. It's as though I've been thrust into a maze of memories I didn't know existed, each twist and turn revealing fragments of a life I never knew I lived.

Holy shit.

"I.. I have a brother?"

PART THREE:

BROTHERS REVENGE

CHAPTER 1:

WHO IS MY BROTHER?

Marcus

Meeting your mother for the first time after being given up as a child is one thing, but discovering in the same breath that you have a brother you never knew existed, is a revelation so overwhelming that it recalibrates your entire existence. A discovery so profound that it redefines your very identity, leaving you to reconcile the fragmented pieces of your past and reframe your understanding of who you are and where you belong.

Unveiling the truth that an entire life has been intertwined with yours, yet hidden in shadow, is like staring at a mirror that reflects a reality that's not your own; like I'm a stranger in my own story.

As I struggle to process this bombshell, my mother's face crumples with worry, her hands trembling as they reach for mine.

"Of course you have a brother." She whispers urgently, shaking her head in disbelief. I shrug, and yes I know that's a pretty pathetic response to such a huge disclosure, but I'm not sure how else I should respond.

How exactly are you supposed to react to finding out you have a sibling you never knew existed?

It's like I'm trapped in a vivid hallucination, where each moment bends and stretches, too strange to be real but too visceral to be dismissed as a dream.

My mother's eyes fill with tears as she takes a deep breath.

"Noah," she says in a defeated sigh, "your brother, sweet. Noah?" The name echoes in my mind, stirring up a whirlpool of confusion and curiosity. The ground beneath me feels shaky, unsteady.

Noah.
I have a brother named Noah.
Noted.

And he's Somewhere out there, living his own life, possibly wondering the same things I've always wondered.

"I don't know him." I state, the words feeling inadequate. My mother's sobs begin softly but quickly escalate, her body wracked with grief. She covers her face with her hands, and her whole frame shakes as the weight of the past crashes over her. Instinctively, though it feels foreign and awkward, I step forward and pull her into a hug.

Chapter 1

The act feels strange, like wearing clothes that don't fit. Comforting a woman who is biologically my mother, yet whom I've never known, is deeply disorientating.

Her pain is tangible, a raw wound laid bare.

"Hey," I say softly. "It's okay." She looks up at me, her eyes red and glistening with tears, searching my face for something, perhaps a sign that I don't hate her. As she looks at me, I begin to notice our shared features for the first time. I'm struck by the unmistakable resemblance between us.

The curve of her lips, the shape of her nose, even the colour and texture of her hair; all mirroring my own. The recognition is complex, grounding me in the reality of our connection in a way that words alone could never achieve.

This woman, this stranger, is my fucking *mother*.

My flesh and blood.

"I just.. I'm sorry, sweet. I don't understand how this could've happened," she says, her voice quivering. "All the years I spent down there, I kept one sliver of hope that at the very least, my children would have had each other." Her words hit me hard, and I can see the depth of her regret.

"It's okay, mum." I interrupt, though it's not. Nothing about this situation is okay. "We'll figure this out. I'll find him. I'll find Noah, okay?" Her sobbing quiets a little, and she takes a shuddering breath, nodding slowly.

I nod back, more to myself than to her. I've just promised to find a brother I've never met, a person whose existence I only learned about minutes ago. The enormity of the task ahead doesn't fully register, but one thing is clear; I need answers. For myself, for her, and for Noah, wherever he may be.

I start thinking more about him. Would he be taller than me? Shorter? Do we have the same mannerisms, the same laugh? It's fun to envision a brother who might share my quirks and idiosyncrasies. Someone who, despite the years and distance, may feel an inexplicable bond with me simply because we share the same blood.

Though, admittedly, I haven't had the best luck with that concept so far.

I wonder what kind of person he is. Is he funny? Does he know about me? The thought that he might have spent years wondering, as I did, if he had a sibling out there somewhere tugs at my heart. What has his life been like? Has he been happy? The questions multiply, each one bringing with it a new layer of curiosity. The prospect of finding Noah is no longer just about answers; it's about the possibility of forging a bond that was meant to be there all along.

I refuse to let my father's actions set the tone for what family is. After all, I've experienced firsthand the warmth and solidarity of family through Skylar's. I know what family can be.

As I mull over the myriad of questions swirling in my mind, another peculiar realisation dawns on me; I don't even know my own mother's name.

"Uh, mum," I start, "what's your name?" I ask tentatively. She looks up at me, her tear-streaked face momentarily frozen.

"Charlotte." Sienna interjects softly, her voice carrying a mixture of empathy and understanding. I glance back at Sienna to see her smiling. "We met already."

My stomach churns, and I feel a wave of nausea. The way they look at each other, the pain and regret in their eyes. They clearly share an unspoken bond, born of their mutual suffering, and in their gazes, I see the reflection of what they must have endured in that basement.

My mother's eyes are red and swollen, but there's a glimmer of hope and gratitude as she looks at Sienna.

"I never imagined I'd meet my son's girlfriend in such a way," she says, her voice laced with a hint of sadness. "But I'm very happy that my son has such a beautiful angel in his life." Sienna blushes and glances up to me.

"Thank you, but I'm not his girlfriend," she says, with a cheeky smile. "Marcus doesn't really *do* labels." I roll my eyes, a small smile tugging at the corners of my mouth.

"*Oh*, I see. You're too cool for that are you, Marcus Bear?" My mother chips in, crossing her arms and giving me a look that feels very stereotypically motherly. I blink, taken aback. "Hm?" She adds. Sienna stifles a laugh beside me, clearly enjoying this. I raise my hands in mock surrender.

"Alright, alright. How about we hold off on the lectures for a little while?" I suggest with a smile,

"I wanna know more about Noah. When did you last see him?"

"The same evening that I last saw you, my sweet." She replies softly, as if it's obvious. "You went into that house *together*."

"That makes no sense." I blurt out instinctively. "I would know him, or at least vaguely remember him." She takes a deep breath, gathering her thoughts before speaking again.

"You were both so young," she begins, her voice trembling. "If somebody had come to collect him early on, you probably *wouldn't* remember."

"I guess." I nod slowly, feeling a slow, simmering rage beneath my skin. The question that has been burning inside me for as long as I can remember, and now it bursts forth like a wildfire.

"Why did you give us up?" The words hang in the air like a challenge, heavy with accusation. My mother flinches as if I'd struck her, her eyes welling up with tears. But not just tears of sadness; there's a deeper pain there, a sorrow that seems to transcend words.

"It was never my choice." She replies bluntly, causing the room to stand still.

The weight of her words settles over me, suffocating in their implication. I feel the rage flare up again, this time directed not at her, but at the man I called my dad. My mother's voice breaks through my tumultuous thoughts.

"I never wanted to give you up," she says, her voice cracking, "I fought *so* hard, sweet." As I stand there, absorbing her words, my mind churns. My entire life, I've operated under the assumption that my mother had given us up, that she had chosen to abandon us. But now, hearing her say it wasn't her choice, it shatters the narrative I had constructed to make sense of my past.

My thoughts, of course, drift to my father. He was the one who *'found'* me. I trusted him, believing he had rescued me from that home. But if my mother had been forced to give us up, it begs the question; what role did my father play in all this? Considering his actions in locking her up in a basement, it's obvious to me now that he's behind it all. Yet, it's still jarring to get confirmation of his deceit.

Despite our problematic relationship, I had always seen my father as a kind of saviour. Yet, this man I had trusted implicitly had actually orchestrated this entire nightmare. He didn't just take me from my mother; he condemned her to a life of darkness, hiding her from me all these years.

Chapter 1

"You have to believe me, Marcus," she pleads, her eyes searching mine for any sign of understanding. "I never stopped fighting for you. Not for a single day." I swallow hard, the lump in my throat making it difficult to speak.

"I believe you," I whisper, the anger slowly giving way to a deep, aching sadness. "It's just a hard pill to swallow."

CHAPTER 2:

WHAT'S HIS IS YOURS

Sienna

Well, now those fucking eyes make sense. The revelation hits me like a freight train and everything is starting to come together. Each piece of the puzzle clicks into place with a sudden clarity that leaves me reeling. Noah, the tall guy from the basement, is Marcus' brother.

He was part of that nightmare, and though it's irrational, it's insane, Noah was different. The memory of him is a whirlwind of emotions; fear, confusion, and strangely, a kind of reluctant fondness. It's a messy, contradictory cocktail that defies logic, but it's undeniable; there was something about him that made me feel.. safe? Even if just for a moment.

This morning when he brought me breakfast. His demeanour had changed slightly; he was almost gentle in a way that felt genuine. We talked. It was bizarre, having this normal conversation in such an abnormal place. I never imagined I would find myself here, unravelling the revelation that he is Marcus' brother. Marcus' *brother*. The words echo in my mind, a surreal twist on the reality I thought I knew.

I had breakfast with Marcus' brother this morning.

Glancing at Marcus, I see his face awash with emotions. He's grappling with the truth of his past, the lies his father told him, and the reality of a brother he never knew existed. How could I possibly ever tell him that I've already met Noah? Knowing him, he would brutally murder Noah if he found out the truth, especially after what happened in the basement.

But Noah ended up being strangely humane with me. He even opened up about how his mother is dead, which now I know isn't true of course. In hindsight, it's evident that he, in his own tumultuous way, is just as much a victim of their father's insidious manipulation and cruelty as Marcus is.

The weight of my secret presses down on me like a leaden stone, but I know I must keep it to myself. This is Marcus' moment, a chance he's yearned for all his life. He has always longed for family, and I can't deprive him of this opportunity to connect with Noah.

Birdie interrupts the silence,

"how are we gonna find him then?" she asks. Marcus, visibly lost in thought, takes a moment to process the question. His brow furrows slightly as he considers the practicalities of locating Noah, whom I know is a lot closer than everyone likely suspects. A determined glint flashes in his eyes, a spark of resolve amidst the turmoil. He moves with purpose, striding toward his father's motionless form. The room seems to hold its breath as he kneels beside his father, his fingers deftly searching through the pockets of the lifeless body. With deliberate fingers, he begins to search through the pockets of that cold, unyielding flesh, a macabre scavenger in a place that once held the remnants of a father's authority.

As Marcus extracts his hand, a triumphant glare illuminates his eyes, and he holds up a phone and a set of jangling keys like trophies. The metal clinks softly as he swiftly unlocks the device, the screen casting an ethereal glow on his face. For a moment, his expression remains inscrutable as he scrolls through the applications in silence. Then, a smirk tugs at the corner of his mouth, a glimmer of amusement and triumph dancing in his eyes.

Without a word, he turns the phone towards us, revealing the screen that displays messages from a contact named 'Noah', confirming not only Noah's existence in their father's phonebook but also their recent communication.

"They were texting just last night." Marcus announces, his voice tinged with a mixture of disbelief and pride. "And, I can see his location."

Dean leans in, his brows scrunched as he processes the revelation.

"So, he's nearby?" he asks, his voice edged with anticipation. Marcus nods slowly, his gaze fixed on the phone screen.

"Yeah," he confirms, his voice steadier now and a sweet smile creeping onto his face. "He's not far at all." Marcus locks eyes with me and I grin back, a silent acknowledgment of the journey ahead and the unspoken support between us.

"Go. Go see him." I happily instruct. He takes a few steps closer to me and grasps my hands, pressing a firm kiss to my knuckles.

"There's no rush, sweet," he says. "I need to get you out of here first. You've been through so much. We need to get you cleaned up and-"

"No." I insist with a smile. "You have to go and find him. I'll be fine with everyone else." Skylar steps forward, her expression resolute.

"Don't worry, Marcus. I'll take care of her. Everyone can come back to my place." Marcus hesitates, staring intensely into my eyes. The determination in his gaze is palpable, but so is the worry.

"Sweet, are you sure?" he asks, his voice barely above a whisper.

"Yes. Go. This is important."

"Nothing is as important as you-"

"Go. I'll be fine, I promise." He searches my face for reassurance before finally nodding and releasing my hands.

As I raise my gaze, Delilah comes into focus. Our eyes lock in a silent understanding. Time seems to halt, the world holding its breath. Then, with an unspoken pact, the trio converges on me. Delilah, Skylar, and Birdie all rush over to me. They pull me into a warm, supportive embrace, their arms wrapping around me tightly. The comforting pressure of their bodies against mine is like a gentle rain shower on parched skin. The familiar scent of their hair, and the gentle murmur of their voices all blend together; grounding me. As I breathe in their scents, I feel my worries melt away.

We slowly pull away from each other, and I notice that Skylar's eyes are glistening with unshed tears.

"Hey, what's wrong?" I ask. Skylar's gaze drops, and she looks down at her feet before speaking in a shaky voice.

"I'm just.. I'm so sorry, Sienna. I should have been paying more attention. I was in my own world and I didn't hear a thing. I could've helped you." I reach out and gently take her hand, giving it a reassuring squeeze.

"Sky," I say softly. "There was no way you could have stopped this."

"I know," she whispers. "I just feel so useless." I shake my head, trying to convey the futility of her words. I take a deep breath and try to think of something to say that will ease her guilt.

"We were *both* in danger."

"But I should have been there for you."

"You were there for me, Sky. You always are," I say. "You're here right now." Skylar nods, still looking a bit tearful, but her expression softens.

I take a step forward and wrap my arms around her, pulling her into another tight embrace. Her body relaxes slightly as she leans into me, her tears finally beginning to subside.

"Okay," she whispers, her voice steady now. "Let's get going. We need to get you cleaned up." I nod, feeling a sense of relief wash over me.

As we begin to pull away, Skylar takes my hand preparing to leave and head to her house. Suddenly Marcus' voice cuts through the quiet.

"Wait." We all turn to look at him as he strides over to his mother. Reaching into his pocket, he pulls out the keys to his father's house; the metal glinting in the dim light. Holding them out to her, his voice is steady, but I can hear the mixture of resolve and tenderness in his words. "What's his is yours."

Charlotte stares at the keys, her eyes welling up with tears. She reaches out with a trembling hand, taking them from Marcus. The keys jingle softly as they change hands, a poignant transfer of power and responsibility. Her expression is a mix of sorrow, gratitude, and something else; perhaps a sense of bittersweet closure.

"Thank you," she breathes, her voice thick with emotion. Marcus nods, his jaw set with determination. He then turns back to me, his eyes softening. The unspoken promise in his gaze reassures me.

"I'll see you tonight, sweet." he says before turning his attention to the girls, "Keep her safe. Please."

CHAPTER 3:
BACK TO ORCHID'S

Dean

The room empties out, leaving just myself, Marcus and Marcus' dead dad. I've always known my life was pretty fucked, but the sheer number of corpses I've now witnessed has left me wondering if 'fucked' is too tame a term. If I were the type to go to therapy, I'd probably need to get my therapist their own therapist after explaining all of this shit.

I walk over to Marcus, who's staring down at the lifeless body with an expression I can't quite read. Maybe it's sorrow, maybe it's relief, maybe it's something in between. It's hard to tell with Marcus; his emotions have always been a mixed bag.

"Yo," I say, my voice softer than usual. "You sure you're ready to do this?" After a few moments, he tears his gaze away from his dad and looks at me. His eyes are bloodshot, and there's a vulnerability in them I'm not used to seeing. He's always been the strong one, the one who never lets anything get to him. But right now, he looks as lost as I feel.

"Yeah," he replies after a long pause. "Yeah, I'm ready. Let's go find our brother." I raise an eyebrow, confused.

"*Our* brother?" I respond. Marcus offers a small, proud smile.

"Yeah, *our* brother. You were here first."

For a moment, I'm taken aback. Marcus and I have been through hell together, but we've never put it into words like this. It's strange, hearing it out loud, but it's also.. kind of nice. Wholesome, even. And for two guys like us, moments like these are rare. I nod, feeling a lump in my throat.

"Alright. Let's go find our brother."

As we head out of the room, I can't help but glance back at Marcus' dad one last time. A part of me wonders if we'll end up like him; victims of a past we can't escape. But another part of me, the part that's still clinging to hope, believes we can break the cycle. We have to.

We step outside into the evening air, the cool breeze hitting us like a wake-up call. The city sounds in the background of music blaring, people shouting, the distant wail of a siren, remind us that we're back home. Back to the devil we know. It's a strange comfort, knowing that despite everything, the world keeps turning.

As we reach the road just outside the house where his dad now lies dead, Marcus slows his pace. He turns his head, casting a glance back, the shadows playing tricks on his expression.

"You okay?" I ask quietly, sensing the hesitation radiating from him. Marcus nods, his expression unreadable in the half-light.

"Yeah," he murmurs. "Just.. taking it in." I don't press further, respecting the silence that surrounds his grief. Instead, we cross the road to where our car is parked. I slip into the driver's seat, and Marcus settles into the passenger side, the door closing with a muted thud. The cool leather interior and the faint scent of rain-soaked asphalt bring a sense of grounding.

I adjust the rearview mirror with a determined flick, my other hand steady on the wheel. I glance at Marcus, catching the set of his jaw and the resolve in his eyes. I start the engine, its gentle hum filling the quiet evening air.

"What's the address?" I ask. Marcus shakes his head slightly.

"Not yet. Head to Orchid's first."

The gate, now hanging off its hinges from Skylar's reckless entrance, greets us with a crooked smile. Along with lines of crime scene tape fluttering in the breeze. I park the car nearby, the engine ticking as it cools down.

"What exactly are we doing here?" I ask, my voice low.

"Since dad mentioned the book before he.." He trails off, unable to finish the sentence. "I wanna make sure I have it. Clearly it's still important."

Of course, the book. Ever since that night we 'closed' it, an uneasy feeling has been gnawing at me, intensifying with every brush with death. The car crash that should have killed me, the tree that nearly crushed my skull, the combine that mercilessly claimed a couple of my fingers but somehow left the rest of me intact. It's as if some unseen force has been toying with my life, pulling me back from the brink time and again. And now, hearing Marcus mention the book, it all seems to connect in a way that makes my skin crawl. I can't share this with Marcus. Not yet. Not just because it would worry him, but because saying it out loud would make it all too real. And I'm not ready to face that reality just yet.

As we step out of the car, Marcus strides purposefully toward the tangled underbrush at the edge of the car park. I follow him, curiosity piqued, watching as he navigates the uneven ground with familiarity. The air is heavy with the damp scent of earth and foliage, the recent rain draping a shroud of moisture over the leaves and grass. He plunges his hand into the shadows of the bush where he'd tossed the book, his arm disappearing into the darkness. For a moment, he's still, as if considering whether he's in the right place. Then, with a slight tug, he pulls the book free from the muck.

What's interesting is that, although it had been raining and lying in mud, the book is entirely spotless. Not a speck of dirt mars its surface, the cover and pages seemingly unscathed by the elements. It's as if it had been shielded by an invisible barrier, untouched by the rain and the grime that surrounds it. The contrast is unnerving.

The mud clings to Marcus's fingers, darkening his jeans with stubborn smudges, yet the book remains pristine, its pages crisp and dry as if shielded by some invisible force. I suppose it's no surprise, considering the fact that we couldn't even put a fucking dent on this book before. But perhaps I assumed that closing the book would have broken the spell, diminishing its mystique.

"Alright, we got it. Let's get out of here," I say, assuming we'd be heading back to the car. But Marcus shakes his head.

"There's one more thing I wanna grab from inside."

As we approach the building, I spot the window we shattered last time, now hastily boarded up yet again. We come to a halt, both of us fixated on the crude patchwork; a jagged barrier held together by nails driven in at awkward angles, struggling to contain the splintered wood beneath.

"Round two, huh?" I nod towards the freshly boarded window.

"Seems like we're making a habit of this." Marcus replies with a wry smile. We step closer, our hands brushing against the weathered wood as we examine the handiwork. Without a word, we set to work, our fingers probing the gaps between the boards. The wood creaks and groans in protest as we apply pressure, our hands moving in tandem as if choreographed.

With practised ease, we pull and tug until the boards yield, exposing the shattered window beneath, shards of glass still stubbornly clinging to the frame. I toss the boards aside with a grunt, then follow Marcus as he climbs inside. As we navigate the debris and jagged glass strewn across the floor, the familiar crunch underfoot echoes through the silent building. Soft moonlight filters through the broken windows, casting long shadows that dance across the dusty surfaces.

We ascend the creaking staircase, the wooden treads complaining softly beneath our footsteps, the sound echoing through the silent hallway like a mournful sigh. Marcus bursts into the room, his gaze fixed on the floor behind the door, his attention razor-sharp and unyielding as he scans the space.

As Marcus crouches down to lift the floorboard where we originally found the book, I watch curiously, memories of our childhood flooding back.

"How did I never know about this?" I ask, incredulous. Marcus chuckles softly, his eyes crinkling at the corners, a spark of pride illuminating his expression.

"In the wise words of Dean Douglas," he replies, "we've been hiding forever." We lock eyes, and for a moment, everything just stops. There's a connection; strong and undeniable. I'm not sure what I'm feeling exactly, whether it's nostalgia, sadness, happiness or something else, but it's there.

Ironically, our childhoods weren't exactly storybook material. We became the 'bad kids' not because we enjoyed causing trouble, but because it was the only way we knew how to cope with the darkness that surrounded us. Breaking rules wasn't rebellion, it was survival. We turned to trouble and chaos as an escape, a way to bury the pain and trauma deep enough that it couldn't hurt us anymore. Or at least deep enough that we forgot about how badly it was hurting us.

Despite how close we are as a group, there are certain topics we just never touched. We never really talked about the shit that went down in our pasts. We were a family in that house. We'd kill and die for each other, no questions asked. But talk about the reasons we were in that home in the first place? No chance. It was like an unspoken rule; don't dredge up the past. Just hide and keep moving forward, no matter what.

And look at where that got us.
We've become complete monsters.

Marcus pulls out the small box from beneath the floorboards, opening it carelessly and immediately grabbing the ripped photograph of his mother from the back of the pile; its edges frayed and corners dog-eared. He shakes it in his hand a few times, as if confirming to himself that this is what he wanted, before stuffing it in his pocket.

I pause, taking a moment to absorb the desolate atmosphere of the room. Wandering towards the remains of my side of the bedroom; my focus lands on the endless array of scratches and slices in the wall. I remember every single one, somehow. The slits seem to ripple through my memory. When my parents sent me here, I had managed to smuggle in a couple of knives in my pockets. I used to stay up all night just slicing the walls. It was my way of dealing with all the shit.

While everyone else tried to sleep, I'd be there, carving away like a madman. Sometimes I'd imagine the plaster was my old man's face or the endless parade of social workers who came in and out of the revolving door; not giving a single fuck about us. Other times, it was just about feeling something, anything, to drown out the numbness.

But those slashes in the wall didn't stay just slashes for long. The anger grew, and so did the violence. It wasn't just walls getting cut up anymore; it was knuckles, then faces. Fights became a regular thing. I'd brawl with anyone, everyone, as if beating the crap out of someone else would somehow beat the crap out of my own thoughts.

Then I spent some more time with Dot, the only social worker who ever seemed to genuinely care. She had this way about her, like she saw through all our bullshit. She'd sit with us, talk with us, actually listen. I don't know how she did it, but she got through. She got through to me. One morning, she brought in these cans of spray paint. She figured if I needed to leave my mark, it might as well be something worth looking at.

It wasn't long before I traded my knives for those cans. Instead of slicing walls, I started tagging them. Graffiti became my thing. It was a way to express all the shit I felt without tearing anything or anyone apart. It was colour and life in a place that felt grey and dead. Every tag was a piece of me, a burst of creativity where there used to be destruction. My aggression never left, but I learnt how to keep it controlled.

Which is of course why I shot somebody in the head this week.

Marcus snaps the floorboard back into place with a final, decisive thud. He stands up, dusting off his hands, and we look at each other.

"You ready?" he asks, trying to keep his voice steady.

"Am *I* ready?" I retort, raising an eyebrow. He chuckles softly and rubs his forehead.

"I'm not sure I'll ever be ready," he admits. "So let's get it done."

CHAPTER 4:
NICE TO MEET YOU

Marcus

As we pull up into Noah's estate, I can't help but stare in awe. In its centre stands a huge, old, classical-English mansion, the kind you see in movies or on postcards, but never in real life. Ivy crawls up the stone walls like nature's own wallpaper, and there's even a fountain in the driveway, water trickling down in a way that seems both elegant and incredibly unnecessary.

I glance at Dean, and his jaw is practically on the floor. He looks like he's just seen a UFO land in front of him, complete with little green men.

"You seein' this?" He mutters, more to himself than to me. I shake my head slowly.

"Oh, I'm seein' it."

433

"*Fuck*," he smiles. "You think he'll lend me a tenner?"
I chuckle at his irreverent humour.

"Maybe if you ask nicely."

We step out of the car, and I feel like I'm in some kind of weird dream. The gravel crunches under our feet as we walk as slow as humanly possible toward the massive front door. I half-expect a butler to come out and shoo us away for lowering the property value by just being here.

"You sure this is the right place?" Dean asks.

"It's the only house here." I reply straightforwardly. Dean whistles low, shaking his head in disbelief.

The irony stings. My dad and I were scraping by in a rundown shithole, a place that barely held together. I always wondered why he was rarely home. Now, seeing this mansion, it all clicks. He'd been raising my brother too, but Noah got the mansion while I got the scraps.

We continue our slow approach, each step echoing in the dark silence, until we stand before the towering door. Just as we raise our hands to knock, the door swings open with a suddenness that startles us both. Standing there, framed by the opulent doorway, is a man who can only be Noah. His face is hard, eyes sharp and calculating, his presence exuding an air of quiet menace. In his hand, steady as stone, he holds a gun; its barrel aimed squarely at Dean.

Good start.

"Unless you're begging for a bullet in your skull, I suggest you get the fuck off my property, Douglas." Noah's voice slices through the air like a blade, cold and firm. The threat in his tone is undeniable, sharp enough to make the hairs on my neck stand up. He looms in the doorway, his towering frame filling the space, exuding a dark authority that demands attention. His presence is intimidating, like the air itself is bending to his will.

Noah shares my dark hair and hazel eyes, but that's where the similarities end. He looms at least 6 foot 7. He's built like a fortress, not dramatically bulky but undeniably muscular, every line of his frame exuding strength and athleticism. His jaw is chiselled, his features hardened. There's no denying, he's a scary guy.

"Nice to meet you too." Dean mumbles as his eyes dart over to me; a silent plea for me to handle this. I swallow hard and consider the best way to navigate the conversation.

"Noah, wait." I interrupt. Noah's eyes narrow, his grip on the gun unwavering as he looks me up and down, sizing me up.

"Who the fuck are you?" He demands, suspicion and hostility clear in his tone. He looks me up and down another time.

"I'm your brother."

A smirk forms on his lips.

"You think you're funny?"

"No joke," I say, trying to keep my voice steady. "I know it sounds crazy, but it's the truth." Noah stares at me, a mocking smile spreading across his face before he turns to Dean, eyebrows raised.

"You gonna tell your little sidekick to shut the fuck up, or what?"

"I'm serious." I reply, standing my ground. Noah's eyes linger on Dean for a moment longer and then back to me, his smirk fading slightly but his grip on the gun still tight.

"Prove it. "

I nod cautiously, my hand inching toward the pocket of my tracksuit bottoms where I'd stashed the photograph. Just as my fingers brush the edge of it, Noah's gun snaps toward me like a coiled viper, his eyes locked on mine with a deadly intensity. I freeze, heart hammering in my chest, the weight of his gaze heavier than the cold steel aimed at my head.

"I'm just grabbing a photo, bro." I stammer, holding my hands up in a placating gesture. "It's proof." Noah's eyes continue to bore into mine, and it's clear he's not easily convinced.

"Slowly," he growls. "And if you pull out anything other than a photo, you're both dead." I nod again, moving deliberately this time, my fingers finding the edges of the worn photograph.

As I cautiously retrieve the photograph from my pocket, Noah's eyes track my every move, his stare sharp and assessing. In that tense moment, it's clear that Noah is a force to be reckoned with, far beyond anything I've encountered before. I retrieve it from my pocket and hold it up; a faded photograph capturing my mother and I before I ended up in Orchid's. Along the left edge, the photo is torn, leaving me to assume my dad and Noah once filled the missing half.

Noah doesn't relax, but his gaze flickers briefly to the image. I can sense the gears turning in his mind, processing the implications of what he sees. He remains silent, his expression unreadable, weighing his options with the careful consideration of a seasoned strategist. Dean stands beside me, tense but alert. I feel him holding his breath, waiting to see how my brother will react. Noah squints his eyes slightly as he studies the photograph, then looks back at me, his stare piercing.

"Which one of you killed my dad?" Noah asks bluntly, his tone harsh. We pause, considering our approach. "I saw you both on the cameras so don't fucking lie to me."

"That would be my girlfriend." Dean replies, surprisingly chirpy, proud even. Noah's reaction is icy and detached, a chasm of emotional numbness

"Your *girlfriend,* huh?" he says, his tone dripping with disdain and a mocking inflection.

The laugh that follows is brief and chilling, betraying more embarrassment and annoyance than genuine sorrow. It's clear that in Noah's mind, such vulnerability, even in death, is a sign of weakness rather than tragedy. He steps back slightly, gesturing with the gun for us to enter. Dean and I hesitate, glancing at each other.

"Do you need a written invitation?" Noah snaps, his patience visibly thinning rapidly.

As we step inside, the opulent atmosphere envelops us; the place screams luxury. The marble floors, polished to a mirror-like sheen, stretch out like a rich tapestry, while the room's modern and antique accents blend seamlessly, evoking the grandeur of a bygone era. It's as if we've entered the lair of a cinematic mafia kingpin. Dim lighting casts shadows across the room, making the rich wood panelling and ornate furniture look even more imposing. Chandeliers suspended from the high ceiling cast intricate patterns of light, dancing across the walls like fireflies on a summer night. Every aspect of the decor exudes an aura of power and wealth.

The air is thick with the scent of cigars, leather, and burning fire, giving the place an old-world charm mixed with a dangerous edge. A grand staircase, swathed in a black runner, curves upward to the next floor like a crimson ribbon. To its right, a massive stone fireplace dominates the room, its mantle adorned with statues and a very fucking rich looking cigar box.

"Sit," Noah commands, gesturing toward a huge black leather sofa. We move to the sofa and sit, the leather cold and unbending beneath us. Noah's grip on the gun doesn't waver as he steps back, making his threat clear. "If either of you get up, I'll shoot." Noah strides over to a large, intricately carved chest in the corner of the room. He opens it, rummaging through the contents before pulling out a small wooden box. He opens the box, sifting through old papers and trinkets until he finds what he's looking for. Holding what looks like the other half of the photograph, he saunters back toward us, but not before grabbing a cigar from the case on the mantel. With a flick of his lighter, he ignites the tip, drawing in a deep breath that fills the air with the rich, heady aroma of smoke. As Noah advances, the photograph clutched in one hand and his gun still aimed in the other, the cigar hangs casually from his mouth.

In this moment I can't help but think,
fuck, my brother's really cool.

Without a word, he holds out his hand to me, expecting the other half of the photo. I hand it over, and he fits the two pieces together. As he studies the now-complete image, the room falls into an uncomfortable silence. The photograph confirms our shared history, but Noah's expression remains hard, unreadable. The seconds tick by like hours, until finally, he utters a low, contemplative 'Hm,' content that I've told the truth before tucking his gun away, a subtle release of tension.

He strides over to a plush armchair opposite the sofa where Dean and I sit. He sinks into the cushions, relaxing into a languid pose. His eyes remain fixed on mine, burning with an intensity that makes my skin prickle, as he savours another slow, considerate drag on his cigar.

"So," he says, his words dripping with quiet authority. "You're my little brother, huh?"

"Yeah." I nod, and for the first time, Noah smiles at me, a genuine smile.

"It's good to see you again, Marcus."

"You know my name?"

"I'm 4 years older than you, little man," he says, his eyes glinting with a knowing light. "I have memories that you don't." Noah's smile grows, and he leans back in his chair, the cigar still smouldering between his fingers. "I always knew you were out there somewhere. As I got old enough to start asking questions, Dad would tell me my memories of you were just fabricated, but I remembered you vividly."

I'm stunned, struggling to process the bombshell he's dropped. Noah's words are like a punch to the gut, shaking me to my core.

"He denied that I was your brother?" I confirm. Noah nods, his expression darkening.

"Yeah," he says gruffly.

"Why would he do that?" I ask, feeling a mix of anger and confusion. Noah shrugs, his shoulders rolling in a gesture of resignation.

"He's a confusing man." he says, his voice low and even. "Always was." I shake my head, trying to clear the haze of confusion from my mind.

"Where've you been?" he asks, interrupting my silence; curiosity and a hint of warmth in his tone. I take a deep breath and relax my body.

"Well, I didn't leave Orchid's until 2018." I reply, trying to sound casual despite the flutter in my chest.

"*Shit.* I almost forgot about that place." he says with a smirk, his eyes crinkling at the corners. "Where'd you go after that?"

"Dad came to collect me," I say. "I've been living with him ever since." Noah's brow furrows, confusion etched across his face.

"With Dad? How's that possible?" His words are laced with scepticism, and I can sense his mind racing to piece together the puzzle. I take another deep breath, trying to make sense of it all myself, but the more I think about it, the more tangled it becomes.

"He wasn't home much. I never understood why. He'd come back for a few days, then disappear for weeks. Now, of course, it makes sense. Apparently, he was living two *very* different lives." Noah exhales a slow, deliberate stream of smoke, his eyes clouding over as he absorbs the revelation. He takes a moment to collect his thoughts before speaking again, his voice low and contemplative.

"As I said, he's a confusing man."

"Now," he starts again, leaning forward. "Let's address the elephant in the room. Why the fuck are you hanging around with this prick?" He jerks his chin toward Dean, who stiffens at the insult. I take a deep breath, bracing myself.

"Look, I don't know what issues you have with Dean, but he's been with me since Orchid's. He's got my back." Noah's gaze sharpens, an icy veneer sliding over his features as he zeroes in on Dean.

"I should put a bullet in your brain, right here right now," he says coldly. "But I'll spare you for my brother's sake, on one condition. You better stop taking our fucking business, Douglas." He points a finger at Dean, the threat clear.

Dean, instead of flinching, looks Noah dead in the eye, his posture relaxed and defiant.

"No need to worry, I'm not dealing anymore. I'm out of the game." Noah raises an eyebrow, his interest piqued.

"Huh. Why the sudden change of heart?" Dean shrugs nonchalantly.

"Things got ugly. Too many feds, too many enemies. I've decided it ain't worth the hassle." He admits. Noah's expression hardens.

"If you say so. But mark my words; if you ever think about crossing me or slipping back into the business, you won't get another warning."

"Understood." Dean nods with a sarcastic grin.

Noah leans back in his chair, finally relaxing a bit. He takes another drag from his cigar, the smoke swirling around his head like a halo of menace.

"Do you remember Mum?" He asks suddenly, his voice softer, almost hesitant.

"Not really," I admit. "All I've ever had was that photograph." I hesitate, then continue, "But I finally met her today." Noah's eyes widen, disbelief etched across his face.

"Met her?" he laughs, "Our mum's dead." I take a deep breath, the truth heavy on my tongue.

"She's not dead, Noah." I share. For a moment, I see a flicker of vulnerability beneath his hardened exterior.

"What do you mean she's not dead?"

"I met her earlier today." I admit, my voice trembling slightly. "She's been locked in Dad's basement all these years." Noah's expression shifts from confusion to a mix of shock and rage.

"The basement?" he echoes, his voice rising. I nod, swallowing hard.

"Yes. She's safe now. But she's been through hell down there."

Noah's face contorts with rage, a flash of anger that seems almost too intense to contain. His jaw clenches, and for a moment, I think he might explode. Then, just as suddenly as it appeared, his anger dissipates, replaced by a chilling calmness. He turns slowly to Dean, his eyes burning with intensity.

"Well," Noah says, his voice dangerously smooth, "tell your girlfriend I said thank you." Dean stiffens, clearly caught off guard.

"Thank you?" he repeats, confusion evident in his voice.

"Yeah. Thank you for taking him out. Saves me the trouble."

We sit in silence for a moment, the only sound being the soft echo of our breathing. His eyes, which had been locked intensely on mine for what felt like an eternity, finally drop to the marble floor, tracing the intricate patterns etched into the stone with a newfound introspection.

"I'd like to see her," Noah says suddenly, breaking the silence. His voice is steady, but there's an underlying urgency to his words. "Take me to her." I nod, feeling a strange mix of relief and apprehension.

"She's in dad's old house. The one we shared together." I tell him. Noah's expression shifts to one of disgust. He sneers, shaking his head in disdain.

"I'll get her a nice place. A *new* place." I nod again. That's exactly what she needs.

We stand up, ready to leave the house and Noah grabs a set of keys from an extremely impressive array of car keys on the back wall.

"Noah," I start. "I need to ask you one more thing."

"Make it quick," he replies, his tone still guarded but slightly more open.

"Do you have any idea why dad would have asked me about a book?"

For the first time since we arrived, Noah laughs; a genuine, hearty laugh that echoes through the grand room. He stands and walks back over to the chest, rummaging through its contents before pulling out a book very similar to mine. With a cocky grin dancing on his lips, he extends it toward me.

"Take it," he says, "I'm sick of hearing about that fucking thing."

CHAPTER 5:

PINK-HAIRED PRINCESS

Noah

I've just met her for the first time, my real mother, not the ghostly figure my father let me believe was dead and buried. Seeing her, broken and frail, was a punch to the gut. I hadn't felt that much anger in years, a rage so potent it made my blood boil. But I couldn't show it. Not in front of Marcus. Not in front of anyone.

I can't believe she was in that 'empty' room in the basement this whole time. They never gave me the keys to that room. They told me it was untouched. All the years I've spent torturing and murdering men down there, in the room next door, and my father managed to hide her from me. He and his loyal minion, Moth, who had always been like a shadow, always lingering around, always knowing more than he let on. More than he ever fucking should've. My old man and his henchman were more cunning than I ever gave them credit for. But now, they're both rotting, and good riddance.

Chapter 5

When Marcus told me he had murdered Moth himself, I felt a sense of pride. Moth is no easy target. My little brother has shown his strength, and I'm impressed. It must run in the blood.

But then he hit me with the real kicker, the reasoning behind the kill. Apparently, Moth had confessed to the shit he did to Sienna, who I've now learnt is my brother's girlfriend.

Of course.

Little did Marcus know, I had joined Moth in doing so. I, obviously, kept my mouth shut about that. I never wanted to do that to Sienna. As stoic as I may seem, hearing her screams broke me in two. But Moth was high as a fucking kite, crazed, and pushing for us to take the job. Refusing would've been suicide, and worse, with me dead, Sienna would be left with no escape. Moth would drag her to his private warehouse, where he'd subject her to unspeakable horrors; rape, torture, and a slow, brutal, bloody murder. The thought of it was unbearable. I couldn't let that happen.

So I made the only choice I could; I agreed, knowing that I could use the situation to my advantage. I suggested taking Sienna to my father's house instead. It was a risk, but it gave me an opportunity to gain some kind of control of the situation. I had full access to that basement room. If I could persuade them to take her there, I'd eventually be able to get her out alive. It was survival, nothing more.

That basement is a place for grown men; enemies and cunts who deserved every second of pain and fear we inflicted on them. Never for sweet little girls. I tried to do something, anything, to make up for the horror she'd endured. I made and brought Sienna breakfast. Pathetic I know, but it was all I could do for right now. I had every intention of getting her out of there, one way or another. But luckily, Marcus showed up before I had to do anything more.

Thank fuck for that.

The drive over here had been a nightmare. Marcus wouldn't stop droning on about books the entire fucking time. Like father, like son. I'm sick of hearing about it. As if one cursed book wasn't enough, now there are two. Mine has been laying out events like clockwork since I opened it. And considering my father was just killed, the final event in the story, my book is finally complete. Done with.

I feel like I'm the only sane one left. While Marcus and our father have been fucking around with magical books, desperate to change the outcomes, I'm fully aware that they're only doing more harm. You can't mess with what's already set in motion. You can't fuck with fate.

And to top it off, I'm sick of Dean. I'm disgusted to find out that Marcus was his fucking Orchid's roommate and has been chilling with him ever since. I don't approve. The guy has been selling for years, constantly taking my dealers' business and giving them trouble. Not to mention the shit he used to cause for my mates back in the unit. He's a slimy cunt. A thorn in my side; always has been.

But it's okay, he won't be a problem much longer.

The book says so.

And now, here I am, standing outside yet-another house, this one belonging to somebody called 'Skylar', because Marcus wants me to meet his friends. This is the last place I want to be. I've got a business to run, enemies to watch, and a reputation to uphold. But family.. well, *my* family is complicated. So I'm here, against my better judgement, because my little brother asked.

Marcus raises his hand to knock on the door, and we wait. The seconds tick by before the door swings open, revealing a tiny figure standing in the doorway.

As soon as I see her, my entire world goes up in flames. I swear the world tilts on its axis.

I'm powerless to look away.

"This is Noah." Marcus says to her, a faint echo in my distracted mind.

She meets my gaze head-on, bold and unafraid, and something deep inside me stirs. It's possessive, almost primal. She's a goddess. She's a siren, looking up at me; beckoning me closer with those piercing blue eyes. She's got to be the sexiest little creature I've ever seen. It's immediately clear to me that I'd give anything to get my hands on her. Her delicate features, her petite frame; she's the perfect little package of fragility And I know exactly what to do with that.

"Hey," she says, her tone teasingly melodic. "I'm Skylar." With intended grace, I step forward. Each movement is calculated, every stride laden with a magnetism I rarely unveil. My eyes feast on her face, lingering on the curve of her lips as they quirk into a subtle smile.

"Skylar..?" I ask, my voice low and commanding. She raises an eyebrow, a hint of amusement dancing in her eyes. I don't care. I know now that I'm not here to play games.

"A little formal don't you think?" she says, her voice husky and confident. I don't reply, instead I smirk, a slow, conscious movement. She's got no idea what she's gotten herself into. She thinks she's brave, standing there with her big girl talk and her flirty eyes. But I'll break her.

"Skylar Farmer." she continues, like she's giving me permission to know her name.

I close the distance between us, stepping into her space, watching the way her breath hitches as I invade her bubble. I lean in just enough to tower over her, my voice turning smooth and lethal.

"Well, Skylar Farmer," I say. "Pleasure."

I'm an ice-cold man, and this is what I've been missing; the rush of power that comes with possessing something that belongs to no one else. She belongs to me, and I know it immediately. She doesn't know what's coming for her yet, but I do. I'm about to do some bad things. Very bad things. My mind is a maelstrom of dark desires, and Miss Skylar Farmer is the spark setting them ablaze.

I've just found myself a pink-haired princess, and she'll soon know what it means to be owned by me.

She stares intensely into my eyes, almost challenging me. Her stare doesn't waver, and for a moment, we're locked in a silent battle of wills. Then, with a subtle shift of her weight, Skylar yields, her body angling to let us pass. The movement is almost imperceptible, but I know it's deliberate; a calculated surrender. As I pass her, I purposefully brush my shoulder against hers, the contact rough and possessive. It's a claim, a teaser of what's to come.

A warning that I'm no prince charming.

I feel her shiver slightly at the touch, and another satisfied smirk tugs at the corner of my lips. There's an immediate tension in the air. I can feel it. And I know she can too.

Inside, the others introduce themselves but I couldn't give a shit. I pretend I've never met Sienna, Delilah's the girl who shot my dad, the ginger one is a bird.

Blah blah blah.

I'm supposed to care about these introductions, supposed to engage, but they're all a distant hum. I'm a statue, frozen in place, my eyes fixed on Skylar and Skylar only; my mind already plotting. My pupils constrict, focusing all my attention on her. I don't blink. I don't breathe. I'm like a man possessed; half-tempted to kidnap her on the fucking spot.

And then she catches me staring. Her eyes drilling into mine like a hot poker, and I give her a stern look; one that says I won't be deterred, I won't be swayed.

But instead of turning away..
she fucking smiles at me.

Not just any smile; a sly, naughty smile. Her lips curve upward in a subtle, knowing arc, as if she's sharing a private joke with me, one that only we understand. My cock hardens in response, but I don't react. I'm too far gone. Too locked in. I'm lost in the vortex of my own desire.

Birdie shouts over from across the room.

"Sky, can you get me a drink?" Skylar lets out a frustrated sigh and rolls her eyes, her irritation palpable as she begins to make her way towards the door behind me. As she approaches, her intensity doesn't waver. The room seems to shrink around us, every step she takes drawing her closer, until finally, she stops right beside me.

She stands close, her eyes locked onto mine with an inexorable stare. Leaning in just enough to invade my personal space, she whispers,

"Can I get you anything, Sir?" Her tone is dripping with mock politeness and formality. Brave girl. She's playing with fire, but what she doesn't realise is that I'm more than willing to get burned.

I narrow my eyes, a smirk curling my lips as I reply in a low, dangerous murmur,

"Just your cooperation, princess. Think you can manage that?" She lingers for a heartbeat longer, letting the tension build, then straightens and continues to the door; this time, her shoulder brushes mine as she passes.

It seems she's keeping score.

Marcus calls me over, his voice cutting through the haze of my thoughts.

"Noah, come join," he says, gesturing towards the group. Reluctantly, I make my way over to where they're gathered. I try to focus on the general chit-chat, nodding at the right moments, but my mind keeps drifting back to Skylar. The conversations around me blur into a background hum until I catch something that piques my interest.

"So, where are you planning on going now?" Delilah asks, her voice tinged with worry. "The police are still on your backs." She says. Marcus sighs, rubbing the back of his neck.

"I'm not sure, but it's getting late. We'll figure something out in the morning."

I see an opening, sliding in with casual ease.

"You could all stay at my place for a couple weeks. It's secure, not too far but it's out of the way, and you wouldn't have to worry about the feds. They wouldn't step foot on my property." I suggest, my tone casual. Delilah looks sceptical.

"I don't think we're all gonna fit in one house." she says. I chuckle, low and sure of myself. Dean joins in, shaking his head with a grin.

"Except it's not a house, darling. It's a fucking estate." He says. Marcus laughs and nods in agreement. I give a nonchalant shrug, pretending like it's no big deal.

"Consider it an open invitation. You'll be safe there, and it'll give you all some time to figure out your next move."

The truth, of course, is that I have an ulterior motive. With Skylar under my roof, I can keep her precisely where I want her; at my mercy, under my watchful eye, and within my grasp. As I observe her, study her, and unravel the secrets of her psyche, I'll gain the upper hand. And once I know exactly what makes her tick, I'll use that knowledge to prey on her. Manipulate her. Bend her to my will.

And the best part? She won't even realise it until it's too late.

"Well, I'm down." Marcus says, looking around, waiting for the others to follow. The nods come quickly, murmured agreements, everyone falling into line. Except Dean. "Dean?" Marcus asks. He doesn't respond right away, too busy rolling a joint, his hands moving faster than they should. I can see the tension in his shoulders, the way his jaw clenches. He hates this idea. Not because of the house, but because of me. I can't resist the urge to poke at him, to remind him of the shift in dynamics.

"Ah, come on, Douglas." I taunt with faux-genuinity "It'll be nice for Marcus to spend some time with his big brother." Dean's jaw tightens slightly, his eyes screwing as he glances briefly at Marcus, then back down at his joint. He doesn't dignify my jab with a response, but I can see I've struck a nerve.

Dean grunts noncommittally, lighting and taking a drag from his joint. The smoke swirls around his face as he exhales slowly, his gaze fixed somewhere in the distance.

"Yeah," Dean finally mutters with a nod. "Sounds good."

As Dean begrudgingly agrees, I smirk inwardly, relishing the subtle power play. He knows who holds the reins here, and it's not him. Marcus values me and I have qualities that Dean simply can't match. I see through his attempts at composure. He knows better than to challenge me openly. He sees me as untouchable, and he's not wrong.

Dean's bravado doesn't impress me. He likes to think he's dangerous, dealing his shitty weed and throwing fists around like it means something. But now, I'm here. He's used to being the big fish in a small pond, but in my ocean, he's just another minnow. His life has been a parade of petty crimes and adolescent bravado. I knew a few guys he had beaten up back in the young offenders' unit. Always picking fights he knew he'd win, thinking it made him hard.

But he's stepping into my world now, a world where I've carved out my place. A world where every single decision is life or death.

I exude arrogance because I've fucking earned it.

The group starts to disperse, everyone moving towards the door. I hang back with Sienna, making sure we're out of earshot from the others. She's been through hell, and I need to make sure she's okay. Considering I'm largely to blame.

"Sienna," I say softly, catching her attention. "How you doing?" She looks up, her eyes a mix of vulnerability and strength.

"I'm surprisingly okay, Noah." she replies, her voice barely above a whisper. I take a deep breath, the weight of my actions heavy on my chest.

"I'm so sorry, Sienna. I'm a fucking monster. I played a role I never wanted to play, but if I had refused, I would've been killed." I explain, "and with me dead, you'd be in a hell you'd have no chance of escaping from." She nods, understanding but still wounded.

"I forgive you."

"I want you to know," I continue, my voice earnest, "I wasn't going to rest until I got you out of there." Her eyes search mine, as if trying to decipher my soul.

"I believe you, Noah. And weirdly, you made me feel safer there." Her words bring a strange sense of relief. I've done unspeakable things, but her forgiveness feels like a lifeline.

She glances around, making sure no one is listening.

"Please, can you keep this between us?"

"If that's what you want." I promise, my tone firm and sincere. "I swear." She extends her little finger towards me, a gesture so innocent it almost breaks my heart. I hook my pinky with hers, sealing the promise, and meaning it.

CHAPTER 6:
SUSPICIOUS

Dean

I linger by the door, my hand on the knob, ready to leave. But something makes me turn. My eyes lock onto the scene unfolding behind me; Noah and Sienna, huddled close, making a pinky promise and smiling at each other like they've known each other forever. The sight makes my stomach churn. They've supposedly just met, yet there's an ease between them that doesn't sit right with me.

I grind my teeth, trying to keep my composure, but I can't shake the suspicion that Noah had something to do with Sienna's capture. He just appears out of nowhere, in full contact with Grizzly and his gang, but for some reason the group is all for him. I know better than to challenge Noah openly. He's got this aura of untouchability, and I can see why Marcus is drawn to him. But it doesn't make it any easier to stomach. Marcus might be eager to get to know his real brother, but I'm not convinced.

There's something off about Noah, something that doesn't add up. And until I figure out what it is, I'll be watching him like a fucking hawk.

He finally notices me standing there. As he glances over, our eyes lock for a brief, tense moment. He gives me that infuriating smirk, the one that makes me want to reach up and punch his cocky face in. He knows exactly what he's doing, jabbing at me, pushing my buttons. And I hate to admit it, but it's working.

Noah strides towards the door, his towering frame casting a shadow over the room. As he approaches, he stops right in front of me.

"Something wrong, Douglas?" he asks, his voice dripping with condescension, his tone implying that he knows better. I don't flinch.

"All good. Just keeping an eye out," I reply evenly as I take a drag of my joint, my tone suggesting more than casual concern.

"Keeping an eye out for what, exactly?" he presses.

"I just wanna make sure you know where you stand," I say, my voice low and measured, each word laced with underlying threat. He smiles, his face dripping with arrogance.

"Oh, I think I've got a pretty good idea," he says. I lean in closer, my voice low and serious.

"Don't mistake Marcus' trust for an open invitation. I don't trust you as far as I could fucking throw you." I warn. Noah laughs, a cold, mocking sound that sets my teeth on edge. He glances down at my hand, a sneer forming on his lips.

"How'd you lose your fingers?" he asks, not out of genuine concern, but as if hinting that I'm an easy fight.

I hesitate for a split second, the truth flashing through my mind of Skylar turning on that fucking combine harvester, but I decide on a different narrative.

"It's a long story," I say, keeping my voice steady, hinting at something darker and more dangerous. I smirk slightly, letting him fill in the blanks with whatever badass scenario he can conjure up. Noah smiles arrogantly and pats me on the shoulder in a patronising gesture.

"See you at the house, yeah?" he says as he swerves around me and heads out the door.

Prick.

I trudge over to where Sienna stands, her demeanour fragile yet resilient, a stark contrast to the tension that just transpired with Noah. I approach her cautiously,

"You good?" I ask. She looks up at me with tired eyes, offering a faint smile.

"Yeah I'm good. A little tired, but good." I pause for a moment, choosing my words carefully.

"I saw you guys making a little pinky promise. What was that all about?" Sienna's shoulders tense slightly, but she manages a small, sheepish smile.

"Oh, we were just joking around." She lies. I nod, trying to keep the conversation light.

"Got it. So, what do you think of him?" I ask, hoping to squeeze something out of her.

"He seems nice," she shrugs. I raise an eyebrow slightly, taking another drag of my joint. Sienna's answer is too neat, too practised.

"Nice, huh?" I repeat, letting the smoke curl from my lips. "You know, I get the feeling there's more to him than meets the eye."

She looks away towards the door where Noah exited.

"Yeah, well, it's hard to get a read on someone in just a couple hours," she replies, her tone dismissive. But I'm not buying it. I step closer, lowering my voice.

"Look, Sienna. He's part of the gang that orchestrated this whole thing. You don't think he has secrets?" I hesitate, watching her closely for any reaction, but her expression remains guarded. Her eyes widen slightly, and she shakes her head, though her reaction is more instinctual than convincing.

"I'm not sure what you're suggesting."

"I'm just throwing things out there," I say quickly, attempting to ease the tension. "Just.. trying to make sense of everything, you know?" I watch her carefully, waiting for her response, but her expression is diplomatic.

"Yeah, I understand," she replies softly, her voice tinged with apprehension. I nod slowly, accepting her answer for now.

"Good," I say, my tone thoughtful. "Well, give me a heads up if anything seems off, okay?"

"I will," she assures me, her voice quieter now.

I watch her for a moment longer, then glance towards the door where Noah disappeared moments ago. The unease settles in my gut like a heavy stone.

"Just don't do anything stupid, okay?" She says with a smile. I smirk, but there's no humour in it.

"Don't worry. Stupid's not really my style."

10:43p.m. I pull up in front of Noah's sprawling estate, Delilah sitting beside me in the passenger seat and Skylar lying leisurely in the back. The mansion rises before us, grand and dramatic, surrounded by well-manicured gardens and imposing gates.

"Holy shit." Skylar gasps. "I might just have to suck him off for some spending money."

"Skylar, what the actual fuck?" I say, head in hand.

"What? It's called a strategy."

Delilah's eyes widen as she takes in the sight.

"Woah, this place is huge," she breathes out, her voice tinged with a mix of awe and uncertainty.

"Yeah I know," I mutter, more to myself than to her. Something about this whole setup feels off, like we're walking right into the lion's den without realising it. But for Marcus' sake, I'll play nice.

As we tread through the gates, into the driveway, I trail my fingers through the fountain, the cool water soothing against my skin. The sound of trickling water blends with the soft rustle of leaves in the breeze, creating an atmosphere that should be serene but instead feels strangely tense.

I'm drawn to the row of expensive cars parked along the driveway, their sleek bodies angled in an intended, intimidating line. Of course he'd have his collection of supercars parked as if they're poised to spring into action at any moment.

We get it, you're big and scary.
And really fucking rich.

Noah pushes open the double doors in a slow, easy motion.

"Welcome home." He says casually. He guides us to the left, bypassing the gigantic staircase, and into a spacious living room adorned with modern art pieces and dark, comfortable furniture arranged around a sleek fireplace. It's all so.. moody. "Feel free to hang out here if you want," he mentions, gesturing towards the large sofa before leading us further into the expansive kitchen.

The kitchen is a chef's dream, with state-of-the-art appliances, and a large island that doubles as a breakfast bar.

"Help yourselves to anything in here," Noah says, opening the cabinets and double-door fridge to reveal a variety of snacks and beverages neatly arranged. "And there are four bathrooms scattered around the house, so no need to worry about waiting."

As he continues the tour, Noah moves swiftly, almost as if he's done this countless times. He leads us down a hallway branching off from the kitchen, stopping at various doors to point out the layout. When we circle back to the foyer, he gestures towards a sleek, vintage black phone mounted on the wall.

"If you need anything ordered in, just use this phone," he explains. "My driver will pick it up and bring it over."

I roll my eyes.
Of course he has a constantly-available driver.

As we ascend the grand staircase, Noah leads us down a sleek corridor that reeks of old money and the pungent scent of cigars. The second floor opens up to another staircase and a wide hallway. Floor-to-ceiling windows allow the moonlight to filter in, bathing the hallway in a soft glow. The walls are adorned with modern wood panelling, adding a touch of sophistication. Polished brown-stain concrete floors beneath our feet give a subtle echo as we follow his lead.

He points us towards the row of closed doors lining each side.

"This floor has enough bedrooms, so just take your pick. They're all pretty comfortable." he says with a careless wave.

"Yes, I'm sure they are." I mutter under my breath. But no one seems to notice my sarcasm. Instead, they're all oohing and ahhing over the opulence like a bunch of groupies at a rockstar's tour bus.

"I gotta finish up some stuff in my office. Just give me a shout if you need anything," Noah adds, his tone relaxed. He starts to turn away, his steps leisurely as he moves back towards the staircase leading down. Just as everyone starts to disperse, he pauses and looks back towards Skylar.

"Oh, and Farmer," he says with a slight grin, his eyes twinkling with mischief, "your room is up on the third floor. First door on the left."

Skylar blushes slightly as Noah proceeds to wink at her; her cheeks turning a faint shade of pink. Birdie and Sienna exchange knowing glances, their smiles widening as they giggle and squeal softly to Skylar about the flirtatious gesture. I stand a few steps away, watching the interaction with a furrowed brow and tight jaw. Sky's excitement over Noah's advances is hard to ignore; she's too gullible, too fucking naive.

I keep a close eye on his retreating figure, my scepticism about him only growing stronger as I watch him disappear into the opulence of the mansion. The lavish decor and sparkling chandeliers may try to dazzle me, but my instincts remain firmly rooted in the conviction that Noah is trouble; and nothing about this gilded cage can change my mind.

I'm pulled back into reality by Delilah calling me over to the room she's picked.

"Dean! Check this out!" Even *she's* all happy and excited; in awe about the room and the mansion in general. I feel like an outlier, aware of the storm brewing while everyone else remains oblivious.

With a sigh, I mutter under my breath.

"Coming."

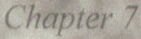

CHAPTER 7:
TOGETHER AT LAST

Marcus

I follow Sienna into her chosen room, closing the door softly behind us. The moment we're alone, I turn to her, my heart pounding with relief and overwhelming emotion.

"Sweet," I whisper, my voice thick with unshed tears. She looks up at me, her eyes shining with a mixture of exhaustion and trust. I can't hold back any longer. I yank her into a fierce hug, wrapping my arms around her like a shield against the pain and fear she's endured. She melts into my embrace, her body trembling as she clings to me, burying her face in my chest.

"I was so scared," she whispers.

"I know. I snap, my eyes locked on hers with fierce intensity. "But I'll always find you. It doesn't matter what trail of blood I have to leave behind."

We stand there for a long time, just holding each other, the room's silence filled with the steady beat of our hearts.

Gradually, her trembling subsides, and she pulls back slightly, looking up at me with a soft smile.

"Is Butter okay?" She asks. I smile, my thumb brushing a stray strand of hair away from her face as I answer.

"Yes, Butter's fine, sweet." I reassure her, "I have to go back tomorrow to get my bike. I'll bring her back for you." Her eyes light up at the mention of her beloved little butterfly.

"Can I come with you?" she asks, her voice hopeful.

I hesitate, the protective part of me wanting to keep her locked in the house forever and as far away from any potential danger as humanly possible. But then I look into her eyes and I'm done. How could I deny that face? She's been through so much, and if this will bring her a bit of comfort, then I'll make it happen.

"Of course," I say, smiling down at her.

She beams up at me, the shadow of fear lifting from her face for the first time since I found her. I pull her into another hug, kissing the top of her head. The scent of her freshly washed hair fills my senses, clean and familiar. I breathe deeply, letting the fragrance wash over me like a soothing balm. After being in that basement, her hair had been tangled and smelled unlike it ever had before. Now, it feels like I've truly got my angel back, the way she's meant to be.

"You must be exhausted." I state.

"I've never been so tired, Marcus." she shares. I nod sympathetically, trying to hide my own emotions.

"Did Sky lend you anything to sleep in?" I ask, trying to sound normal, as I gently sit her down on the edge of the bed. She nods, pointing to a small bag on the floor. I grab the bag and pull out a pair of soft pyjamas, then kneel slowly on the floor in front of her, just like I've done so many times before.

But this time, as I carefully remove her borrowed clothes, I'm met with the bruises and cuts marring her thighs and behind; my heart clenching painfully at the sight. The moonlight casts an eerie glow over the room, making everything feel like a bad dream. I carefully slide off her underwear, my fingers tracing the lines of her bruised skin like a map of pain. Each touch is like a tiny betrayal, like I'm complicit in her suffering. My breath catches in my throat as I realise the true extent of the damage; her thighs have actually been sliced, the dark bruises interspersed with deep, angry gashes.

I always put her pyjamas on for her, tuck her in and whisper sweet nothings in her ear. It's a ritual that's supposed to be about care and protection. But now, it just feels like a cruel fucking joke. Because underneath these innocent little pyjamas, she's been savaged in the most intimate way.

I gently tug on the fabric of her new, borrowed garments, as if the fabric could somehow scrub away the brutal reality. The soft cotton whispers against her skin like a mournful sigh, and I feel like I'm trying to erase the evidence of what I allowed to happen to her. But it's too late for that.

I'm putting a plaster on a broken bone.

As I pull up the bottoms, I try to be as gentle as possible, my touch feather-light against her damaged skin. I have to fight to keep my expression neutral for her sake.

I kiss her body gently, starting from her toes and moving upwards, savouring the warmth and softness of her skin. Each kiss is a tender gesture, reassuring and loving. Her curls spill across her face like a curtain of innocence, adding to her deservedly-peaceful appearance. I take my time, making sure to cover every inch of her skin, lingering on the gentle curves of her neck and the soft slope of her shoulders. Once I've kissed her body to my satisfaction, I slide the pyjama top over her head, trying not to jostle her too much.

I burrow her into the bed snugly, making sure the duvet wraps around her comfortably. Leaning over, I stroke her forehead and run my fingers through her curls, gently smoothing them out. My tired angel closes her eyes immediately.

"Sleep tight, sweet," I whisper, before I withdraw and turn off the light.

Walking towards the window, I light a blunt, seeking a moment of respite from the endless emotional turmoil from today's unfathomable events.

I started the day in a shitty B&B without Sienna.
Now I'm ending it in a mansion with Sienna back, a dead dad and a new brother and mother thrown into the mix.

Pretty fucking normal.

The sweet, pungent aroma of marijuana fills the air, and I take a deep drag, feeling the smoke curl around my tongue and down my throat. The instant rush of relaxation washes over me, easing the tension in my shoulders and calming the racing thoughts in my mind. As I exhale, my eyes droop slightly, and I let out a slow sigh, feeling my muscles relax and my breathing slow. The smoke has a way of quieting the noise in my head; like a twisted rubber band snapping back into shape.

I take another hit, feeling the effects intensify. My vision blurs a little as the cannabis takes hold. I lean against the window, feeling the cool breeze on my skin as I watch the smoke curl out into the night air; hearing Sienna's tiny breaths in the background. It's not perfect, but it's a small moment of peace in a day that's been one giant clusterfuck.

"Marcus?" Sienna's soft voice interrupts my thoughts, drawing me back to her side.

God I missed that beautiful little voice.

I turn to see her gazing at me with those big, innocent doe-eyes.

"Yes, sweet?" I respond, my voice gentle.

"Will I ever be your girlfriend?" she asks, quiet and hesitant. The question catches me off guard and I chuckle lightly, taking another long drag.

"No, sweet," I say. "I don't think so." Her expression falls slightly, but she nods.

"I love you, Marcus."

"I love you too, sweet. More than anything."

With a small sigh, Sienna's eyelids flutter closed, exhaustion finally claiming her. I watch over her for a while longer, feeling a swell of protectiveness and gratitude that she's safe with me now.

CHAPTER 8:
HARD TO GET

Noah

2:35a.m. I finish up downstairs, making sure everything is in order. I've been on the phone non-stop, dealing with the fallout from Moth and, more importantly, my father's death. Calls to trusted dealers, whispered conversations about retaliation and alliances shifting in the underworld. I have a more important role now that my dad is gone. A role I've been primed for since I could crawl.

The house is quiet again, thank *God*. Having to keep everyone here just to ensure Skylar will be close by is a fucking hassle. I prefer my peace and quiet, and a full house grates on my nerves. I'm not exactly the most social person to begin with, and the fact that I have to force chatter and smiles with an entire group, just to get to know my brother and keep Skylar under my watch, is already driving me fucking nuts.

Then on top of that, you toss Dean Douglas into the equation, and I'm seriously considering offing myself.

Every time a door slams or someone laughs, my muscles tense. But I remind myself that this is temporary. The noise, the small talk, the tension with Dean; it's all part of the game. A game I intend to win. Keeping Skylar here, keeping her off-balance, is worth every bit of discomfort.

Heading upstairs, I catch movement behind one of the doors; the one I gave to Skylar. There's banging, movement, the sound of drawers being yanked open and slammed shut. My curiosity spikes, and I stop in front of the door, listening. She's up to something.

I knock on the door, waiting for a response. Silence. I rap again, more firmly this time, but there's still no reply. A bit concerned, I decide to open the door. Skylar is there of course, rummaging through the drawers, her back to me. She spins around, her eyes narrowing when she sees me.

"I didn't say come in," she snaps, her voice icy and her posture defensive.

"I knocked," I reply smoothly, stepping into the room. "You didn't answer."

"That usually means fuck off, genius."

Her unnecessary verbal abuse should piss me off, but instead, I bite down on a chuckle. My eyes rake over her, taking in the way her body moves; the way she seethes. God.

She's sexy when she's mad.

"What are you looking for?" I ask, my voice calm and collected. In actuality, I'd like to teach her a lesson for that sharp tongue of hers; show her what happens when she talks back. She huffs and turns back to the drawers, clearly unwilling to share. I lean against the doorframe, watching her every move.

"You know, Farmer," I say, letting the condescension drip off my words. "If you need something, you could just ask. This is my house, after all." Skylar freezes, her hands paused mid-reach, before continuing her search.

"I don't need anything from you," she spits out, her tone dripping with venom. I step closer.

"I think you're going to need me more than you realise."

She stops rummaging and looks at me, her eyes challenging mine.

"Is that so?" She questions. I nod, holding her gaze with an intensity that I know unsettles her.

"Yes. And the sooner you accept that, the easier things will be for you, princess." For a moment, we stand there, locked in a silent battle of wills.

"Well, since you decided to put me in your weird little sex dungeon, I have no room for my clothes!" She snaps. I stop, raising an eyebrow.

"Sex dungeon?" I repeat with a grin. Skylar glares at me, her cheeks flushing slightly.

"Yes! The hooks, the.. other stuff. What is all this shit?"

I chuckle, the sound low and amused.

"I see you've been exploring."

"Listen, fuckface-"

"*Fuckface?*"

"I don't know what you think you're going to accomplish by putting me in this room," she spits out, her tone acidulous, "but I'm not interested, and I *really* don't appreciate the lack of drawer space."

Did she seriously just call me fuckface?

I raise an eyebrow, a slow, predatory smile spreading.

"Don't worry, I'll make sure you have room for your things." I step closer, my voice dropping to a whisper, "but don't pretend you're not curious."

Her breath catches, just for a second. Gotcha.

She doesn't reply, her defiance faltering for a split second. I press on, enjoying her discomfort.

"What's with the attitude, princess? I have to say I preferred it when you were calling me sir."

"Well don't hold your breath," she laughs. "I can assure you that'll never happen again."

"I wouldn't be so sure."

"You're beyond delusional," she says with a scowl, but the aggression in her voice is tinged with something else; something that excites me. I step closer again, enjoying the way she stiffens as I invade her space.

"Oh yeah?" I murmur, my voice dripping with confidence. She doesn't reply.

I chuckle softly, taking a few more steps closer until there's barely any space left between us.

"You're in my house now, princess." I warn, lifting a hand to brush a stray lock of pastel pink hair away from her face. "And if you keep pushing, I might have to put this room to use." Her skin prickles under my touch, but she doesn't pull away. Her cheeks flush deeper with anger and frustration as she looks me up and down like a high school bully.

"Good luck with that." She shoots back, clearly unimpressed. I take one last lingering look at her, my smirk widening.

The pretty-pink hair gets more ironic the more she opens her mouth. It's like I'm looking at this adorable little candyfloss dream and thinking she's all sweetness; but then she hits me with these witty, spiteful comebacks out of nowhere. She's a tough nut to crack. Unpredictable. I wouldn't be surprised to learn that she's plotting world domination in her spare time. And I'm all for it.

"I think it's about time someone taught you how to behave." I suggest, my voice low, as I turn to leave. I can feel her eyes burning into my back as I take a step away from her, leaving a silent challenge hanging between us like a thread. "Goodnight, Farmer." I say over my shoulder.

I close the door behind me with a soft click, the sound echoing through the silent hallway. A sly smile spreads across my face, a thrill of satisfaction coursing through my veins. Her discovery means she's fully aware of my intentions towards her. The realization is sinking in, and fuck, it's delicious.

She's just uncovered a tiny piece of my world, and now she'll be on edge, wondering what I'm going to do about it. She thinks she's got me figured out, but she's only seen the tip of the iceberg. It's like a game of cat and mouse, and what she doesn't know yet is that this game only ends one way. I take a deep breath, feeling my pulse race with excitement. This is what it means to be alive; to be a predator, to be a hunter. I smile to myself, savouring the thrill of the chase.

But fuck, she's a firecracker. This is going to be a much bigger challenge than I thought. Her insufferable, sassy little attitude was certainly unexpected. Every snarky comment, every raised eyebrow made me harder than a rock. She's feisty, rude, and unyielding, and I fucking love it. The thrill of breaking through that tough exterior, of showing her who's boss, is more exhilarating than I could have imagined.

She has no idea what I'm capable of, what depths of depravity I'm willing to sink to in order to get what I want.

And what I want is her.

CHAPTER 9:

WAKEY WAKEY

Marcus

The morning light seeps through the curtains, casting a soft glow over the room. I wake slowly, aware of Sienna nestled against me, her warmth a comforting weight. Her eyes flutter open, still heavy with sleep, and she smiles drowsily at me.

"Good morning," she mumbles, her voice still thick with sleep.

"Morning, sleepy," I reply softly. The relief of having her safe and sound washes over me anew.

"How are you feeling?"

"Happy," she says simply, her smile widening as she snuggles closer. I raise an eyebrow. 'Happy' is probably the best, and least expected, reply she could've given to that question.

We lay there for a while, savouring the quiet intimacy. Her steady breathing, the way her body moulds to mine. After a few moments, I shift slightly.

"I'm gonna get up and make us some breakfast." I say, my voice low and husky. Sienna pouts, her eyes barely open, her face scrunched up like a child who's been told it's time to leave the playground.

"It's only 8a.m. You're never up this early. Can't we stay here a tiny little while longer?" she whimpers with a faux-sad expression. I chuckle and then, without warning, tickle her sides. She squeals, squirming in my arms. I follow it with a light smack on her behind, and she swats at me playfully.

I grin, standing up and pulling on classic my tracksuit bottoms and white t-shirt.

"You get up whenever you feel like it, sweet," I say. Sienna splays herself out on the bed dramatically, stretching her limbs like a cat and sighing theatrically.

"Never," she declares with mock defiance, "this bed is *so* cosy." I laugh softly, watching her indulge in the comfort of the bed. For a moment, I just stand there, admiring her. Her natural beauty, the way her hair fans out on the pillow, the serene expression on her face; she looks like pure perfection. It's a sight I could get used to waking up to every single morning.

"Alright, sweet," I say, leaning against the doorframe. "But don't blame me if you miss out on your favourite breakfast." She cracks one eye open and looks at me sceptically.

"What are you making?" she asks, curiosity piqued despite her dramatics. I grin, turning to leave the room.

"A full English of course," I say through the crack in the door, my voice teasing. "But if you don't want any, that's fine, I'm sure Dean would be delighted to take yours off your hands," I add with a wink.

I can hear her groan of protest just as I close the door, a smile tugging at my lips. As I head downstairs to the mansion kitchen,

I still can't believe this is my brother's house. The sheer size and opulence of it is overwhelming. This could've been me too.
Man, my dad is a prick.

Reaching the kitchen, I open the massive fridge, its coolness washing over me as I grab all the ingredients. The sizzle of bacon hitting the hot pan fills the room. I move efficiently, cracking eggs into another pan, their edges crisp and turning golden. The tomatoes and mushrooms release a mouthwatering scent as they cook, mingling with the savoury smell of the sausages.

I'm just starting on the baked beans, stirring them gently in a saucepan, when I hear footsteps behind me. Turning, I see my brother Noah entering the room, his hair is tousled under a cap and he's still shaking off sleep. He's wearing a compression top that highlights just how ripped he is. The guy looks like he could bench press a small car.

"Morning," he says, yawning. "What's all this?"

"Just making breakfast," I reply. Noah raises an eyebrow, glancing at the spread.

"Nice." He smirks, grabbing a mug and pouring himself some coffee. "It smells good."

"Thanks, man." I smile.

The kitchen is filled with the sounds and smells of cooking, the beautiful aroma of breakfast foods blending together. I plate the bacon and sausages, setting them on the counter next to the fried eggs. The beans are simmering nicely, and I give them one last stir before turning off the heat.

Noah leans against the counter, sipping his coffee. Despite the early hour and his sleepy demeanour, he's got this constant alert look. It's honestly quite unnatural how someone can look that menacing before 9a.m.

"So, how's Sienna?" he asks.

"She's good," I say, smiling to myself as I think about her upstairs, likely still sprawled out on the bed. "She's happy. Which is all that matters." He nods, watching me work.

"You're doing pretty well with this. Got the timing down and everything."

"Yeah, I've always liked cooking." I admit. Noah's face softens a bit, a rare expression for him.

"Mum does too." he shares. I pause, turning to look at him fully. He nods, looking over at my bacon.

"You know, she had this trick for getting the crispy edges on the bacon while keeping it tender in the middle."

He steps up, taking the tongs from my hand and showing me how to arrange the bacon in the pan just so, and then lowering the heat slightly.

"You let it cook slower, give it time. Keeps it from getting too tough." he shares. I watch him, absorbing the information. He hands the tongs back to me. "See how that goes," he says. "She taught me that as a kid. I used to help her in the kitchen all the time."

There's a moment of silence between us, filled only with the sounds of cooking. It's a comfortable silence, a new thing for us.

"I wish I had some memories with her." I acknowledge. Noah looks at me, his expression unreadable.

"Yeah I know, I wish you did too. But at least you can make some new ones now, right?" He says. I smile, feeling a strange warmth in my chest.

"True that."

Just as I'm flipping the last of the sausages, I hear soft footsteps padding down the stairs. I turn to see Sienna, still sleepy-eyed and in her borrowed-pyjamas, looking adorably rumpled. She stifles a yawn as she enters the kitchen, her eyes lighting up at the sight of the food.

"There she is." I greet her with a grin.

"Yum," she smiles, rubbing her eyes. "This smells amazing, guys."

"I knew the promise of food would get you out of bed." I tease, grabbing a plate and arranging the food with a flourish. I shape some of the food into a heart; the sausages forming the outline, and the eggs and tomatoes filling the centre. "Just in time to get the first plate while it's hot," I say. She giggles, taking the plate from me and giving me a grateful smile.

"Thank you."

As she makes her way to the huge dining table, Birdie, Dean and Delilah follow behind her, all looking a bit more awake.

"Mmm," Birdie sings, skipping across the kitchen. She grabs a plate and holds it out for me to dish up. Dean gives a nod of approval as he sees the spread laid out before them.

"Mornin', all," He says, grabbing a plate and starting to serve himself.

"Wow, you guys really went all out," Delilah adds, her eyes wide with appreciation. Noah shakes his head.

"Credit goes to Marcus here," He says, clapping a hand on my shoulder. "He's the one running the show this morning."

"Hey, we worked as a team."

"Jeez, could you guys get any further up each other's arses?" Dean says, screwing up his face dramatically. The room goes quiet for a beat, the tension palpable. Noah's jaw tightens slightly, but he keeps his cool.

"Feeling left out, mate?" He says, raising an eyebrow.

"Nah, just making an observation." Dean shrugs grumpily. Noah smiles and replies,

"You always this charming in the morning?"

"Yeah, what's up with you today?" I chime in. Dean shrugs and takes a rough bite of a piece of bacon.

"Just hungry." He says nonchalantly, before heading over to the dining table with his plate.

As I plate up mine and Noah's breakfast, carefully arranging the food with a bit of flair, I notice Noah's gaze darting towards the entrance of the kitchen. He seems to be waiting for someone, his attention divided between his coffee and the doorway.

"There you go, man." I say, sliding his plate over to him. He doesn't hear me; his mind occupied. "Hellooo," I say as I wave my hand in front of his face to get his attention. He snaps quickly out of his daydream, giving me a brief smile. "Your food," I remind him, gesturing down to his plate.

"Yes, sorry. Thanks, bro." Noah finally acknowledges. He takes the plate with a distracted nod, clearly still waiting for someone.

"Shouldn't we wait for Skylar?" He asks, glancing over his shoulder again. I laugh softly, shaking my head as I grab a knife and fork for myself.

"If you wait for Skylar, you'll starve."

I take a seat at the table, grabbing a piece of toast and starting to spread some butter on it. As I glance back towards the kitchen, I see Noah still hanging around, seemingly lost in thought. He's leaning against the counter, his eyes fixed on the doorway once again.

Curious, I watch him as he carefully begins plating up an extra serving of breakfast. He dishes up a generous amount of food, more bacon, sausages, eggs, and beans; taking his time to make sure it's all perfectly arranged. He then wraps the plate meticulously in kitchen foil. He takes extra care to ensure it's well-wrapped and secure, pressing down to keep everything insulated and hot. His attention to detail is clear.

Once he's satisfied with his work, Noah leaves the foil-wrapped plate on the kitchen island before heading over to join the rest of us at the table. As he takes his seat, I catch his eye and give him a teasing, knowing smile. Noah catches my eye and immediately knows what I'm smiling about. He tries to suppress a smirk but fails.

Hm, I think my brother has a little crush.

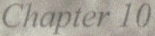

CHAPTER 10:
SHADOWS OF DOUBT

Breakfast is over, *thank God*.

The whole meal had been like a boxing match, Noah and I exchanging verbal jabs beneath the surface of the casual conversation. Every comment had felt like a strategic shot, each of us trying to come out on top without outright throwing a punch. Round one might be over, but I know this fight is far from finished.

As the group slowly disperses, I follow Delilah back upstairs. The mansion's grand staircase seems to echo each step, a rhythmic reminder of the irritation simmering inside of me. The sun streams through the tall windows, casting long, golden shadows that flicker as we ascend.

When we reach our room, Delilah closes the door softly behind us. She turns to me, her expression a mix of concern and curiosity, eyes searching mine for answers.

"What on earth has gotten into you today?" She asks. "You were snappy all through breakfast." I let out a heavy sigh, running a hand through my hair in frustration. The plush carpet beneath my feet does little to ground my scattered thoughts.

"It's Noah." I say immediately, not bothering to soften the edges of my frustration. "I've got a real bad feeling about him."

She raises an eyebrow, her curiosity piqued but still tinged with scepticism.

"Noah? Really? He seems chill." she questions. I shake my head, pacing up and down.

"No, baby. There's something off about him, and it's driving me fucking crazy that nobody else seems to see it." Delilah sits down on the edge of the bed, patting the spot next to her, a concerned look in her eyes. I join her, my mind racing as I try to articulate my thoughts.

"It's everything, Delilah. The way he talks, the way he looks at people. The constant, arrogant fucking smirk on his face. He's hiding something, I know it." I continue. She tilts her head, considering my words.

"Okay, I hear you." She responds softly. "But.. hiding what exactly?"

I hesitate for a moment, then decide to voice the suspicion that's been lurking at the back of my mind. To share my little sprinkle of information.

"I saw him with Sienna last night, they were making a pinky promise with each other. And neither of them would tell me what it was about"

"Dean, *really*? A pinky promise? That's not exactly a crime." She states, with a confused smile.

"My point is, there's no way they only met yesterday." I let out a deep breath, "You don't think it's possible he had any involvement in Sienna's abduction? He was talking to Moth and

Grizzly on a regular basis. He must have an important role in their operations. I mean, just look at his fucking house!"

Delilah's expression turns serious, her eyes narrowing.

"So, you're suggesting that he kidnapped Sienna?" she clarifies. I shake my head, feeling the need for some quick damage control. My Delilah is a blabber-mouth after all.

"I don't know that for sure, Delilah. I'm just throwing it out there." I mumble, backing down slightly. "But I *know* something's up with this guy."

She looks at me with a mix of concern, confusion, and warmth for a few moments, her eyes searching mine. Her brow furrows as she wraps her arm around me, drawing me in for a gentle hug. I lean into her touch, rubbing my temples in frustration.

"I'll keep an eye on Noah," she whispers, her voice soothing. "We'll work it out together." Her words wash over me like a soothing tide, and I nod, feeling a profound sense of relief. Delilah has always had a way of knowing exactly how to calm me down. She's not trying to offer grand solutions or promise that everything will be perfect, nor is she dismissing my concerns as absolute fucking paranoia. Instead, she's simply being present.

We sit in silence for a long while, our eyes locked on each other's, the connection between us like a gentle thrumming in my chest. Her features are soft and relaxed. Time seems to stretch out as we sit there, lost in each other's eyes. The world outside recedes, leaving only the two of us, suspended in this moment of quiet intimacy. As I place my hand on her thigh, I can feel my heart rate slowing, my breathing evening out.

And then, something shifts. It's as if a switch has been flipped, and her eyes darken, growing more intense. Her pupils dilate, and her lips part slightly, inviting me in. I feel my own eyes responding hungrily, my heart rate quickening as I drink in the sight of her. I know that look on her face all too well. I raise an eyebrow, a silent question of, 'what happens now?' And then she sucks in her bottom lip, her eyes never leaving mine.

Her breathing grows shallow, and before I can fully process what's happening, she pounces on me. Her lips crash into mine with an eager, desperate fervour. She grabs my face with both hands, her fingers digging in gently as she pulls me closer. The kiss is fierce and consuming, a mix of relief and passion that erupts between us. I'm caught off guard by the sudden surge of intensity but quickly respond, sliding my hands around her waist and pulling her onto my lap.

Delilah's weight settles onto my lap as she straddles me, her body pressing firmly against mine. The kiss grows even more desperate, her lips moving with an urgency that mirrors the pounding of my heart. My hands instinctively grip her waist, pulling her closer, feeling the heat and intensity of her touch.

Her hands slowly shift down, guiding my fingers to her lower back and then further, until they rest firmly on her ass. She lets out a soft, approving moan, her body arching into my touch as if savouring every second. I let out a breathy laugh.

"You know exactly what you want, don't you?" I murmur between kisses, my voice rough with desire.

She grinds against me, her hips circling in a slow, sensual motion. My fingers dig into her ass, controlling her movements. Delilah's breath hitches as I guide her rhythm, my fingers pressing deeper into her flesh. Her eyes flutter shut, lost in the sensation. My hands roam up her back, feeling the smoothness of her skin beneath her shirt. I tug it upwards, exposing more of her, and she raises her arms to let me pull it off completely. I toss it aside, and she's already working on my belt, her fingers nimble and insistent.

"Fuck," I mutter as she grinds harder, the friction driving me wild. Her hands are everywhere, exploring my chest, tracing the lines of my abs. I capture her mouth again, kissing her fiercely, our tongues tangling as the heat between us intensifies. She whimpers, her hands sliding down to my crotch. She teases me through my tracksuit bottoms, her touch light and maddening. I can't take it anymore. I flip us over, pinning her beneath me on the bed, my mouth trailing hot kisses down her neck.

She moans, arching into me, her hands clawing at my back. I hook my fingers into the waistband of her shorts, pulling them down slowly, savouring the sight of her. She's breathtaking, her skin flushed, her eyes dark with need. I position myself between her legs, my body thrumming with need. She pulls me closer with her legs wrapped around me, her eyes begging me to take her hard.

Just as I'm about to lose myself in her, a sharp knock on the door shatters the moment. We both freeze, our eyes snapping open in unison. Delilah sighs deeply, rolling her head back against the bed in frustration.

"Seriously?" She pants, her voice dripping with exasperation. "Right now?" Still leaning over her, I can't help but smirk as I let out a resigned breath through my nose. The smirk lingers on my lips as I slowly push myself off her, both of us trying to reorient ourselves after the abrupt interruption. Just then, the door knocks again, followed by Birdie's loud shout from the other side.

"Hey, stop fucking for a minute! I have to tell you something!"

Delilah grabs her top, pulling it back on as she shakes her head; clearly frustrated but also unable to suppress a small, rueful smile.

"We'll continue this later." I say, winking at her as I saunter towards the door. Opening it, I'm met with a disapproving Birdie; her pink, sparkly phone glued firmly to her hand. Her gaze moves from me, looking a bit dishevelled, to Delilah, who's now hastily adjusting her shorts. Birdie's eyebrows raise in a knowing look, her expression a blend of teasing and judgement.

"Knew it," she declares matter-of-factly, her tone equally playful and serious. Without a response, she struts past me like a sassy cat and heads straight for Delilah.

Birdie shows Delilah her phone screen, and Delilah's eyes light up with excitement as she reads the message. She lets out a delighted squeal, jumping up and down and throwing her arms around Birdie.

"No way! You got it?" Delilah exclaims, her voice bubbling with happiness. Birdie beams, nodding enthusiastically.

"Yup."

"That's amazing, Bird!"

I walk over, curious.

"Got what?" I ask. Birdie, grinning from ear to ear, turns the phone towards me.

"I've been accepted as a lifeguard at the best surf beach in the country!" She shares. Delilah hugs her again, practically bouncing with joy. I blink, then break into a wide grin.

"Wow. The bar must be pretty low if they're letting you in," I tease, nudging her playfully. "You know that means you'll have to get your precious hair wet, right?" Birdie rolls her eyes but can't suppress her smile. It's quite sweet really.

"Yes, Dean. I'm aware."

"For real though, congrats. That's actually pretty sick. Just make sure you don't drown." Birdie gives me a mock-serious look.

"Thanks, Dean. It means a lot coming from someone who probably thinks 'Baywatch' is a documentary."

"Hey, I know my way around a pool," I retort, unable to hide my genuine happiness for her. "I just prefer to leave the life-saving to the pros like you." Birdie laughs, her eyes sparkling with pride.

"I start next month!" she squeals.

"How long will you be down there?" Delilah asks.

"Until the spring," Birdie replies. Delilah's face falls, and she pouts, sad and dramatic.

"Oh Bird, I'm gonna miss you."

"I'm gonna to miss you too," Birdie says, giving her a reassuring squeeze. "But my parents rented me this incredible beach-front apartment so you can all come and visit, whenever you want." Delilah's eyes brighten at this.

"Absolutely! We'll make it work."

CHAPTER 11:
BOOK TALK

Marcus

I stand in the kitchen, the lingering scent of breakfast still in the air. I start clearing the plates from the table, my movements deliberate as I stack them in the sink. Noah is washing up, and I take a moment to watch him, noticing how out of place he seems. I don't picture Noah as the type of guy to do much housework. I'm sure he has a maid who does this for him.

But it doesn't take long to realise why he's doing it. His gaze keeps flicking towards Skylar, who's sitting at the table, eating the breakfast he kept warm for her. Every time she looks up, he straightens, ensuring he's in her eyeline.

"You've got a good chance with her, you know," I say with a casual smirk. Noah glances at me, a hint of confusion in his eyes.

"Why's that?" He asks. I let a grin slide across my face.

"Oh, she's really into drug dealers."

489

Yes, I'm aware that my brother isn't exactly a 'drug dealer'. But I figure being the leader of a criminal empire as big as his, there's enough overlap to make the comparison. Also, I'm yet to have any banter with my long-lost big brother, and this seems like a good place to start. Noah's eyebrows shoot up.

"What you on about?" he snaps. I chuckle, nodding towards Skylar.

"It's a running joke with us. She fucked a couple of her dealers. She has a thing for '*bad boys*'. So, I figure you kinda fit the bill."

Noah's expression shifts subtly. There's a flicker of irritation in his eyes as he processes what I said.

"Really?" he says, his voice low and edged with something I can't quite place. Noah's gaze returns to Skylar, and I can see the change in his demeanour. The playful glint is gone, replaced by a harder edge. Despite my attempt at humour, it's clear that Noah isn't happy.

Change the subject, Marcus.

"So," I begin, my voice steady but curious, "do you have any idea why Dad asked me about the book before he died?" I ask. Noah sighs deeply, setting a plate in the drying rack with more force than necessary, seemingly annoyed that I'm interfering with his Skylar fantasies.

"Because he was desperate to change the outcome."

"The outcome?" I echo.

"Yeah," Noah says. "Dad gets murdered at the end of my book."

I'm suddenly struck by two realisations at once, the chilling thought that the events of Noah's book have unfolded in reality, and the unsettling fact that he has already read and finished it. I had assumed that, since the book was sealed, he hadn't opened it yet.

"Wait, yours is completed?" I ask, my voice barely above a whisper.

"Yeah, Dad died. It is what it is." Noah replies nonchalantly, his focus still more on Skylar than on our conversation. His tone is detached, almost cold, which strikes me as strange. He seems surprisingly unfazed, considering our dad has just been murdered, and that he knew it was coming.

"Mine is closed too, but Dean.. he's still having near-death experiences." I share. Noah glances at me briefly, a flicker of possible interest crossing his face before he turns back to Skylar.

"That's weird, man." He says, clearly distracted once more.

"What was the story you wrote?" I press, trying to keep him engaged.

"It wasn't really a story," he replies, scrunching his eyebrows in thought. "It was more like a wishlist."

"A wishlist?" I ask, intrigued despite his evident distraction.

"Yeah," he says, finally looking at me. "I just wrote stuff like 'Mum is still alive', 'I'm going to be fucking rich', 'Dad needs to die'. You know? Cringy shit like that."

I stare at him, processing his words. It dawns on me that the magic must not have come from the story but from the book itself. Noah and I had the exact same book, yet what we had written inside was entirely different.

The book's power lies in the pages, not the content.
Noted. =

"So it's the book itself," I murmur, more to myself than to him. Noah nods absently, his attention drifting back to Skylar.

"What was yours about?" He asks. I launch into a brief summary, explaining the plot without going into too much detail. Noah definitely listens, but whether he's actually absorbing the information is another question entirely.

"So, how did you seal it if it's not completed?" He asks with a puzzled look.

"I went and found Millie and we were able to close it together. The book was glowing like crazy." I explain.

"It glowed?"

"Yours didn't?" I ask, intrigued.

"No. There was a '*boom*' noise but that's about it." Noah shares as he turns to face me fully now, his focus finally breaking away from Skylar. "What happened after you closed it?" He asks.

I take a deep breath, trying to gather my thoughts.

"Dean looked better," I say, my voice steady. "He wasn't sick anymore. But then an argument started. It got pretty heated. I could hear police sirens approaching and, long story short, the night ended with Skylar running Millie over." Noah raises an eyebrow, a mix of intrigue and an odd sort of admiration crossing his face.

"What do you mean she ran her over?"

"Sky stole a car and got into a chase," I explain.

"Stole a car? Wow." Noah lets out a low whistle, smirking in Skylar's direction. "So the queen is dead, huh?" He continues with a jokey tone.

"Yeah," I reply, letting out an awkward laugh at his cold response, but it quickly dies in my throat. I sit with it for a second, the weight of his words settling over me. I think more. And more. And then it hits me like a ton of bricks.

"Holy fuck," I mumble, my eyes widening in disbelief. "The queen is dead." Noah looks at me confused, a frown creasing his brow.

"Yeah, I just said that."

"No," I say, my voice trembling with realisation. "The queen is dead. That's why the story is still playing out."

Noah stares at me like I've lost my mind, the smirk slipping from his lips, replaced by a look of quiet disbelief. The coldness in his eyes unsettles meso sharp and detached, it's as if nothing can touch him. Not our father's death. Not Millie's. Not even the looming danger of the book's unresolved magic. He's an island, standing apart from it all, indifferent. Unbothered. The implications of Millie's death and what it means for the book's narrative weigh heavily on my mind, a burden that becomes increasingly harder to bear alone.

He stops washing up and turns off the tap, his movements intentional. He picks up a tea towel and dries his hands roughly, the fabric making a harsh sound against his skin. Each movement seems precise. He strides toward me, halting just inches away, his gaze locked onto mine.

"Stop stressing about the book," he says, his tone low. "What will be, will be." Before I can respond, he presses the tea towel to my chest with an intentional push. The gesture is forceful but not aggressive, like he's giving me an order. He then swerves past me, his shoulder brushing mine as he walks away, his posture relaxed and confident.

Noah's footsteps echo as he strides away, leaving me standing in the kitchen, clutching the tea towel to my chest. The cloth is now a physical token of the power play that just unfolded. As I stand there, I can't shake the sense that his words were more than just a casual remark. It felt like a definitive statement, a final word on a subject that I refuse to accept as settled. The implication was clear; the outcome of the book, the events that are unfolding, are beyond our control. That sense of inevitability, of resignation to fate, is something I can't afford to entertain.

The more I think about it, the angrier I become. The idea that we should simply accept Dean's hinted death as an unavoidable part of our fate is unacceptable to me. Noah's dismissive attitude towards the gravity of our situation stings. It's almost as if he's suggesting we should all just roll over and accept the hand fate dealt us. As if the best we can do is turn Dean's possible demise into a dramatic, tragic finale. I, for one, plan to rewrite that ending with every ounce of determination I've got.

I start drying up, the rhythmic motions of scrubbing and rinsing grounding me as I try to process the implications. The kitchen, now quiet except for the gentle hum of the refrigerator, feels almost serene. Just then, Skylar strolls up, her breakfast plate in hand, clearly in no rush. Without so much as a glance, she flicks her wrist and drops the plate into the sink. It clatters against the metal, but she's already tossing me a lazy grin and sauntering off. I look at the plate, now the lone occupant of the sink, and let out a dry, resigned laugh. Because of course, just as I think I'm done, there's always one more thing to handle.

CHAPTER 12:
GIRLFRIEND?

Sienna

I'm standing in Skylar's room, wearing a pair of flared low-rise jeans with an obnoxious heart-shaped buckle; along with a pink tank top that shows way more skin than I'm used to. I'm suddenly very aware of my bruises and cuts. The clothes feel like they're mocking me, highlighting the marks that I'm struggling to come to terms with.

As I tug at the hem, trying to make it cover just a bit more, I'm caught in a tug-of-war between two conflicting emotions. On one hand, I feel like I should hide the bruises. They're a reminder of something painful, something I'd rather not have others see. Hiding them feels like a protective barrier, a way to maintain some semblance of control over my own vulnerability. But on the other hand, there's this nagging feeling that hiding them is a form of surrender; like admitting that they have power over me, that I'm afraid of how others might perceive them. I glance in the mirror, realising quickly that it's not just as simple as 'this outfit shows off the bruises'; it's that it makes me feel like I'm being forced to confront them in a way that's uncomfortable.

I feel a surge of sadness. Each mark tells a story I'm not ready to share, a story that's still unfolding within me. The choice to cover them or not feels like a choice between vulnerability and strength, between acceptance and denial. The more I think about it, the more I realise that the conflict isn't just about what others might see; it's about how I see myself. How I reconcile the person I am now with the person I was before, and how to navigate a world that seems cruelly determined to remind me of both.

"I don't think this is quite my style," I admit, glancing at Skylar, who has made herself right at home on the bed, legs swinging back and forth as she's absorbed in her DS game. She glances up for exactly two seconds, takes in my outfit, and then dives back into her game as though it's a matter of life and death.

"You look cute." She chirps helpfully.

I roll my eyes and start rummaging through her bags and drawers again, looking for something that feels more like me. Her clothes look like they belong to a Bratz doll; crop tops, miniskirts, and low rise everything as far as the eye can see. I pull out a tiny leopard-print cami, trimmed with pink lace along the top, and hold it up, giving her a look.

"Seriously, Sky? How do you even breathe in this?" I ask, holding the top up for her inspection, feeling both amused and slightly horrified.

"It's called fashion, Sienna." She declares with such confidence that I almost want to salute her.

"Fashion or torture device, I can't tell." I mutter under my breath. Sensing my struggle, Skylar puts her game down and sits up, determined to save me from my fashion crisis.

"Here, let me help you find something." She says as she starts digging through a drawer, tossing aside crop tops and miniskirts with a flourish. "There's got to be something in here that works."

After a bit of digging, she finally pulls out a simple pair of cream trousers and a soft blue top. "What about these?" She asks, holding them up like a prize; hoping for my approval. I take a deep breath, feeling a wave of relief wash over me at the sight of the clothes; nothing outrageous, nothing that seems designed to squeeze my body and spirit into submission.

"Much better. Thanks," I reply, a genuine smile breaking through.

Just as I'm adjusting the waistband and smoothing out any wrinkles, the door creaks open. Marcus strides into the room with the kind of casual confidence that makes you feel like he's always been here. Skylar looks up from her spot on the bed, her DS game momentarily forgotten.

"Seriously Marcus? No knock?" She scoffs. Marcus raises an eyebrow, giving a mock bow.

"So sorry, your majesty." He says with a sarcastic grin. Skylar rolls her eyes dramatically and goes back to her game, clearly unperturbed.

Marcus' gaze shifts to me, and his expression softens.

"You look beautiful, sweet," he says with a sincere smile. I feel a small blush creep up my cheeks.

"Thank you."

Marcus then glances around the room, taking in the piles of discarded clothes scattered across the floor. He raises an eyebrow in mock concern.

"You ready to go?" he asks, his tone a mix of amusement and worry.

"Please," I reply, eager to leave the chaos of the room behind. As we turn to head out the door, his eyes land on a particularly suspicious ring-hook on the wall. His brow furrows in genuine concern this time.

"What's with the hooks?" He asks Skylar, his voice low and serious. Before Skylar can retort, I quickly grab Marcus's arm, tugging him along.

"Don't ask," I say firmly, trying to stifle my own discomfort.

As we step out into the warm summer afternoon, the sun bathes everything in a golden glow, casting long shadows across the driveway. Marcus and I are heading towards Dean's stolen ride when I notice Noah standing by one of his many cars, the boot wide open. Curiosity gets the better of me, and as I pass by, I peer inside. My eyes widen at the sight of an array of guns neatly lined up inside.

"Nice collection, Noah," I joke. "Looks like you're preparing for the apocalypse." Noah turns around, a wry smile tugging at the corner of his mouth.

"Something like that," he says. "With the two biggest players gone, I'm in charge now. That alone puts a target on my back. And believe me, their deaths? It's blood in the water. Our enemies are already circling, thinking we're vulnerable." I nod, pretending to understand the gravity of pressure on his shoulders.

"Well, good luck with that," I say, trying to inject some levity. "Just don't count on us for backup." Noah chuckles, though the sound is devoid of real humour.

"I'll try not to," he replies, closing the boot with a decisive thud.

We continue toward Dean's stolen car, but before we reach it, Noah calls out.

"Why don't you take one of my cars instead?" He asks. Marcus shakes his head.

"Thanks bro, but we can't bring it back. We're gonna go get my bike," he says. Noah smirks and tosses Marcus a set of keys.

"No worries. Take the Range Rover, I've never been a big fan of it. Makes me feel like some rich yoga-mum. Call it a loan." He says. I raise an eyebrow at Noah's nonchalant attitude. It's almost impressive how literally throwing away a car is just a casual thing for him; must be nice to be that rich. Marcus catches the keys, gives them a quick once-over, then looks back at Noah as if trying to decide if he's joking.

"Thanks, man." Marcus says, slightly hesitant but grateful.

We climb into the Range Rover, the interior exuding an aura of expensive luxury. As we drive away from Noah's place, the car's smooth, quiet ride feels almost surreal compared to the chaos we've been through. The leather seats are buttery soft, and the dashboard gleams with high-end tech. I sink back, letting the comfort momentarily wash away my lingering anxiety.

The drive to the B&B is peaceful, the sun casting elongated shadows across the road as the afternoon wears on. For a while, we don't speak, content to let the quiet hum of the engine fill the space between us. Marcus keeps one hand on the wheel, the other resting comfortably on my knee.

As we pull up outside the cottage, the familiar sight stirs a whirlwind of emotions within me. The quaint façade feels tainted by what I endured during my time there. As the engine purrs to a stop, the silence looms heavy between us, and I can feel the tension coiling in my stomach.

Marcus turns to me, concern etched into his features.

"You wanna wait outside?" He asks, low and gentle. I shake my head, a shaky breath escaping my lips. The idea of him doing it for me is tempting, a protective gesture that feels warm and safe. But there's a part of me that knows I need to face this. I take a moment, gathering my thoughts, and despite the anxiety gnawing at me, I respond,

"No, I want to go in."

Marcus studies me for a moment, his hazel eyes searching mine for any hint of doubt. I can almost see the battle between wanting to protect me and believing in my strength.

"Okay," he concedes, his tone reluctant but supportive. We step out of the car under the warm embrace of a summer afternoon, the sunbathing everything in a golden hue that feels almost idyllic. However, despite the beauty of the day, a sense of dread tinges the air around me. With each step towards the front door, my heart races, thudding relentlessly in my chest.

As we get closer, my stomach drops at the sight of the door hanging ominously off its hinges; a gentle breeze whispering through the entryway. A wave of anxiety crashes over me, flooding my senses with the memories of that horrific moment; the thunderous sound of the door being kicked open, the chaos that ensued as I was ripped from everything I held dear. I can still hear the echoes of panic and fear that reverberated through that moment.

Could Butter have left?

Gritting my teeth, I take a hesitant step forward, each footfall heavy with the weight of dread and uncertainty. My mind races as I cross the threshold, instinctively scanning the dim interior for any sign of movement. As I venture deeper into the room, the wooden floor feels cool beneath my feet, grounding me in a reality I desperately want to escape. That's when I see them; patches of dried blood smeared across the floor, stark and grotesque against the sunlit wood. A chill snakes through me, my breath hitching in my throat as a wave of confusion washes over.

It's unsettling, but rather than evoking the panic I expected, it leaves me feeling strangely numb. How can something so visceral and horrifying feel so removed from my own existence? I blink, trying to process what I'm seeing. The blood shouldn't belong to me; it couldn't be mine. But even as I tell myself that, a part of me wants to recoil, to walk away from this gruesome evidence of violence. But I'm not sad.

Instead, I'm left with an unsettling yet promising sense of detachment, as though I'm watching someone else's nightmare unfold. The images in my mind refuse to align with the horror at my feet; I can't connect the dots between the bloodstains and my own reality. Yet, amidst the chaos of my racing thoughts, something catches my eye. There, perched calmly on a shelf, is Butter, her silhouette bathed in golden sunlight.
She is here.
She stayed.

"Butter," I whisper, tears welling in my eyes as I marvel at her fragility and beauty. She flutters her wings gently, her presence a small, comforting constant in a world that feels so unstable. Butter, my steadfast little companion, flits gracefully from the shelf to my finger. "I missed you." I murmur, my voice quivering with emotion. She responds with a gentle flutter of her wings, almost as if she's saying she missed me too. I cradle her gently in my palm, captivated by the way her wings glimmer like stained glass. I can't help but smile through my tears, the connection between us feeling more precious than ever.

A giggle escapes my lips as I extend my finger, inviting her to take flight. With a graceful leap, Butter flutters into the air, and I spin around in delight, laughter bubbling up from somewhere deep inside me. As I turn, I catch Marcus' presence in the corner of my eye. He's leaning against the doorframe. Time seems to freeze as I meet his gaze. He isn't smiling, at least not fully, but oh, the way he looks at me makes my heart skip.

His hazel eyes are locked onto mine, filled with something so deep it nearly takes my breath away. In that moment, it feels like I am the only thing that matters in the entire universe. Everything else dissolves into a shadowy haze, as if the rest of existence could burn to ash, crumble into dust, leaving no trace behind, and he would remain unfazed; enthralled only by the essence of me.

Marcus' expression is intense, his eyes filled with a beautiful kind of admiration. I can see it in the way he watches me, as if he's witnessing something precious and rare. It's the way he sees me, completely and without reservation, that makes me feel like I'm alive, rather than surviving.

He ambles past me without a word, his focus shifting to the task at hand. He places his duffel bag on the bed, the soft thud breaking the quiet. Without hesitation, he begins to methodically gather our clothes and belongings, his hands moving with practised ease. Each item is carefully folded and placed inside the bag. I watch him, momentarily mesmerised by the quiet strength in his actions. There's something comforting about the way he takes charge; his calm demeanour contrasting with the chaos that's surrounded us.

His broad shoulders move with confidence, muscles flexing subtly beneath his shirt as he works. In his quiet steadiness, I find an anchor for my own tumultuous thoughts; a deep sense of calm washes over me, reassuring me that no matter the storm, he is here, and he knows what to do.

After a few minutes, Marcus finishes packing and turns to face me. He reaches for Butter's enclosure, which is resting on the bedside table, and hands it to me with a gentle touch; his fingers lingering against mine for a brief second. Just as I take hold of the enclosure, Marcus' hands slip around my legs, his strong arms lifting me effortlessly. I see Butter fluttering nearby and, with my free hand, I reach out, catching her gently in mid-air.

A soft gasp escapes my lips as I'm hoisted higher into the air, my world tilting as I'm slung over his shoulder like I weigh nothing at all. Marcus chuckles, the sound rich and low, vibrating through me as he holds me securely against him. My laughter mingles with the soft flutter of Butter's wings. Everything feels surreal, like we're in a world of our own.

His hand rests on the back of my thigh, steadying me as he strides toward the door. As he carries us out of the room and toward his beloved bike, I find myself feeling lighter. I look back at the cottage and small smile tugs at the corners of my lips. It's a quiet smile, one that holds no bitterness, just a gentle acknowledgment that the worst is over. The cottage no longer feels like a place of torment, but rather a setting in a book of my own.

A book finally closed.

As we ride back to Noah's, I can feel the exhilarating zip of wind against my face. I never thought I'd admit it, but I missed the bike. Marcus leans into the curves with effortless precision, the bike slicing through the air at a hundred miles an hour as though it's a part of him. Each acceleration sends a jolt through me, the speed blurring everything around us into streaks of green and grey.

It's funny, really. I'm gripping him so firmly, literally hanging on for dear life, and yet instead of feeling terrified, I'm completely enchanted. The wind rushes around us like a wild melody, and I can't help but marvel at how his reckless abandon feels oddly.. sexy.

Sure, we may be one small jolt away from certain death. But you know what? If I die in a fiery explosion, I might as well go out swooning, right?

As we continue down the winding road, I notice that Marcus isn't heading back the way we came. My curiosity piques as we veer off onto a path I recognize. The landscape starts to look familiar, and my heart skips a beat when I realise where we're headed.

"This isn't the way home," I shout over the roar of the engine, my voice barely audible. Marcus doesn't respond immediately, his focus clearly on the road.

"I know."

The anticipation builds as we approach a spot that has become etched in my memory. I can barely make out the glint of sunlight reflecting off the river's surface as we draw nearer. Memories flood back; the river where I'd found a tiny bunny and then, quite dramatically, ended up taking an unintended dip. It feels like a lifetime ago.

Marcus pulls the bike over to the side of the road, bringing us to a smooth stop beside the familiar riverbank. As the engine quiets, I feel the exhilarating rush of speed give way to the calmness of this peaceful spot.

He removes my helmet with a tender touch, his fingers brushing against my skin. I look up at him, my heart still racing from the ride, and see a soft, knowing smile on his face.

"Remember this place?" he asks, his voice low and warm. I nod, a smile spreading across my face.

"How could I forget?"

The riverbank where everything had felt so perfect yet so complicated.

I stare at the water, my thoughts drifting back to that day. It was here that everything changed for us. Marcus had confessed his love for me; raw and honest. And unexpected. I can still picture the moment we leaned in for that kiss; his eyes sparkled with hope and sincerity, reflecting a vulnerability that took my breath away.

But instead of leaning in, I panicked. A wave of fear crashed over me, and in my haste, I pulled away; not just physically, but emotionally as well. I remember the harsh words that tumbled from my mouth, unkind and unfiltered. I was unable to embrace the gift he was offering so freely, and that decision weighed heavily on my heart. Even now, as I watch the river flow, I can't help but wonder how different things might have been if I hadn't let fear take control.

We walk hand in hand to the riverbank, the only sound around us the soft rush of the water over the rocks. The sun is lower now, bathing the world in a warm, golden glow that softens the edges of reality, almost like a memory. We reach the edge of the river, and without a word, we sit down on the grass. The ground is slightly damp, but I don't mind. It feels good to be here, away from everything, just the two of us. I watch the water flow by, its surface catching the last of the sunlight, sparkling in the quiet.

There's a peace in this moment that I haven't felt in a long time. It's like all the chaos and fear that's been swirling around us has finally settled, if only for a little while. I glance over at Marcus, who's staring out at the river with a thoughtful expression, and I feel a wave of warmth towards him. Being here with him, in this familiar place, feels right.

The stillness of the river is comforting, but I begin to notice that something is off. Marcus is quiet. His usual confident demeanour replaced by something I can't quite put my finger on. His eyes are fixed on the water, but I can see his mind is somewhere else entirely.

"So.." I start, my voice breaking the silence, "what are we doing here?"

He glances at me, the corner of his mouth twitching into a half-smile, but there's a seriousness in his eyes that makes me nervous; like whatever he's about to say matters, a lot. He finally breaks the silence, his voice steady.

"Last night, when I told you that you'll never be my girlfriend," he pauses, his eyes locked on the flowing river as if searching for the right words. "Well, I meant it."

My heart drops like a stone, the weight of his words sinking in before I can fully process them. A sudden tightness grips my chest, a wave of sadness swelling that I wasn't prepared for. I try to mask the hurt welling inside, forcing a laugh that falls flat, barely masking the tremor in my voice.

"Because you don't do labels, right?" I joke, but even I can hear how hollow my attempt sounds. Marcus' expression doesn't change, his brow furrowing like he's grappling with something crucial. My attempt to brush off his words doesn't seem to ease the tension hanging between us.

"You're right, I don't do labels," His voice sends a cold shiver down my spine, the pit in my stomach growing heavier. My mind races with confusion.

"It's not because I'm afraid of commitment or because I don't care about you. It's because.." he begins, his voice measured, almost too calm. "It's because that label doesn't feel right for us." The words hit me like a cold splash of water, and my heart sinks. I can't comprehend why he wouldn't want to be my boyfriend, to make this official. "I've never been one for doing things the typical way. *We've* never been typical, have we?" He asks.

I shake my head, more out of reflex than anything else. I'm still trying to wrap my head around what he's saying. His words cut deeper than he probably realises. It's true, we've never been typical. My whole life has never been conventional, never followed the normal paths that everyone else seems to navigate so effortlessly. I've always craved something solid, something secure, and I want that with Marcus. Calling him my boyfriend would be something normal, something to hold onto in a life that has never felt particularly stable. And now, it feels like even that is slipping through my fingers. My thoughts are a whirlwind of confusion and hurt, spinning faster with every word he says.

"So, when I said you'll never be my girlfriend," his voice drops, colder now, sharper, "I meant it." He states flatly, and in that instant, I feel as if my heart is fracturing into a thousand pieces.

He really doesn't want to be with me.

But then, Marcus shifts, his hand reaching into his pocket. My breath catches as I watch, time slowing as he pulls out a small box. For a second, my mind goes blank, unable to comprehend what's unfolding before me.

He opens it to reveal a delicate gold ring, shimmering softly under the fading light. The sight is breathtaking and surreal, but it does little to calm the storm brewing inside me.

"I don't ever want you to be my girlfriend, sweet," he says, his voice firm yet tender. "I want to skip that part. I want to go straight to the part where you're my wife."

I freeze, heart racing in a frenzy that feels both exhilarating and terrifying. His hazel eyes hold an unwavering depth as he gazes at me, and all at once, I'm overwhelmed.

"Sienna Saunders, will you marry me?"

My heart races, every beat echoing louder than the last. The shock is too great, the emotions too raw, and for a moment, everything inside me seems to freeze.

Tears well up in my eyes, blurring my vision. I'm overcome with a tidal wave of relief and joy; a deep, undeniable love that makes my chest ache. I try to speak, but the words catch in my throat, too choked by the overwhelming emotion. All I can do is nod, a silent, tearful confirmation of what I can't find the words to express.

As soon as the first tear spills down my cheek, I can't hold back the flood. I'm sobbing, the tears streaming freely as I look up at Marcus. My vision is clouded, but I can see the tears brimming in his eyes too. They reflect the same raw, intense emotion that's surging through me. Without thinking, I crash into him, flinging my arms around his neck, clinging to him as if I can't bear to be apart. Marcus' one hand settles on the small of my back, his hold is both strong and gentle, comforting me as I bury my face in his shoulder, letting the tears flow uncontrollably.

"So, is that a yes, sweet?" He whispers teasingly. I nod vigorously, my smile breaking through the tears.

"Yes, Marcus. Yes, a million times."

CHAPTER 13:
ART OF SEDUCTION

Noah

11:49p.m. I push through the door, the weight of the day dragging on me like a chain. The soft click of my keys echoes through the silence as I hang them up, the tension still coiled tight in my muscles. Today was hell; hiring new people, managing the internal power struggles of my organisation, and taking care of a few dealers who clearly didn't know their place. The weight of it all is pressing heavily on my shoulders, and I long for the rare calm of my space. I grab myself a bottle of water and drag myself through the expansive hallways, the echo of my footsteps amplifying the solitude of the night.

I push open the door to my bedroom ready to collapse, but as the door swings open, all thoughts come to a screeching halt.

My little pink-haired menace, sitting on my bed like she owns it.

Yes, I never explicitly said nobody was allowed in my room, but I gathered it wasn't something I'd need to spell out. It's the kind of thing that goes without saying. It's strictly off-limits by default. But little Miss Skylar? She's breaking every unspoken rule without even flinching. It pisses me off, but at the same time, it's.. hot. Real fucking hot.

My first impulse is to slam the door, pin her down on the mattress and fuck her as a punishment. But as I take in her provocative, effortless allure, I find myself oddly impressed. She's not just invading my space; she's owning it with an air of audacious confidence that's undeniably sexy. *How long has she been here?* The question pulses in my mind as I take in her strong, almost smug demeanour. It's such a daring move, so unlike anyone else I've encountered.

I smirk as I close the door behind me, the soft click of the latch echoing in the quiet room. My gaze locks onto her with a predatory intensity. I stand there for a moment, just watching her, letting the silence stretch.

"Skylar Farmer." I say, my voice low and charged with an edge of amusement.

"Noah Bear."

"No, not personally." I reply. Skylar's expression shifts to one of puzzled disapproval, her eyebrows knitting together as she looks at me. "Get it? Noah Bear. Know-a-bear?" I explain, attempting to make the pun land. She blinks at me, clearly unimpressed.

She stares at me, unimpressed, and I exhale, dropping the joke like the waste of breath it is. My voice turns serious, my eyes narrowing as I take a step closer.

"Why are you in my room, Farmer?" I ask. Skylar's eyes narrow, and she shoots back almost immediately.

"Why do you like me?" She snaps.

511

"What's not to like?" I say simply. She doesn't skip a beat, her frustration mounting as she gets up from the bed and begins to pace like a caged animal.

"I'm serious! What do you want from me?"

"Sorry?"

"Do you want sex? Is that it? Or are you just bored? Because I'm not some trophy to be won, Noah! I'm not-" She continues to pace, her steps growing more erratic before she catches me smiling and stops right in front of me.

Yeah that definitely didn't help.

"Is this some kind of game to you? Do you have a checklist of women you need to fuck to make yourself feel better? Huh? Because let me tell you, *sir*, I'm not interested in being another mark on your list! I'm not here for you to prove a point or for you to get some sort of thrill. I have my own life, my own goals! Okay?" Her voice trails off, and she stops abruptly. She looks at me, her eyebrows scrunched together in a mixture of defiance and confusion.

Meanwhile, I'm standing there, utterly bemused. I hadn't expected this kind of reaction.

"Sit down." I order with a single chuckle. Skylar's eyes flare with irritation.

"No." she snaps, her voice sharp. I clench my jaw, my expression turning more serious.

"I'm not gonna ask you again."

Her defiant stance begins to falter under my intense gaze, and she sighs heavily; frustration evident in every line of her face. After a moment, she relents, dropping onto the edge of the bed. She crosses her arms tightly, her posture rigid, trying to look as mad as she can manage. But even in her attempt at anger, she's far more adorable than intimidating. Tempting.

I lean against the doorframe, watching her silently. I give her the space to process, letting the room settle into a quiet that feels almost tangible. Gradually, her defiant stance softens. Her eyes drop to the floor, and I can see the tension in her shoulders ease, even if just a little. The irritation in her expression fades, replaced by something deeper. As I observe her, it's already crystal clear to me what's going on in that pretty little mind.

I think back to what I learned earlier, to the dealers I dealt with today. It's obvious to me that they were the kind who use and discard without a second thought. If she's let herself get close to men like that, men who don't give a damn beyond their own gain, then I know exactly why she's standing here so guarded now, her defences sharp, ready for the next hit.

She expects me to be no different. She's bracing for the same treatment; waiting for me to take what I want and leave her hollow like the rest. Her attitude is just a mask, a way to protect herself from more disappointment. I can see the fear she's trying to hide, the vulnerability she doesn't want me to touch. But she has no idea what she's dealing with. I'm not like them. Her fear, her insecurities, they don't stand a chance against the weight of what I intend to take; and I won't be leaving her in pieces.

I let out a heavy sigh, pushing off from the doorframe.

"I'm not here to use you, Farmer." I say sternly. I take a step closer, voice low and firm. "Let me make something real fucking clear." I continue, "This isn't some fling. You don't get to walk away. I'm going to fucking own you, every part of you. You can hate me, scream, fight, it doesn't matter." I look deeper into her pretty blue eyes, "I'll be under your skin, in your fucking bones, haunting your every thought. You think you can run? I'll hunt you down, drag you back, and remind you exactly who the fuck you belong to."

There's a finality in my tone, something that leaves no room for argument. There's nothing soft about it, nothing sweet. Just the hard truth. I'm not letting her go, and she better get used to the idea. When she doesn't respond, I let out a slow breath, steadying myself. I'm not frustrated, just feeling the weight of her uncertainty. I cross the room, the silence thick. Reaching the large cabinet against the wall, I yank it open, rummaging through until I find what I'm looking for, a fucking huge box. I stroll back to her, noticing how her eyes follow my every move, cautious but curious. I set the box down in front of her with a solid thud.

"Now that we've got that out of the way," I say, my tone firm but softer, "let's paint."

She stares at the box, her confusion plain as day.

"Excuse me?" she asks, her voice laced with bewilderment. I don't respond. Instead, I crouch down and open the box, revealing its contents; paints, brushes, canvases, everything. I start taking them out, one by one, spreading them across the floor in front of her. She watches me, still trying to figure out what the fuck I'm doing, but I stay focused on the task, letting the action speak for itself.

Once everything is laid out, I pick up a canvas and a brush, holding them out to her. She's still staring at me like I've lost my mind, but I don't waver.

"C'mon," I say, my voice steady. She hesitates, eyes flicking between the canvas and my face, trying to make sense of this sudden shift. When she finally takes the canvas and brush, I nod, satisfied. "Paint." I tell her, as if it's the most natural thing in the world.

I shift from a crouch to sitting on the floor, getting comfortable as I squeeze out the colours onto a palette. Skylar watches me intently, her eyes narrowing slightly as she glances between the paintbrush in her hand and me. I can sense her hesitation, the internal struggle playing out behind her guarded expression. Finally, she exhales deeply; her shoulders relax just enough for me to notice before she shifts to sit down beside me on the floor.

"Atta girl." I murmur.

Dipping the brush into the colour of her choice, she starts to paint, her strokes hesitant at first. It's clear she's not thrilled about this, but she's doing it. Begrudgingly. Skylar continues painting, her brush moving more fluidly with each stroke. The tension in her face starts to fade, the lines of stress and anger slowly melting away. I sit there in silence, just watching her. Every flick of her wrist, every dip into the paint, it's like I'm seeing her unravel bit by bit.

Her focus shifts entirely to the painting in her hand. The raw, chaotic energy she came in with is being transferred onto the canvas, leaving her features calmer, softer. She's letting go, even if she doesn't realise it. And all I do is watch, taking in every subtle change.

After a little longer, Skylar stops painting and turns the canvas around to face me, her expression dead serious. I glance at the painting, and for a split second, I'm unsure how to react. The artwork is.. definitely something.

She's painted us.
In a way.

As I study the painting, I realise it's not just poorly done, it's also disturbingly graphic. The scenes she's conjured are twisted, depicting her figure torturing mine in various brutal and unsettling ways.

We both stare at the painting, trying to keep straight faces, holding onto whatever sternness we can muster. But it doesn't take long before I see the corners of her mouth twitch, and I feel my own restraint slipping. Skylar's the first to break, a small giggle escaping her lips, and I can't help but follow. The laughter builds until we're both genuinely laughing, the sound filling the room, and for a moment, all the tension and unspoken words dissolve.

As our laughter fades, we lock eyes, and I notice something different in her gaze; hope, maybe, and a certain calm that wasn't there before. The tension that had gripped her earlier seems to have unravelled, leaving her looking more relaxed, almost at ease. I reach out and take the canvas from her hands, examining it with a thoughtful expression. With my other hand, I surreptitiously dip my finger into some light blue paint, making sure she doesn't notice.

"You know," I say, keeping my voice casual, "I think it's missing something." Her brow furrows slightly as she leans in.

"What?" she asks, looking like she's ready to dive into a deep art critique.

That's my moment. Without missing a beat, I swipe my paint-covered finger across her cheek, leaving a streak of blue. Her eyes widen in shock, and then her expression hardens so fast I barely have time to react.

Oh yeah, she wants to kill me.

I watch, amused, as she processes the violation, her expression growing darker by the second. She's quiet, too quiet, and I notice her hand tightening around the paintbrush in her hand like it's a weapon. That little face of hers scrunches up in fury, but all I can think is how damn cute she looks.

It's like I'm battling with a very abusive Strawberry Shortcake.

I try to keep my amusement under control, but I can't resist. The corner of my mouth tugs up into a smirk.
That's all it takes.

She lunges at me with the paintbrush, violent and fast, but I'm faster. I easily knock it out of her hand, my leer growing wider. But then I see the determination in her eyes, and before I know it, she's going for the palette. I yank it out of her reach with a smug grin, enjoying this a little too much.

"You've gotta do better than that, baby." I chuckle. She huffs, clearly annoyed, but the fire in her eyes hasn't dimmed one bit. She's relentless. Her eyes dart to the open tubes of paint, and I catch on to what she's planning a split second before she moves.

As she makes a move for the paint, I catch her wrist midair and, without a second thought, twist it around, using just enough force to guide her down to the floor. In one swift motion, I grab the other wrist and pin her there, her back against the hardwood. I hover over her, my grip on her wrists firm as I hold them above her head. My other hand presses down on the floor beside her, keeping her in place. My jaw clenches as I look down at her, my gaze stern and threatening; her piercing, ice-blue eyes staring back at me.

"You really think you've got a chance?" I say, my voice low and controlled. There's a weight to my words that goes beyond the paintbrush and palette.

She meets my eyes, and we both know exactly what I mean. It's not just about the little fight we're having over art supplies. I'm telling her, without needing to say it outright, that she's not going to win against me in any sense. She can't fight it. Whatever it is that I want from her, I'll have it. She glares up at me, her frustration blatant.

"You think you can just pull out some paints and now everything's cool? That's not how this fucking works."

I smirk, unfazed by her attitude.

"Princess, if you wanna play with paints, we can play with paints." I use my free hand and dip it into a blob of black paint, before pressing my paint-covered palm firmly against her throat. The paint leaves a dark handprint around her neck, and I tighten my grip just that little bit more than necessary, my fingers pressing into her skin in a way that's both possessive and intense.

"This stuff doesn't wash off easily," I murmur, my voice dropping to a dangerous purr. "So why don't we make sure everyone knows exactly what we've been up to?" As she struggles to gulp, her throat constricted by my hand, I can feel her pulse thrumming beneath my fingers. Hot and alive. Her efforts to break free heighten my awareness of the control I wield over her. My breath quickens, an animalistic growl rumbling deep in my chest. When I finally release her, it's slow, with a controlled exhale, like I'm granting her a gift she doesn't deserve.

I sit down on the edge of the bed, my eyes never leaving her as she stands up in front of me. The black handprint around her throat is stark and sharp against her skin. A slow, satisfied smile creeps across my face as I take in the sight. I pull off my shirt, tossing it aside. She crinkles her nose, a mix of distaste and intrigue, but I catch her eyes wandering down to my abs, lingering just a heartbeat longer than she probably intends. Then, her eyes crawl up again, landing on my chest, and her face drops.

"That's a lot of scars." She says bluntly, both eyebrows raising. I smirk.

"Proof I'm hard to kill, sweetheart."

"Go crazy," I say, my tone suggestive, as I stretch out on the bed with a casual, dominant ease. I gesture to the array of paints and brushes on the floor, a smirk playing at the corners of my lips as I watch her reaction. She gives me a disdainful look and replies bluntly,

"I despise you." I don't respond at first; instead, a genuine smile blooms on my face. With a defiant huff and an exaggerated roll of her eyes, she snatches the palette from the floor, her movements brimming with resolve. As she strides over to me, she plants her hands on my chest and delivers a firm shove. Although it doesn't budge me an inch, I can feel the anger coursing through her touch. I'm momentarily caught off guard, not used to being manhandled like this, but *fuck* is it turning me on.

I let myself fall back onto the bed, arms crossing behind my head as I settle in comfortably, the smirk on my lips never wavering. She straddles me, and I look up at her, savouring the unexpected thrill of being under her control. Her eyes are fierce, but I can see the flicker of excitement in them, matching my own. She works on my chest with the palette in hand, painting in silence. Every stroke of the brush, every flick of her wrist, is mesmerising. I stay completely still, just watching her. Her focused expression, the way her brows furrow in concentration, and the subtle sway of her hips as she moves. The silence stretches between us, but it's not uncomfortable.

As Skylar finishes painting my chest, tilting back to admire her work, I pull my phone from my pocket. I hold it out to her with confidence.

"Take a picture," I say, offering the phone with a casual flick of my wrist. "The password's 221515." She glances at the phone and then back at me, a look of genuine incredulity crossing her face.

"Why the fuck would you give me your password? Have you ever met me?" She asks. I chuckle softly, meeting her gaze with a mixture of arrogance and genuine interest.

"I don't have a thing to hide from you, my princess."

Her expression shifts, and I catch the faintest hint of a smile tugging at the corners of her mouth. She tries to suppress it, but she can't hide from me. Skylar snaps a picture with my phone and then turns it around to show me. As the screen lights up, I see the painting she's done; a stunning galaxy spread across my chest and up my neck. The colours swirl together in vibrant hues of blue, purple, and pink, capturing the essence of the cosmos with an impressive depth.

I tilt my head, examining her work. The intricate patterns and the way the colours blend together are surprisingly impressive. It's clear she's put a lot of effort into it, and the result is striking. I let out a low whistle, genuinely impressed.

Then, I pause, my eyes locking onto the middle of my chest. Right where my sword tattoo should be. My brow furrows. The sword's still there, but it's been transformed; the blade now

521

serves as the body of a butterfly, its wings spreading outward, delicate and vivid, blending seamlessly into the stars around it. She hasn't just covered up the tattoo; she's used it, turning something hard and sharp into something graceful and alive. Beautiful.

"A butterfly?" I murmur, half-amused, half-bemused. She shrugs, still fighting that smile.

"It suits you." She says. I can't help but chuckle. Somehow, she's turned my darkness into something light, and against all odds, it doesn't feel wrong; it feels strangely right.

"Not bad at all, Farmer." I admit. She raises an eyebrow, a mix of pride and defiance in her expression.

"You doubted me?"

"Never." I say, flashing her a grin. She snorts, rolling her eyes with an obviously fake disgust.

"If it's so good, maybe I should charge you for it."

With that, I stand up, brushing off some of the dried paint and giving her a once-over.

"Alright, missy, I think you need to get some rest," I say, my tone firm but with a hint of a smirk. "You know, cool off a bit before you try to kill me again." She scrunches her eyebrows, but there's a flicker of a smile. I lean in slightly, adding with a casual tone, "and if you're feeling brave, you're welcome to stay in my bed tonight." Skylar raises an eyebrow judgmentally.

"Rest? It's not even 2 a.m."

I'm about to respond when she suddenly grabs the hem of her top and yanks it over her head, tossing it aside without a second thought. It drops to the floor, and without warning, she's standing there, half-naked, like it's no big deal. My brain short-circuits for a second. Women don't do this around me. They don't have the balls to pull a stunt like this. But Skylar? She's got no fucking fear.

I'm rooted to the spot, caught completely off guard. My eyes rake over her body, taking in every curve, every inch of exposed skin, and it's driving me insane. My pulse kicks up, thoughts spiralling.

What the fuck is she doing?

"What, you've never seen a pair of tits before?" She says. My jaw clenches so hard I can feel the tension in every muscle. I'm fighting the urge to lose control, to just take her right here. But there's something about that attitude of hers that gets under my skin in a way I can't ignore. Normally, I wouldn't tolerate this kind of disrespect from anyone, but with her, it's different. I hate it, and I love it at the same time. Skylar casually flops onto the bed, sprawling out on her stomach as if she's completely at ease. Her bare back exposed and inviting.

"Your turn," she says bluntly. My mind races as I take in the sight of her, and I'm struck by how she's completely shifting the dynamic between us. This isn't how things usually go. Women I deal with are usually more compliant, less daring. But here she is, making me question myself. Despite the shock, a grin creeps onto my face. I can't deny that I'm impressed. Her audacity is disarming, and it's got me intrigued.

I move to the box of paints, my steps steady but my mind racing. How the hell am I letting this happen? I'm supposed to be the one in control, but here I am, eagerly complying with her demands. There's a part of me that wonders why I'm allowing this shift without enforcing some kind of punishment. But nonetheless, I lean over her, the mix of colours spread out on the palette in my hand.

"Alright, princess," I say, my tone both mocking and indulgent. "What you want, you shall receive." I start painting her back, and it quickly becomes apparent that I'm not just applying colour; I'm deliberately making this as intimate as it gets. I use both the brush and my fingers, letting the paint blend and smear in ways that are both intentional and teasing. My fingers glide along her skin, sometimes tracing light, almost ticklish strokes, and at other times pressing firmly enough to make her squirm. I make sure to take my time, savouring each touch, each shift of her body under my hands. Every time I move my hand, I'm acutely aware of the way she reacts.

As I paint, my mind drifts to darker, more primal thoughts. I'm painfully aware of how easily I could have her right now. How effortlessly I could hold her still. I focus momentarily on her flimsy little shorts and knickers that cling to her hips. The sight of them, so easily removable, is driving me wild. All it would take is one firm grip, a quick tear, and I'd be having my way. My body responds to the fantasy, a hard, urgent pressure that I'm struggling to control. I try to stay focused on the task at hand, but it's almost impossible not to let the images of what I could do seep into my mind.

I finish painting, the final strokes of colour blending seamlessly across her skin. I step back, admiring my work with a smirk.

"Job done." I murmur, my voice tinged with satisfaction. Reaching into my pocket, I pull out my phone and snap a picture of the masterpiece. I throw the phone down onto the bed beside her, my grin widening as she glances at the screen. Her eyes go wide, taking in the intricate sunset I've painted. The colours are vivid and mesmerising, capturing the last light of day in a breathtaking way. She's genuinely stunned, her usual tough exterior softening as she looks at the painting. I watch as she sits up, her eyes still glued to the phone screen.

"Woah, what the fuck," she says, her tone a mix of surprise and genuine admiration. "That's actually sick."

"Thank you, princess," I reply smoothly, leaning back and letting the compliment roll off me. She continues to examine the photo, zooming in and scrutinising every detail, clearly impressed. Meanwhile, my gaze drifts over her half-naked body, unable to ignore the way her bare skin looks in the dim light. It's a battle not to let my eyes linger too long, and the sight is becoming harder to ignore.

Finally, I reach my breaking point. I grab her shirt from the bed and toss it at her in a firm gesture.

"Alright, now be a good girl and get to bed." I command, trying to sound stern but probably just sounding grumpy. She catches the shirt and shoots me a begrudging look, her attitude still firmly intact. As she puts her top back on, she drops my phone onto the bed and stands up. She heads for the door, glancing back with a smirk.

"*Yeah*, sorry to break it to you," she starts, "but I'm not a good girl." She says with a laugh, the sound echoing in the room as she walks out.

I watch her glide out, a mix of frustration and fascination simmering inside me like a pot that's slightly too full. This girl is anything but predictable, and it's becoming increasingly clear that she's not going to make things easy for me.

CHAPTER 14:
HE'S NEW HERE

Marcus

The sun is high, and I step out into the garden just as lunchtime is in full swing. Before me lies the sprawling estate; a mafia-king style mansion garden. It's an absurdly huge expanse of green that's probably visible from space. Seriously, this place is so big, I'm half expecting to find a lost civilization hiding in one of the hedges. But, hey, I guess that's what you get when your rich brother's idea of a home is a royal fucking palace.

I make my way across the stone path, the sound of my footsteps echoing in the open space. The stones are immaculate, almost offensively so, like even the earth itself bends to Noah's will, too afraid to leave a single mark on his kingdom. Everything here screams control, order. Power. Their voices float over, and I catch the tail end of a conversation that makes me smirk.

"I just think it's too much hassle," Birdie's saying, her tone dripping with that rich-girl apathy. "Being chased by a snail for the rest of your entire life? No thanks." She continues. Skylar snorts, clearly not impressed.

"Of course *you* wouldn't take the money, Birdie. You're already fucking swimming in it." Birdie shrugs, not even denying it. Skylar grins, mischief written all over her face. "Personally, I'd trap the little bastard in a safe, chuck it in the ocean, and call it a day." Noah, lounging next to her, raises an eyebrow, clearly ready to pick apart her plan.

"Yeah okay, and what happens when the safe rusts and the snail breaks out? Or better yet, what if someone finds it, opens it up, and accidentally sets the snail free?"

"You got a better solution?" Skylar asks.
"Just shoot it," Noah says, deadpan, as if that's the end of the discussion. Skylar whips her head toward him, eyes blazing.

"The snail is invincible, you moron. You can't just shoot everything that pisses you off." She replies. Noah leans back, giving her a lazy, amused look.
"Clearly. If that was the case, I'd have shot you days ago." He snaps back. Sienna, sitting off to the side with Butter on her hand, sighs and jumps in with a more practical approach.

"Or you could just move to a different country every couple of years. The snail's slow. It'd take forever to catch up."

My sweet, always the voice of reason.

Birdie rolls her eyes, crossing her arms. "Honestly, this whole thing is just ridiculous." She mumbles. Skylar's eyes light up with a new idea.

"Oo, okay, what if I just keep it in a glass tank as a pet? That way, I can watch over it all the time." She suggests. Noah raises an eyebrow.

"What if someone smashes the glass?" He questions. Skylar scowls at him.

"Why the fuck are you so obsessed with violence?" She shrieks.

"Did you seriously just ask that?" Birdie interjects, "the guy kills people for a living." Noah shrugs, a smirk playing on his   lips.

"I'm just thinking practically. Not everyone has the patience to be a fucking snail babysitter."

I finally sigh and sit down next to Sienna, grabbing a handful of crisps from the table. Their back-and-forth is entertaining, but I've heard enough. As Noah and Skylar continue their relentless bickering about the stupid snail scenario, Dean strolls over with a scowl on his face, clearly unimpressed. His mood is anything but cheerful, and the ongoing argument only seems to irritate him further.

I'm desperately trying to think of a way to move the conversation along when I notice that both of them have tiny smudges of black paint on their necks. Noah has dark remnants that look almost deliberate, and Skylar has a couple of telltale black lines across her throat. It's a curious detail, considering their current tension, and it immediately grabs my attention.

I smirk, unable to resist the urge to dig a little deeper.

"What's with the paint?" I blurt out before I can stop myself. The effect is instant and almost comical. Noah and Skylar both turn their heads sharply in my direction, Sky's face going pale as if she's seen a ghost. It's clear they weren't expecting anyone to notice, let alone call them out on it.

I guess they've had a busy night.

Skylar's face flushes with embarrassment and she becomes instantly defensive. Her eyes dart around, clearly uncomfortable. It's as if I've unearthed a secret she wasn't prepared to expose. Her shoulders stiffen, and she's suddenly very intent on avoiding eye contact. Noah, on the other hand, remains calm, his expression shifting to a smug, knowing grin. It's clear he's fully aware of what's going on and doesn't mind flaunting it. He leans back with a self-satisfied smirk.

"Just a little late-night art," he says smoothly. "You know how it goes."

I see Noah's enjoyment. His calm demeanour and the arrogant glint in his eyes show that he's not only aware of the situation but is relishing the attention. Across from him, I see Dean's expression darken, tension rolling off him in waves. He's clearly irritated and wants to change the topic fast.

"Wow, isn't that interesting." He snaps, sarcastically. Immediately, the conversation comes to a halt. Everyone goes quiet, leaving a thick, uncomfortable silence. The tension between Dean and Noah is electric; it's clear this isn't just a casual disagreement. They're staring each other down; their eyes locked in a silent, deadly standoff. The hostility radiates off them like heat from a fire, each man's gaze sharp enough to cut through steel.

Delilah, sensing the hostility and desperate to break the uncomfortable silence, suddenly pipes up, her voice just a little too obnoxiously bright,

"So, Marcus, what's the deal with the books?" The question comes out rushed, almost like she's grabbing at the first thing that comes to mind. I clear my throat, grateful for the distraction.

"I don't know," I say, leaning forward, resting my elbows on my knees. "I've got a lot to think about. I'm trying to put the puzzle together, but I just need some time."

Before I can say anything else, Dean chops in, his voice sharp and clearly teetering on the edge.

"What if we don't have time?" He snaps, his frustration palpable. "The universe is fucking me at every single turn. I've lost two fingers, for fuck's sake. When is the next time gonna be the time that this book actually finishes me off?"

His words strike with a daunting weight, bringing the harsh reality of the situation home to everyone present. The tension is thick, and no one seems to know what to say. Dean's eyes blaze with a fierce mix of anger and fear, and for a fleeting moment, the only sound cutting through the stillness is the soft whisper of the wind rustling through the towering trees.

An uneasy silence blankets the garden, the weight of Dean's words lingering like a spectre. My brother, seated directly across from him, can't fully suppress the faint smirk that tugs at the corner of his mouth, though he quickly attempts to mask it. Dean catches the gesture, his glare intensifying, but instead of responding with words, he grabs a drink from the table and downs it in a swift gulp. Without uttering another word, he pushes back his chair, the legs scraping sharply against the stone as he rises and storms inside, the tension discernible in his wake.

Delilah shoots up from her seat, quickly trailing after Dean as he storms off. I let out a heavy sigh, rubbing my forehead as if that could somehow ease the stress that's been building in my mind. My thoughts are a tangled mess, and every time I try to piece them together, it feels like I'm only making it worse. I glance around at the others, noticing how everyone is avoiding eye contact. The pressure's getting to us all. I'm supposed to have this figured out, supposed to be the one keeping everything together. But right now, it feels like everything's slipping through my fingers. I lean back in my chair, staring up at the sky, wishing for some kind of clarity. The sun's bright, almost mocking in how cheerful it is compared to the storm that feels like it's inevitably brewing.

Skylar pipes up, her voice cutting through the heavy silence.
"Why don't we all go and hang out at the tunnel? It might make everyone feel better." I glance over at her, trying to gauge if she's serious. The idea of heading down to the tunnel doesn't exactly scream 'stress-free' to me, especially considering the fact that Skinny Jeans body was just found down there. But I mean, Skylar's trying, and I can see she's desperate to lift the mood.

"The tunnel?" Noah questions, raising an eyebrow. Skylar rolls her eyes, exasperated.
"Ugh, noob." She mutters. Sienna giggles softly, stepping in to explain.

"It's just our spot. We've been hanging out there since we were kids. It's where we go to chill." Noah looks between them, clearly intrigued. I'm not thrilled about the idea, but I'm also not ready to shoot it down just yet. I glance at Skylar, giving her a look that says, *'Are you sure about this?'*; to which, she smiles, doubling down on her suggestion. The tunnel has too much baggage for my liking, but honestly, it could be exactly what we need to clear the air.

CHAPTER 15:
UNCOVERED SECRETS

Dean

Some genius had the bright idea of dragging us down to the tunnel, and somehow, I got roped into it. Now here I am, trudging through the woods, getting closer to that shitty little spot we've claimed as our hideout for years. There's an old, ratty sofa abandoned there, like it's some kind of living room for ghosts. We've been coming here forever to chill, smoke, paint and pretend we're not *completely* fucked up.

But now, this place feels different. Heavy. And surprisingly, it's not just because there's a massive gap in the floor where some dead guy was buried. It's because Noah's here. I can't even put my finger on why I fucking hate him so much. Sure, we've got some history; old street dealer bullshit involving his crew, but it's nothing personal. He's a smug bastard, sure, always hanging around like he thinks he's the king of the world. But there's something deeper gnawing at me. Maybe it's that cocky way he carries himself, all calm and collected, like nothing rattles him. Or maybe it's *because* I can't quite figure him out, and that's what pisses me off the most.

Then there's the whole Sienna situation. I've got a gut feeling he's tied up in her abduction, but with no proof, it's all just speculation. And the worst part? Sienna seems perfectly fine around him. Happy even. Which just makes me feel even more off-balance.

Ah fuck, I don't know.

I'm the first to make a beeline for the old sofa, throwing myself down into its worn-out cushions like it's the only thing that makes sense anymore. The others are still milling around outside, but I'm not about to waste time pretending I'm thrilled to be here. I pull out my rolling papers and start working on a joint, trying to drown out the nagging thoughts about Noah and everything else that's been getting under my skin lately.

Delilah wanders over and plops down next to me, her presence as familiar as it is comforting. She watches me roll the joint for a moment before nudging me with her elbow.
"You okay?" she asks, her voice soft, but there's a hint of concern there too. I give her a genuine smile, one that actually reaches my eyes.

"Yeah, I'm fine," She smiles back, and it's one of those rare, unguarded moments that remind me why I keep her close.

"Well, you better be. We're not doing the whole brooding thing again tonight, okay?" She jokes playfully. I let out a small laugh, appreciating her attempt to lighten the mood.
"Yes, ma'am." I laugh, my smile lingering as I light up the joint.

535

The rest of the group starts to settle in, each finding their spot. I watch as Noah strides past, all tough-guy swagger, as if he owns the place. His eyes scan the walls of the tunnel, and he points at the graffiti.

"Has this always been here?" He asks. I don't even bother looking up from my blunt.

"No," I mutter, keeping my tone flat, "I did all the graffiti." He glances at me, one eyebrow raised, and I can feel him waiting for some kind of reaction. I just keep rolling, ignoring the weight of his stare. I'm not giving him anything. Let him wonder if I'm pissed off or if I even care. The truth is, I don't know which it is myself.

"Looks nice, man." He says.

I glance up, just for a second, catching the genuine tone in his voice. It's almost unsettling. I don't know if he's messing with me or what, but I'm not interested in figuring it out. I go back to rolling my joint, keeping my expression blank. I don't give two fucks if he thinks it's nice. I didn't do it for him, and I'm not about to start caring what Noah thinks.

As I finish rolling the joint, I hear Noah mutter, "You're welcome," dripping with sarcasm. I don't bother looking up. The flick of the lighter follows. As I take a drag, letting the smoke fill my lungs, I finally glance up and catch sight of Noah settling onto one of the logs. He's got a cigar in hand, the tip glowing as he lights it. Of course, he'd pick a cigar; gotta one-up me, even with something as simple as what he's smoking.

He meets my gaze, puffing out a cloud of smoke, his eyes locked on mine like he's daring me to say something. I won't lie, despite all my talk, the guy is fucking intimidating. There's something in his eyes, a coldness that sends a chill down your spine. It's not just that he's tough; he looks like a killer.

Probably because he *is* a killer.

That sadistic stare of his is a reminder of exactly who I'm dealing with. I'm a fighter, sure, but *fuck*. Noah's on a whole different level. The kind of guy who looks like he could end you without breaking a sweat. It's enough to make me think twice, just for a second. I exhale, the blunt's smoke swirling up around me, and look away. Not giving him the satisfaction.

We've been sitting around for hours now, the sun beginning to set, everyone trying to act like we're here to unwind. Birdie, always the one to lighten the mood, suggests,
    "How about a game of 'Never Have I Ever'?" I don't have the energy to protest, so I go along with the idea. Skylar's all in, of course.

    "Fuck yeah! I'll start." She squeals.

    "Never have I ever been arrested?" Skylar, Birdie and I all put a finger down without hesitation. I watch as Noah's hand stays perfectly still, not a finger budging. Skylar narrows her eyes at him, disbelief written all over her face.
    "Hold on, you're telling me you've never been arrested? You, of all people?" she asks, incredulous. "You're literally an open criminal." Noah leans back, giving her that arrogant smirk he's perfected.

    "I don't get caught, princess." He replies nonchalantly. Skylar scoffs, but I catch a hint of amusement in her expression.

It's my turn next, and I decide to raise the stakes.

"Never have I ever killed someone." There's a pause, a noticeable shift in the air. Slowly, Skylar, Marcus, Noah, and Delilah each put a finger down. An awkward pause follows, before the group bursts into giggles. Then it's Noah's turn, and he seems ready to dive right in.

"Never have I ever betrayed someone." He says it casually, like it's just another question, but his eyes are locked on mine. For a fleeting moment, I wonder if he's hinting at something specific or if it's just my overactive imagination. I maintain a neutral expression, even as my mind races with paranoia.

Sienna, Butter in hand, takes her turn next.

"Never have I ever done drugs." She says. Everyone except her drops a finger, and Delilah wastes no time calling her out, a playful grin on her face.

"Sienna, don't lie, you've smoked weed before." Sienna rolls her eyes, looking a bit defensive.

"Yeah, against my will. And it was awful!" There's some laughter, and it's lightened the mood a bit, but I'm still on edge. I can feel Noah's gaze, like a knife digging into my back.

"Never have I ever dyed my hair." Delilah says. Skylar immediately drops a finger, groaning.

"Woah, that's not fair." Skylar protests. We all chuckle, but I can't help but notice how Noah's still watching me.

"Never have I ever been caught trying to steal from someone," he says, and this time his gaze isn't just calculating, it's predatory. My stomach twists. I know exactly what he's alluding to. There was a situation back in the young offenders unit. I tried to lift some cash off a guy who looked like an easy target. Got the absolute shit beaten out of me instead.

How the fuck does Noah know about that?

I shift in my seat, trying to play it off, but my mind is spinning. He's got dirt on me, and he's making sure I know it. Delilah takes her turn, but her words drift over me like background noise. All I can think about is Noah, about how much he knows. How he's peeling back my layers in front of everyone, one question at a time.

Before I can steady my nerves it's Noah's turn again, and I brace myself.

"Never have I ever," he starts, his eyes stabbing into me, "kept a secret that could've changed everything." As soon as the words leave his mouth, it's like the world stops spinning. The ground drops from under me. My mind goes blank for a second, and all I can think is; he knows.

Oh my God, he fucking knows.

I feel the blood drain from my face, a sudden coldness washing over me, followed by a wave of heat that makes me break out in a sweat. My heart pounds so loudly in my chest, I can barely hear anything else. My vision narrows, the edges of my vision blurring as I focus on Noah, on the way he's looking at me.

The joint I'm holding wobbles between my fingers, and I barely notice as ash falls to the dirt. I try to stay still, but I can't. My hands are trembling, and I shift on the spot, desperate to draw air into my lungs. It's futile. The woods around us seem to close in, the trees pressing down like they're suffocating me. The world narrows down to the space between us, and all I can feel is panic, pure and raw. My stomach twists, a sick feeling crawling up my throat.

I can't stem the tide of memories rushing back, my long-buried secret clawing its way to the surface.

Marcus can't find out. He can't find out that I knew.

He *can't.*

I remember the day I found the file, like it was yesterday. We were just kids, stuck in that shitty children's home, with peeling wallpaper and a stench that never went away. I was in our bedroom, trying to kill time by moving the furniture around; anything to distract from how miserable that place was. That's when I spotted it, dusty and yellowing, wedged behind the wardrobe, waiting to be unearthed.

I pulled it out, flipping it open. And there it was, plain as day; Marcus had a brother. A real, biological brother, out there somewhere. The kind of family connection I'd never have. My first instinct was to tell him. I should've told him. But then, the selfish part of me kicked in. What if he found his family and left? I'd be stuck in that hellhole alone, without my best friend, without the only person who made that place bearable. I couldn't let that happen. So, I burned the file. I never spoke a word.

But I knew.

I kept that secret buried deep, convincing myself it was for Marcus' sake. But deep down, I knew the reality; I was terrified of being left behind. Terrified of losing the only family I'd ever known. Noah's stare is cutting into me, and there's a twisted satisfaction in his eyes. He's got me cornered, and he knows it. The smug bastard knows exactly what he's doing. I'm struggling to keep my breathing steady, trying not to let the others see just how fucked I am right now. But I can feel it, everything I've tried so hard to protect is slipping through my fingers like sand.

I can't take it. The pressure in my chest is too much, my vision blurring as everything starts to spin. I stand up, needing to escape before I completely lose it. Marcus glances up, concern etched on his face.

"You alright, mate?" he asks. I can't even look at him. The guilt is clawing at my insides, but I force myself to nod.

"You look a little pale." Noah adds, his voice dripping with mock concern as he takes a puff on his cigar.

"I'm fine, bro." I manage to get out, my voice tight. "I just.. need a minute."

I turn to leave, but suddenly Sienna's butterfly starts flapping in my face, wings fluttering wildly as if it senses the chaos inside me. The tiny thing buzzes around, adding to the disorienting swirl in my head. I swat at it, not hard, just enough to get it out of my way, but my movements are rougher than I intend.

"Dean!" Sienna's voice is sharp, a mix of surprise and anger. I can feel everyone's eyes on me, but I can't control my body. I can barely think straight, my mind is a mess of panic and regret, and this fucking butterfly won't leave me alone! I push at it again, stumbling forward, my hands trembling as I try to get away from the group, away from Noah's smirk and the memories that are ripping me apart inside. But the butterfly just keeps coming, its tiny wings beating around my head.

"Dean, what's going on with you?" Delilah asks. I can't reply. I see Marcus reach up and snatch the butterfly from the air. The tiny creature flutters in his hand, finally stilling as he cups it gently. Sadly, I don't have the luxury to appreciate the gesture. As I stagger away from the group, I feel a jarring snag on my foot. I look down to see my shoe wedged tight in the metal of the old train track, the iron teeth catching with an unforgiving grip.

I try to yank my foot free, but the track's metal seems to hold on with an almost mocking tenacity. Panic rises in my chest, my breaths coming out in short, frantic bursts. Every pull only makes the situation worse, my foot feeling more and more trapped. My vision starts to blur, not just from the dizziness but from the growing realisation that I'm stuck.
"No fucking way." I mutter under my breath, tugging desperately. I can't believe this is happening, not now. The metal track seems to laugh at my struggle, remaining obstinately fixed.

The butterfly launches itself from Marcus' grasp, immediately diving back toward my foot, its wings beating frantically around the spot where I'm ensnared. I swat at it, struggling to concentrate, but it seems determined to pester me.

Then, from somewhere in the distance, a low, ominous rumble begins to swell, gradually growing louder and reverberating through the air. Everyone freezes, the sound pulling us all into a sharp, tense silence. It takes a moment for the realisation to sink in, but when it does, it hits like a punch to the gut.

A train.

The distant roll sharpens into something more defined, transforming into the unmistakable clamour of metal grinding against metal. The train's whistle pierces the air, a haunting sound that starts as a faint echo, but grows, blaring progressively louder with each passing second. My heart races, each frantic beat mirroring the threat that looms closer. I pull at my foot with renewed desperation, panic flooding every nerve in my body.

"Dean!" Delilah's scream slashes through the air, raw and filled with terror. The sound jolts me, but my foot stays stuck, the track holding on tight, refusing to let go.

The group around me bursts into frantic motion, but I'm only vaguely aware of their urgent shouts and scrambling bodies; my whole world narrowing down to the sight of my foot caught in the track and the menacing roar of that train barrelling toward us. I pull harder, the metal digging into my shoe, but nothing gives.

The train's growl gets louder, closer, and I can almost feel the vibrations through the ground. Panic surges, cold and sharp, as I begin to understand just how little time I have. Frantic hands claw at me, tugging desperately at my leg, my foot; anything they can grasp in a desperate bid to liberate me from the unyielding embrace of the track. The light from the approaching train becomes visible now. A blinding beacon, a searing beam that intensifies with each pounding heartbeat. The ground beneath us shudders, the vibrations building into a deafening, earth-shaking roar that rattles my very bones.

"God, this is it," I whisper, my words lost in the atmosphere. I close my eyes, bracing myself for the onslaught of inevitability. The thunderous clatter of the train envelops me, a monstrous force that seems to consume the world whole.

And then, just when the end feels unavoidable, Marcus delivers one final, desperate tug. Pain shoots through my ankle as it twists free, a sharp, burning sensation that ignites my nerves. In an instant, I'm yanked through the air, flung backward with a force that knocks the wind from my chest. The train surges past, a colossal blur of metal and noise, the wind from its speed whipping violently across my face. It's so close that it warps my mind.

For a moment, the world falls into stillness. Sprawled on the ground, I gaze up at the canopy of trees, my chest heaving as I struggle to reclaim my breath. My heart pounds a relentless tattoo in my ears, the echo of survival ringing in my head.

The others are on the opposite side, likely staring towards me through the blur of the passing train. It feels as if a colossal wall of steel has risen between us, the engine so loud it drowns out everything else. I can't hear a thing, except the train and the knelling in my ears.

The moment unfurls like an eternity, a surreal freeze-frame where time itself seems to stretch thin. At last, the train roars past, its cacophony gradually dissipating into the distance, leaving in its wake an eerie stillness. Straining against the ground, I push myself up onto my elbows, the gritty earth rough beneath my palms, and gaze across the tracks.

The group stands frozen in place, their faces a tumultuous mix of shock, fear, and something more sinister; a flicker of darkness that betrays their thoughts. No one says a word. They fix their stares on me, and I can see it in their eyes, a shared recognition.

This shit just got very real.

CHAPTER 16:

YES, ANOTHER FUCKING CHASE

Marcus

What the actual *fuck* is going on?

First Dean freaks out over Noah's question in a stupid game of 'Never Have I Ever,' and then nearly gets himself flattened by a fucking train. I can't wrap my head around it. I look at Dean across the tracks. He's pale and shaken, and the rest of us aren't far behind. We're all rooted to the spot, not really sure what to do next. One minute, it's a game; the next, we're staring death in the face.

Delilah bolts across the tracks, throwing her arms around Dean as soon as she reaches him. He's still catching his breath, but he holds onto her like she's the only thing keeping him grounded. She probably is. The rest of us just stand there, looking at each other, and it's clear we're all thinking the same thing. No one says it, but the looks passing between us say everything.

Dean's not safe. Not even close.

The book isn't done with him yet.

If I were a normal person at this moment, I'd probably be thinking, 'Well, at least that's over.' But I've learned the hard way not to be too quick to assume everything's wrapped up nicely. Optimism and I don't mix well these days. And apparently, my instinct is right. As if on cue, I hear a shout from down the track. My head snaps around, and I'm met with three police officers marching toward us.

Shit.

The group shifts uneasily, the weight of the moment sinking in. Everyone's eyes dart around, clearly unsure of the next move. Noah takes a step forward, positioning himself between the group and the approaching police officers; his cigar still clamped between his fingers. His demeanour is unyielding, and he remains cool and collected as he faces them. The officers, recognizing him immediately, address him with a mix of respect and wariness.

"Noah Bear," one of them says, clearly familiar with his reputation. Noah meets their gaze, his expression hard and unphased.

"Is there an issue?" he asks, his voice low and assertive, cutting through the tense air. His confidence is palpable, and he doesn't flinch under their scrutiny.

One of the officers begins to reach for his walkie-talkie, presumably to call for backup. Noah reacts in a split second. He unexpectedly pulls out a gun and, without hesitation, fires at the walkie-talkie. The device explodes into pieces, clattering to the ground.

"You *really* don't wanna do that." he warns, a sinister grin spreading across his face. I'm struck dumb. My eyes widen, and my mouth probably falls open as I watch the whole thing unfold. It's like watching a scene from an action movie, except this is real life, and it's happening right in front of me. I glance at the others, their faces reflecting the same stunned amazement I'm feeling. Noah isn't just playing the game, he's redefining it. I can't lie, my brother is pretty fucking sick.

The officers look completely thrown off, their confusion and surprise evident. His casual handling of the situation flips the script entirely. He just stands there, gun in one hand, smoking his cigar with the other like he rules the world. Noah doesn't take his eyes off the police as he speaks, his voice steady and low.

"Marcus, take everyone to the cars," he says. "I'll be there in a minute."

I hesitate, my eyes flicking between Noah and the officers. There's a part of me that wants to stay, to see how this all plays out, but I know better. When somebody like Noah gives an order, you don't question it. I start backing away, leading the group toward the cars. The coppers aren't just standing there, though, they're getting antsy.

"Don't fucking move!" one of the officers shouts, his voice cutting through the air like a whip. But I don't stop. None of us do. We're getting the fuck out of here.

The moment we're out of the police's line of sight, we all break into a run, feet pounding against the dirt and gravel as we race toward the cars. We reach the cars, breathless but moving fast. Sienna and Skylar bundle into the backseat and I slide into the driver's seat, hands gripping the wheel. I watch the others speed off, the car kicking up dust in its wake.

As we huddle in the car, the silence is deafening. Skylar's staring out the window, chewing her lip, while Sienna fidgets in the backseat, her knee bouncing anxiously. I glance around, but there's no sign of Noah yet. The seconds tick by, stretching out unbearably. Then, faintly at first, I hear sirens in the distance. My chest tightens.

I tap my fingers on the steering wheel, trying to keep calm, but my patience is wearing thin. I grip the wheel harder, urgency pounding in my veins.

"Come on, Noah," I mutter, the words escaping through gritted teeth. Every second that passes cranks up the pressure.

The flash of blue lights appears in the distance and I can't wait any longer. I reach for the keys, jamming them into the ignition with trembling hands, ready to floor it. But just as I'm about to start the engine, Noah strolls out of the woods, still puffing on his cigar like he's got all the time in the world. He's completely unfazed, the picture of calm, and it's actually really pissing me off how cool he looks right now.

He saunters over to the car and slides into the passenger seat, the rich scent of the smoke trailing behind him. For a moment, I just stare at him, caught between relief and disbelief. He looks over at me, raising an eyebrow.

"Drive, then." He says, calm and confused. I blink at him, my astonishment momentarily overriding my panic. I can barely contain a chuckle.

"You're fucked, you know that?" I admit. Without waiting for a response, I slam the car into gear and peel out, making an immediate U-turn; the tires screeching against the asphalt.

The police sirens are deafening, slicing through the night with a relentless wail. Every inch of the road ahead is a battlefield of flashing lights, screeching tires, and the throbbing pulse of adrenaline. I whip the wheel, taking a sharp turn onto a narrow side street. The car skids, tires screeching in protest as we narrowly avoid a row of parked cars. The atmosphere is thick with the scent of burnt rubber and the tang of diesel from the police car closing in behind us.

"Left." Noah barks unexpectedly. I barely have time to think before, just as Noah's command leaves his lips, another police car screeches around a corner up ahead. It's charging straight for us, trying to cut off our escape.

"Do you have x-ray fucking vision or something?" I snap. I wrench the wheel sharply to the left, the tires screaming in protest as they grip the ground, whipping us around the narrow bend in a wild skid.

Each turn feels like a desperate gamble, and the relentless glare of the pursuing police car looms in my mirrors like a dark omen. Suddenly, I hear the distinct click of a window being rolled down. I glance over, only to see Noah calmly puffing on his cigar, the night air whipping into the car. And I thought *I* was relaxed in chases.

"What are you on the run for anyway?" he asks, his voice maddeningly calm, like we're just out for a casual drive. I blink, momentarily thrown off by the absurdity of his question.

"Really? Right now?" I snap, dodging another police car as it veers into our path. The side mirror just misses clipping it, and I slam on the gas, pulling ahead. But Noah just looks at me, waiting for an answer, smoke curling lazily from his cigar.

"I uh," I grit out, swerving to avoid a pedestrian sign. "I killed some guy." Noah doesn't even flinch, understandably, just raises an eyebrow. "I buried him back at the tunnel. I guess they're watching over the area now." I continue as I slam the brakes to avoid yet another police car that suddenly appears in front of us. The car jerks, and I throw it into reverse, speeding backward down the narrow street. Noah just nods, blowing another puff of smoke out the window.

"Got it," he says. "Who'd you kill?"

For a split second, my thoughts spiral back to that night; my first kill. I can still see his face, twisted, the way his eyes widened in shock when he realised he wasn't getting out alive. I remember the cold, detached fury that had washed over me, a part of me I didn't even know existed until that moment. It was like flipping a switch, and once it was done, there was no going back. That night changed everything. It changed me. I'm not the same person I was before that moment, and I never will be.

"A cunt who had it coming," I finally say, my voice cold, as I gun the engine, pulling us much further ahead now.

Noah just nods, like that's all he needed to know. He doesn't press for details, doesn't pry into the twisted mess that led me to that point. I'm sure he gets it, I know he's been there too. Or maybe he just doesn't care.

As we tear through the streets, I notice the police cars are trailing a little further behind. Their lights still flash in the rearview mirror, but they're not as close as they were. There's a chance, a small one, but a chance nonetheless. I know of a tight alleyway up ahead, barely wide enough for the car. It's risky as fuck, but If we can just squeeze through, we'll be out of sight before they even realise where we've gone.

I jerk the wheel with all my strength, causing the car to slide sideways and skid into the cramped alleyway. The car scrapes against the alley walls, the screech of metal against brick is loud; painful, even. The car bucks as it scrapes through, sparks flying from the sides, and for a split second, it feels like we're going to get wedged in tight. But then we're through, bursting out of the other side of the alley. I barely have time to straighten the wheel before I ramp up the speed.

The speedometer climbs past 100mph as I rocket towards Noah's house. My grip on the wheel loosens just a little, and I start to feel that familiar rush.

Marcus Bear has done it again.

The police sirens are distant now, barely a whisper behind us, and the roads ahead are wide open. I hear the girls in the back let out simultaneous sighs of relief, the tension in the car slowly melting. A smile spreads across my face, pride swelling in my chest. It's almost becoming routine at this point, but *fuck* it never gets old.

As we step out and get a good look at the car, it's clear the thing is wrecked on both sides. Scratches, dents, and who knows what else; it's a miracle we even made it here. I glance at Noah, expecting him to be at least a little pissed, but he just looks at the damage and smirks.

"Just a scratch," he says, completely deadpan.

"Hopefully you've got the cash to cover it," I shoot back, glancing mockingly up at the mansion looming behind us. Noah chuckles richly, completely unfazed.

He glances back at the house, then at me.

"Don't worry about the feds. They won't be sniffing around the tunnel anymore. I've taken care of it." He assures. I stare at him, still trying to wrap my head around this level of control. It's the kind of power I thought only existed in movies.

"How do you do it?" I ask, genuinely curious. Noah looks at me, a small smile playing on his lips.

"You're a Bear, Marcus," he says, his voice steady. "You can do it too."

CHAPTER 17:
THREATS, THREATS, THREATS

Noah

I'm thoroughly impressed by what I just heard; yet another kill under Marcus' belt. My little brother is a force, no doubt about it. He's proving himself in ways I didn't expect, showing the kind of grit and ruthlessness that could make him a great partner in the organisation.

I finish off my cigar and step into the house, the door clicking shut behind me. I'm ready to call it a night. My feet carry me up the first flight of stairs, each step echoing in the quiet hallway. Just as I'm about to reach the top of the stairs, I spot none other than Dean-fucking-Douglas; standing at the top of the stairs, blocking my path.

For fuck's sake.

I stop in my tracks, eyeing him with a mix of annoyance and resignation. He's pissed off, and the feeling is mutual.

"What do you want?" I ask, my voice flat. I'm not in the mood for this right now. He doesn't move, just stares down at me like he's got something to prove.

"We need to talk," he says, his tone dripping with the kind of forced intensity he probably thinks is intimidating. It's not. I let out a slow breath, rolling my neck like I'm loosening up before a fight.

"Yeah? Well, I need to sleep. So unless this is life or death, it can wait." I reply. Dean doesn't budge, his expression like stone, but I can tell he's determined to drag this out.

Dean doesn't say anything, just stands there, eyes locked on mine, like he's daring me to take this seriously. I don't. I continue up the last few stairs, intent on walking right around him, but he steps further to the side, purposely blocking my path. The move is subtle, but it's enough to make my blood simmer. We're in my house. He might think he's a big man, but this is my domain, and I won't tolerate being challenged under my own roof.

I stop in front of him, letting the silence hang for a moment. Then I lean in just enough to make sure he gets the message.

"You're in my fucking castle, Douglas. Don't push your luck." I threaten. Dean's face tightens.

"I want answers."

"Yeah, I bet you do." I grin, enjoying the way his frustration bubbles up. "Unfortunately, it doesn't work that way."

"What's your game?" He asks. I chuckle, the sound low and dangerous.

"My game? You brought this on yourself." I say, my voice calm but laced with menace.

He clenches his jaw, staying silent, but I can see the rage burning in his eyes. He wants to say something, to lash out, but he's holding it back.

"If you wanna show me disrespect," I continue, stepping closer, "then I'll be your worst fucking nightmare." I smirk, leaning in slightly. "Don't underestimate what I know, or what I can find out." As I move myself closer to him, Dean tilts his head up, meeting my gaze with that tough look he's always fronting. But it's almost funny, seeing him have to look up at me like that.

Being this tall, towering over people, it makes everything I do more fitting. I love how it adds to the intimidation factor, and makes my job that much easier. There's something about looking down at someone, especially someone like Dean, that just reaffirms my place at the top. It's an ego boost, really.

"How did you know?" He asks, surprisingly quiet.

"Somebody had to find the file, Douglas. And clearly it wasn't my brother," I smile.

"I'm not fucking scared of you," he spits out, his voice low but firm.

"That's your problem, Douglas." I say, savouring the absurdity of it. "You should be."

"I'm not the only one with secrets." He retorts.

When Dean says it, I can tell he's hoping to get under my skin. But instead of annoyance, I feel a flicker of respect. Decent response for once. I let a slow smile spread across my face.

"The difference is, you're guessing. Putting two and two together and hoping you'll get four. You've got no proof, no context," I laugh, "you're way out of your depth."

Dean's lips curl into a smug smile, and I arch a brow. The fuck is he grinning at? He looks like a Cheshire fucking cat, undeservedly full of himself. I'm not intimidated, never by him, but something about the way he's looking at me stirs my curiosity.

"What if I don't need proof?" he finally says, that shit-eating grin still plastered on his face. I stare at him for a second, barely holding back a laugh. Alright, Douglas. Let's see what you've got.

A low chuckle escapes me, and I rub my jaw, letting the tension roll off as I look down at him.

"Humour me," I say, my voice calm but with that edge I know gets under his skin.

"Do you think Skylar would be happy to know that you and Sienna have been spending time together? Making pinky promises?" He says. The laugh dies in my throat, but my smirk stays. Ah, there it is. He's swinging, and I'll give him credit; it's a decent hit. But not enough. Never enough.

"Though she'd never admit it, Skylar's wrapped around my little finger." I share, "But it's a decent threat, Douglas. You're getting better at this."

I know how to twist people, how to make them loyal without even realising it. Dean's trying to hit me where it hurts, but he doesn't know just how tight my grip is. Dean's smugness falters for a second. Just a flicker, but I catch it.

I start up the stairs again, shoulder brushing past him with force. Dean doesn't move to stop me this time. For a second, I think he's finally getting the hint, but then his voice cuts through the air again.

"What would Skylar think," he says slowly, dragging the words out, "if I told her you've been eyeing Sienna a little too closely?"

I pause, my back still to him, my jaw tightening. That little fucker. He knows that's a lie, but it's just slimy enough to plant doubt. And Skylar.. well, she's clearly got her triggers. I take a breath, letting it slide off my back, keeping the poker face locked in tight. I turn slightly, just enough to glance over my shoulder.

"So you'd lie?" My voice is low, controlled, but there's an edge to it, like a warning beneath the calm exterior.

Dean just shrugs, that smug grin still plastered on his face, like he's enjoying this little game.

"If it gets the job done."

Alright, time to shut this fucking show down.

I turn back fully, stepping into Dean's space so fast his cocky smile falters. I can feel his breath hitch as I get up close, towering over him, looking down with nothing but cold intent.

"You like to lie, don't you, Douglas?" I say, voice barely above a growl, but it lacerates through the atmosphere between us. My eyes lock onto his, unblinking. I lower my voice, letting each word dig under his skin. "You lied to your best friend," I say, slow and intentional. "You knew he had a brother and you kept it quiet. How the fuck do you sleep at night, huh?"

His jaw tightens, but he doesn't say a word. I can tell I'm getting to him, though. He can't hide the guilt flashing across his face.

"You were supposed to *be* like his brother, right? His ride-or-die? But nah, you kept it all to yourself. And for what? So you could stay top dog in his life?" Dean's breathing gets heavier. I'm right there, chipping away at whatever bravado he has left. "You're the one with the big bad secret, Douglas. You went and fucked over the only person who actually trusts you." I let out a low chuckle, shaking my head.

I see his eyes darting away briefly, trying to escape the weight of what I'm saying. But there's no fucking way I'm letting him off that easy; not when he's throwing around threats like that. I've gotta make sure he's too rattled to even think about going through with any of it.

"Why you looking away now, huh?" I growl, stepping even closer, invading his space. "You might be able to lie to Marcus, but you can't lie to me. I know what I'm fucking doing."

Dean's gaze snaps back to mine, more intense now. His jaw clenches so hard I can almost hear it.

"You're not as untouchable as you think." he says, his voice steady but sharp. It's not a full-blown threat, but it's clear he's not about to roll over either. I can see it in his posture, the way his chest rises and falls like he's keeping his nerves in check. He knows I've got him cornered, and we both know I mean business.

I smirk as I glance at him again, noticing the sheen on his forehead.

"I'm not the one sweating, Douglas," I say, my tone mocking as I let out a low, sinister laugh. He doesn't reply, though. He's holding back, and I can tell. I turn slowly and make my way up the stairs. "Remember where you stand in my fucking house." With that, I start climbing the stairs again, every step deliberate and slow. As I reach the top, I can feel his eyes burning into my back, but I don't look back. I don't need to. He knows exactly who runs this shit.

CHAPTER 18:
GUNPLAY

Noah

As I ascend the stairs, I start heading toward my room, planning to unwind from the day. But then, a thought crosses my mind, and I veer off course, deciding to pay Skylar a visit instead.

I reach her door and swing it open without knocking. Skylar's sitting on her bed, scrolling through her phone, her expression focused until she notices me. The second she sees me, her face tightens into an annoyed scowl.

"Why don't men ever fucking knock?" she snaps, her tone sharp and irritated. It's clear she's not in the mood for any interruptions, but I just smirk.

"My mistake, princess." I say calmly, backing out and closing the door. I give it a firm knock and then wait for her to respond. From inside, she shouts,

"Fuck off!" Her voice laced with frustration, but I just chuckle. Ignoring her protest, I open the door once more, stepping back inside with a nonchalant shrug.

As I mosey back in, I head straight for the bed where she's sitting, still absorbed in her phone. I watch her for a moment before I speak up,

"I'm just coming in to check on you." She doesn't look up or acknowledge me, her attention still locked on her screen. I can't help but let my lips curl into a smirk as I watch her. That little attitude is just *so* sexy. I lean in slightly, tilting my head. "Is there a problem, Farmer?" I ask, drawing out the nickname with a touch of dirty amusement.

She looks up at me in slow motion, like something straight out of a horror film. Every inch of her glare seems to crawl up my body with painstaking slowness, as if she's trying to project her fury through sheer willpower. It's both terrifying and hilarious; here I am, a 6 foot 7 criminal kingpin, and she's a tiny ball of sass with baby-pink hair, staring daggers at me like she's about to summon some kind of dark force.

"Yes," she says, her voice dripping with venom. "There is a problem."

She just keeps staring at me, her gaze piercing through the room like a hot knife through butter. It's that kind of stare that makes you think of the old saying, *'If looks could kill.'* But right now, I'm thinking, if her stare could actually manifest into something, she'd probably have me six feet under and buried in the back garden.

"Would you like to elaborate on the problem?" I ask, the edge in my voice more teasing than anything.

"My drug dealer died," she snaps. I raise an eyebrow, unfazed.

"So?" I say, shrugging. "Dealers get killed all the time." Skylar finally breaks her stare, rolling her eyes as if I'm the dumbest person she's ever encountered.

"Yeah," she huffs, "but then I went to go ask my other dealer, and guess what?" I raise my brow again, playing along.

"What?"

"He's dead too!" she shouts, throwing her hands up, clearly pissed. I bite back a smirk, keeping my face as neutral as possible.

"I'm sorry for your loss," I say, layering the words with as much sarcasm as I can manage.

Skylar's face twists with irritation, and before I can even blink, she's shoving past me, her tiny frame packing a surprising force. She starts pacing the room, her steps sharp and furious, like she's trying to incinerate the floor beneath her. I just watch, arms crossed, enjoying the show. Skylar stops dead in her tracks, turns on her heel, and just stares at me. Her eyes narrow, and for a second, I think she might throw something.

"Why did you kill both of my dealers?" She asks, voice sharp as glass.

"Why did you let both of your dealers fuck you?" I shoot back, unflinching.

Skylar's eyes flare wide, and I can tell I've struck a nerve immediately. Her eyes flicker with insecurity, embarrassment even, but she swallows it down fast, quicker than I expected.

"Because I was horny," she fires back, her chin lifted like she's daring me to say something else. I can't help but laugh under my breath. That's Skylar for you.

"You're better than that." Her face darkens with annoyance, and she strides right up into my personal space. This is the second time today I've had someone square up to me in my own house.

A new record.

She rolls her neck and plants her hands on her hips.

"I don't need a lecture from *you* about my sex life." She spits.

"I'm not lecturing you, I'm setting boundaries." I step closer, and the move forces her to take a step back, her defiance momentarily faltering. I can see her fighting to regain her composure as she eyes me. "From now on, nobody touches you, but me." The firmness in my voice leaves no room for argument, my authority clear and uncompromising.

"Sorry?" She laughs, her voice dripping with defiance as she tries to regain her space.

"You heard me, Farmer," I say, my eyes locked on hers. I take another calculated step forward, forcing her to retreat. She tries to stand her ground, but every inch of space I close down on her makes her push back. It's instinct. It's power. She's getting cornered, and she knows it.

"You're insane if you think you can tell me who I can and can't-"

"I don't *think*, baby. I'm telling you. This isn't up for discussion. It's a command. And trust me, you'll want to obey." I cut her off.

"You don't control me, Noah. Nobody does." She says. I let out a low chuckle. My God, it's so hot when she says my name.

"Wanna bet?"

Her back hits the wall, and I take the last step, boxing her in. She's trapped between the wall and me now. She swallows hard, looking up at me, but I can tell her mind's racing, searching. Then, out of nowhere, her lips curl into a smirk, eyes flicking around the room before landing back on me.

"Y'know," she starts, her voice still full of sass. "I think the reason you're so insistent on telling me who I can and can't fuck, is because you're insecure." She says, still giving me that little smirk. "Overcompensating with all of this maybe..?" She tilts her head, mocking me, and her gaze flicks to the ropes and hooks on the walls.

I arch a brow, my expression unchanging, though inside, I can't help but be amused at her pathetic attempt to hit a nerve. A slow smile spreads across my face as I watch her.

"Careful, princess," I growl, my voice low and teasing. "You wouldn't want me to have to punish you for that mouth."

"Oh my God. I'm right, aren't I?" She laughs, "you're boring in bed."

I don't respond immediately, keeping my cool, but she's pushing it. Every word out of her mouth feels like a challenge, like she's begging me to prove her wrong. My grip on my self-control is slipping fast, and my thoughts, well, they're not just dark. They're graphic. Filthy. Her little comment about me being 'boring' in bed? She has no idea. I want to fucking tear her apart, make her regret every word she just said; make her beg for the things she's mocking me for. The ropes in this room? They're not for show, and the thought of her tied up, helpless under me, only makes me more desperate to prove her wrong. I can feel it all playing out in my mind: her eyes wide, attitude gone. *Fuck.*

Skylar keeps pushing, her attitude as fierce as ever.

"I bet even *Sienna's* having more interesting sex than you," she taunts, her eyes dancing with defiance. I watch her, unimpressed but intrigued.

"Keep talking, Farmer." I say, my voice deliberately low and threatening.

"It's true," she says, her voice remaining confident. "She told me he held a knife to her throat while they *did it*." I smirk, feeling a dark satisfaction.

"Well, it's cute that my little brother's been playing with knives.." I take another small step closer, pressing her even more firmly against the wall. My voice drops to a cold whisper, "but big brother plays with guns."

I slowly pull my gun out of my waistband, watching as Skylar's eyes flash with confusion and a hint of fear.

"What's that supposed to mean-" Before she can finish, I yank her wrists up, jerking them hard above her head. She gasps, her protest cutting off into a squeal as I move quickly, grabbing the rope hanging from the hook on the wall. I wrap it around her wrists, pulling it tight, forcing her arms to stretch painfully above her. The rough rope digs into her skin, pinning her against the wall with a brutal finality.

Skylar's breath quickens as she starts to show real fear. I slide the barrel of my gun under her chin, tilting her head up so she has no choice but to look at me. Her eyes widen as she meets my gaze, a mix of resilient defiance and dread swirling in them.

"Noah, what are you doing?"

"Feeling a bit nervous now, are we?" I taunt, the gun's cold metal pressing against her skin, making her shiver. Her lips part, but no words come out. I let the gun hover just beneath her chin, the pressure firm but not enough to hurt.. Yet.

"Tell me, princess," I continue, my voice low and dangerously calm. "Did you really think I'd just stand here and let you run your mouth without consequences?" Her eyes dart around, searching for an escape that isn't there. I keep the gun steady, enjoying the way she's forced to focus entirely on me, her bravado crumbling. "Because, *I* think you know exactly what you're doing," I say as I let the gun press a bit harder, making her flinch slightly.

She tries to squirm,

"I don't know what you're talking about. Fucking untie me, you weirdo!" Her demand hangs in the air, but I ignore her plea, my gaze locked onto hers.

"You want me to prove you wrong, don't you?" I taunt, relishing the way her jaw tightens, the fire in her eyes dimming to a wary flicker. The realisation dawns on her; she wanted to push me, to test the limits, and now she's learning just how perilous that choice was.

"That's not-"

"Well here you go, princess. You've got my attention." She struggles against the ropes, but it's futile. The more I talk, the more I see the panic set in. It's clear she didn't expect me to take her taunts seriously, let alone react like this.

"Now, shut that pretty fucking mouth," I growl, the command rough and final.

With one hand still gripping the gun under her chin, I use my other hand to hook a finger into the waistband of her little shorts. She tries to look down, probably trying to gauge what's happening, but I make it impossible for her by tightening the gun under her chin, forcing her to meet my stern, unyielding stare.

"Noah," she whimpers, her voice suddenly small and pleading. The shift from her usual defiance to this quiet, almost mousy desperation is jarring. It's a tone I've never heard from her before, and it's extremely satisfying.

"I thought I told you to be fucking quiet," I remind her, my voice cold and unfeeling. She swallows hard, her breath coming in shallow, uneven gasps. I can see the tension in her body, the way her muscles tighten with apprehension. This is where I want her; nervous, on edge, completely aware of how little control she has. It's turning me on to see her struggle against the ropes, knowing that the more she fights, the tighter they pull.

I lock eyes with her, the heat in my stare making it clear this isn't some innocent game. My scowl's fierce; I'm not truly angry, but I want her to feel the weight of my intent. With a predatory growl, I hook a finger into the waistband of her shorts again. My grip is ironclad, and in one brutal yank, I rip the fabric away from her, watching it tumble to the ground like a shredded trophy. As that fabric flutters down, my thoughts turn feral.

I let my gaze devour her; the sight of her bare skin, so close and so available. The curves of her thighs and ass now fully revealed. Her knickers, a delicate baby-pink lace with a sweet little bow on the front, remain, now the only barrier. I feel like a fucking animal. I take a deep breath through my nose, my jaw clenched tight. The tightness in my chest and the raw, urgent need surging through me are almost unbearable.

I hook my finger into the lower part of her knickers. Slowly, provokingly, I run the back of my finger over her sensitive skin, teasingly trailing along her clit before descending lower. The second I feel how soaked she is, a low, guttural sound escapes me, and I have to swallow hard to keep myself in check.

"*Oh,*" I murmur, my voice dripping with contempt. "Is someone enjoying herself?" I tilt my head, leaning in closer, watching her carefully. "All that attitude, and here you are, soaking right through your knickers." I look down as I trace her again, savouring the way her body betrays her.

I press my finger in slowly, just enough for her to feel the tip slip past her entrance. Her body responds instantly, a subtle shudder running through her as she clenches around that small intrusion. I can feel the wetness coating my fingertip, and I push in just a little deeper, not enough to give her any real satisfaction but enough to torment her. She's fighting it, trying to squeeze her thighs together, but I keep her pinned, my finger still barely

565

inside her, feeling her body tense with every tiny movement I make. Each slow, intentional push stretches her slightly more, her pussy clinging to my skin as I press in just a fraction deeper before pulling back again.

To my surprise, she lashes out, trying to kick me. I have to give it to her, she's fucking brave. Most people would be begging by now, but not Skylar. She fights. Unfortunately, it's not going to work. I catch her ankle mid-kick and shove her harder against the wall with a force that makes her gasp.

Her entire body is now pressed between the wall and my hand, which is gripping her throat tightly, holding her in place. Her back is arched so severely that only her ass and shoulders touch the wall, leaving her torso suspended, tense and exposed.

"Think you're brave?" I growl, pressing down hard enough to make her panic.

"Okay, I get it! Let me go." She manages to choke out. I smirk, rubbing my thumb back and forth slightly.

"You're not going anywhere until I've made my point, baby." I promise.

With that, I press the gun to her lips, it's cold steel making contact with her warm skin. I tap it lightly twice, each gentle knock a clear, unmalleable order.

"Open your mouth for me, princess." I command softly, though the underlying menace in my voice is unmistakable. Her eyes widen, a tempest of fear and disbelief swirling within their depths. As she thinks, her breaths come in sharp, erratic gasps. She hesitates, her eyes locked on the gun, knowing exactly what this means.

Her voice trembles as she whispers,

"Is the gun loaded?" I let out a soft, mocking chuckle.

"Why would I tell you that? I thought you wanted some excitement?" I taunt. Her pale blue eyes plead with mine. The colour is almost unnaturally vivid, like shards of frozen crystal reflecting the dim light of the room. The hue is almost otherworldly, reminiscent of the clearest winter sky just before dusk; deepening into an iridescent sheen that seems to capture both light and shadow, swirling within their depths like ancient glaciers.

As she slowly parts her lips, the movement is cautious yet resolute. I let a dark, satisfied smile curl at the corners of my mouth.

"Good girl," I say, my voice smooth and dripping with smug approval. I realise, in this charged moment, that beneath all the tension and brutality, I am completely, irrevocably in love.

I press the cold metal of the gun barrel against her tongue, feeling the tremor that runs through her. The gun's weight is solid in my hand, and as I slide it slowly in and out of her mouth, the subtle twist of the barrel is intentional, forcing her to feel every inch of it. Each time I withdraw the barrel, I see her breath catch, her throat working involuntarily. As I push it a bit deeper, I can't help but grin as her eyes widen, her mouth struggling to accommodate the intrusion.

"That's it, baby," I encourage her. "Make it nice and wet." I continue to press the barrel further, inch by inch, until she gags, her body jerking against the wall.

I pull the gun out abruptly, the metal slick and shining with her saliva. A glistening trail follows as it slips free from her mouth. She gasps for air, her chest heaving with the effort to steady her breathing. Her lower lip trembles, a result of the force I've been asserting. I allow her a moment to gather herself, observing her with a blend of satisfaction and cold detachment. Her eyes remain wide, shimmering with unshed tears.

in a way that catches me off guard. For a moment, I swear I catch a small, fleeting smile; barely there, but enough to make me pause. She bites her lip, and I can't tell if it's from pain.. or pleasure.

I feel the slick warmth on my hand, confirming what I'm starting to suspect. It takes me a second to process, and it twists something in my gut. I lean down to her eye level, searching for any hint of hesitation, but all I see is the strange blend of vulnerability and something more. She's turned on.
A slow, mocking grin spreads across my face.

"Are you having fun too, princess?" I ask.

As she looks at me, her lips part slightly, but she doesn't say a word. The moment her eyes flash with that wicked, daring look, something in me snaps again. It's like the animal inside me takes over, feral and hungry. I feel it in my veins, pulsing with adrenaline. I want to see her break. I want to watch her unravel beneath me, and I'm not stopping until I get that. With that primal switch flipped, I push the barrel deeper, twisting it slightly, feeling her thighs tense.

Her wetness coats the gun as I drive it in further, the disinclination of her tight body sending a dark thrill through me. I start pumping it harder, a brutal rhythm, each twist purposeful. Her back arches as I force her to take more, the tension in that tight little body making it clear she's fighting to keep control.

"Come, Skylar." I order firmly as I straighten up once again, towering over her. "Now."

As I pump faster, the movements become more intense, her wetness soaks everything. With each brutal thrust, tiny droplets flick off, splashing against my hand and her thighs. The slick sounds of it fill the room, mixing with her sharp breaths and quiet whimpers, and I feel her trembling under me, losing the battle against herself.

Tears mix with the sweat on her flushed cheeks, and she can barely hold herself together as the waves of ecstasy crash over her. A choked cry escapes her lips, her eyes squeezing shut as she tries to hold it together, but she's completely unravelling, coming hard.

"Atta girl," I praise, pumping harder, ignoring her adorable, desperate pleas as they spill from her lips in broken sobs,

"Please, Noah. Please.."

I hold the gun still, pressed deep inside her, sensing every quiver and tremor as her body tries to recover from the orgasm. I don't move, just watch her. Tears of mascara streak down her cheeks, mixing with the flush of her skin; her pretty little ass is squished hard against the wall. Her legs are weak, barely holding her up, and I can feel the slick trickle of her come reaching my fingers. She's nothing but a trembling mess, and the wetness coating my hand is proof of how much she's given in, whether she'd admit it or not. I keep the pressure steady, savouring how she's completely fallen apart, undone, and knowing I'm the one who's done it. I press in a little deeper, just to hear that pathetic little whimper once more.
There's no fight left in her at this moment, she's just a used-up, panting princess who's exactly where I fucking want her.

I remove the gun and loosen the rope, watching her collapse as soon as her wrists are free. I let the gun drop to my side and look down at her. Her eyes are glassy, and her body is thoroughly spent. I lean over, grabbing a fistful of her hair and yanking her face up to mine; allowing myself a full view of her dishevelled state.

"Am I still boring, princess?" I ask, my voice icy and mocking. My grip tightens slightly, pulling her face closer to mine. "Or have you changed your mind?"

To my surprise, she meets my gaze with a bratty sparkle.

"No," she says, her voice sassy and firm, "I haven't changed my mind." With a sudden, sharp move, she snatches the gun from my hand, pointing it directly up at me. The dynamic of the moment shifts as she pulls the trigger with a quick, wanton motion. The click of the empty chamber reverberates in the room, and a disturbingly sweet smirk blooms across her plump lips.

"The gun wasn't even loaded," she says, her voice dripping with a smug, seductive edge. I stare her down and smile along, a dark thrill coiling in my gut.

Fuck, she's good.

CHAPTER 19: PLOT CHANGES

Sienna

The morning light streams through the sheer curtains, illuminating my room with a soft, golden glow that dances across the floor like a warm embrace. I'm sprawled comfortably on my bed, a slight smile curling my lips as I gently cradle Butter in my outstretched hand. She flutters her delicate wings, a mesmerising display of iridescent hues contrasting beautifully against the pleasant yellow of her wings.

My gaze drifts to the dainty gold ring glimmering on my finger; a stunning little diamond that catches the light in a way that feels almost magical. Yesterday, amidst a whirlwind of emotions, I said yes to a future that just days ago I had believed to be out of reach. It's not just a piece of jewellery; it's the embodiment of everything my heart has whispered for so long. Marcus. Peace. A future suffused with the kind of love that feels like home. And as I watch Butter swirl gracefully through the air, I find solace in the knowledge that I am safe, that I am loved, and that Marcus stands beside me; an unwavering pillar in a world that often feels unmanageable.

The door creaks open, and Marcus walks in, the two magical books in hand. He's got that look in his eyes, serious and focused; he's on a mission. Sitting up with an instinctive rush, a smile blossoms across my face. His gaze softens, melting away the seriousness that often cloaks him. With a loving smile breaking through, he approaches me. His glare is soft, full of tenderness. He leans in and places a gentle kiss on my forehead, before moving over to the desk.

"Whatcha doing?" I ask. He picks up Noah's book and starts flipping through its pages carefully; his brow knitting into a frown of concentration.

"His book didn't glow." he says, his voice edged with a hint of frustration.

"That's weird," I say, settling back against the pillows, watching him work. I watch as Marcus picks up his book, his fingers brushing delicately over the latch. For a moment, I become entranced by the rhythm of his movements. His jaw is clenched tight, and his gaze is still. Locked in. Then, the realisation hits me like a bolt. My eyes shift from his fingers to his taut expression, and it sinks in; Oh my god, he's considering opening it again. My heart races wildly, and a wave of anxiety crashes over me.

I can't hold back.

"Don't, Marcus," I urge, my voice tight with worry. He doesn't look at me, nor does he reply. His focus is entirely on the latch, fingers lingering; almost trembling hesitation. The way he's gripping the book, the deep furrows on his brow, it's clear he's wrestling with himself. His jaw is clenched so tightly that it

573

seems he's grappling with an invisible force. Every second feels heavy with his internal struggle, the weight of whatever decision he's about to make pressing down on him.

I get up from the bed, my heart pounding a little. I walk quietly behind Marcus, not wanting to disturb the intense concentration etched on his face. Gently, I wrap my arms around his shoulders, resting my head by his ear. The warmth of my body against his seems to ground him, just a little. I can feel the tension in his muscles.

My voice comes out soft but worried.

"Marcus.. if you open it, we have no way of closing it. Not without Millie here." Marcus hesitates for a long moment, his fingers still brushing the edge of the book's latch. Finally, he exhales sharply and mutters,

"I'm starting to think it doesn't make any difference whether it's open or closed." His words hang heavy in the air, and I feel a knot form in my stomach. Partly because I wasn't expecting that reply, but mostly because I know exactly what he means.. And I fear that he's right.

"What do you mean by that?" I ask softly, even though I already know. The sadness in my voice betraying me. Marcus turns to face me, and I can tell by the way his expression softens that he's seen the anxiety in my eyes. He offers a small, almost apologetic smile before patting his lap, silently inviting me to sit. I nestle into his lap, and he instinctively reaches up to sweep my curls back over my shoulder, his touch delicate. His hand settles on my thigh, warm and solid, anchoring me in the moment. There's something intense about the way he holds me, like he's trying to reassure me, even though his own thoughts seem far away.

Marcus' eyes bore into me with a fierce intensity, their fervour coiling around my heart like a serpent waiting to strike.

"Sweet, if we don't do something, Dean is gonna die." His voice is a low rumble, thick with strain. He takes a breath, as if gathering strength from the air, his grip on my thigh tightening. "I don't think he has much time." He pauses for a moment, swallowing hard, before placing his hand on the book. "And clearly I've missed a piece of the puzzle." The calamity in his tone is undeniable. His frustration is bedlam beneath the surface, like he's bracing for the storm ahead, hand gripping the book like it holds the answers to everything.

Which we know now, *it does*.

I study him, my brows furrowing in uncertainty. My attention drifts to the book, its worn cover obscuring a trove of perilous secrets. *Is Marcus right?* My thoughts whirl, a cacophony of questions colliding, each one more insistent than the last. After a taut moment, I finally whisper,

"Are you sure you wanna do this?" As soon as the words escape my lips, Butter flits from the bed and gracefully settles on the desk beside the book. Marcus and I freeze, our stares colliding in mutual disbelief. We share a look of astonishment that conveys everything. It's like the universe just handed us a sign.

We exchange a resolute nod, our unspoken concord unmistakable. With measured caution, he reaches for the book, his fingertips grazing its timeworn cover. Gradually, he elevates it from the desk, and an electric tension crackles heavily in the air around us. We both know there's no turning back now.

Marcus's fingers tremble slightly as he pulls open the latch. The room holds its breath, and we exchange a tense glance, bracing ourselves for something; anything. But as the latch clicks open, an unsettling silence falls. There's no explosion, no glowing light, no dramatic noise. Just the quiet, still air and the book lying innocuously in Marcus' hands. We stare at it, our anticipation giving way to bewilderment.

That's a good thing, right?
Is that a good thing?

The absence of any immediate danger is oddly comforting, yet the silence leaves me with a gnawing sense of uncertainty. Marcus and I exchange a look, our expressions a tapestry of relief and mild disappointment. We almost shrug in unison, a shared sense of anticlimax hanging in the air. It's as if we had anticipated something far more dramatic, but instead, we're left with a quiet moment that feels almost underwhelming. Deflating.

Marcus starts flicking through the pages, the faint sound of paper rustling filling the room. We both lean in, carefully reading each line, our eyes scanning assiduously, but nothing jumps out as immediately dangerous. When we reach the last couple of pages, Marcus suddenly pauses, his brow furrowing.

"Hold on," he mutters, his voice low. "It's not the same." He slams his finger down on the page, his voice sharp with urgency.

"Look," he demands, eyes wide with intensity. I snap to attention, following his finger to the line he's pointing at. As I start to read, my stomach drops. The story, it's different.

'Despite their fear, the animals fought back valiantly, determined to defend their beloved home..

In the midst of the chaos, the Queen left the safety of the castle, determined to protect the village herself. As she moved through the smoke and fire, the battle raged on, with spells and arrows flying.

Then, just as suddenly as it had begun, the Derpy Dragon faltered, its strength drained. With a final, shuddering breath, it collapsed to the ground, lifeless. The village was spared, but something else had been lost that day.

The King emerged from the castle, surveying the battlefield, the smouldering ruins of homes, and the faces of the villagers; those who had fought, and those who had fallen. Among the debris, the Queen was nowhere to be seen.
The villagers, their faces etched with exhaustion, gathered together in a solemn circle. They joined hands, forming a tight-knit ring of solidarity and shared grief.

His heart heavy, the King led the animals back toward the castle, their footsteps slow and quiet. As the rain began to pour heavier on the village, the King whispered a promise to the villagers and the fallen, that they would always be his family.

Once they passed through the great gates, the King turned and ordered his trusted guard to close them. The sound of wood and iron sealing shut echoed through the village like a sigh. The King's final gesture, his reassurance and whispered promise, seemed to bind the gates with more than just physical barriers.

And so the gates remained, never to open again. Though the village had survived, the King stood at the walls, staring out beyond them, knowing deep within that nothing—no spell, no courage—could change the course that had been set that day.'

The changes aren't just small, they're unsettling, like pieces of a puzzle rearranged into something dangerous. I look at Marcus, concern and stress etched into my face. He's still staring at the book, his breathing quick and uneven. His eyes flicker with disbelief, and he's subtly shaking his head, as if trying to deny what we're both reading.

Marcus begins flicking through the following pages, his movements frantic. One after another, the pages turn, but they're all the same as before... blank. His frustration builds with each turn, his hands trembling slightly as he searches for something, anything, to make sense of it.

"This can't be it," Marcus says, his voice cracking as panic takes over. He flicks through the pages even faster now, his hands shaking. "There has to be something more!"

The implications of the ending, the story's cruel suggestion that Dean's fate is sealed, that there's no way to change it, are sinking in fast. Marcus' eyes dart across the empty pages, as if willing more words to appear, but all that greets him is an endless void.

"We can't let this happen," he whispers, his voice barely holding it together. I watch his panic and try to steady my own racing thoughts.

"Just wait," I say, trying to keep my voice calm. "There has to be a loophole or a hidden message somewhere. A way we can change this."

My eyes stop on a poignant moment right after the battle.

'The villagers, their faces etched with exhaustion, gathered together in a solemn circle. They joined hands, forming a tight-knit ring of solidarity and shared grief.'

"This has to mean something." I say, pointing to the passage. Marcus peers at the text, his brows knitting together in concentration.

"You think it's important?"

"Yes," I insist, my finger tracing the line. "It's right before the gates are closed, and it's a moment of collective action. It might be a clue that we need to do something similar in order to close the book." Marcus squints at the line I'm showing him, not looking totally convinced.

"So.. you're saying we all hold hands in a circle while I close it?"

He's being polite, but it's obvious he thinks it sounds ridiculous. I can't help but roll my eyes a little.

"I'm not sure, sweet. There has to be something else."

"What do we have to lose?" I question. He scratches his head, clearly a little uncomfortable and trying not to shoot me down. I take a few steps closer to him and look into his eyes, hoping to comfort him. "If it doesn't work, we can come back and look for something else."

Marcus takes a huge breath, his chest rising and falling heavily. His face is tight, and when he looks down at me, he tries to force a smile, but it barely holds together. I can see the stress in his eyes, the hopelessness he's trying to hide. He gently cups my face in his hands, leaning in to kiss my forehead, his touch lingering.

"We'll try everything, sweet," he whispers, his voice shaky but filled with forced reassurance. "Everything."

His words are meant to comfort, but the weight of them presses down on both of us. I can see it, he's holding on by a thread; trying to stay strong, even though he's not sure there's anything left to hold onto.

CHAPTER 20:
GIVE IT UP

Noah

There's a certain satisfaction in being alone in the kitchen. Well.. *my* kitchen. State-of-the-art appliances, countertops gleaming, the fridge stocked with anything I could want; and zero interruptions. No chaos, no noise. Just the gentle hiss of butter melting alongside a hefty ribeye that's sizzling away. The enticing aroma of garlic and rosemary fills the air. No bland sandwiches here.

Lunch, done right.

I let it sear undisturbed for a few minutes, the crust forming a rich-brown colour that promises a juicy interior.

As the steak cooks, I prepare the plate. I swipe a small amount of garlic butter over the surface, letting it melt into a slick sheen. I sprinkle a touch of sea salt on the plate, creating a subtle base.

580

When the steak is nearly done, I use tongs to flip it, watching as the other side takes on a deep, caramelised hue. I add a sprig of rosemary and a couple cloves of garlic to the pan, letting their flavours infuse the meat as it finishes cooking.

With the steak cooked to a perfect medium rare, I transfer it carefully onto the prepared plate, drizzling a bit of the pan juices over it.

I reach for the whiskey bottle from the top shelf. It's a familiar weight in my hand. I twist off the cap and pour a generous measure into a glass, the amber liquid flowing smoothly. The sound of it hitting the glass is sharp, distinct. I set the bottle back on the counter with an adept flick of the wrist.

I take a deep, contented breath, letting the rich aroma of the steak mix with the smoky notes of the whiskey. I cut into the perfectly seared ribeye, the meat tender and juicy. As I take a bite, the flavours burst in my mouth; just the way I like it. I follow it with a generous swig of whiskey, feeling the warmth of the alcohol as it settles comfortably in my gut.

Everything's in its right place; the steak is spot-on, the whiskey smooth, and the kitchen blissfully quiet. I'm fully in my element, enjoying this rare moment of peace. I think back to last night, and a slow smirk tugs at the corner of my mouth. Skylar had stepped out of line, pushed things a little too far, so I had to remind her who was in charge. The gun was the lesson. It was punishment, plain and simple. I made her take it, every cold inch and as it spread her, I watched her eyes; the flicker of fear mixed with that twisted, dirty need.

For the first time, she wasn't acting bratty or full of attitude. The cocky confidence she always wears like armour was gone, replaced by something raw and vulnerable. Whether she hated it or secretly loved it, I couldn't be sure, and I didn't give a fuck either way. She needed it, and she had no choice in the matter. It wasn't about pleasure, not for her anyway. It was about control, and I held it tight. I take another bite of steak, washing it down with a heavy swig of whiskey.

Fuck, life is good sometimes.

Then, as if on cue, the pounding footsteps from upstairs rip through my calm. Marcus barrels into the kitchen, clutching that fucking book again like it's about to explode in his hands.

"Hey, I need to show you something." He says, almost breathless, slamming the book onto the counter. I don't even look up. I sigh and stab another bite of steak, chew, but it doesn't taste the same; the satisfaction quickly fading. The flavours that were perfect a moment ago feel dull now.

Marcus doesn't wait for a response. He dives right into it, flipping open the book.

"Look, the story's changed. It wasn't like this before, there's something new here. I'm almost certain we need everyone's help to close it this time." He says. I hear him, but I'm not listening. Not really. I take another swig of whiskey, staring at my plate as he goes on about villagers and loopholes or whatever the fuck he thinks this book is telling him.

But I already know better. Fate's fate. The book's going to do what it wants, and there's no point in trying to fuck with it. You can't change the ending, it's already written.

Marcus starts from the top, reading out the entire story. I don't show it, but I listen to every word, chewing on my steak as he goes on. He flips through the pages, his finger tracing the words like he's cracked some kind of code, before turning back to a specific line.

"Right here," he says, his voice urgent. "The villagers joined hands in a circle before the gates were closed. I think it's symbolic, maybe even literal. If we do the same thing, it'll give us a shot at stopping this before.. before it's too late."

I stand at the counter, chewing on another bite of steak, barely acknowledging him. The silence hangs between us for a second after he finishes. Then I snort, setting my fork down and letting out a low, sarcastic laugh.

"So, let me get this straight," I say, wiping the corner of my mouth. "You want us all to stand around in a circle holding hands?" I raise an eyebrow, waiting for him to hear how ridiculous that sounds.

Marcus hesitates, his eyes darting between the book and me. He knows it sounds crazy, I can see it in his face, but he's desperate, hanging onto any shred of hope he can find.

"I know it sounds.. like a stretch," he admits, scratching the back of his neck, "but what else do we have? This could be something, right?" I take a sip of whiskey, shaking my head.

"You're grasping at straws, man." I lean forward, voice low and blunt. "Fate's already set. This book? It's just playing out the script. You can't fuck with that."

Marcus lets out a frustrated sigh, slamming the book shut but keeping his hands on it.

"Then what, Noah?" he snaps, his voice tight with tension, though it's not directed at me. "What are we supposed to do? Just let it happen? Let Dean die?" He questions. I shrug, not flinching.

"Look, I'm sorry to be the bad guy, but you're searching for answers in a story that's already written."

He stares at me, his frustration simmering beneath the surface, not at me, but at the situation, the helplessness of it all.

"I know it's a long shot, man. I know it's fucking ridiculous. But I don't know what else to do." His voice cracks slightly.

"Then stop trying to control it," I say, my tone sharper now. "If you don't have the answer, then maybe there isn't one."

"But I'm not like you, Noah!" he snaps, his voice rising. "I can't just switch myself on and off. I can't act like I don't care. I'm not built that way." I don't react, just taking another sip of whiskey, my gaze steady on him. He's worked up, and I know this isn't about me. He's pissed at the situation, at how powerless he feels. I've seen it before, in a thousand different ways.

"That's your problem, Marcus," I say, my voice calm, almost cold. "You think that just because you care about something, that gives you the power to change it. It doesn't."

The words strike a chord in him. He freezes, and for a fleeting moment, our eyes lock. It's a difficult truth, the kind that stings not merely because it's harsh, but because it's undeniably real. I can tell he's taking it in, even if he doesn't want to admit it. Silence overtakes us. Nothing but that unspoken understanding, a hard, brotherly moment where I'm not saying it to be cruel; I'm saying it because he needs to hear it. He looks at me, and I see it in his eyes. He knows I'm right.

Marcus just stares down at the book, his jaw clenched tight, silent as a statue. The tension in the room lingers, thick and heavy. I sigh, glancing at the whiskey bottle, and figure maybe it'll loosen him up. I pour a glass, sliding it across the counter toward him. He doesn't touch it right away. Just stares at it like it holds something more than liquor, his eyes narrowing slightly. I can tell he's thinking about something, feeling something; though what, I have no idea.

I wait, watching him carefully. He's not saying a thing, but something's clearly off. After a beat, he subtly shakes his head, a motion so slight I almost miss it. Then, out of nowhere, he grabs the glass aggressively, knuckles white as he downs the whole thing in one go, like it's nothing.

It's more than nothing, though.
Something's eating at him.

Before I can even take him up on it, Dean Douglas strolls into the room, hood up, heading straight for the fridge. He clearly didn't expect to find anyone here and looks thoroughly pissed to see the two of us standing around. I lean back against the counter, exhaling through my nose; staring at him as he scowls.

Oh boy, here we go.

CHAPTER 21:
TENSIONS FLARE

Dean

I trudge into the kitchen, hood up, mind set on one thing, the fridge. I just need to grab something and get out. But, of course, as soon as I step in, I'm met with Marcus and Noah, both of them already looking my way.

For fuck's sake. Here we go.

Marcus has that intense look on his face, like something's eating at him, and Noah's leaning against the counter, looking like he's already annoyed before I've even opened my mouth. Perfect. I pretend I don't see either of them and head for the fridge, hoping they'll take the hint and let me be. And, of course, that was a stupid thing to hope. Silly me for thinking the complex task of grabbing a drink could ever be straightforward. Before I even get my hand on the fridge door, Marcus speaks up.

"Dean, I've got an update on the book."

Great. I grip the handle tighter, already feeling the headache coming on. I inhale sharply, yanking the fridge door open and grabbing a drink. I twist the cap off, already feeling my patience wearing thin. Turning back to them, I take a swig before muttering,

"What is it now?"

Marcus dives into his explanation about how the story in the book changed. I listen, but it feels more draining than anything. The book used to mean something, used to offer a sliver of hope. Now? It's just a reminder that things are spiralling, and I've pretty much given up on it. When he finally finishes, I take another swig.

"So you want us all to hold hands in a circle?" I ask, bluntly. Noah snorts.

"Yeah, that was my response too."

I rub a hand down my face, the weight of everything just crashing in. This whole situation is exhausting. Before I can say anything else, Marcus snaps,

"I'm fucking trying, alright?" But to his surprise, I lower my hand and look at him, dead serious.

"Well, stop."

The room goes quiet. I know it's the last thing he expected to hear, considering I'm the one with a death sentence hanging over my head. I look Marcus in the eyes, feeling the weight of every word. He looks stunned, but I don't care.

"Stop," I say again, harsher this time, though my voice cracks just a little. There's a hint of desperation behind the words. I'm tired of the constant fight. I've given up hope and, right now, I would rather just ignore the problem than keep pretending we can fix it. Marcus looks at me, eyes pleading, the kind of look that digs deep.

His voice shakes as he speaks,

"How can I just stop? How can I sit back and watch this happen?" I see the desperation in him, the fear of losing me. I'm just as scared. But I can't give him the answer he wants. I exhale, feeling the weight of everything.

"I don't know, man. But I can't keep getting my hopes up, only to watch them crumble over and over again." Before I can even finish, Marcus steps toward me, quick and determined.

"We already closed it once," he states. I laugh, the sound bitter and hopeless. I throw my hands out to the side, gesturing at everything around us, like it's obvious.

"Yeah, and look where that fucking got us." The frustration bubbling up in me spills out with those words, and I can't help it.

Marcus' voice cuts through my frustration, sharp and laced with anger.

"What is your fucking problem lately?" He starts. "The grumpiness, the isolating yourself, and walking off the other night at the tunnel. What the fuck is going on with you?" I clench my jaw, feeling my pulse quicken. I don't need this right now. Not from him. Not from anyone. But he keeps pushing, his words striking at the raw spots. "What, you think I didn't notice?" He asks. His eyes bore into me, and I can tell he's hurt, frustrated, confused. But it's too much. He's too much.

I grit my teeth, trying to keep my voice steady.

"It's nothing, alright? You're making a big deal out of nothing. I'm just fucking knackered." The words feel hollow even as I say them, and I know Marcus isn't buying it. He's never been one to fall for bullshit, especially mine.

"The Dean I know wouldn't fucking rest until he worked this out," Marcus says, his voice rising. "You've given up."

His words hit harder than I want to admit. My head starts to blur with the weight of everything, his voice becoming more distant as my thoughts spiral. I'm trying so hard not to snap because deep down, I know he's right. I know I'm wrong for keeping the secret, for shutting down, for pushing everybody away. But my mind is so full of stress, tangled up with everything that's been happening. Noah, the book, the fear of what's coming; it's suffocating.

"Marcus, I-" I start, but he keeps going, his words hammering in my skull.

"It's like you've just decided to roll over and die. What the fuck is going on with you?" Marcus' voice doesn't soften; it sharpens, each word hitting like a slap. He slams his fist down on the counter, rattling the glass next to him. "I'm trying to help you, man. Why won't you let me?" he shouts, and the sound echoes in the kitchen. I feel my pulse spike, the tension in the room thickening like smoke. My head is spinning, trying to keep everything together, but Marcus isn't letting up. His anger is raw, cutting through the air, and I can't escape it. He's right there, in my face, pushing me, demanding answers, and all I can think is how much I want him to stop. How much I want to just shut down and forget about all of this. But he's not letting me.

"I didn't ask for your fucking help!" I snap back, my voice harsher than I intended, but I can't stop it.

"I didn't ask for any of this shit!" I shout, the anger burning through me as I throw my hands up. "I didn't ask to be beaten up and tossed away as a kid. I didn't ask to be dealing drugs on the streets by the time I was fourteen. I didn't ask for you to write that stupid fucking book that's ruined everything, and I *definitely* didn't ask to be stuck here with this cunt!" I point sharply at Noah, who just raises an eyebrow like he couldn't care less. My chest is heaving, and I'm so wound up I can barely see straight. All the shit I've kept locked down just keeps pouring out. "I didn't ask for any of it" The room falls silent, my heart pounding in my ears.

"I never even wanted to live this long." I say, my voice breaking as the words leave my mouth. The world freezes. Every breath feels heavy, the ambience thick with disbelief. Even Marcus, that ball of frustration, stands frozen, as if my words have knocked the wind out of him. His expression shifts, haunted.

"Are we done?" I ask defensively, my voice rough and strained. Marcus' face tightens with anger and frustration. Without saying a word, he turns and walks over to Noah, who's still standing by the counter. Marcus slams the book down in front of him with a finality that's almost palpable.

"Do whatever you fucking want with it," he says, his voice cold and clipped.

As he storms past me on his way out, he halts just long enough to shoot me a burning glance, fury simmering in his eyes.

"What would Delilah think of you giving up now? Huh?" he asks, each word laced with accusation. "Ever stop to consider what she would want?"

He lets out a short, harsh laugh; more of an angry exhale through his nose; sharp as a blade. It's a sound of disbelief and raw frustration, as if to say he can't believe I'm being this selfish.

The echo of his disbelief carves through me.
I know he's right.
And I can't believe it either.

CHAPTER 22:
INTERESTING

Noah

Dean stays in the room for a second longer, his glare sharp, full of anger and blame. Like he's waiting for me to say something. As if everything that's happening is somehow my fault. I glance over at him and shrug my shoulders, indifferent. What does he expect? A cuddle? A pep talk? I've got nothing for him. He shakes his head, muttering,

"Fuck you," through gritted teeth as he storms out.

I lean back against the counter, letting the significance of the moment settle in the air for a bit. Marcus leaving, all dramatic. Dean, doing his whole emo, tortured-soul act. I'm supposed to care, I guess. But, of course I don't. I've got enough shit of my own. I never thought I'd say it, but I actually agree with Dean Douglas. Marcus is running around like a headless chicken, frantic, desperate. It's like watching a dog chase its own tail. He's not thinking straight, just clinging to this idea that he can somehow fix everything if he just tries hard enough. The guy's lost the plot.

My eyes drift to the book sitting in front of me, and I feel a strange sense of relief. It's here. In my possession. And that's where I like it. It means I've got control, not just over the book but over where it ends up; whose hands it falls into. Everyone's so caught up in what the book might do, but they forget the most important part; who owns it. And right now, that's me.

I slide the book off the counter, tossing it up and catching it almost playfully. The weight of it feels good in my hands; familiar. It's funny when I think about it; Marcus and I, the stories we'd written for ourselves, both literally and figuratively. While Marcus was stuck in the orphanage, lost in his own world of fairytales, scribbling stories about animal characters and dragons, I was already knee-deep in the real world.

From a young age, I was moulded by a world of crime and brutality. By the time I became a teenager, I was already living a life of violence and corruption that no child should ever have to know. My book was not a collection of whimsical tales but a detailed record and wish list of my rise within my father's criminal empire. I wrote wishes of how my mother wasn't dead, and how I'd eventually kill my way to the top of the organisation. I detailed how my father would be murdered, leaving me to take his place. Every page was a blueprint of my rise through the criminal world. And it all came true; murder, corruption, and absolute power became my reality.

It's almost tragic, really. While I was groomed for a life of crime and abuse, Marcus was sheltered in his imagination, thinking his minor rebellions and petty crimes made him something he wasn't. He's got a lot to learn, and he has no idea just how harsh the world can be.

I walk upstairs, the book clutched in my hand. The early evening light filters through the windows, casting a glow on the walls. The idea is to head to my room just to put the book away before diving into some work. I'm not planning on sticking around for anything else.

But when I open the door, I freeze. Skylar is lying on the sofa in my room.. asleep. Her chest rises and falls steadily, her expression peaceful, completely unaware that I've walked in. A slow, smug smile spreads across my face. After last night, I figured she'd be avoiding me, or at least keeping her distance. But here she is, asleep in my space, like she's made herself at home.

The thought amuses me. After what I put her through last night, she should be wary, should be thinking twice before being anywhere near me. Yet here she is, asleep and completely vulnerable, in my room. It's almost too easy. Not the smartest move. I thought my princess would know better. She clearly has no idea how easily that could backfire.

But then I catch myself. Maybe she's not as clueless as she looks. Maybe, on some level, she feels safe around me. I can't help but feel a bit flattered. After all, if she really thought I was a threat, she wouldn't have let her guard down like this.

I toss the book on the table, eyes still on her. The smirk remains still on my face as I prowl toward her. I can't help but take in how beautiful she looks right now. There's a fragility to her that I don't usually get to see, like all the attitude has melted away, leaving just this peaceful, serene version of her behind.

As I stand over her, watching her sleep, something unexpected stirs in me. It's rare that I look at anyone this way, but there's something about Skylar right now that makes it hard to tear my eyes away. Her pink hair, usually wild and untamed, falls perfectly around her face, soft and delicate. It frames her like some kind of halo, the strands resting gently against her skin; skin that looks so smooth, almost porcelain in this light. There isn't a flaw to be found, like she's carved out of something more fragile than the world around her.

Her lips catch my attention, full and plump, parted just slightly as she breathes. They look softer now than they ever have, like she's left all the fight behind. There's a sweetness to her in this moment that almost doesn't fit with the Skylar I've come to know; the one who challenges me at every turn. Right now, she's delicate, peaceful, like something that could break if touched too roughly.

I'm not used to seeing her like this. I'm not used to thinking about anyone like this. I've trained myself to ignore that kind of beauty, to see it as nothing more than a distraction. I've spent my life in a world where humans are just tools, commodities to be used and discarded. I've seen more death than most people can fathom, more abuse, more trafficking, more torture. It's desensitised me, numbed me to the point where I don't view people as human anymore.

I grew up in a world where survival was paramount, where the mantra was kill or be killed, trust no one, and never let your guard down. Emotions were a liability, a weakness to be exploited or, worse, a vulnerability to be eliminated. I learned early on to shut them off, to see people as mere functions in a ruthless game, never allowing myself to connect, to feel. They're just moving parts in a machine I know all too well.

I had always despised when my father's men would drag women in for torture or worse. It wasn't part of the game I ever enjoyed, not like the others did. I'd make it my mission to get them out, find the easiest way to give them an out; no matter how slim the chances were. I'd never let them suffer more than necessary, not if I could help it. But it was never about connection. I never pretended to connect with them. I didn't feel anything for them. It was just a matter of principle.

But I'm realising quickly that Skylar is different.

Looking at her now, asleep on my sofa, I'm confronted with a side of her that I've never allowed myself to see in anyone. I realise that I've grown accustomed to viewing others as robotic entities, devoid of real substance or emotion. It's how I've survived, how I've kept myself from caring too much, from losing control. By keeping my own humanity at arm's length, viewing the world through a lens of cold detachment.

For the first time, I can't do that. For the first time, I'm *feeling*. Really feeling. She looks so human to me. This revelation is terrifying. I'm afraid of what it means to actually care for someone beyond myself. It's as if my control, the very essence of what I've been taught to uphold, is slipping away. I understand that I've been isolated from everything that makes life human. Skylar's presence forces me to confront the depth of that isolation, and the facade I've built around myself. It's a new, frightening frontier; one that threatens to unravel absolutely everything I've ever known, everything drilled into my head from the start, everything I've been told to believe.

And I hate it.

I pull my mind back from the tangled mess of emotions threatening to overtake me. The soft hum of Skylar's breathing is the only sound in the room. I draw in a slow, controlled breath, then gently exhale near Skylar's ear, the warmth of my breath stirring her from sleep. It's a technique I've learned. She stirs, her body tensing as she becomes aware of my presence.

Her eyes snap open, and the shock of waking in such an intimate, unexpected way causes her to gasp. Before she can fully react, I swiftly cover her mouth with my hand. I don't mean to hurt her, but the urgency in my grip is unmistakable. Her eyes widen in alarm, and she tries to wriggle free, but my hold is firm.

I keep my hand over her mouth until her breathing steadies, and the initial panic in her eyes begins to fade. The moment stretches taut with tension, and I watch as her frantic energy calms, her breaths becoming more measured.

"Farmer," I murmur with a chilling calmness. "What are you doing in my room?" I hold her gaze as I slowly lift my hand from her mouth, my fingers brushing against her skin. As if in slow motion, I move a strand of her hair from her face, the gesture almost tender.

I watch as Skylar gulps, trying to steady herself before speaking. Her voice comes out in a hesitant murmur.

"I needed a first aid kit." She says. I raise an eyebrow, my curiosity piqued.

"A first aid kit? Why?" I ask. She meets my gaze steadily, her voice calm.

"I've got an injury. I couldn't find a first aid kit anywhere, so I came here to ask you for one. When you weren't around, I must have fallen asleep waiting."

I scrunch my eyebrows, processing her request. Without a word, I walk into the adjacent box room. The door creaks slightly as I open it, revealing a space cluttered with mundane items; an ironing board, various tools, and the first aid kit I need. The sterile scent of the room mingles with the faint odour of dust. I

598

pull open the cabinet, the rustle of the kit's contents against the plastic is faint but distinct. I grab the first aid kit and head back, the door clicking shut behind me.

When I return, Skylar is sitting up on the sofa, rubbing her eyes. I approach her.

"Where are you hurt?" I ask bluntly. She keeps steady eye contact with me.

"My legs." She says. I nod towards her tracksuit bottoms with a curt gesture.

"Take them off, then." I crouch down to the floor, keeping my eyes on her. Skylar hesitates briefly, but then slowly begins to pull down her tracksuit bottoms. As the fabric slides down, the full extent of her injuries is revealed.

My gaze sharpens as I see the gashes and cuts scattered across her thighs, extending down to just below her knees. Blossoming bruises mar her skin in vivid purples and reds. The sight of these injuries triggers a deep, immediate anger within me. They're reminiscent of knife cuts and marks from a brutal fall, and the thought that someone might have done this to her stirs a surge of fury. My hands clench around the first aid kit, my mind racing as I struggle to keep my cool.

I stare up at Skylar, my anger barely contained.

"Who did this to you?" I ask, my voice strained with concern. Her face briefly registers confusion before shifting to a hint of amusement. She looks at me with a touch of irony in her eyes.

"Nobody, you freak," she says, her tone light and dismissive. "I fell off the roof."

Huh?

I blink, completely thrown off. The absurdity of her explanation hits me, and despite myself, I can't help but let out a short, incredulous laugh. It's somehow such a typical Skylar thing to do, yet still completely unexpected. I'm momentarily stunned.

"You were on my roof?" I ask, the disbelief clear in my voice. She nods in response, as if it's the most normal thing in the world. I let out a weary sigh, rubbing my forehead with disbelief and confusion.

"Skylar, why were you on my roof?" She huffs, clearly annoyed by what she perceives as an obvious question.

"I like to climb onto my roof at home to stargaze," she explains, her tone carrying a hint of irritation. "I was trying to find a good spot here, but I slipped and fell onto the balcony."

I'm still processing her casual tone and the absurdity of the situation. My concern for her well-being remains, but the way she's handling it is almost surreal. I raise an eyebrow, trying to gauge her seriousness. Shaking my head, it's still hard to wrap my mind around this bizarre situation. As I start treating her wounds, my movements are precise, almost mechanical. Antiseptic is applied to the cuts, bandages to the bruises; the clinical routine providing a sense of grounding amid the absurdity.

After a few moments of working in silence, I look up at her, puzzled.

"Why can't you just stargaze on the ground?" I ask. Skylar shrugs, a hint of wistfulness in her voice.

"It's not the same down low," she says softly. "I like looking at the stars from high up." Her words, tinged with a subtle sadness, catch me off guard. It's unexpectedly cute and wholesome. Despite my usual stoicism, I find myself smiling slightly at the sincerity in her voice.

As I finish tending to her wounds, I keep my focus on the bandages, my hands moving with practised efficiency.

"I'll figure something out for you," I promise. I pause briefly, "and Skylar, don't ever climb on my roof again." Only then do I glance up, my eyes meeting hers just before I continue. "That's an order." Skylar looks back at me, her expression softening as she nods in acknowledgment.

I stand up, towering over her as she sits there. I look down at her, and for the first time in my life, my first instinct isn't to be cold. It's something else, something softer, and it startles me. It scares me. I'm losing myself-

Ah, fuck it.

Before I can think, I grab her face, fingers pressing into her skin a little too hard, and pull her towards me, kissing her authentically. I crush my lips against hers with raw intensity, and she gasps, startled. For a split second, I expect her to push me away, to fight back; but then she melts into it, kissing me back. The kiss spirals quickly into something chaotic, frenzied; like we're both starved for it, for each other. Our hands grasp at whatever we can reach, and the air between us thickens with heat. It's reckless, unrestrained, like everything we've kept locked away is erupting all at once. Her breath mingles with mine, and the wildness of it makes me feel like I'm on the edge of losing myself; but I can't bring myself to stop.
And I don't want to.

I lift her off the sofa, my hands gripping her ass, fingers slipping just beneath the edge of her knickers. Her body tenses in my hold, and I push her against the wall, the cool surface a contrast to the heat building between us. Our lips never part, the kiss becoming more frenzied, more desperate, like we're drowning in each other.

I trail my mouth down to her neck, tasting her skin, the soft gasp she lets out driving me further. It's messy, unrelenting, my grip tightening as I press her harder against the wall, completely lost in the intensity of the moment. She lets out a sharp squeal as I kiss and suck on her neck, hard enough to leave marks. My hands dig deeper into her asscheeks, pulling her closer, my grip rough and passionate. Her body squirms against mine, reacting to the intensity, but she doesn't pull away. Instead, she grips onto me tighter, her breath coming in short gasps as I continue my sweet assault on her neck, each sound she makes only spurring me on.

She whimpers my name, a sound that hits me like a spark to gasoline. Before I know it, I spin her around and slam her down onto the bed, her stomach pressed against the mattress. My hand grips the back of her neck, pinning her, but she's not entirely still. She shifts beneath me, her movements hesitant; like she's toying with herself. It's not complete submission, but it's enough to stir that need.

With a rough motion, I rip away her underwear, her cry swallowed by the mattress. I spit onto my fingers, then shove them inside her with a brutal, relentless speed. My movements are chaotic, desperate, as if I'm trying to claw my way back into the familiar coldness I know so well. Each thrust is frenzied, a frantic attempt to drown out the unsettling warmth that's threatening to consume me. Her body jolts, her cries muffled by the bed, and I can barely think straight, lost in the struggle to revert to the monster I'm used to.

As she tries to scream and wriggle, I press her harder into the mattress, the rough fabric biting into her skin. My voice is cold, devoid of any warmth.

"Shut the fuck up," I growl, the words harsh and uncompromising. My grip tightens, my movements relentless, as if trying to suffocate any trace of vulnerability that might linger. "Shut your mouth and fucking take it." I order harshly.

I keep my focus on the task, my fingers moving with a relentless rhythm. The wetness against my fingers increases, her reactions growing more pronounced. I twist my fingers deeper, my gaze locked onto the way her body shifts under me. I watch as her hips squirm, her body arching slightly with each movement. Her gasps are muffled against the mattress, and I see her muscles contract rhythmically. Her body's reactions grow more pronounced, her ass jiggling with every thrust.

"Keep still, baby, or I'll make it worse," I threaten, tightening my grip on her neck.

I keep going, in a trance. I lose myself in the rhythm. Hypnotic. Her body begins to shake under my touch, her reactions almost distant. I keep going. My focus narrows to a single point, and my mind goes blank. I persist, each motion driven by an instinct I can't fully grasp. I keep going. Her screams and cries are there, but they blur into an eerie silence, a world where nothing else exists. The sounds blend into a muted cacophony, like static on an old radio. I keep going, the repetition unending.

Then, without warning, I feel it. Her body convulses violently, a signal that she's reached her peak. She's coming. It jolts me from the trance, dragging me into harsh reality. I realise that I'm sweating, my breath ragged and uneven. The sensation is foreign, a visceral shock to my system. I pull my fingers out abruptly, the brusqueness shocking even me. The slap I deliver to her ass is brutal, and it reverberates with raw energy. It's as if I'm merely a vessel for a violent impulse, my body acting on its own accord.

I stand up straight, my body trembling with an unnerving energy. Adrenaline surges through me, but it's not the kind I'm used to;

it's erratic, unsettling. Tingling. My entire being feels charged, electric, like a live wire barely contained. I stare down at her, to my shock, she looks up at me with a flush of obvious pain and subtle satisfaction. Her eyes are half-lidded, her breathing steady, and there's an unsettling calm in her expression, as if the tumult we've just experienced has left her feeling fulfilled. My body feels alien to me. I'm a storm of feelings I don't understand, and I'm desperately trying to shut them down with the only weapon I know..

Cruelty.

I yank open the drawer of the side table, my fingers fumbling slightly as I grab a cigar. I flick open my lighter, the flame hissing to life. The familiar scent of tobacco fills the air as I draw in a long, steadying breath. With the cigar firmly between my lips, I collapse onto the sofa, my body sinking heavily into the cushions. I lean forward, resting my forearms on my knees, my eyes locked on the floor, trying to ground myself. From the outside, I'm sure I look calm and collected. But inside, it's a different story. A tempest of adrenaline and confusion roars through me. Every nerve ending feels alive with a jittery energy.
I draw another puff from the cigar, letting the smoke curl around me, and with a deep breath, I finally force myself to look over at Skylar. She lies there, still and unnervingly silent, her body trembling ever so slightly. The shaking seems approaching deliberate. Her breaths come in uneven gasps, shallow and almost imperceptible, making her seem more like a marionette whose strings have gone slack. I look back to the ground.

We sit in the oppressive silence for nearly twenty minutes, the only sound being the faint crackle of my cigar and the occasional shuffling from Skylar as she tries to find a more comfortable position. The room feels like it's holding its breath, heavy with unspoken words and the residue of what just happened. Finally, breaking the stillness, Skylar whispers, her voice barely above a breath.

"Did I do something to make you angry?" Her tone is laced with the usual sarcasm, a defence mechanism she uses so well. The question hangs in the air, a strange mix of jest and genuine inquiry. It's clear she's trying to keep things light, but there's an undercurrent of real concern.

I can't answer immediately. The question pricks at the edge of my brain. I exhale a cloud of smoke, my gaze still locked on the ground.

"No," I finally say, my voice devoid of emotion. There's a pause, a stretch of silence that seems to stretch on forever. Then, I let out a low, gravelly laugh. "The problem is, I don't think you could ever make me angry, Farmer."

I look up at her then, I don't expect a reply, but she snaps back quickly.

"Why is that a problem?" she asks, her tone moulded with genuine curiosity. I let out a short breath, the cigar smoke curling between us.

"Because that means you're in charge."

CHAPTER 23:
SWEET HEAT

Sienna

It's now 9 p.m., and the tension in this house could cut glass. About an hour and a half ago, Noah ordered pizza; probably his attempt to keep us all grounded in some shred of normalcy. Not that it worked. Everyone ate separately, like we were strangers. We've never been like this before. Fragmented. like a mirror that's shattered but still pretending to hold its shape.

It's ridiculous, really, when I think about it. I was in a basement, practically counting my breaths in the dark, and yet, now? *Now* we're all sulking. And for what? Dean, Marcus, everyone's too wrapped up in their own misery, their own secrets. What are we even doing anymore?

Marcus has been sitting at the window, smoking since dinner. His posture is rigid, a constant cloud of smoke swirling around him, eyes barely open. It frustrates me, more than it should. I get it; he's stressed. Everyone's on edge right now, but the way he just sinks into himself, blocking everything out.. it's making things worse. I cross the room, standing right beside him. He doesn't move or even acknowledge me.

"You've got to get out of this room," I say firmly, but with care.

Marcus exhales a cloud of smoke, barely turning his head as he mutters,

"I'm fine here, sweet." His bluntness stings, but I don't let it show.

"Do you think this is gonna help?" I ask. Marcus just looks at me, his eyes heavy and dark, like he's barely present. He doesn't say a word, but the stress is etched deep into his features; his clenched jaw, the lines on his forehead. I almost back off. But I don't.

"Life is shit, Marcus," I tell him, my voice sharper than I expect it to be. "It's shit, and it's unfair, and it's hard. We all know that better than most." I continue, gesturing to the others in the house. "But I can't keep doing this. I can't keep spending every day in a slump just waiting for the next shitty thing to happen." I pause, hoping something I'm saying is getting through to him.

I'm almost pleading with him now, my usual sunny demeanour replaced with something raw and desperate.

"I owe it to my parents to make something out of this, to live a life that means something, even if it's not the life they wanted for me. I owe them the chance to look down and see me not just surviving, but actually living. To see me not fucking losing anymore." He's listening, really listening now. I take a deep breath, trying to steady my voice.

"If we don't have any unity left in us, if we let this break us, then we're done for." The room is heavy with my words, with the grim reality of our situation. "We owe Dean more than that." He takes a deep breath and gives a slight nod, looking a little more resolute.

"I'll talk to Dean tomorrow," he says, his tone still weighted with stress. I walk over to Marcus, gently leaning in to place a soft kiss on his cheek.

"Do you want to come downstairs with me?" I ask, trying to offer a little warmth despite the chill in the room. He looks at me with tired eyes, shaking his head slightly.

"Maybe in a little while," he replies, his voice quiet. I feel a twinge of disappointment, but I understand.

"Alright."

I head downstairs, hoping that diving into something that brings me joy might also help lift the spirits of everyone else. The clatter of the house is subdued now, but I need a distraction, something grounding. Baking should do the trick. I glance around the foyer, spotting the phone Noah had mentioned earlier. I pick it up, dial, and wait for the line to connect. After a few rings, someone answers with a crisp,

"What do you need?"

"Hi," I say, trying to sound upbeat despite the heaviness of the day. "I need some ingredients."

After a brief exchange, I rattle off my list:

-Butter
-Caster sugar
-Light brown sugar
-Eggs
-Flour
-Chocolate

Not long after, a delivery arrives with all the ingredients neatly crammed. I unpack everything and lay it out on the counter, feeling a bit lighter as I anticipate the scent of freshly baked cookies filling the air. The oven hums to life as I preheat it, and I catch myself softly humming too, my fingers already itching to get started. First, I take the butter and sugars, blending them together until they're a smooth, creamy mixture, like sunshine in a bowl. I tap the egg against the edge of the counter, feeling oddly proud as I crack it perfectly. In it goes, blending in with the sugar and butter like they're meant to be together.

Then comes the flour. It always makes me feel like a little kid, scooping it out carefully and watching it puff in little clouds. As I stir it in, the dough starts to form; thick, golden, and just begging for those chunks of chocolate. I can't help but sneak a taste, grinning as the rich sweetness hits my tongue. Once the chocolate chunks are mixed in, the dough looks absolutely perfect. I grab my spoon and scoop it onto the baking trays, making cute little mounds, all evenly spaced.

I slide the trays into the oven and wipe my hands clean, taking a moment to twirl around the kitchen, feeling lighter than I have all day. The scent of melting chocolate and butter beginning to fill the room, and I can't wait to share this little bit of happiness with everyone else.

I pull the tray out of the oven, the edges of the cookies perfectly set, and the centres just soft enough; exactly how I love them. The kitchen smells incredible, rich with warm chocolate and butter.

Grabbing a spatula, I lift one of the cookies carefully, feeling its warmth through my fingers. I take a bite, the chocolate melting in my mouth, the dough soft and chewy, sweet but not too sweet. It's perfect. A tiny, happy sigh escapes me, and I feel a sense of accomplishment.

As I turn around, still savouring the warmth of the kitchen, I nearly jump out of my skin when I see Marcus standing in the dark doorway, leaning against the frame. His presence, silent and brooding, feels almost spectral, like an apparition that has silently materialised

He's smiling, but not quite. His eyes are locked on me, deeper than usual, like he's seeing me in a way that's both familiar and intense. It's not intimidating, but the atmosphere feels charged, a mix of quiet admiration and that unspoken tension that always lingers between us. I don't say anything. Neither does he. We just stand there, caught in the moment, as if words would break whatever this is.

"How long have you been standing there?" I ask, my voice quiet. Pushing off from the doorway slowly, his eyes never leaving mine, he replies,

"long enough." Marcus walks over, his movements unhurried and knowing. Without saying a word, he places his hands on my waist and lifts me onto the counter with ease. My breath catches as he leans in, pressing soft kisses against my neck, his lips warm against my skin.

"You don't even realise it, do you?" he murmurs against my ear, his voice low and rough. "How much I need you.. how you keep me together when everything else is falling apart." He pulls back just enough to meet my eyes, his gaze intense. I smile softly at him, my heart swelling.

"I love you," I whisper. He doesn't hesitate, his voice deep as he responds,

"I do more than love you, sweet." He pauses, "You're in my blood. Loving you is instinct, but the way I *need* you, that's a hunger I can never satisfy."

Marcus' words hang in the air between us, his voice deep, like a whisper brushing against the heat of my skin. My heart skips, my breath catching as I feel his hands still holding me. I kiss him softly, letting the moment pull me in, but as it starts to heat up, I pull away. I don't want it to end, but at the same time, the cookies are still sitting there, and I can see the flour and sugar scattered across the counter.

"I should probably clean up the mess," I say, feeling a bit breathless. Marcus smirks at me, his eyes dark and teasing.

"Why clean up the mess," he starts, his voice deep and low, "when we could make some more?" I bite my lip, pretending to consider his offer as if I'm weighing the pros and cons. My eyes flicker to the mess on the counter, flour, sugar, chocolate chips scattered everywhere; but in reality, I've already caved. I nod very softly, tilting my head to the side as if I'm still thinking.

But he knows me too well.

And he knows that cookies are the last thing on my mind now.

Before I know it, Marcus' lips find mine again, pulling me into a kiss that quickly deepens. His hands slide up my waist, pulling me closer as I wrap my arms around his neck, letting the moment take me. I feel the heat between us rising, the air thick with everything unspoken, but then, just as things start to get more intense, he pauses.

His breath is warm against my ear as he lingers there for a moment, his hands steady but gentle.

"You're okay with this, right?" His voice is low, careful. I feel a flicker of frustration, not at him but at the situation. I don't want what happened to change this. To change us. I won't let it. I nod against him, closing my eyes for a second.

"Don't be gentle with me," I say, voice firm. His grip stays tense for a moment, like he's still unsure, but I meet his gaze and push harder. "Do what you always do. I'm not fragile, Marcus."

Marcus smiles deeply as his lips brush my ear.

"Anything but," he pulls back slightly to look me in the eyes, his gaze intense and unwavering. "Which is good," he growls, voice rough with satisfaction. "Because gentle isn't really my thing." Before I can respond, his mouth finds mine again, the kiss fierce and demanding. He's unapologetically rough, and I'm more than ready for it.

Without hesitation, he pushes me down onto my back, making me gasp as I find myself splayed out on the cool surface of the counter. His hands are relentless, gripping my thighs tightly as he leans in. His mouth trails fiery kisses up and down my legs, each touch a mix of heat and hunger. I know he can see my scars, but he doesn't comment on them. Doesn't avoid them. He does as I've asked. He sucks and nips at the sensitive skin. I can feel the intensity in every kiss, every touch, as he devours my skin with a fervour that makes my breath catch.

Marcus pulls away slightly, his eyes glinting with a predatory gleam. He looks me over, taking in the contrast between the warm, sugary cookies and the raw desire in his gaze. His voice is low and gritty.

"Looks like I've got more than cookies to feast on tonight," he says, a dark promise in his tone. He maintains a firm grip on my thigh, his fingers pressing in with a possessive urgency. With his other hand, he pushes up my 'nightdress', a simple, oversized t-shirt, exposing my bare skin. His touch is rough, unapologetic, as he grabs my breast, his fingers kneading with a fierce intensity.

Without breaking his gaze, he leans down, biting onto my underwear. The fabric stretches and tears under the pressure of his teeth, and I feel a shiver run through me as he pulls them away. He moves his mouth down, and I shudder as he spits slowly; followed by the sting of his tongue, barely making contact with my clit but sending jolts through me. His touch is calculated, almost cruel in its teasing.

His fingers dig into my flesh, rolling my nipple with a fierce pressure that makes me gasp and whimper; and he begins to feast. Roughly. Passionately. Sucking, licking with raw ferocity. My body responds instinctively. My back arches, lifting me from the counter as if drawn by an invisible thread. Each swipe of his tongue is like a spark that ignites a firestorm within me. The sensation is an electric current coursing through my veins, sending jolts of molten pleasure radiating from my core.

His tongue is a relentless force, tracing patterns that feel like both a caress and a demand. As I arch further, my body responds to his relentless rhythm. My skin feels like it's on fire, each movement a plea for more, my whimpers a soundtrack to the visceral dance we're engaged in.

He suddenly shifts, his demeanour turning fierce and primal. Without warning, he yanks me up, his grip hard and unyielding. I barely have time to react before he drags me toward the stairs in the foyer. The sudden shift sends a jolt through me, my breath catching as he hauls me across the room.

He slams me down onto the steps, my front hitting the cold surface with a harsh thud. I feel his weight press down on me, his hand gripping my neck with a firm, controlling hold.

In a dark, hushed tone, he leans in close, "Now, you have to be quiet, sweet," he orders, the edge in his voice sharp and commanding. "We wouldn't want anyone knowing what a good little slut you are for me. Right?"

He waits for a response, but when I don't immediately reply, he slams his hand down on my ass with a sharp, stinging slap that makes me squeal. The pain is immediate and intense, causing me to squirm. Before I can make another sound, he clamps his hand over my mouth, his grip forceful and unyielding.

"Behave." He warns. I can feel his grip tighten on my waist, his fingers pressing into my skin as if marking his claim. He keeps his hand clamped over my mouth, his fingers pressing hard against my cheek. There's no escape, not that I'd ever try.

I nod quickly this time, not daring to disobey, the tension in the air thick enough to choke on. He positions himself at my entrance, slowly, deliberately, and I can feel the sheer force of his presence. The anticipation claws at me, and then, suddenly, there's nothing soft about it. He presses forward into me, hard and unforgiving, and the sensation tears through me like a shockwave. There's no space left for anything but this moment; raw, consuming, and relentless.

Each thrust is intended, slow but rough, the intensity building with every movement. My body arches instinctively, my senses overwhelmed by the mixture of pain and pleasure, every nerve alight with sensation. The weight of his body, the sound of his breath, the friction; it all blends together, driving deeper and deeper into something primal, something I can't control.

His grip tightens, his fingers digging into my waist, and I can feel him claiming every inch of my body. The rawness of it, the way he commands every part of me, leaves no room for thought; only the burning need that consumes us both. His hand stays firmly over my mouth, silencing the muffled cries that escape as he pushes deeper, rough and relentless.

"Feel that?" He asks quietly. His voice is rough, full of raw possession. "You're mine. Every fucking part of you."

I'm trembling beneath him, caught between wanting to cry out and knowing I can't. His hand presses tighter, stifling the sounds of my struggle, leaving me helpless under his control. The pressure in my body builds, a tension that threatens to break me completely, and he feels it too.

"*God*, you feel so fucking good," he growls. "You're taking it so well, sweet." His hand presses down harder, keeping me silent, while his voice and movements make it clear that he's revelling in how well I'm responding. "So fucking tight. You love this," he breathes, his grip firm. "Don't you?"

I try to nod, my body betraying me, and a muffled moan breaks free from my throat, trembling against his hand. He chuckles darkly, satisfied with the response, and slams harder, his voice thick with authority. The room is filled with the sounds of our movements, the rhythmic pounding punctuated by my soft, muffled gasps as he keeps me pinned in place.

"*Fuck,*" he moans. "Keep taking it like this, and you're gonna make me lose it," he growls, the promise of his own release mingling with his praise.

Every nerve in my body is on high alert as Marcus continues. The relentless rhythm drives me to a breaking point, pushing me past the edge. The intensity builds and builds until I can't hold back any longer. I'm overcome by a powerful release, my body arching and trembling with the force of it. The sensation is overwhelming, a hot, pulsating force that fills me entirely. I feel as though I'm caught in a vortex, being pulled into a whirlpool of intense pleasure that drowns out everything else. The stairs beneath me are cold and hard against my skin. My fingers claw at the steps, gripping desperately.

The pleasure is so powerful it seems to stretch time, each moment dragging out into a prolonged, exquisite agony. My legs tremble, unable to hold me steady as the final waves of release crash over me. My body quivers uncontrollably.

But the pleasure is marred by a sharp, stinging pain. The pain is a fierce, almost unbearable reminder. But I consciously ignore it. The pleasure is what I deserve, what I want to feel, and I concentrate on it with everything I have.

The lingering pain fades into the background as I bask in the aftershocks of pure ecstasy. My body still tingles, every nerve ending alive with the remnants of the experience. The discomfort is just a shadow, an insignificant part of the broader spectrum of what I'm feeling. My focus is entirely on the pleasure, the satisfaction that eclipses the pain, making every ache worthwhile. He leans in, his voice a dark, mocking whisper.

"Already coming, huh? Didn't even wait for permission?" His tone is rough, filled with an edge of satisfaction that makes my skin prickle. "Well, I'm not fucking finished yet."

Before I can even fully process his words, he's moving again, increasing his pace with a relentless drive. The sudden intensity takes me by surprise. Each thrust is harder, faster, and the sensation is beyond anything I could have imagined. My body, already spent and on edge, is thrust into a new realm of sensation. It's as if every nerve is alight, heightened and exposed. Through the haze of sensation, I can distinctly feel his focus and the depth of his enjoyment.

As he reaches his peak, he grips a fistful of my hair, pulling me closer into his rhythm. I can feel the warmth of his release inside me, a powerful and all-encompassing sensation. The moment is a jolt of ardour, spreading through me in waves that mix with the lingering pleasure.

"You feel that?" he growls, his tone cold. "You better take it all, you hear me?"

I whimper his name, a soft, broken sound that escapes my lips as he continues. After a few more intense moments, he pulls out, and I can feel the heat of his come trickle down my thigh, a slow, dripping stream. The sharp edges of the stairs dig into my skin as I collapse onto them, the coarse, unforgiving surface a brutal counterpoint to the intense, throbbing pleasure that still pulses within me.

"Aww," he mocks with a slight chuckle and dirty tone. "Look at all the come dripping from that pretty little cunt." he towers over me, staring down as if to admire his handiwork.

Then, with a swift motion, he picks me up, draping me over his shoulder. He strides confidently into the kitchen, the sound of his footsteps echoing slightly against the crisp floor. The shift from the stairs to the kitchen is jarring, the cool air of the room a stark contrast to the heat we left behind. He sets me down, and I brace against the counter as he grabs a damp cloth.

His hands are steady as he wipes me clean, each motion charged with a dark satisfaction. There's a casual, yet intense pleasure in his gaze, his words a testament to the pride he takes in how well I've handled him. Marcus finishes wiping me clean, his touch lingering for a moment longer before he sets the cloth aside. With a smooth, confident motion, he wraps his arms around me from behind, pulling me close against his chest.

His breath fans against my neck as he begins to press soft, languorous kisses along my skin. Each kiss is purposeful, a feather-light caress. His lips trace a slow, reverent path from the nape of my neck to just below my ear. Each kiss is imbued with a languid sensuality, a blend of devotion and desire that sends shivers cascading down my spine.

"I vow to spend my entire life worshipping you, Sienna." As he finishes speaking, he deepens his attention, his lips now sucking harder on my neck, leaving a trail of heated marks. His touch is insistent, a blend of rough and passionate, as he demonstrates his devotion in the most physical way.

After a moment, he pulls back slightly,

"I should've been your safety," he says, his voice heavy with regret and intensity. "I'll never forgive myself for letting you slip away, my sweet. But I'd die before I let it happen again."

CHAPTER 24:
BAD MOVE

Dean

It's late afternoon, and I traipse into the living room, a quiet sigh escaping me as I notice Delilah, Skylar, and Birdie lounging around. The room feels different, lighter somehow, despite the weight that's been hanging over me. My hood is up as usual, a habit I've fallen into lately, cocooning myself in a shell of solitude.

As I take a seat next to Delilah, I can already feel her eyes on me. She's had enough of my constant gloom, and I know what's coming. Without a word, she reaches over and pushes my hood down, exposing my face to the room's soft light.

I look at her, seeing the mix of frustration and care in her eyes. It's a gesture that cuts through my self-imposed darkness, reminding me of the warmth and support I've been trying to shut out. I manage a small, apologetic smile.

Chapter 24

"Sorry," I mumble, the word carrying more weight than I intend. It's an apology for not just being down, but for letting it affect everyone around me. I know Delilah's been trying to pull me out of this, and her action is both a reprimand and a reminder of how much she cares.

But as I sit there, surrounded by their light-heartedness, a grim thought settles in my mind. Death is literally knocking on my door; every step I take feels like a march toward something inevitable. How am I supposed to enjoy life when I'm so clearly running out of time? The heavy knowledge that my days might be numbered makes it hard to fully engage with the small moments of joy around me.

Am I crazy for feeling this way?
Or are they all crazy for not feeling it?
I guess I should take some comfort in the fact that they don't seem overly concerned. Maybe their apparent ease is a sign that they've accepted the uncertainty of life in a way I haven't. Or maybe it's just a smarter way of coping. Delilah gives me a soft, encouraging look, her touch lingering on my shoulder for a moment before she settles back into her spot.

I glance around at the others, trying to distract myself from the relentless tick of my internal clock.

"So, what's today's conversation, ladies?" I ask with a rasp, as if the words are struggling to escape. Delilah glances up from her spot on the couch.

"We were just talking about Birdie's new lifeguard job," she says. Birdie beams, practically bouncing with excitement.

"So, Dad's rented me a place right by the beachfront. It's pretty sick." She says. Delilah raises an eyebrow, a playful grin tugging at her lips.

"So, does that mean there's room for a sleepover?"

"Sleepover? *Girl*, I plan on throwing parties every weekend. It's gonna be a non-stop scene."

Skylar, sitting with one leg draped over the arm of the opposite couch, perks up.

"But please tell me you're not inviting your snobby private school friends. I don't think I can handle their whole *'I don't do sand'* routine." She pleads, and I agree. Birdie snorts.

"Definitely not. I only plan on inviting people with a personality." I glance over at Skylar, a grin tugging at the corner of my mouth.

"Well, I guess that means Skylar's not invited then." The reaction is instant; Birdie and Delilah both burst into exaggerated gasps, their voices ringing out in unison,

"Ooohhhhh!"

For a second, the tension in me breaks, and I let out a real laugh. It's been a while since I've heard that sound from myself, and it feels.. strange. But good, in a way. The girls are laughing too, the room feeling lighter for a moment. Skylar crosses her arms, shooting me a sharp look.

"I've got more personality than you, Mr. Dodgy Dealer." I let out a low laugh, settling back deeper into the couch, stretching my arms across the back of it.

"Your only personality trait is being a little fucking brat."

She scoffs, rolling her eyes dramatically, but the smirk on her lips betrays her. There's a flicker of something almost like warmth in the room, the kind of energy we used to have when we'd tease each other relentlessly. For a moment, the heaviness that's been clinging to me all week seems to lift, just enough to let me breathe.

It's the first time in days that I've had even an ounce of my usual banter with Skylar, and it feels uncanny, but nice; like I've grabbed onto a piece of normalcy in the middle of the mess my life has become. Skylar smirks, leaning in with a mischievous glint in her eyes.

"How many fingers you got there, Dean?" She starts counting her fingers dramatically, her gaze lingering on my hands. "One, two, three, fo- Oh, shit, I think you're missing a couple. "

I glance down at my hands, feeling the faint sting of her words.

"Yeah, thanks for the reminder." I chuckle. Delilah laughs softly, shaking her head.

"Skylar, you're evil."

Birdie and Skylar's conversation about Birdie's new lifeguard job continues in the background, their voices blending into a low murmur. They're animated, clearly excited about the upcoming changes, and I can't help but overhear snippets about beach parties and new decorations.

My attention, however, is drawn to Delilah. She stands up gracefully and walks over to the other side of the room. Her movements are smooth, almost soothing in their deliberate calm. I watch as she grabs a tupperware container full of cookies. She returns, her movements fluid as she carries the tupperware container like a prized possession. She places it on the coffee table with a soft thud, the lid popping open to reveal a tempting stack of cookies.

"Sienna made these last night," she announces cheerfully. "They're *incredible*."

Skylar's hand shoots out almost instinctively, snagging a cookie with a satisfied grin. Birdie, never one to miss an opportunity, takes three, her expression one of pure indulgence. Skylar can't resist a jab, her tone dripping with playful sarcasm.

"Typical rich kid." She states. Birdie arches an eyebrow, unfazed.

"And *that* attitude is exactly why you're not rich, Sky."

Delilah's laughter is warm, a soft counterpoint to their banter. She turns her gaze to me, her smile inviting.

"Dean, aren't you gonna have one?" She asks. I shake my head, offering a faint smile.

"Nah, I'm good." Skylar's gaze lingers on me with a puzzled frown.

"Why aren't you taking a cookie?" She asks. I glance back at her, feeling a slight tightness in my chest.

"Not really in the mood for one right now," I reply, trying to keep my tone casual. Skylar doesn't let it slide.

"You didn't eat dinner last night either."

"I just wasn't hungry. No big deal."

Skylar tilts her head, then suddenly breaks into an exaggerated, over-the-top tone.

"*Mmm!* Oh my god, this is literally the best cookie in the entire world!" she announces dramatically, waving the cookie in the air. It's clear she's trying to make me feel like I'm missing out, her showy performance a blatant attempt to get a reaction from me. Her efforts are well-intentioned, but they only seem to highlight the chasm between her world and mine. The truth is, sometimes it feels like the end of the world is closer than anyone realises. Everyone's attempts to lighten my mood are earnest, but they miss the mark. Death is knocking on my door, and no amount of cookies or jokes can change that.

I force a chuckle, even as my irritation simmers beneath the surface.

"Very funny." I say. Skylar, still holding her cookie, gives me a sideways look.

"Seriously, what's your deal with not eating? It's just a cookie." Delilah senses the shift in my mood and steps in, her voice calm but firm.

"Skylar, just leave it. Let him be." She says. I glance over at Delilah, her concerned eyes meeting mine. A flicker of gratitude passes through me, and I give her a small, weary smile. I reach out and place my hand gently on her thigh, a silent thank you for stepping in. The warmth of her skin beneath my palm a significant comfort.

Skylar sighs dramatically, clearly annoyed but relenting.

"Fine," she relents. I seize the opportunity to let my irritation surface.

"Thanks for the support, Skylar. Really appreciate the concern." I reply. Skylar's eyes narrow, her tone sharp.

"Oh, don't get all grumpy on *us* now too. Marcus offered to help you, and you wouldn't even let him, so what do you actually fucking want?" Her words hit harder than she realises. My jaw tightens, and I don't reply. I don't have a response. I can feel the anger rising, my patience wearing thin. Delilah notices the change in my demeanour and leans in to whisper softly,

"Skylar shh."

Skylar doesn't relent, her tone growing more insistent.

"No, seriously, what are we supposed to do? Just sit here and mope around? We wanted to help you, but you don't wanna help yourself." The frustration in her voice only fuels my own anger. I feel a surge of heat and the sharp sting of her words. My anger spikes, and I snap,

"Sky, shut the fuck up." She raises an eyebrow, her lips curling into a smirk.

"What happened to tough guy Dean, huh? Can't even finish a game of 'Never Have I Ever' without running off these

624

days." She mocks with a jokey smile. I let out a harsh laugh, the sound almost a growl.

"Yeah, well, believe it or not I'm not exactly in the mood for games right now."

Skylar, undeterred, stands up and shifts closer. Her voice drops into a sarcastic baby tone.

"Aww, is big bad Noah too intimidating for you?" She says. I shoot her a steely look.

"I can assure you, your boyfriend doesn't intimidate me." She smirks, wiggling her fingers in a teasing manner as she edges closer. The playful gesture only heightens my irritation. She inches closer, her grin widening as she continues her relentless teasing.

"Are you *scared?*" As she reaches right in front of me, I bat her hands away, my voice sharp.

"Sky, stop."

She misinterprets my tone and keeps on, her voice dripping with playful mockery.

"Ooo, is Noah *scary?*" I feel my body tensing, my chest tightening with each inch she closes. The space around me feels smaller, as if the room itself is closing in. My skin is crawling, every sound and movement around me amplifying my stress. I'm overwhelmed, overstimulated, my breath coming in short, sharp bursts. I grip the arm of the couch, my knuckles white.

"Seriously, stop," I growl, my voice strained, but Skylar seems to think I'm still playing along. The playful banter, once a welcomed distraction, now feels like an assault. I'm suffocating, each touch and word from her only intensifying the pressure building inside me.

The building tension snaps like a taut wire. I rise abruptly, my movements driven by a storm of pent-up frustration and a suffocating sense of inevitability. With a force I barely comprehend, I shove Skylar. The shove is more than a push; it's a violent expulsion of every suppressed emotion, propelling her backwards onto the unforgiving wooden floor.

The sound of her hitting the floor is like the shattering of glass, a stark and jarring contrast to the otherwise muted room. The impact is immediate, the wind knocked out of her. She's sitting there, her knees drawn up and her arms splayed out, her breath coming in quick, uneven gasps. She looks up at me, eyes wide and brimming with confusion and fear. I stand there, rooted to the spot, as the realisation of what I've done floods over me. My heart pounds like a war drum, each beat echoing the horror and regret crashing through me.

My hands, which moments ago were just extensions of my anger, now feel like foreign entities. They tremble and seem almost translucent, as if they've betrayed me in the most profound way. I feel utterly isolated, trapped in a moment of profound regret, knowing immediately that there's no easy way to undo the damage I've just caused.

"Sky, I'm so sorry-" The words tumble out, but they are abruptly swallowed by a deafening crack. The sharp, clean sound of a gunshot splits the air, and a bullet buries itself into the wall just inches behind my head, leaving a jagged hole and a whiff of burning gunpowder. Dread floods my veins.

I'm fucked.

I turn slowly towards the doorway, my heart hammering in my chest. I know exactly who I'm about to see holding the gun. Noah stands in the doorway, his presence as formidable as a thunderstorm. The gun is lowered but still clutched in his hand, the steel of it cold and unforgiving. His eyes, dark and burning with a righteous fury, fixate on me with an intensity that feels like a physical assault. It's not just anger; it's a tempest of rage and resolve, and it makes my blood run cold.

Noah's voice lacerates through the charged silence, controlled but laced with deadly firmness.

"Put your hands on my girl again, and I'll cut them off," he says, his tone a chilling whisper of menace. Noah's eyes burn. The room falls into a heavy, suffocating silence. I can't breathe. My mind is a whirlwind. Thoughts collide. I'm fucked. I'm so fucked, and rightly so. I can't move. I can't think. Just his gaze is enough to paralyse me. "Is that fucking clear?" Noah's voice rises, sharp and commanding. I inhale sharply, the oxygen burning in my chest. I nod, barely moving.

"Clear."

CHAPTER 25:
RUNNING IN THE RAIN
Noah

The night is still as I mosey down the long stretch of the front drive, my footsteps echoing faintly off the stone beneath me. A low fog blankets the ground, swirling around the edges of the stone path, creeping up the dirt paths and manicured lawns before me. The mansion looms behind, a silent giant, its vastness fading into the murk as I leave it behind. The estate feels endless, the emptiness sprawling out like a ghost town with no life, just shadows and mist. I pull out a cigar, the weight of it familiar between my fingers. I take my time lighting it, watching the orange glow flare up as I inhale the first drag. The smoke curls into the haze, vanishing into the cold air.

The silence is thick. Too thick. The kind of quiet that feels unnatural, like the whole world is holding its breath, waiting for something to break. The stillness presses in on me, heavy, but I welcome it. A chill seeps into the space around me, but it doesn't reach my bones. Not much does anymore. I breathe it in, the smoke mixing with the brume, both lingering in the air like ghosts. I stand there, letting the cigar burn slowly.

Everything's quiet. The trees stand tall and unmoving, shadows cast long and dark across the ground. The wind shifts slightly, carrying the smell of wet earth and old stone, like something ancient, something untouched. The fog rolls across the dirt paths like it's bowing at my feet. There's power in the quiet, in knowing everything around me is under my control. Mine. I don't need to speak or move to prove it.

The silence quickly breaks with the soft sound of footsteps behind me. I don't flinch, but my grip on the cigar tightens slightly. Turning, I catch sight of Skylar, her figure cutting through the mist, her steps light but purposeful as she struts toward me. Or so I think. As she gets right up to me, close enough that I can smell the faint hint of whatever sweet perfume she wears, she gives a slight nod.

"Noah," she says, her voice steady, before continuing past me without breaking stride.

It's calm, almost too casual, like she's acknowledging me without really engaging, as if I'm just part of the scenery. I watch her walk ahead, the fog swallowing her up a little more with each step. I let her have her moment. But as always, I'm never far behind. I fall into a slow, calculated pace, letting the silence stretch for a beat before I speak.

"Going somewhere, princess?" My voice cuts through the stillness, low and smooth, a warning wrapped in calm.

Skylar keeps walking, her back to me as she mutters simply,

"Out." It's enough to make me chuckle, a subtle sound that barely leaves my chest. I take a long, slow puff of my cigar, savouring the taste before crushing it out under my boot. I watch her figure in the mist, each step taking her farther into the night, and my lips curl into a smirk. I take a few steps closer, just enough so she knows I'm right behind her.

"Not at this time of night you're not," I say, my tone smooth but firm, like I've already decided for her. Because I have. She doesn't stop right away, but I know she heard me.

She always hears me.

As she flips her hair with a dramatic sass, her voice dances with defiance.

"I'm not spending another minute locked up in this house. I'll lose my mind." She says. My lip curls into a smirk as I fall into step beside her.

"And where exactly are you planning on going?" I ask, my voice smooth and deliberately casual. My tone is laced with a touch of smugness, knowing full well that the sprawling estate around us is nothing but country lanes and empty fields beyond the gates. She shrugs nonchalantly, her gaze fixed ahead.

"I don't know. Somewhere high up." She says.
A flicker of amusement dances across my face as the pieces fall into place. She's looking for a high vantage point to stargaze. It's a small, almost endearing detail; her need to escape the confines of the house and lose herself in the night sky. I find it oddly charming, this simple pursuit of a celestial view.

If stargazing is what she wants, stargazing is what she gets.

I turn slowly, my boots crunching on the gravel as I head back towards my line of sleek, darkened cars parked near the mansion. The haze clings to the polished surfaces, casting an eerie glow that seems to pulse with the subtle movements of the night air. The car I approach is a black silhouette against the mist, its form both imposing and elegant. As I draw closer, the headlights cut through the mist with a sharp brilliance, piercing through the monochromatic gloom.

I slip into the driver's seat with purposive ease, the leather cool beneath my touch. The engine roars to life with a throaty growl that shatters the night's stillness. I rev it with intention, the sound echoing ominously across the vast estate. With a smooth motion, I ease the car out of its spot, the tires gripping the damp gravel as the vehicle glides forward. The headlights cut through the haze in sharp, slitting beams, creating a serpentine path through the swirling mist.

I drive the car smoothly out of the driveway, the engine's purr a steady companion to the night's quiet. As I ease the car alongside Skylar, the vehicle appears to glide like a phantom through the mist, barely making a sound. I lower the passenger window with a soft hiss and lean slightly across the seat.

Skylar glances over at me, her face illuminated by the harsh light of the car. She lets out a weary sigh, clearly irritated. Without a word, she turns away, her steps resolute as she continues traipsing through the night.

"Get in the car, Farmer," I say, my voice low and teasing. Skylar doesn't even break stride. She glances at me again, her brows furrowing, a hint of defiance in her eyes.

"No," she snaps, turning her head away. "I don't need you watching over me. I'm fine on my own."

"You don't even know where you're going." My voice drips with that smug, knowing tone. Skylar quickens her pace, her chin tilted defiantly upward, that familiar stubbornness igniting within her as she strives to prove a point.

"I'll figure it out," she retorts, her voice resolute yet tinged with a trace of uncertainty.

Chapter 25

The thing I love is that she genuinely believes that. She has that reckless confidence, the kind that would probably land her somewhere eventually, even if she had no fucking clue where she was going. Odds are, being the obstinate person she is, she'd find a spot; might even be a good one.

But unfortunately for her, there's no way I'm letting her walk out here alone in the middle of the night. Not even on my estate. Not anywhere.

"If you don't get your pretty little ass in the car right now," I say, voice low and steady, "I'll come out there and drag you in myself." Skylar stops, turning to look at me with a raised brow, her face saying *'Really?'*. She thinks I'm being dramatic, but I'm dead serious. "Don't think I won't," I add, not breaking eye contact.

"I'll set your fucking car on fire." She snaps.

Hot.

When she still ignores my instruction, I turn the wheel abruptly, the car lurching forward just enough to cut her off, forcing her to stop. The tires grind against the dirt path, kicking up small stones. She spins around, eyes blazing with anger.

"Are you fucking crazy?" she shouts, fury spilling out as she glares at me. I don't rush. She knows I won't back down. I just let a slow, calculated smile stretch across my lips.

"I think you already know the answer to that." I reply, my voice smooth as glass.

She stands there for a moment, staring at me like she's weighing her options, the defiance still simmering in her eyes. Then, slowly, she does that little move; her tongue sliding across her top teeth in frustration, like she's biting back a string of curses. I just sit there, watching her fight it out with herself. And then, as

I knew she would, she turns with a huff and pulls open the passenger door. Without a word, she slips into the seat beside me, the car door shutting with a solid thud.

I settle back into my seat, one hand casually gripping the top of the wheel. The other rests on the gearshift, fingers drumming lightly.

"Good girl," I mock, my tone considered, almost purring. "See, baby? That wasn't so hard." I let the words linger in the air, the smirk on my face barely visible but unmistakable. Skylar doesn't say a word. She just shoots me a look of pure annoyance before turning her attention to the window.

I flick the car back into gear, my fingers barely touching the steering wheel as I guide it with a smooth, practised roll of my palm. The wheels hum against the gravel, the sound slicing through the night.

As the car lurches forward, I glance over at my princess, her profile illuminated by the headlights. A sliver of moonlight catches her face, revealing her tight-lipped irritation. I can't help but chuckle softly, the sound blending with the growl of the engine. With a final roll of the wheel, I turn the car onto the darkened road, the landscape outside merging into a blur of shadow and fog. The night stretches out ahead, and I drive into it.

I cruise in silence for a while, the roar of the engine slicing through the stillness of the night. The road unfurls ahead, and I press the pedal, pushing the car into a blur of speed. The headlights cut through the dense mist, illuminating the path with a stark, penetrating glow. Skylar's presence beside me is a mix of calm defiance and quiet amusement. She occasionally grabs the side handles, her fingers gripping them tightly during sharper turns or sudden accelerations.

After about ten minutes, she breaks the quiet.

"So, where exactly are you taking me, anyway? Or is this some sort of kidnapping plot?" Her voice is light, laced with playful sarcasm. I cast a sidelong glance at her, a smirk tugging at the corners of my lips.

"You wanna stargaze, we stargaze." I say, matter of fact. Skylar's eyes dart to me for a moment, and I catch a glimmer of a cheeky smile tugging at her lips. She tries to mask it, but I can see the satisfaction in her expression. She leans back in her seat, her posture relaxing slightly as if my words have validated her desire.

After almost two hours of driving through quiet roads and dense trees, the road begins to open up. I ease the car to a halt in a large, secluded clearing right at the edge of a cliff. The forest encircles the space like a protective barrier, the trees towering high and casting deep shadows around us. The cliff drops sharply beyond the clearing, offering an unobstructed view of the night sky, where stars are scattered like diamonds across a velvet canvas.

I shift the gear into neutral and kill the engine, the sudden silence contrasting sharply with the previous roar. The only light comes from the moon, which bathes the clearing in a soft, eerie glow. I step out of the car, my movements smooth and headstrong, and look back at Skylar.

She exits the vehicle, her eyes scanning the vast, open space before her. The edge of the cliff looms ahead, but the forest provides a natural barrier, keeping the view both stunning and secure. I lean against the car, watching as Skylar takes in the scene. Her expression shifts from curiosity to something softer; a mix of appreciation and contentment.

Her eyes widen slightly, reflecting the myriad of stars above. She looks up at the sky, a gentle, almost breathless awe in her gaze. The glow from the distant stars casts a delicate sheen on her face, highlighting her piercing, ice-blue eyes that are now softened by the night's splendour.

Her usual careless attitude seems to melt away in the presence of such beauty. It's as if she's momentarily lost in a world far removed from the one we've been navigating. The way she stands, with her head tilted back slightly and her eyes locked on the vast, glittering expanse, speaks volumes. For a moment, she's just a girl, spellbound by the sheer magnificence of the universe.

I remain still, observing her with a quiet fascination. There's something enchanting about watching her like this.

"Is this to your liking, princess?" I ask. She turns her gaze away from the heavens and looks at me. Her eyes, though still shimmering with starlight, carry a subtle smile.

"It'll do," she replies, her tone carrying that familiar sarcastic edge but tempered by the quiet wonder that still lingers in her voice. She doesn't need to say more. The way her eyes instantly dart back to the sky, the way her body seems to relax in this place, tells me all I need to know. This moment, this place; it's exactly what she was looking for.

Skylar slowly lowers herself to the ground, lying flat on her back in the middle of the open space. Her eyes stay fixed on the sky as if she's trying to memorise each star. I stand there, hands in my pockets, watching her; content in her own little world. She turns her head slightly, glancing over at me.

"So, are you gonna join me," she says with a hint of playful teasing in her voice, "or just watch over me like a creep?"

Chapter 25

A low chuckle escapes my lips, but I don't move. I just keep staring down at her, a calm admiration flickering in my chest. She rolls her eyes and looks back up at the sky, her lips curling into a half-smile.

"Ahh, I get it," she sighs, shaking her head slightly. "You're too cool for fun." I let out a loud, exaggerated sigh, playing along with her little jab, before stepping toward her. It's not that I mind, but I like making her think it's more of a hassle than it is.

I settle down beside her, the ground solid beneath me. The world feels still, untouched, save for the faint rustling of trees swaying in the breeze, the distant call of an owl, and the rhythmic chirping of crickets. The quiet presses in, the kind that's thick with space; where the silence speaks louder than words.

Above, the sky is a jagged expanse of obsidian, dotted with fractured shards of starlight. Each one pulses faintly, distant but alive, shimmering through the fog that clings to the edges of the horizon. The stars provide little respite from the void that seems to swallow everything. It's the kind of night sky that makes you feel small, insignificant under its vastness, like you're standing on the edge of something unfathomable.

The moon hangs, not just in the sky, but like a weight pressing on the world; an ancient eye, cold and watchful. Its light dominates the night, washing the landscape in pale luminescence, sharp and cold like the gleam of steel. The stars struggle to compete. It's sharp, cutting through the darkness like truth slicing through lies; yet so soft, so lenient. There's something unnerving about it tonight, something eternal, like it's seen a thousand lives begin and end and will see a thousand more. It hangs there, full and unapologetic, as if daring the night to swallow it. But the night can't. No matter how thick the dark, the moon pierces through, exposing everything. Bone-deep. a ghost's caress; soft, but full of weight, carrying every secret ever whispered under its watch, every glance exchanged in the shadows. And tonight, it feels personal, as if it knows.

The moon doesn't hide.
It bares all.

I point up at the sky.

"See that?" I start, cutting through the quiet. She follows my finger.

"Yeah," she answers, her voice soft beneath the moonlight.

"That's Saturn," I share. Her laughter bubbles up, light and genuine.

"Nerd." The word dances across the silence, a playful jab that catches me off guard, a smile tugging at my lips. She turns her head, curiosity glinting in her eyes. "How do you know that?" She asks.

I shrug, my gaze still fixed on the sky.

"I don't know. I've always quite liked astronomy." It's a simple truth, but in the moon's harsh light, it feels like more than that. To me, it feels almost monumental, sharing something so trivial about myself. I've never had anyone in my life who knew me on any kind of a personal level; not even my father. It's like I'm revealing a deep, dark secret. It's strange because, in reality, it's just a hobby. Something pretty mundane.

"Well, you learn something new everyday."

As I watch her, taking in the night's spectacle, I'm struck by a sudden clarity. This is real. I'm here. Down on the grass, looking at the stars with a girl who's quickly woven herself into the fabric of my existence. So unexpectedly important to me. Sharing something so simple and human, yet so profoundly different from anything I've ever known.

"Skylar," I start. "Why don't you hate me?" The question escapes my lips before I can second-guess it. Skylar turns to me, her pale blue eyes reflecting the soft luminescence of the moon. There's a genuine tenderness in her gaze, something that catches me off guard. A gentle smile curves her lips, and she says,

"I do," her tone light and teasing. For a moment, we both laugh. Genuinely laugh.

As the laughter fades, we turn to face each other once more.

"I mean it," I say. "After all the things I've done, why don't you hate me?" Her eyes hold a quiet vulnerability, and her smile is timid, small but sincere. The soft moonlight highlights the delicate curve of her lips as she answers,

"Because I'm broken too." The words linger in the night, a fragile confession that deepens the stillness around us. She pauses, then continues, "because I've also gone through life playing a role I never really wanted to play." There's a delicate pause as we both absorb her words.

"You make it really fucking hard to stay in character, Farmer." I admit, my voice a low growl, laced with frustration and something like reluctant admiration. I can see the way my admission affects her, a flicker of joy crossing her features. It's not just that she's unsettled my carefully maintained facade; it's that she's done it with an unexpected ease, peeling back layers I thought were impenetrable. The night feels charged with a raw honesty, the distance between us shrinking with every breath. She glances away, her eyes shifting back up to the star-studded sky. There's a moment of silence as she absorbs my words, her posture relaxing slightly. I see a new edge in her expression; contentment, or maybe even relief.

We lie there, side by side, lost in conversation as the stars shift subtly across the sky. Our talk drifts from light-hearted banter to deeper revelations, the line between flirting and genuine connection blurring effortlessly. Her laughter punctuates the night air, and each shared glance feels like a thread weaving us closer together.

Hours pass in this intimate dance, our words and touches blending with the tranquil backdrop of the universe. After a while, I notice a change in the sky. The stars that once twinkled brightly are gradually obscured by a blanket of clouds, their dark mass creeping in from the horizon. The atmosphere grows heavier, and the once-clear expanse begins to take on a greyish hue. Skylar, too, seems to sense the shift. She glances up, as the first wisps of clouds drift across the sky.

"Looks like we've got company," she says.

Tiny droplets start to fall, the first hints of rain catching the edge of the moonlight. I feel the light patter against my skin, and then a few more drops hit, quickly turning into a steady drizzle. I sit up and stretch, my clothes beginning to cling uncomfortably to my skin. I glance over at Skylar, who's still seated now too; her head tilted back, letting the raindrops cascade over her.

"Come on, let's get going," I say, standing up and offering my hand to her. She stays put, her eyes closed as she revels in the sensation of the rain.

"But this is fun," she replies, her voice light and carefree. I shake my head with a wry smile,

"You'll catch a cold if you stay out here like this." She looks up at me, her eyes reflecting the raindrops, but she doesn't move; almost captivated by the rain.

"That's a myth," she says with a small, defiant smile. I shake my head, half-amused and half-exasperated.

"Come on, princess." I say, trying to keep my tone firm.

"No," she replies, disobediently.

I step closer and gently but insistently pull her to her feet. I start striding towards the car, rain dripping from the tips of my hair and soaking through my clothes. She resists, her feet stubbornly planted.

"I'm not moving," she declares, crossing her arms, her voice resolute even as the rain grows heavier; droplets cascading down her face and shoulders.

I halt and turn back, the rain now pouring down steadily, creating a curtain of droplets around us. I can see the raindrops clinging to her lashes and the soft, defiant smile playing on her lips.

"We can't stand here all night" I insist, my voice raised to cut through the relentless sound of the rain. "Get in the car." We stand there, locked in a silent standoff, our gazes holding each other's despite the downpour. The rain coming down in a torrential cascade that blurs the world around us. The sky is an expanse of relentless grey, and each drop feels like it's racing to join the flood gathering around our feet.

Her pastel-pink hair is plastered to her forehead, and water streams down her cheeks, but the playful smile never fades. There's a spark of challenge in her eyes, as though she's daring me to do something about it. I can't help but be impressed by her stubbornness, even as the rain soaks through.

The torrential rain continues its unrelenting descent, drumming loudly against the roof of the car and the ground beneath us. I realise that if I want to get her into the car, I'm going to have to take matters into my own hands. I take a few intentional, yet subtly quiet steps toward her, trying to close the distance without startling her.

Just as I'm close enough to reach out and grab her, Skylar takes one large, premeditated step backward, her eyes still locked on mine, her mischievous grin widening as she dances just out of my reach. I feel a laugh bubbling but keep my expression firm.

"Alright, that's enough." As I hold my ground, her gaze drifts momentarily toward the dense forest beside us. Before she can make a move, I catch her intent and cut in sharply, "Don't even think about it, Farmer."

Her eyes flicker back to me, the playful challenge momentarily replaced by a flash of contemplation. I step closer, letting the weight of my warning hang heavy in the air.

"If you try to run, there will be consequences. I'm not playing games anymore."

The rain pelts down with increasing intensity, the droplets blurring the edges of the world around us. The forest stands in stark contrast to the storm, a tempting escape, but I'm resolute. My tone is firm and unyielding, making it clear that there's no room for negotiation. Skylar's smile fades slightly, but her eyes still hold a glint of mischief, tempered by the seriousness of my warning.

She doesn't obey.
She runs.

I stretch out a hand, trying to catch her, but she's already out of reach, her laughter mingling with the roar of the rain. She disappears into the dense undergrowth, leaving me standing in the storm, drenched and momentarily stunned. I pause for a moment, rubbing my jaw with a mixture of frustration and intrigue. The rain continues to hammer down around me, a relentless downpour that soaks me through.

Okay, princess.
You run, I hunt.

I take a deep breath, shaking off the water, and start moving toward the forest. The rain splashes around me, a veil of atmosphere, but I maintain a steady pace, my movements deliberate against the storm's fury. My eyes lock on the dark silhouette of the trees, which seem to swallow her presence whole. The forest's shadows deepen, becoming an ominous labyrinth where she's chosen to hide.

There's no rush in my approach. I walk steadily, the rain cascading off my shoulders and dripping from the strands of hair, hanging in front of my eyeline. The forest looms ahead, its dark, tangled branches reaching out like twisted fingers, beckoning me into its depths. I hear her footsteps, a distant echo through the dense foliage. The sound is faint but clear. A mere whisper compared to the storm's roar, but it's enough to guide me.

I move through the rain, my face set in a focused expression, every muscle in my body attuned to the hunt. The air is cool and thick with moisture, each breath I take mingling with the midnight chill. My eyes are sharp, scanning the shadows for any hint of her presence; the rain lashing against my skin. I catch glimpses of movement in the periphery; quick flashes of her silhouette darting between the trees. Her flight is desperate, but the darkness and the downpour make her elusive. Every now and then, a splash of water or a snapped twig betrays her position, but I only quicken my pace slightly, never breaking my steady, calculated stride.

The forest grows denser as I push deeper. My senses are heightened, attuned to every sound, every shift in the shadows. She's moving faster now, but so am I, the thrill of the pursuit sharpening my focus. Suddenly, I catch a clearer sight of her; a fleeting shadow against the dark green of the trees. I adjust my path, drawing closer, the distance between us narrowing.

I stop next to a particular tree, its gnarled trunk slick with rain. The forest around me is a dark, rain-soaked expanse, but In the darkness, I notice a stray, pink hair. She's hiding behind this very tree, her breath a faint shudder. A slow, dark smirk curls on my lips as I stand facing the trunk, my body casting a looming shadow. The rain hisses around me.

"I know you're there, my princess." I say, my voice low and smooth, dripping with a predatory edge. "I can hear your heartbeat."

I shift slightly, my face close to the rough bark. My voice is a whisper, intentionally distorted by the wood between us, creating an eerie, intimate proximity.

"Come out and face me," I taunt, my voice a velvety purr that slashes through the storm. "Or should I come around and pull you out?" I continue, my voice dripping with a cruel, seductive promise. I pause, letting the words linger in the rain-soaked air, relishing in the silence that follows. The anticipation crackles like electricity between us, and I can almost feel her trembling just out of sight. I smile, savouring the thrill of knowing she's so close, so vulnerable.

"Are you scared, Skylar?" I ask, my voice a low, predatory whisper. No reply. "Do you want to know what I'm gonna do to you when you finally come out of your little hiding spot?" I wait, the darkness and the storm swirling around us, my eyes fixed on the wet strands of pink hair creeping around the tree trunk.

I lean in, pressing my face close to the rough bark, the cold, wet air mixing with my breath.

"I'll make sure every second of your fear is stretched out until you're begging for it to stop." I let my fingers trace the grooves of the tree, the sensation cold and almost comforting against the dark intent simmering beneath. "I'm going to savour every fucking moment of this," I continue, my voice now a cold whisper that wraps around her like a noose.

My hand grips the tree tighter, as if holding onto the thrill of the hunt.

"You're hiding now, but soon, I'll have you right where I want you," I say, my voice a dangerous, dark caress. "And when I do get my hands on you..." I let the words hang, dripping with malevolent intent. "I'll make sure you never forget what it means to run from me."

I press against the tree, the rain streaming down in relentless sheets, drenching everything around us. The storm's fury is nothing compared to the dark anticipation crackling in the night. Her fear is a tangible thing, seeping through the rain, guiding me.

"So what's it gonna be, baby?" I growl, my voice a low, dangerous rumble. "Are you going to come out and face me, or am I going to have to drag you from your little sanctuary?"
The sky is a roiling, black sea, unleashing its fury. It pours from the heavens like a thousand vengeful eyes, watching, waiting. I clench my jaw, the tension in my muscles mirroring the storm's ferocity. My patience is wearing thin, the seconds stretching like a taut wire.

"You have five seconds, Farmer." I say, my voice harsh and edged with a dangerous finality. "I'm starting to lose my patience."

I count down, my tone dropping to a low, threatening whisper.
"Five.. four.. three.." The rain continues its relentless assault, each drop a small, insistent drumbeat, driving the tension higher. "Two... one..."

At the final count, her tiny figure emerges from behind the tree, stepping into the open, drenched. I let my eyes rake over her, noting how her soaked top clings to every curve with a transparency that leaves little to the imagination. Her eyes lift to meet mine, wide and glistening, the storm's reflection dancing in their depths. There's a mixture of guilt and resignation in her stare.

I take a slow, menacing step toward her, the mud squelching underneath me. As I take a step closer, I notice her shuffling back, trying to put some distance between us. Not happening. My reaction is immediate and ruthless. I close the distance in an instant, my hand shooting out and grabbing her by the throat. The grip is ironclad, merciless. I slam her against the tree, the rough bark biting into her back as the impact jolts through her. Her eyes widen in shock and fear, her breath coming in shallow, ragged gasps.

"You think I'm gonna let you keep running from me?" I hiss, leaning in close. "You should be begging for fucking mercy right now." I feel her chest heaving against my grip, her breaths coming in strained gasps. "Does it make you wet, knowing that I control your breath, your life?" I can feel her struggling, her body pressing harder against the tree as she tries to pull away.

"Be a good little girl, Skylar." I continue, my fingers digging deeper into her flesh, restricting her airflow. "Beg me to stop."

Her eyes are wide, pleading, but the words she wants to scream are choked off by my unyielding grip. I can feel her desperation, her inability to beg me as I've commanded. The realisation only deepens the cruel satisfaction I find in her helplessness.

"Look at you," I say, my voice dripping with disdain and mockery. "You can't even beg, can you? Too weak to even form the words. And I haven't even fucking started." I maintain my grip a moment longer, savouring her futile struggles and the shiver that runs through her. "You might think you're a big girl with that sharp mouth of yours when you're out there, showing off in front of everyone else. But I'm not everyone else, princess."

Then, without warning, I release her throat with a rough shove, watching as she gasps for air, her breath coming in ragged, uneven bursts. In one fluid motion, I haul her up over my shoulder. Her body shifts and adjusts, the wet fabric of her clothes clinging to me. With her draped across my shoulder, I begin to walk back towards the car, the rain slashing against us in a relentless cascade.

As she struggles on my shoulder, her movements are fierce and driven by desperation. She pounds my back with surprising force, her kicks and wriggles intense enough to make me feel her frustration. Despite the strength and energy she puts into her attempts to break free, her resistance is nothing compared to the iron grip I have on her. A wild storm against an immovable mountain.

With a cold smirk, I decide to make her discomfort even more palpable. I lean in and sink my teeth into her exposed thigh, the bite sharp and unmistakable. Her body tenses and jolts, and I relish the way she reacts to the sudden, intense sensation.

"Keep it up." I threaten.

I reach the car, the open space around it now drenched through by the relentless downpour. The rain cascades off the edges of the car, pooling into muddy puddles beneath it. With her still draped over my shoulder, her struggles having subsided to occasional, exhausted twitches, I stop beside the car. The water running in rivulets off the roof.

"Now, let's see how much you can really endure." I say, my tone a menacing promise.

With a swift, forceful movement, I slam her down onto the car's bonnet. The metal is slick and cold beneath her. Her body hits with a sharp thud, and the sound of her startled yell pierces through the storm. The impact reverberates up my arm, but her reaction, pure, unfiltered, sends a thrill through me.

The rain pours over us, relentless, soaking into her skin, her clothes translucent and plastered to her body. I keep her pinned there, one hand pressing down hard on the back of her neck, forcing her to stay face down against the car.

"Scream all you want," I growl, leaning over her, my mouth close to her ear. "No one's gonna hear you, sweetheart. Not out here." The scream that tore from her lips was satisfying, but it's her silence now, her stunned, breathless surrender, that really does it. "Go on, scream louder for me."

I press down harder, feeling her body tense beneath me. With a chilling calm, I grip the waistband of her shorts, ripping them down with disturbing ease. The sound of fabric tearing is sharp in the air, and her body jolts in shock. I let out a dark chuckle, my hand grazing her exposed skin as I toss the scraps of clothing aside like they're nothing.

"You fucking prick!" she spits, her breath ragged as she tries to push back against the fear tightening in her chest.

"That's not very polite, princess." I reply coolly, my voice dripping with dark amusement. "You should know by now that I'm not one to tolerate disrespect."

I look down at her, my gaze sweeping over her drenched, vulnerable form. The rain cascades relentlessly, soaking her to the bone, each drop clinging to her curves and tracing a path down her body. Her hair, once perfectly styled, now falls in wet, tangled curls, sticking to her back and shoulders. The rain trickles down from her body, streaking down the car bonnet. Her skin glistens under the downpour, each droplet accentuating the curve of her spine and the swell of her hips. The car bonnet beneath her is slick with rain, making her every movement a slippery, tantalising sight.

I spread her legs apart, the wet fabric of her clothing now discarded on the ground, leaving her exposed to the elements and to me. I position myself at the entrance of her pussy. Leaning in close, my voice drops to a low, sinister murmur, meant only for her ears.

"Any last words?" I ask, my breath warm against her cold skin.

"Fuck you." She whispers.

With that, I begin to ravage her.

I thrust into her forcefully. Her tight cunt stretching around my length. Her body tenses and she lets out a strangled gasp, her fingers scrabbling for purchase on the slick metal of the car hood. I give her no time to adjust, setting a punishing pace as I slam into her again and again. The rain lashes down around us, each droplet stinging against my skin as I drive into her mercilessly. I can feel her resistance, her muscles clenching around me as if trying to push me out. But I'm unyielding, my pace brutal and unforgiving. The car rocks beneath us, creaking in protest with each forceful thrust.

Her screams pierce through the night air, mingling with the storm, a haunting symphony of pain and surrender. My hands roam with a dark satisfaction, feeling her shudder with every powerful movement before I pin her face against the car with a bruising force.

"Try to run now, princess." I taunt. I let a stream of spit fall onto her back, the warmth mingling with the rain. The act is intentional, meant to further degrade and break her down.

Chapter 25

I drive deep, each thrust calculated, slow, a haunting rhythm in the night. I'm relentless, carving my path with a measured intensity. Her gasps, raw and fragmented, dance in the dark. The downpour slicks her skin, a translucent sheen that glistens under the dim moonlight, each droplet cascading down her spine like a cruel, mocking caress.

"Keep struggling if you want," I taunt softly. "It'll give me a reason to push harder." My hands grip her with an almost reverent force, fingers digging into her flesh as if to imprint my mark, to brand her with my presence.

Leaning in close, I murmur in a low, menacing tone,

"How's this feel, princess? You like that?" I pull back slightly, teasing her before plunging back in with a fierce, almost cruel intensity. I grab a fistful of her hair and pull her head back, her back arching uncomfortably.

"Think you're ready to be full of my come? Are you going to beg for it like a good little girl?" I smack her hard, the sound sharp and biting against the roar of the rain. Her head jerks with the impact, and I yank roughly on her hair, pulling her back against me. "Come on, baby," I growl, my voice thick with dark satisfaction. "Let me hear you say it." Her voice comes out in a desperate plea, barely audible over the storm.

"Please, Noah. *Oh God*, please." She manages to utter, her voice trembling with vulnerability and need. I lean in closer, my voice a dark murmur in her ear.

"Yes, atta girl," I rasp, my tone laden with malicious approval. "I am your fucking God."

With a fierce, almost savage delight, I slam into her again, my movements now frantic and wild. I press deeper, pushing through her, feeling the intense heat and tightness around me. As I reach the deepest point, I stay there, unloading inside her pretty cunt. Her body quivers uncontrollably, her screams slicing through my eardrums.

"*Fuck*, princess." I moan as I throb inside her, my body pulsing with intense release. Each spasm is a testament to the raw, consuming pleasure that grips me.

After emptying myself deep inside her, I pull out and immediately yank her up from the car hood. I crush against her, my hands grabbing her face, holding it with a desperate, hungry intensity; as if she's my last tether to sanity. Our lips meet in a fierce, passionate kiss. The kiss is a savage reckoning, a collision of need and possession. The rain continues to pour, relentless, drowning us. Our breaths mix, heavy and laboured.

I'm in love.
I'm so in love it hurts.
I'm terrified.

I pull back, my breath coming hard and heavy. I grip her face, forcing her to look at me.

"I claimed you, Farmer. You fucking belong to me. Understand?" I rasp.

She nods, gently.

"And I'm fucking in love with you." I growl, my voice rough and unrelenting. Her eyes widen, the fierce light in them matching the storm's fury.

"I love you too," she breathes, her voice trembling yet sure. Her smile is sharp; hitting me like a punch to the gut. My own smile is jagged, a blend of triumph and disbelief. I've been holding my breath for so long, finally exhaling. It's like peeling away layers of steel and ice to find a beating heart. A recognition of the fact that, despite all my attempts to stay detached, I've let someone in.

I can't help it. A low, genuine laugh escapes me. Skylar's laugh follows, a light, infectious giggle that makes the ambience between us feel lighter, more open. They mingle. And then, she says the most Skylar Farmer thing she could possibly say.

"So.." she starts. "Round two?"

CHAPTER 26:
BLOOD

Marcus

11:27p.m. The storm outside mirrors the tension I've been feeling all day. Thunder rumbles in the distance, and the rain's been relentless, drenching everything in sight. I need to talk to Dean, and I know exactly where to find him. I always do.

I don't even have to think about it. The moment I heard the rain slamming against the windows, heavy and relentless, I knew exactly where he'd go. Dean has always loved storms. While most people run inside, he thrives in them. There's something about the chaos, the unpredictability of it all; he always says it makes him feel alive. So when I hear the downpour, I already know I'll find him outside, under some half-assed shelter, using the storm as an excuse to light up a blunt and disappear into his own head.

I throw on a plain, black hoodie and head for the front door. The mansion feels empty as I move through it, the sound of the rain drowning out any noise inside. But I can feel the tension hanging in the air, thick and heavy like the storm itself. Everyone's on edge, and I know Dean's no different. He's been avoiding me, avoiding all of us, sinking deeper into the dark place he's been living in lately.

The moment I step outside, cold raindrops pelt my skin, but I barely register it. Dean's right where I knew he'd be, huddled on the front step, blunt pinched between his fingers, smoke curling up into the dark air. His hood's pulled low over his face, but I can still see his eyes, sharp and distant, staring out at the storm like it's got answers.

He looks up when I walk out, our eyes catching for the briefest second. Then, just as quickly, he looks away, taking a long, slow drag like he didn't see me at all. He doesn't say anything. Neither do I. I sit down next to him, the step cold and slick beneath me, the rain coming down so hard it's bouncing off the concrete. The space between us is thick; years of knowing each other too well, of seeing too much, and yet probably not saying enough.

I pull a pack of papers and some weed from my pocket, the familiar motions grounding me as I start to roll my own blunt. The sound of the rain hitting the porch blends with the subtle crinkle of paper in my hands, a rhythm I've known for years. It's easy, automatic, something to do with my hands. He doesn't look at me, still lost in the storm, his own blunt burning down to a slow ember. I lick the paper, seal the blunt with precision, and spark it up. The flame catches instantly, glowing bright for a second before it dulls into a slow burn. I inhale deeply, the smoke filling my lungs, harsh but welcome.

I glance at Dean out of the corner of my eye. His face is set, jaw clenched, staring straight ahead like if he stares hard enough, something out there in the rain might fix what's broken. The silence stretches out, thick and unbroken, but somehow there's no edge to it, no awkwardness. It's like we've settled into a space where words aren't needed.

I break the silence, my voice rough from the chill and the smoke.

"I'm sorry, man," I say, the words feeling heavy as they leave my mouth. The sound of the rain almost swallows them, but I know he heard. He doesn't respond. His eyes stay locked on the storm, his profile unmoving. I let out a slow breath, the smoke curling lazily around me. "I didn't mean to get so angry with you," I continue, trying to keep my voice steady. "I'm just scared."

Dean's silence is heavy, but it's not hostile.

"I'm scared too," he says, his tone raw. "Terrified, actually." He pauses, his shoulders tightening as he clears his throat, a gesture that seems to strain against the dam of emotion he's fighting to control. "You were trying to help and I-" he pauses, the words coming out in a low murmur, almost swallowed by the storm. He clenches his jaw, as if to keep his emotions from spilling over. His gaze remains fixed ahead, not meeting mine.

I watch him struggle with his words, my own breath hanging heavy in the air.

"It's okay," I say, my voice soft. Dean finally turns to face me, his eyes glistening with a mix of rain and unspoken emotion.

"I just wanted to avoid it altogether, you know?" he says, his voice carrying a tremor of regret. "Pretend it wasn't real."

He looks down, the weight of his words settling between us.

"But you were right. I should've accepted your help. If not for me, then for Delilah." He drags his hand across his face, as if trying to wipe away the heavy truth. The lines on his face deepen. The blunt between his fingers is almost forgotten, the smoke curling aimlessly in the air. The silence stretches for a beat longer, until I can't fight the urge to ask him the question on my mind any longer.

"Did you mean what you said?" I ask, my voice barely above a whisper. The question hangs in the air, loaded with the gravity of our shared pain. "About not wanting to live this long?" Dean's jaw tightens, a muscle in his cheek twitching. He looks away, struggling with the turmoil in his mind. The weight of his words is too much for him to bear alone. His hand clenches the blunt so tightly I can see the strain in his knuckles.

"I don't know," he says finally, but the way he says it, I can tell there's more tangled in those words than he's letting on. "I've been through hell, bro. I'm fucking tired. I thought I'd be gone by now, you know? I figured if someone hadn't taken me out by now, the drugs surely would've." He looks up at me, his gaze weary and haunted.

"I didn't think I'd have anything worth fighting for," he says, his voice rough but tinged with a strange clarity. "I figured, why bother? Nothing mattered much. But now," he pauses, looking deep into my eyes with an earnest intensity; raw and unguarded. "Now I've got Delilah, and I've got you. And I uh.. I'm realising that having nothing to lose was a lot easier than having everything to lose. But now you have Noah and I-"

"Dean." I take a deep breath, the cold air sharp against my lungs as I cut him off.

"You'll never lose me, man. Just like I'm never gonna lose you." I'm watching him, my eyes starting to burn. My voice shakes a little as I continue. "We might not share blood, but our lives have bled into each other. We're carved into each other's flesh." My throat tightens, and I blink rapidly, trying to hold back the tears. "Our bond is stitched into the very marrow of who we are. Not even death can erase this. If we lose each other in this lifetime, I'll find you in another." A single tear escapes, rolling down my cheek, as I finish with a raw, trembling voice. "And I'll still annoy the fuck out of you."

Dean lets out a shaky laugh, and it's like a sudden crack in the dam. Tears cut paths down our faces, mixing with the rain, forming rivulets of our shared pain. It's a messy, beautiful collision of the storm and our sorrow, as if the universe itself is weeping and laughing with us. Our laughter is an uneven cadence, punctuated by the tremors of our breath and the raw honesty of the moment. I see his eyes, those deep pools of emotion, glistening with a vulnerability that lays everything bare.

He wipes his face with a grimy sleeve, attempting to regain a semblance of composure. Through his tears, he smirks, a bittersweet glint in his eyes.

"*Fuck*, bro. Look at us," he says, his voice thick with emotion yet trying to carry a hint of his old defiant humour. "A couple of pussies, crying in the fucking rain." I chuckle through my tears, shaking my head.

"Yeah, who woulda thought," I reply, my voice rough but steady. He takes a puff of his joint, looking up at the sky.

"You know," he begins, his voice cracking slightly, "for the longest time, I really felt like the world owed me something. I used to think if I held on long enough, if I fought hard enough, it'd all pay off. Like, someday, the universe would hand me some kind of fucking trophy for just surviving." He lets out a thoughtful, almost rueful laugh. "But the stupid part is, my trophies were already on the shelf."

He shakes his head, another chuckle escaping him even through the tears. "Delilah, you, everyone who's stuck around. I was so busy looking for some grand prize that meant fuck all, that I missed what was standing right in front of me." He says. I let the words settle between us, my voice soft but filled with sincerity.

"I love you, bro." I tell him, "you'll always be my family."

His eyes glimmer with something close to relief as he smiles, a simple,

"I know" slipping from his lips. With a shared glance, we tap the ends of our blunts together; a silent toast to our brotherhood. The quiet gesture feeling like a promise.

There's no one like Dean. He's the brother fate forgot to name but the universe delivered anyway.

And I'm gonna save him.

CHAPTER 27:
SURPRISE!

Noah

We're trampling through the woods, branches snapping under our feet; the usual banter bouncing between the group. It's normal. There's a buzz of curiosity hanging between them; they're all wondering what the fuck I've dragged them out here for. Except for Dean. He hasn't looked me in the eye once, and I don't blame him.

The way he shoved Skylar, her body hitting the floor like she was nothing. My blood boiled the second it happened. It took every ounce of control not to put a bullet in his skull right there and then. I fired that shot as close as I could, I wanted him to feel it. To let him know what I could've done. I wanted to see him flinch. Killing him then would've been the easiest thing I've ever done. But easy wasn't what he deserved.

And now, I've got a surprise up my sleeve.

We're getting closer to the tunnel now. I can feel it. The trees are thinning out, and the air's shifting, getting cooler as we near the entrance. Every step brings us closer, and my pulse picks up. I'm trying to keep my face neutral, but there's this buzz under my skin, this electric hum that only gets louder the closer we get. The tunnel's just a few yards away, the mouth of it dark and yawning, like it's been waiting for us. I stop short, turning to face them.

"Alright," I say, holding up a hand. "Everybody close your eyes." Skylar's the first to speak, her voice tinged with suspicion.

"Noah, what's going on-"

"Shh," I cut her off, giving her a look that tells her to trust me. "Eyes closed." They hesitate, but one by one, they close or cover their eyes. Dean, well, he's still not looking at me, but he closes his eyes too, his jaw tight, hands shoved into his pockets like he's bracing himself. "Keep 'em closed," I say, walking backward toward the tunnel, guiding them.

"I'll cut to the chase," I begin, "I couldn't help but notice that Miss Sienna has been sporting a new little ring on her finger." I say, letting a hint of satisfaction creep into my voice. I've always had a sharp eye for detail, and I spotted the ring immediately. It was the sort of thing that didn't escape me; subtle changes, small shifts. It's in my nature to notice these things.

The reaction is almost instantaneous. Skylar's eyebrows knit together in confusion, followed by a sharp,

"What?" Her voice carries an undertone of curiosity mixed with surprise. Birdie's soft,

"Wait, what?" follows, and the excitement is palpable even through their muffled responses. Sienna's face flushes with a mix of embarrassment and excitement.

"Oh my God, Noah," she protests. Marcus, predictably, has a proud smirk on his face. I let the anticipation build, savouring the way the atmosphere is thick with expectation.

"So," I say, the corners of my mouth lifting slightly, "to mark this occasion, I've got a little surprise." A genuine yet menacing grin stretches across my face as I watch them. "On the count of three," I say, my voice smooth but carrying a dark undertone. "Open your eyes."

Here we go.

"One.." I draw out, letting the word hang in the dense, expectant silence. "Two.." I let the pause linger.

"Three."

When they open their eyes, the silence that follows is heavy, weighted with disbelief. The tunnel, once marked by years of Dean's graffiti, has been transformed into something completely unrecognisable. It's beautiful. Dominating the wall, stretching across one side of the concrete, I've painted a massive mural; Butter, Sienna's pet butterfly, rendered in painstaking, vivid detail. Her bright yellow wings painted with an almost ethereal glow, so vivid they seem to flutter against the background.

She soars through the air, delicately carrying two intertwined wedding rings. The whole piece radiates a sense of beauty, almost innocence. It's deceptively sweet.

But sweet, it's anything but.

I watch as the reactions unfold. Sienna is first, of course; her eyes widen with pure astonishment, her hands covering her mouth as a breathy,

"Oh my God.." escapes her. She steps closer, her voice catching. "Noah! This is beautiful. It's Butter."

"Yeah," I say, my voice smooth, almost casual, watching her eyes light up. "Thought she deserved some attention."

Her eyes are wet now, clearly touched by the gesture. She doesn't know. She doesn't know that this wasn't just for her.

Dean knows.

I can feel the heat coming off him. His eyes are locked on the mural, and I can see the recognition hit; this was *his* tunnel. His canvas. Years of his own work, his art, layered in spray paint across that wall, and now? Gone. Erased. His years of expression, pride, and escape wiped clean beneath a yellow butterfly. And I did it with precision. I see it; how his chest rises with a sharp breath, how his teeth clench. But he holds it in. He's good at that.

Skylar steps closer to the mural, brushing her fingers lightly over the painted surface.

"It's amazing," she whispers. "Butter looks so real!"

"Thank you, princess." I reply. Delilah stands a few feet away from Dean, her eyes lingering on him, filled with concern. She knows him better than anyone, knows exactly what's boiling beneath his silent exterior. Her hand hovers near his arm, like she wants to comfort him but isn't sure it's the right time. She's waiting for him to crack, to say something.
But Dean just stands there, stiff, his gaze locked on the mural like it's mocking him. Delilah bites her lip, her brow furrowing

with worry. Marcus steps up to Dean, clapping a hand on his shoulder in what's meant to be a comforting gesture.

"You okay, bro?" His voice is casual, but there's an edge to it, a knowing look in his eyes as he peers at Dean. Marcus can sense the tension too, even if he doesn't fully understand the layers underneath it.

Dean doesn't answer. He just nods, barely a movement, more like a twitch. His jaw is tight, and he keeps his hands shoved deep in his pockets. His eyes never leave the butterfly, never leave the rings that dangle beneath it like an insult, a claim to something sacred. Marcus looks between us for a moment longer, clearly confused, before he steps over to me. Closer now, his voice dropping as he leans in, speaking low enough for only me to hear.

"It looks great, man. Really. Thank you." I flash him a small smile; just enough to keep him satisfied.

"No problem," I say, my voice cool and collected. "Sienna deserved something special."

And that part's true. I'm not lying. Sienna does deserve something special, something that shows I care. She's been through hell, and even if she despises me, which she should, I want her to have this. It's *her* butterfly, *her* symbol, something light and beautiful amidst all the darkness.

I'm killing two birds with one stone. Sienna gets her sweet gesture, something that'll make her smile, something light and beautiful in a world that's anything but. And Dean? Dean gets his punishment, handed to him in broad daylight, with everyone thinking I did it out of the goodness of my heart. I get to watch him burn, and no one's the wiser.

The sun is dipping low, casting a golden glow that's just warm enough to be comfortable but with a chill starting to creep in.

The group is animated, the girls chattering excitedly about Sienna's engagement, their laughter ringing through the clearing. It's a pleasant scene for once. Dean is sitting alone on one of the logs, his posture slouched, his hood up. He's a shadow on the edge of the celebration, and I can see the tension radiating off him. He's clearly trying to distance himself from the group, the cheerfulness of the moment seemingly just out of reach for him.

I watch him for a moment, letting the silence stretch between us. The sounds of laughter and conversation filter through, almost mockingly, as I push off from where I was standing and make my way over to him. My boots crunch softly on the underbrush, breaking the silence just enough to announce my approach.

I sit down next to him on the log, keeping my distance but close enough to make my presence known. The warmth from the fire does nothing to touch the cold, deliberate edge in the air between us. Dean doesn't look at me, his gaze fixed somewhere beyond the trees. His shoulders are tight, and I can see the way his hands are clenched into fists.

Dean's gaze stays fixed ahead. To my surprise, he speaks first, his voice barely above a whisper.

"So, is this your way of apologising to Sienna?" He asks. Brave, but not very smart. I let a thin, almost imperceptible smile curl my lips. I let out a slow breath, my voice steady and cold.

"This is me letting you know I'm still on your fucking back, Douglas. Especially now," I start, "You fucked with my girl and I don't take that lightly."

"I never meant to shove her like that. It was wrong." He admits immediately. Too little too late.

"I should've fucking killed you."

"I agree, I'm sorry." he murmurs. "If anybody pushed Delilah like that, I'd have killed them too."

Dean finally turns his head, his eyes locking onto mine. The air between us thickens, tension rising with every second of silence. His jaw clenches as if he's weighing his next words carefully, knowing anything he says could push me further. He's saying all the right things, so far. But unfortunately, I don't give a fuck.

"You think a quick apology means shit to me?" I ask with a laugh.

"Then what do you want?" he asks. His lip curls slightly, a flicker of anger, but he keeps his voice level controlled. "You just waiting for me to fuck up again?"

"That's exactly what I'm doing." I nod, not bothering to hide the cold truth in my eyes.

For a moment, neither of us says anything, the silence thick and heavy, like the calm before a storm. Dean shifts on the log, and I can see the decision form in his mind before he even speaks.

"Well, you don't have to worry." He says quietly, his voice carrying a finality that catches me off guard. "I'm off." I raise an eyebrow.

"Off?" I repeat. He stands up slowly, brushing the dirt off his hands; his eyes drift back to the tunnel, then to the group laughing around the fire. His jaw tightens, and he looks back at me, a grim sort of resignation in his eyes.

"Yeah, I'm leaving. Going home."

For a second, I'm thrown. He's really leaving? I didn't think it would be this easy. My surprise fades quickly though, replaced by a cold satisfaction. Maybe I've actually gotten rid of him.

"Smart move, Douglas." I say, my voice cold. "But don't think for a second that this means you're off my radar," I continue, standing up, lowering my voice. "I'll still be watching,"

"I figured as much," he says, voice steady. He gives me one last look before turning away, walking toward the edge of the clearing. I watch him go, my eyes narrowing as he disappears into the trees.

As Dean trudges off, I can't help but feel a flicker of confusion beneath the surface. I mean, don't get me wrong, I'm over the fucking moon. He's leaving. That's what I wanted. But still, this? This was all it took? The tunnel was nothing compared to what I should've done to him, and yet here he is, walking away like some wounded animal, tail tucked between his legs.

I expected more from him. I expected a fight, some kind of pushback, something that made this feel like it was worth the effort. Instead, he's going home in a sulk, like a kid who just lost a playground scrap. It's almost.. anticlimactic. Well, whatever the reason for his sudden retreat, it doesn't matter.
Mission accomplished.

Dean's gone.
Well, that was easier than expected.

CHAPTER 28:
BARBED WORDS

Dean

I've had enough of Noah's place. The hours here are dragging by like I'm in some kind of purgatory. I've spent the last couple of hours with Delilah, who decided she wants to spend one more night here with Birdie. For her, this whole mess has been like one big sleepover. I get it, she's trying to stay positive, trying to hold onto whatever normalcy she can find. But I can't do it. Not anymore.

I grab my stuff, shoving everything into my duffel bag, and head out. The stairs creak beneath me as I head down; every step feels heavier than the last, like the air in this house is weighing me down. When I reach the front door, I drop my bag beside me and bend down to pull on my shoes; the soles worn and the laces fraying. I'm halfway through tying the second shoe when I sense movement behind me.

"Where are you going?" Her voice catches me off guard, but I don't let it show. I finish tying the knot, then stand up, dusting off my jeans. I take a slow breath, steeling myself as I turn to face her. She's standing in the doorway to the kitchen, arms crossed, looking at me like I'm some kind of alien.

"Home, Skylar." I say, flat and final; the word *'home'* feeling strangely foreign on my tongue. I had almost forgotten my shitty little flat had even existed.

"Now?"

"Yeah." I reply, keeping my gaze fixed on the floor, trying to muster the energy for another conversation.

"Does Delilah know?"

"Yeah, she knows," I say, my tone clipped. I'm not in the mood for small talk. "Where's Marcus?"

"Why are you leaving?" She asks, ignoring me completely.

"I just wanna leave, Skylar. Where's Marcus?" I press, trying to keep my frustration in check.

"He went over to his mum's new place. Now you answer *my* question. Why are you leaving?" She repeats, her eyes narrowing.

I let out a long sigh, running a hand through my hair, feeling the messy strands beneath my fingers.

"I can't be here, Sky. I can't deal with all of this right now."

"*Ahh*, so you're running away?" She mocks. I'm feeling the weight of her words. She has a right to be annoyed at me. I know I should probably be apologising after shoving her, but my frustration and need to escape are overpowering me.

"Look, Marcus is gonna start working on the book again. He'll text me any updates." I explain, my voice a low murmur, every syllable laced with resignation. "Until then, I need to be alone, okay?"

"What's your problem with Noah?" She asks, her voice laced with challenge. I huff, feeling my irritation spike even more. Of course she's bringing him up.

"I'm not getting into this," I state, attempting to deflect.

"Why not?"

"I said I don't wanna talk about it, alright? Can you stop fucking grilling me?" I say, my voice harsher than I intended. Skylar's tone hardens, the weight of her frustration matching mine.

"You can't keep giving all of us the silent treatment," she counters. "Clearly Noah's winding you up."

"Why do you even care?" I snap back, anger pulsing through me like a live wire. I can feel my temper fraying at the edges, but I'm too wrapped up in my own chaos to care enough to rein it in. All I want is to get out of here. Away from her questions, away from everything. She glares at me, her eyes darkening as she takes a step closer, refusing to let this go.

"I care because you, of all people, should be happy for me," she says. It catches me off guard. I feel my breath catch in my chest, like an unseen hand squeezing my heart.

"What do you mean?" My reply comes out quieter than I wanted, a threadbare whisper that betrays just how cornered I feel.

"You told me I deserved to find someone," she presses, her voice tight with emotion, her eyes searching mine for something I can't give her right now. She's right, I did tell her that.

I swallow hard, trying to keep my voice level, but all I manage is a rough,

"I don't know what you want me to say."

"Something.. anything," she pleads, desperation lacing her voice like an urgent melody. I can feel the intensity of her gaze bearing down on me. My chest tightens, and I'm seconds away from just walking out without another word, but the frustration spills over.

"I just don't like him, Sky," I finally say, my voice flat. "It's as simple as that." She scoffs, shaking her head in disbelief. Skylar's voice rises, her words tumbling out in a rush.

"You told me I should find someone who doesn't care about my past, who likes me the way I am.. Someone who's a good guy-" I bite down, hard. My jaw tightens, and before I can stop myself, the words spill out, sharp and biting.

"He's not a good guy!" I yell, my voice reverberating. Her eyes flare with emotion, a wildfire of hurt and defiance igniting within them. She snaps back immediately, the vulnerability in her voice cracking like fragile glass.

"He's good to *me!*"

Her eyes are wide, brimming with tears, and for a second, I just freeze. I stare into her eyes, unable to move, unable to speak. My chest tightens. I'm dying to explain everything, but I know she's too far in. She's in love. Deeply. She wipes at her face, frustration building as her voice cracks.

"He doesn't make me cry, Dean. He makes me feel like I'm enough." She continues, her voice rising slightly with the intensity of her emotions. "Noah is the first person who's *ever* looked at me and didn't just see some broken girl from an orphanage. He doesn't treat me like I'm damaged goods, like someone too messed up to ever be loved properly."

Her eyes fill with tears again, and she doesn't bother wiping them this time.

"You have no idea what it's like, Dean. Every guy I've ever been with, they either pity me or try to 'fix' me. Nobody wants anything fucking real with me. Like I've got too much trauma to be worth any actual effort."

Her voice cracks, and I feel like someone's twisting a knife in my gut. She's never been this vulnerable, not with me, not with anyone. I can't look away from her, but I still can't bring myself to say anything. Her words hit me hard, and guilt seeps in deeper, because I know she's right. She deserves to feel the way Noah makes her feel. I should be glad for her. I should be happy she's finally found someone who sees her for more than her scars, more than her trauma.

But I know Noah. I know the kind of man he is, the things he's capable of.

"I don't understand why you can't be happy for me. Why can't you just let me have this?"

"Skylar, I really have to go," I mutter, my voice low and strained as I turn towards the door. I can't stay here, not with her looking at me like that.

"Fine. Go." Her words tremble, but there's something sharp in her tone, something bitter. "It's easier for you, right? To walk away."

"Because there's shit you don't know, Sky!" I snap, the raw edge to my voice catching her off guard.

"Then fucking tell me!"

And then I feel it; this terrible guilt creeping up on me, twisting everything in my chest. My throat tightens, and I can't keep it in any longer. I'm breaking right in front of her, the pressure too much, the weight unbearable.

"I've seen the way he looks at Sienna, okay?!" I blurt out, my voice shaking with emotion. My chest heaves with the lie, the guilt immediately eating at me. I see Skylar's face crumble, her eyes widening as if I've just torn her heart in two. Which I have. Yet I keep going. "He fancies her, alright? He flirts with her all the time. It's fucking obvious."

It's a lie. It's all a lie.
But I can't tell Skylar the real reason.
It's not my story to tell.

673

If Noah was involved in Sienna's abduction as I suspect, then Sienna is the only one who deserves to share that. So I let this lie, this twisted half-truth, fall between us, hoping it'll keep her safe. Hoping it'll be enough to push her away from him. The silence is deafening, her lips trembling as she tries to process what I've just said.

"What?" she whispers, barely audible. I can't bring myself to say anything else. I'm already too far gone, choking on the regret, watching her fall apart. It's killing her. And I'm the one who's doing it. "Are you sure?" She asks, almost begging me to change my story. Her tears spill over, and I feel something in me crumble at the sight.

"Sky, I'm sorry." I say. My voice is hoarse, almost pleading. She's searching for something, anything to hold onto. But I've just ripped it all away. Her sobs fill the room, quiet but sharp, like they're stabbing into me with every breath she takes. "I have to go." The words barely make it out of my throat, low and broken.

I turn away, moving toward the door, my shoes scuffing against the wooden floor. Each step feels like I'm dragging a lead weight behind me. As I reach for the handle, Sienna's voice suddenly echoes from upstairs.

"Butter!" The shout reverberates off the walls, and in an instant, the familiar fluttering of wings fills the air. Butter zooms down the staircase, her vibrant yellow wings catching the light peaking through from the kitchen. She begins to flutter around the door handle. My heart sinks. The last time she appeared like this, it was chaos; a moment that nearly cost me everything.

"Please," I mutter, freezing mid-motion. The instinct to flee wrestles with the memory of Butter's chaotic energy, and I tug the handle. In a flurry of frantic movement, Butter begins to batter herself against the door, her tiny frame colliding with the sturdy wood. I wrench the door open wider, and Butter is knocked back momentarily, but she doesn't give up. I make it out of the door and she hurls herself right in front of me, her wings beating wildly a blur of colour and fervour. With relentless zeal, she thumps against my chest again and again, as if trying to force me back into the house.

"What the fuck are you doing?" I growl, my frustration spiking again. She keeps at it, relentless, and I grab her, holding her tiny body in my hands.

For a moment, I just stare at her.

Thoughts whirl chaotically in my mind, a turbulent storm of emotions that refuses to settle. There's an overwhelming weight of expectations, but at the core, it's a void; an aching emptiness that clings to me like a shadow. I know I should feel something profound at this moment, a surge of longing or perhaps regret, but instead, I'm met with silence; a dissonant echo of feelings that should be there but aren't.

I slowly release my grip, letting her slip from my fingers, like a feather drifting back into the confines of the house. Butter flutters backward, confused, but I don't turn.

I walk away.

CHAPTER 29:
BEYOND SALVATION

Noah

I pull into the driveway just after eleven, rain pouring down in relentless sheets; the sound of it drums against the roof of my car. The window wipers struggle to keep pace, smearing the world outside into a blurred canvas. I had a few jobs to wrap up; deals to finalise and a couple of threats to manage. The headlights cut through the darkness, illuminating the slick gravel, where puddles shimmer like scattered silver coins under the faint glow.

As I step out, the chill in the air seeps through my clothes, wrapping around me like a damp shroud. I make my way to the front door, each footfall muffled by the rain-soaked ground. There's a lightness in my chest tonight, knowing Dean isn't here. I head straight to Skylar's room.

I knock on her door, the sound nearly drowned by the storm outside. No answer. I knock again, louder this time, my knuckles rapping against the wood. Silence hangs heavy. So I go in. Inside, the dim light casts long shadows. There she is, sitting on the bed, her back to me, engrossed in her phone. The glow of the screen illuminates her silhouette, but she doesn't turn to acknowledge me. I take a step forward.

"Before you shout at me, I knocked twice," I say, trying to keep my tone firm yet playful, ready to disarm her usual sassy retorts.

Still, she doesn't move. Something feels off. I reach the side of the bed, and she's still glued to her phone, her fingers scrolling with focused determination. Confusion prickles at the back of my mind, but I suppose it's typical for her to pull this kind of silent treatment.

"Farmer," I say. No reaction. I bend down, fingers sliding under her chin, forcing her to look at me. Her eyes finally meet mine, but they're distant; hollow. A cold, unsettling emptiness that gnaws at me in a way I can't ignore. "What's going on?" I ask, the lightness in my voice fading, replaced by a thread of concern. She swats my hand away, the defiance in her voice sharp.

"Don't touch me."

What the fuck?

I step closer, trying to bridge the gap between us.

"Who do you think you're talking to?" I ask, forcing a smirk, hoping to lighten the moment. But instead, she whips her head around to glare at me, and the intensity in her eyes makes my chest tighten.

"You!" she spits, her voice brittle, cracking something shattered beyond repair. The hurt is so thick it clings to every syllable, and I see the glimmer of unshed tears pooling in her eyes. My heart sinks as I realise this isn't just a passing annoyance; she's genuinely upset.

I take a step back, my playfulness evaporating into thin air.

"What's wrong?" I push gently, my voice low and steady, hoping to draw her out. Skylar doesn't reply, her silence heavy in the air. I narrow my eyes. "What have I done?" I ask, my voice low and incredulous.

She finally looks at me, eyes clouded with confusion and raw hurt.

"Leave me alone. You're a fucking liar." She swallows hard, and I can see the fight in her fading. Her words slam into me, and I blink, caught completely off guard.

"What?"

Skylar pushes off the bed, pacing like she's trying to outrun the mess between us. Her body's shaking, fury rolling off her in waves, but I'm left standing here, clueless; no idea what the hell I did. She won't even look at me, like the very sight of me turns her stomach.

"Sky, what the fuck are you talking about?"

"You're just like everyone else! You pretend you care, pretend you're different, but you're fucking not." A cold feeling settles in my gut.

"Of course I fucking care." I say.

She keeps pacing, her steps frantic, like she's trying to burn off the anger, but the storm in her eyes just keeps getting worse.

"Bullshit." Her voice cracks, betraying the real pain underneath the rage. I step toward her, but she whirls around, throwing up her hands again as if to block me out.

"I haven't lied about anything."

"You think I don't know what's going on? You think I'm fucking stupid?" My head's spinning. I rack my brain, trying to piece together what's gotten her so worked up. But nothing makes sense.

"Sky, I don't know what you think I've done, but I haven't lied to you."

She stops, her lip quivering, biting it down like she's struggling to hold back a flood. I can see her walls crumbling, the tears she's so desperately trying not to let fall. Her fists are clenched at her sides, shaking with the effort of keeping it all together. And then, finally, her voice breaks, barely above a whisper, but filled with the kind of pain that cuts straight through me.

"You've been flirting with Sienna."

The words hit like a sledgehammer, and I just stand there, frozen. For a second, I'm too stunned to even react. But as fast as the shock hits, it's gone, replaced with a searing rage that almost knocks the wind out of me. Dean fucking Douglas.

"Dean told you that, didn't he?" My voice is tight, but the anger simmers just beneath the surface. I'm barely holding it back. She doesn't speak, but she nods, her lips pressed together. She wipes at her eyes like it's taking everything not to fall apart in front of me. But I already know. It's written all over her face.

She looks destroyed.
And that rips me apart.

"Farmer, listen to me." I say, stepping toward her slowly, like I'm trying not to spook her.

"There's nothing to say."

"He's lying to you." My voice is low, strained. The anger boiling inside me is begging to be let out, but not now. Not with her. I swallow it down, keeping it in check, because right now, she's breaking in front of me, and she needs to be reassured. The rage can wait.

She laughs, sharp and bitter, and it tears at me more than I'd ever admit.

"Why the fuck would he lie, Noah?" She asks. I step closer, keeping my voice steady, calm, like I'm trying to soothe a cornered animal.

"Because I know some shit he doesn't want getting out." I tell her, genuinely. I watch her carefully, and I can see the shift in her demeanour almost in an instant. That harsh, defensive edge softens, just slightly, and there's something in her eyes, like a hint of belief. Or maybe it's just that she wants to believe me. Would prefer to believe me.

I can work with that.

She shakes her head, her confusion clear as she whispers,

"I don't believe you." I watch as a single tear finally slips free, tracing a path down her flushed cheek, and for a second, everything else fades. That tear hits harder than any bullet, harder than anything I've felt before.

"Look at me." My fingers twitch, wanting to wipe that tear away, but I hold back. "Now." Her lips part, the confusion still clouding her eyes as she stares at me, searching for something to hold onto.

"Dean's been keeping a secret for a long time," I say, voice steady, low, because I know she'll hear every word. "He knows I know, and he's scared." Her eyes widen a little, the disbelief softening around the edges. I can see her mind working, trying to process it, to fit the pieces together; but it's not enough. She's not fully convinced. I see that flicker of doubt, that

680

hesitation in her eyes. She wants to believe me. I just need to push a little harder.

"But why would he lie? Why would he ever want to hurt me like that?" She chops in. Her voice trembles, her brows furrowing as she tries to make sense of it all. Her eyes search mine, desperate for answers.

"Because he doesn't want me around, Farmer." I say slowly, forcing the calm in my voice despite the fire threatening to break loose. "I know too much. I'm too big of a threat to him."

Her breath hitches, a spark of hope flickering in her eyes for a second, like maybe, just maybe, this could be true. She's clinging to it, desperate to believe me, and I see the crack in her defences, the way her lips part as if she's about to speak; but she doesn't. Instead, her face crumples, and she shakes her head, trying to reject what I'm telling her, like she's terrified of trusting it. But then, Skylar freezes, her eyes narrowing slightly as if her mind is piecing together something monumental. I can practically see her brain ticking, the gears turning slowly.

"Never have I ever kept a secret that could've changed everything." She mumbles. I can't help it; my smile is small, but it's genuine. That's my smart girl.

"Yes, princess," I say softly, the words coming out low, calm, and steady. "You got it." Her expression shifts, and though there's still confusion, there's also a flicker of something else; maybe clarity, maybe disbelief. It's like a veil's been lifted, and she's standing at the edge, ready to see things as they really are.

"What is he hiding?" She asks, with a shred of anger and hesitation; as if unsure of whether or not she actually wants the answer.

I pause, staring at her. The question hangs heavy in the air, and I can feel her eyes drilling into me; and for a second, I debate whether or not I should even tell her. It would put Marcus in the crossfire. But at this point.. fuck it. Fuck Dean. He made his bed. He's the one who pushed this, crossed lines he knew better than to touch.

I never would've gone here.

The silence between us stretches tight, and I can feel her anxiety building with every second that ticks by.

"Dean knew Marcus had a brother," I start, my voice low but steady. "He knew my name. He knew everything. He found my file." Skylar's eyes go wide, her whole body tensing. She looks like I just told her the world was ending.

"What? H-how do you know Dean found it?" Her voice trembles, the disbelief and shock swirling together, fighting to make sense of what I'm saying.

I stare at her, my pulse picking up, trying to keep my frustration buried for her sake.

"*Someone* had to find it, baby," I mutter. "And it sure as hell wasn't Marcus."

"But.. Oh my God.. But," she stammers, completely thrown. "That makes no sense. Why wouldn't you go back for him? For Marcus? If you knew he existed-"

"I didn't," I cut her off, sharp. I let out a breath, trying to pull it back, trying not to let my anger leak out. "I was a kid." I say, my voice steady but tinged with memory. "My father had me almost entirely convinced that Marcus was all in my head. I couldn't even leave his side to find out," I share. "By the time I was old enough to start questioning things again, Marcus had been picked up. Now, of course, I know it was my father who had him at that point." Her expression falters, her lips parting slightly as she stares at me. It's a lot. I know it is. The way she looks at me, so much confusion, pain, disbelief; I can feel it cutting me too.

"And.. Dean knew?"

"Yes. For a long time."

Skylar just stares at me, speechless. Her eyes, wide and stormy, search mine for answers I don't think she's fully ready for. Another tear falls from her eye, rolling slowly down her cheek. The room feels heavy; so heavy it's sinking into my stomach, twisting everything inside me. I take a breath, fighting back the strange ache building up inside me.

"Skylar," I start, my voice quieter than usual, rougher, the words slipping out before I can second guess them. "You think I'd ever look at someone else? Flirt with someone else?" I let out a harsh laugh, the kind that comes from somewhere deep. "I don't even fucking *see* anyone else. No one exists for me but you. You're the only thing I feel, the only thing I've ever felt." Her lips tremble, but she still doesn't speak. She doesn't have to. My voice is low, dark, like the truth clawing its way out of me.

I move closer, my eyes locked on her.

"It's not some passing obsession. You're in my blood. You're in every fucking breath I take." I reach for her, cupping her chin with more force than I probably should, but I need her to see this in my eyes. To *feel* it. She has to see what she's done to me. "It's not something I can turn off, Farmer. You own me. Every part of me. Body, mind, soul, whatever the fuck is left of it, it's all yours."

I hold her face in my hands, hard, pulling her closer so there's barely an inch of space between us. Her breath hitches, but she doesn't move, doesn't resist. I need her to hear every fucking word.

683

Because it's the truth.
Every single word.

I run my thumb along her jaw, softer now, but my grip stays firm.

"Do you understand?" I whisper, my voice still laced with that dark, consuming edge. "I don't just love you. I'm ruined by you." Her lips part, but no words come out, just shallow breaths. I can feel her trembling, can see the cracks forming in her walls. Good. Let them break. "You've hollowed me out. Crawled into the darkest parts of me, and now you live there. There's no way out." Her lips tremble as another tear falls, and I swipe it away with my thumb, softer now, but my eyes are still locked on hers, still burning with that obsession that she's unleashed in me.

The silence stretches between us, thick and suffocating, like the room can't hold the weight of everything unsaid. She's crying, tears slipping down her face like they're falling from somewhere deeper, somewhere even she can't reach. I watch her shatter, piece by piece, and I stand there, letting it happen.

I don't say anything. I just let it sit, let her absorb every single word, every piece of the obsession I've just laid bare. Her chest rises and falls, her breath shaky, eyes glassy with the weight of it all. I lean in, my voice low and cold.

"Do you understand?" I repeat. I'm not asking. I'm demanding. Her silence isn't enough.

She nods, shaky and fragile, like one wrong move might break her for good. Then, without warning, she throws herself into my arms. The impact of her body against mine sends a ripple through me, but I don't flinch. I hold her, feel the way she clings to me like I'm the only thing keeping her from drowning. And maybe I am.

Her sobs are soft, muffled against my chest, but I feel them. Every tremor, every jagged breath. It echoes through me, stirs something dark, something primal. This is what I wanted; to be her everything. To be the one she runs to, no matter what. The only one who can piece her back together. I tighten my arms around her, pulling her closer, feeling her pulse against mine, syncing. Becoming one.

She's mine. She's always been mine.
And now, she's sure of it too.

I hold her, just feeling the weight of her in my arms as her sobs slowly fade. Time blurs, the world outside this room disappearing into nothing. It's just us. Just her heartbeat against mine, her breath steadying as she calms. She looks up at me, something raw and quiet burning in her gaze. Her voice is barely above a whisper, but every word sinks into me.

"I should be terrified of you," she says, "but I'm not. In fact, this is the first time I've ever felt secure. The first time I'd ever trust someone else to control me. A power I never thought I'd crave." I laugh softly,

"Nobody can control you, Skylar Farmer," I say with a smile. "But I can protect you."

The words slip out, heavy with meaning. I watch her eyes flicker with understanding. It's not about control; it's about survival, about keeping her safe in a world that's anything but. I'm offering her a shield, a promise wrapped in shadows.

"I feel lost," she says suddenly, her voice shaky. "I finally found the one thing I wanted more than anything. And the person who's supposed to be my best friend would rather destroy it than face his fucking secrets."

"I'm sorry," I murmur.

"It's okay." she replies, but I see the hurt in her eyes. "And.. how could he do that to Marcus?" she mumbles, the disbelief clear in her voice. It's a rhetorical question, but one I'd also like an answer to. I look at her, the softness in her voice catching me off guard.

"I think I'm gonna get some sleep."

"Good idea, baby," I reply, keeping my tone steady.

I step toward the door, the tension from our conversation still crackling in the air. Just as my fingers brush the handle, her voice pulls me back.

"Noah," she calls, and I pause, turning back to face her. "Goodnight," she whispers. I'm struck by the vulnerability in her eyes. It's a mix of hope and sadness, and I can feel the weight of her unguarded heart in that single word. She looks so small, so delicate, like a candle's fragile flame flickering against the dark.

In that moment, everything sharpens into focus. My world, filled with chaos and shadows, narrows down to her. She's what I want. My life revolves around this tiny pink-haired girl standing before me, the one who makes me feel something I thought I'd lost forever.

"Let's go somewhere," I suggest, the words tumbling out before I can second-guess myself. "I have other estates. We can get away from all this shit. Just for a while." She pauses, her brow knitting as she considers the offer. Then, that smile, a radiant spark breaking through the gloom, lights up her face.

"I'd like that." She says softly, an edge of relief in her tone. A wicked grin spreads across my lips, something dark and possessive swelling within me.

"Pack a bag, princess. I'll be back."

I step out and ease the door shut behind me, the soft click resonating like a heartbeat in the heavy stillness. But the moment it closes, my smirk evaporates, leaving a tightness in my chest. My jaw clenches involuntarily, anger coiling within me like a serpent ready to strike. Concentration floods my senses, sharpening every sound, every flicker of movement in the shadows.

I have one more thing to deal with.

I stride into my bedroom, the dim light casting jagged silhouettes across the walls. My gaze sweeps the room, finally landing on two vital objects that lie on my desk. The book.. and my handgun.

I slide into the car, the door slamming shut like a declaration. Every movement is tight, precise; like a wound spring ready to snap. I crank the key, the engine roaring to life, a beast awakened. With a growl, I floor the gas; the tires screaming like a banshee wail that shatters the night, while the downpour transforms the roads into slick, shimmering ribbons.

The city unfurls before me, a sprawling maze of shadows and flickering lights. I cut through the streets at 100 mph, the world outside dissolving into a blur; just noise, just chaos. My focus is razor-sharp, every heartbeat synchronised with the thrum of the engine. I'm not driving; I'm stalking my fucking prey.

I cut the engine and step out into the downpour, the rain drenching me instantly. It's a cold slap against my skin, but I welcome it. My gaze fixes on the rundown block of flats ahead, a crumbling monument to despair and decay. It looms like a grave, each cracked window a hollow eye. The rain drips from the eaves, each drop echoing like a countdown in my skull, relentless. The world around me is silent, eerily still, as if holding its breath. The only sound piercing the quiet is the furious thrum of my blood in my ears.

I stride toward the entrance, the flickering light above sputtering, casting grotesque shapes on the walls. I step inside, the door groaning like a wounded beast. The air is heavy, saturated with mildew and despair. A chill snakes down my spine. The hallway stretches ahead, long and narrow, like a throat waiting to be cut. The stairs creak beneath my feet. The wood groans, whispering secrets to the silence around me. I let it speak. Let it fill the space, stretch it out. The railing brushes my fingers, cold as death. I grip it once, hard, then let go. Let it breathe. I reach the top.

Flat number 2. Faded numbers, paint peeling away, like this place forgot what it was a long time ago. I stand there, just staring at the door. Flat number 2. I trace the edges of the doorframe with my eyes. There's nothing special about it. Just another door in a rundown block of forgotten lives. Flat number 2. I whisper it under my breath, just to hear how it sounds. Just to feel it on my tongue.

I slam my fist against the door. Hard. It echoes down the empty stairwell, rattling in the silence like a warning. I take a step back, just far enough. The door creaks open. For a second, he looks normal. A split second. But then our eyes lock, and the light drains from his face, replaced by a cold, hollow emptiness. His pupils widen, reflecting nothing but black. There's a flicker of realisation, a flash of fear that he can't hide, but it's swallowed by a void. It's the look of a man who knows he's cornered, a recognition.

"Don't say I didn't fucking warn you, Douglas."

"Look, man. I can explain-"
I raise the gun.
I pull the trigger.
Then.. I close the book.

After all, I am the trusted guard.

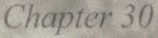

CHAPTER 30:

GOODBYE, FOREVERMORE

Marcus

The shovel hits the dirt, a hollow thud. The sun hangs low, bleeding into the sky, drowning the field in gold and fire.

Dean's dead.

Two days, and it still feels like a lie. Murdered. A word that burns every time it crosses my mind. I never thought this moment would come, not like this. Not standing in this forgotten, unkempt field.

I never imagined I'd be the one to bury him.
But here I am.

I stare at the freshly turned earth, my body heavy, my heart hollow. The grave is raw, a gaping wound in the middle of nowhere. It feels wrong. No flowers. No words. Just a rough, ugly hole, because that's all we could manage. Because he's gone, and there's no way to make sense of it.

No tears. I've cried them all. My chest aches, but there's nothing left to spill. Not here. Not now. Dean wouldn't want it. He didn't believe in tears. He believed in moving forward, even when everything felt like it was crumbling around us.

Now look where we are, brother.

The sky is a palette of bruised colours; deep pinks, orange streaks, as if the world is mourning with me. The sun slips further, casting long shadows over the grass, the light barely touching the grave. But he's not here to see it. I swallow hard, the lump in my throat refusing to budge. My hands shake, but not from the cold. It's a strange kind of numbness, something that creeps into my bones and sits there, heavy and unmoving. It settles in, and I let it.

I wish I could say I'm angry, but I'm not. Not anymore. That fire burned out the moment I saw his body, lifeless and cold, when everything went still inside me. Now, all that's left is this void where he used to be. We were supposed to grow old together. All of us. That was the plan. A bunch of screw-ups from a children's home who made it out. We were gonna make it, no matter what the world threw at us.

But the world threw more than we could catch.

I exhale, my breath shaky. I should say something; some final words, some kind of closure. But everything feels too big for words, too tangled to unravel. What do you say? I don't know. I'm not sure I ever will.

The sunset blurs, the edges of the world softening, the darkness creeping in slowly. My hands are filthy, covered in earth, sweat and death. I step back from the grave, the hole now just another part of the landscape. I feel like I'm floating, like nothing's real. It's too quiet here. Too peaceful. Dean would hate it. I hate it.

"I'm sorry," I whisper, the words barely audible. Maybe he can hear me. Maybe he can't. I don't know if I believe in any of that anymore. But I still say it. Somehow, it still feels like he's standing right behind me. Like I'll turn around and see him there, grinning that reckless grin of his, ready for the next disaster. But I won't. Because he's not here. He's buried underneath my feet.

I turn around, and there they stand. Sienna, Birdie, and.. Delilah. *Oh God*, Delilah.

Her face is gaunt, eyes vacant, like the life's been drained out of her, like she's buried too. She loved him- *loves* him- and now she's here, staring at the same grave, the same patch of dirt, and all I can think is how much more she has to lose. How much death can a person take before they just fucking break?

She's trembling, her lips quivering like she's about to say something, but there are no words. There never were. She looks at me for a second, and I feel it; the weight of her grief, her confusion. And all I can do is stand there, just as lost, just as broken, with nothing to offer her. No comfort. No answers.

Sienna's eyes are red-rimmed, her hands stuffed deep into her jacket pockets, like if she just keeps them there, keeps them still, maybe the world will stop spinning for a second. Maybe she'll stop feeling like everything's falling apart. Birdie's standing beside her. Her sobs break through the silence, sharp and raw. Her cheeks are a burned red, streaked with tears. That perfect, prided hair of hers now lies dishevelled, flat.

But there's one face missing.
No Skylar.

She should be here. She was the light in all this darkness. Dean's best friend, his sister in every way that mattered. Always loud, always laughing, filling the room with her chaotic energy. She would've thrown her arms around Delilah right now, whispered something stupid, something only Skylar could get away with saying that'd somehow make you want to laugh even in the middle of this hell.

But she's not here. She and Noah disappeared without a trace. Gone. Like smoke in the wind. Noah. My brother. My blood. The one who tore into my life like a hurricane, and now he's left just as suddenly. Leaving a trail of death and sorrow in his wake. I'll never get to ask him why. Why he did it.

I wonder if that was always the plan. For him to tear through everything, to rip apart what was already fragile, and then vanish, leaving me to clean up the mess. The deaths. The grief. The emptiness.

He left, just like he came.
And I don't know if I'll ever see him again.

The wind picks up again, cold and biting, as if the earth itself is reminding me that nothing stays, that everything slips away sooner or later. I close my eyes for a second, trying to breathe, trying to steady the storm brewing inside me. But it's no use. I open them and see Delilah again. Her eyes filled with unshed tears, staring at the place where Dean's body lies, and I know there's no peace to be found. Not here.

Not anymore.

I glance over at Sienna. Her butterfly, that fragile little thing she's carried through so much, is perched on her shoulder, wings still, unmoving. Just like her. We lock eyes, and there's a quiet knowing. My sweet, broken yet again, shattered by this life we've been forced to endure. Her strength cracks, but it doesn't crumble; Sienna always finds a way to hold on, even when the world rips her apart piece by piece. I walk to her, wrapping her in my arms. Keeping her.

Delilah takes a step forward, her body moving on instinct, like she's walking through a dream she can't wake up from. She kneels at the patch where Dean's buried, and places down a note, written in her delicate handwriting, along with a single flower. A rock goes on top to keep it all in place, like she's trying to hold onto something, anything, that won't be taken by the wind.

Then she stands, slowly, and turns back to us, her face a blank slate, her eyes distant.

"I can't believe this is real," she whispers, and her voice trembles like a leaf caught in a storm. Then it steadies, and she looks up, eyes burning with something darker. Something that hurts to look at. "He's gone. Actually gone. And now.. now I have to carry him with me. Not in some sweet memory. Not in some photo I can look at when I miss him. No. I have to carry him like a fucking wound. An open wound that will never close. I have to carry his death with me, every single day." She pauses, wipes a tear from her cheek, but it's like trying to stop the rain. It just keeps coming. "And I don't know how to do it. I don't know how to live in a world where he doesn't exist."

Her words crack like thunder in the stillness, shaking the ground beneath us. My chest tightens, and I can't breathe, but I still can't cry. I'm too far gone for that.

"The last thing I told him was *'Be safe'*." She says. "*'Always'* he told me. Always." The irony twists like a knife, and her breath catches. Her eyes blaze with sorrow, reflecting the dying sun.

I wish I could turn back time, erase the moment he walked away. I want to scream his name, to shake the universe until it gives him back. But all I have are memories; flashes of a boy who was fierce and loving, a brother who deserved more than this cruel end.

I close my eyes, and the memories flood back; those golden moments that feel like they belong to someone else, another life. Riding bikes down cracked pavement, the wind whipping through our hair as we raced under the sun, laughter echoing like a song of freedom. Playing pranks. Running. Jumping. Scratches and doodles on the peeling walls, our fingerprints marking a chaotic canvas, proof of our innocence, proof we existed.

Sneaking out under a blanket of stars, hearts racing, shadows dancing in the dark. The thrill of rebellion, tiptoeing past creaky floorboards, bursting into the cool night air; stealing sweets, drinks, freedom on our tongues. We thought we were invincible, a force of nature, untouchable.

Those memories soon shifted. Smoking together in the stillness of midnight, clouds swirling like the secrets we kept. Stored, for each other. Those endless conversations, the world dissolving, every whispered hope, a promise, a bond forged in smoke and laughter. Stealing cars, adrenaline pumping. Fights that left us bruised, bloodied, but laughing. Those moments, woven tightly, the fabric of who we were, now frayed at the edges, unravelling before my eyes.

But those are the only memories I'll ever have. That's it. There will never be a new one. This is the end of our story, the last chapter unwritten, and it crushes me. The memories wrap around me like barbed wire, each one a reminder of a bond severed too soon. No more adventures. No more anything.

The world keeps spinning, but I'm standing still.

I shift my gaze to the left, and something catches my eye; a flash of vibrant blue against the muted backdrop of grief. A butterfly, beautiful and serene. A butterfly, suspended in the air, not fluttering aimlessly but hovering, poised as if the universe itself has held its breath, watching us.

I extend my hand, palm open, an invitation wrapped in thick hesitation. To my surprise, the delicate creature alights on my

Chapter 30

skin, a featherweight against the weight of everything I've lost. It feels like a whisper, a secret, a connection that transcends this world. Then it lifts. A spirit set free. It drifts toward Delilah. Dances around her head, a soft glow.

Her eyes widen, captivated. The atmosphere thickens with magic; fragile yet potent. The butterfly flutters gently, lingering deliberately near her stomach, before landing on the rock she placed. The world falls away, leaving only this sacred exchange. A spirit, dancing through the air. It transforms. Transcends. Becomes something eternal.

In that instant, I'm reminded, not even death can erase this.

Fate may carve its path,
but what we've built endures,
for fate intended this as well.
Goodbye, forevermore.

THE END.

ABOUT THE AUTHOR

Amber Fawn, born 2002, is a Cornwall-based indie author, specialising in Romance & Dark romance. Her passion for reading and writing began as early as 3 years old when she forced herself to learn how to read. Her preferred writing style is often on the darker side, experimenting with elements of gore and psychological trauma.

Website: amberfawnwrites.com
Instagram: @amberfawnauthor